The ROSES OF
ROAZON

Cherith Baldry was born in Lancaster, England, and studied at Manchester University and St Anne's College, Oxford. She subsequently worked as a teacher, including a spell as a lecturer at the University of Sierra Leone. Cherith is now a full-time writer of fiction for both children and adults – her children's fantasy, the 'Eaglesmount' trilogy, was published by Macmillan in 2001. Her adult novels are *Exiled from Camelot*, followed by *The Reliquary Ring* which was published by Macmillan and Tor.

CHERITH BALDRY

The ROSES OF ROAZON

TOR

First published 2004 by Tor

This edition published 2013 by Tor
an imprint of Pan Macmillan, a division of Macmillan Publishers Limited
Pan Macmillan, 20 New Wharf Road, London N1 9RR
Basingstoke and Oxford
Associated companies throughout the world
www.panmacmillan.com
www.toruk.com

ISBN 978-1-4472-5556-7

A CIP catalogue record for this book is available from
the British Library.

Typeset by SetSystems Ltd, Saffron Walden, Essex

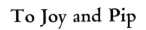

To Joy and Pip

PROLOGUE

Triptych

The room was large, its corners lost in a darkness of heavy tapestries. A stifling vapour, from the copper bowl that bubbled on the brazier, hung in the air. Its aromatic perfume overlaid a sour stench of decay.

In the bed, beneath the gold embroidered canopy, a man was dying. The straggling white hair was soaked with sweat. The stringy throat convulsed for each rattling breath. The eyes were bright with hatred.

'My lord!' One of the watchers by the bed spoke harshly. 'You must send for your heir.'

The old man clutched the bedcover as he fought to raise himself. Strangling sounds came from his throat as if he tried to speak. Then he spat.

'My lord, you will plunge the whole land into war if you die without an heir.'

The dying man struggled again, this time rasping out words. 'Do it then. And God ... God damn him — and you.' He fell back on his pillows in a spasm of choking laughter.

2

The pale light of early morning filled the courtyard. In the centre a fountain played its perpetual soft music. A creeper climbed the walls, starred with flowers even before the leaves came. They rippled silver against the greyish stems as a breeze stirred them.

He stood staring at the fountain, not seeing it. His inward trouble did not disturb a face schooled to calm.

'Where are you?' he whispered. 'Who are you?' And then, 'Who am I?'

As flakes of sun glittered on the surface of the pool, the fountain leaped into light. Stars seared his eyes. Silence became charged with an immanent revelation.

The breeze sighed cool against his face, the fountain played, the starflowers shone against the grey walls.

From somewhere up above, a bell began to sound its imperative summons.

3

The cathedral was hushed, its pillars like winter trees half lost in a grey twilight. At the foot of the sanctuary steps, the dead lord lay on his bier, his face composed to a serenity it had never shown in life, his hands folded in the gesture of prayer that had been so foreign to him. The rest of his body was covered in silver and black brocade, the folds of it sweeping down to the stone floor.

From the door into the vestry came a tall man in a black cassock, a taper in one hand, the other cupped to shield its flame. He bowed to the Holy Knot above the altar, and then began to light the six tall candles that stood around the bier. Gradually the light of them grew, until a golden radiance surrounded the dead man.

When all the candles were lit, the priest bowed once more, and stood before the Knot for a long moment.

'Dear God,' he murmured at last, 'his life is over, and you will judge him. But we still remain, here where the fields are barren, the people sicken, and even the air hangs heavy with his sin. I pray you, show us the road we must travel. Heal us and make all things new.'

PART ONE

Civitas Dei

One

Sir Valery de Vaux edged his way towards the doors of the cathedral in the wake of the departing procession. The interior was dim, hung with gauzy veils of incense; outside the sun shone. Impatient for a first breath of clear air, Val felt a hand grip his shoulder, and straightened reflexively as he turned to see his commanding officer.

'Val, you're off duty now?' Sir Guy de Karanteg, Captain of the Knights Companions, spoke rapidly, in a whisper.

'Yes, sir, once I've set the guard.'

'Don't go yet. I must see the procession on its way, and then I want a word.'

The Captain left Val scarcely time for an assent before he was off, expertly snaking his way through the departing congregation, towards the banner bearer who brought up the rear of the procession.

Val followed him out into the square. The relief guard was filing out of the citadel, the newest recruit, Lucien de Gwern, fumbling with his belt buckle as he brought up the rear. They formed a ragged line, which straightened noticeably as Val strode over to them.

He saluted and ran an expert eye over them. On this day of all days, with so many visitors in Roazon, the Knights Companions must look their best. They were the bodyguard of the Duke of Roazon, a small, elite group of the Legion of God, and they had a reputation to live up to.

Some of the Knights were already off attending Duke Joscelin in the procession. Val despatched others to relieve the ceremonial guards on the causeway gate, and the citadel gate, and in the citadel itself to wait for Duke Joscelin's return.

At the end of the line, Lucien de Gwern stood rigid, staring straight in front of him. Val flicked at a barely visible spot on the boy's burnished armour.

'Relax, Sir Lucien,' he murmured. 'You're doing very well.'

Smiling, he sent the lad with a couple of the older men across the lake to supervise the preparations for the grand tournament that would take place two days from now.

Sir Guy had still not returned, so while he waited, Val rested his hands on the low wall that bounded one side of the cathedral square, and looked out over the city and the lake below him. The water, reflecting the blue of a summer sky, was beginning to kindle now with the blaze of the sun as it turned towards setting. A breeze stirred Val's hair and fluttered the white surcoat of his Order, dissipating the smell of incense that still clung to it.

The far shore of the lake was edged with ships at anchor, their sails all neatly furled, and the gaudily painted barges that had brought the nobility from the south to Roazon for this Day of Memories. On the shore itself stood clumps of bright pavilions, and banners snapped in the breeze, too far away for Val to make out their devices.

Beyond lay gently sloping fields that rippled with ripening corn. From this distant vantage point they promised plenty, but Val had seen how sparse the crop was, the ears of corn scanty, mildewed and riddled with blight. There would be a poor harvest for the third year running and, for all the bravery of the banners, there would be empty bellies in Arvorig this winter.

Behind him Val was aware, as always, of the soaring bulk of the cathedral, joy bells clamouring from its topmost tower. The Offering was over and the procession was winding its way down through the many levels of the city towards the harbour gate, and the bridge that led to the Pearl of Arvorig. When Val looked down he could see it as a twisting golden snake threading between grey stones and the spilling green of rose bushes. The chanting of the choristers floated up to him, a pure thread of counterpoint against the hurrying bells.

Val drew a deep breath. He was off duty now until the night watch. Time to get out of this cumbersome ceremonial armour, and to enjoy a bath, before he had to escort his mother to the ceremony and there light the candle for his father. And then be polite to her dinner guests afterwards . . .

Always supposing that Sir Guy de Karenteg did not have other plans for him.

Turning away from the wall, he saw his captain crossing the square towards him, with long strides that made his cloak billow out behind him.

'Good,' the man said as soon as he was in earshot. 'Come with me. I won't keep you long.'

He led the way down some steps, through a postern gate into the citadel, and into his own quarters lodged in a turret between the end of the barracks and the outer wall. Val followed him inside, leaving the door partly open to let in the light and warm air of the summer afternoon.

The walls of the turret room were bare, except for a large map of Arvorig hanging opposite the door. A plan of the city of Roazon itself was skewered to the window shutter with a rusty dagger. The only furnishings were a scarred table and a single chair, with a bench under the window.

Guy unfastened his ceremonial cloak and slung it over the back of the chair. Taking up a leather bottle from the table, he poured wine into two horn cups and gave one to Val.

'To memories,' he said solemnly, took a mouthful, and gagged. 'Rot it – I can't taste anything but that damn' incense.' He banged the cup down on the table and turned to face Val. 'I'm leaving the city,' he said.

'Sir?' Val wasn't sure he had heard right. Guy had been Captain of the Knights Companions for as long as he could remember. As a small boy, Val had come here to the citadel with his father, the armourer, and it was Guy who had first shown him how to use a sword.

'Leaving, boy. Don't look so surprised.'

'You – are you retiring, sir?'

'Do I look senile yet?' A grin creased Guy's weathered face. 'No, I'm promoted Commander – to lead the Legion in Gwened.'

Val opened his mouth to offer congratulations, then hesitated and took a sip of wine instead. He was not sure this promotion was a matter for congratulation.

Cautiously, he asked, 'Are you pleased about that, sir?'

Guy took another gulp of wine. 'No, I'm not pleased, rot it. Count Fragan of Gwened is a tricky bastard, and he doesn't like having an order of knighthood within his territory which isn't personally sworn to him.'

'Then your new post should be ... interesting, sir.'

Guy snorted. 'I'm getting too old for "interesting". Though I reckon that's why Father Reynaud is sending me there. I'm a soldier, and I've never pretended to be anything else. Maybe our respected Grand Master thinks I'll get on better with the Count than one of these priestly types of knight.'

He drained the wine and put his cup down. 'This is wasting time. You haven't yet asked why I wanted to talk to you.' Amusement glinted in his sharp, black eyes. 'Or even who is going to be the new Captain of the Knights Companions.'

Val waited for him to continue, saw his superior's amusement flare into laughter, and suddenly understood what the commander meant. He nearly dropped his wine cup. 'But Father Reynaud doesn't like me. I assumed Girec . . .'

'Girec d'Evron! That rat-faced, boot-licking excuse for a man, commanding the Knights? Over my dead body.' Sir Guy took a breath. 'As for Father Reynaud, he's hard, but fair. You've been lieutenant now for over a year. You've done well. And, as departing captain, my recommendation carries weight.'

For a moment Val felt as if he couldn't breathe. The captaincy had long been his dream, but one he felt he would never realize. And now, in this small, shabby room, he felt as if his whole world had changed. As if the sun was dancing.

'This is unofficial as yet,' Guy went on. 'Father Reynaud will send for you tomorrow. But I'm clearing out of these rooms now – you can move in as soon as you want.'

'Yes,' Val still felt dazed. 'Yes . . . thank you, sir.'

Guy held out a hand, and the rough clasp of that calloused palm brought Val back to reality, elation swelling inside him.

'Count Fragan is visiting for the ceremony,' Guy said.

'So I'll stay a night or two at the Plume, and go on to Gwened with him. You and I will find a time to talk before then, but you'll need to get away to your family now.'

Still in a daze, Val saluted and left. Returning to the barracks, he found that the other off-duty Knights had long gone, so he had the dortour and the bathhouse all to himself. This was a relief, as he didn't want to talk about his promotion – not until it was officially announced – but he feared he would have been incapable of talking about anything else.

Dressed in the robe of undyed linen normally worn off duty, he left the citadel and took the stair which led most steeply, and most swiftly, down through the levels of the city to the street in which his mother lived.

He had lived there too, all his childhood and youth, until he left for the barracks of the Legion. It was a tall, narrow house, whose austere grey walls were lightened only by the flowers that cascaded from troughs at every window. Steep steps led up to the front door where Val gave the bell a single tug and went in without waiting for an answer.

The hallway was cool and quiet, though sunlight lay on the flagged floor and touched the icon of the Warrior which hung on the wall. The wooden treads of the staircase and the carved eagles on the newel posts were polished to a soft sheen.

Master Pernet, the old steward, appeared through the door leading to the kitchens, but bowed and withdrew without speaking as Val waved him away with a smile.

Briefly he stood, drinking in the silence, but almost immediately a voice called out from somewhere above him. 'Valery, is that you?'

'Yes, Mother.'

Regine de Vaux appeared at the head of the stairs. She

was a small woman whose smooth black hair, braided into a coronet, was beginning to silver, but she carried herself with immense dignity. Now, dressed for the forthcoming ceremony, she wore a gown of black velvet, unrelieved except for a belt of linked silver rings which held her chatelaine.

Val met her at the foot of the stairs and stooped to kiss her cheek. Smiling, he said, 'I've news.'

'News?' Regine's thin brows rose. 'Don't tell me Duke Joscelin has named his wedding day at last?'

'No, nothing like that.' Val paused for a moment, savouring his triumph. 'I'm promoted Captain.'

Regine was betrayed into a gasp. 'Valery ... my dear! Truly?'

'Truly. Since Sir Guy is promoted to command the Legion in Gwened.'

His mother's face broke into a warm smile. She was just raising a hand to his face when the street door crashed open.

Regine's face froze, her eyes wide. 'Bertrand!'

Val spun round to see the squat figure of his cousin standing in the doorway. Sweat plastered his black hair down over his forehead. His tunic was torn and filthy, and a gash in one exposed knee was bleeding freely. Incongruously he was carrying over one arm a hood of scarlet velvet, trimmed with miniver.

His face bore a triumphant grin from ear to ear.

'What have you been doing?'

Bertrand kicked the door closed behind him and advanced into the hall. 'I had a wrestling match with some lads in the square,' he said cheerfully. 'Look what I won.' He held out the scarlet hood towards her.

Regine squeezed her eyes shut. 'Wrestling in a public square?' she whispered. 'With tradesmen's sons?'

Bertrand's jubilant smile began to fade. 'I hoped to please you, Aunt.'

'Please me?' Regine's tone was edged with steel. 'You are Bertrand d'Acquin. You have a family name. You do not trail that name in the gutter, by wrestling with grooms and fishermen.'

Bertrand's happiness in his victory had now quite gone. Something inside Val twisted at his dejected look.

Staring at his feet, Bertrand muttered, 'I thought you would like it.'

'Oh, Bertrand!' Regine's voice was warmer again. She went to her nephew and took one of the filthy hands in both her own. 'My dear, that was kindness ... but I could not wear such a thing. It would not be seemly.'

Flushing, Bertrand nodded. 'I don't know these things. I don't know anything. I'm not good for anything.'

'That's not true,' Regine said, gently now. 'All will be well, my dear. But for now, you must promise me, no more wrestling in the streets. Give me your word that you will never fight again, unless you have a knightly weapon in your hands, and a noble cause to fight for.'

Bertrand shrugged uncomfortably. 'Very well, Aunt.'

'Good.' Regine released his hand, saying briskly, 'Now Valery and I must go to the ceremony. While we are away, you must bathe and put on a new tunic. Your parents are here in Roazon, and I have invited them to supper.'

Bertrand's head swung up, a stony look in his black eyes. 'My mother and father? No!'

'Bertrand ...'

'I won't meet them. I won't sit down at table with them.'

'Bertrand, you will do exactly as I wish. You must show your parents that you, at least, are capable of civilized behaviour. What *they* may be capable of,' she added acidly, 'is something else.'

Looking away again, Bertrand muttered agreement.

Regine smiled. 'Come now, Valery.'

She held out a hand, and laid it on Val's arm. Glancing back as they left the house, he saw Bertrand still standing motionless in the hall, the scarlet velvet hood crushed between his grubby hands.

2

Alissende arrived in Roazon as the Day of Memories was drawing to its close. The road wound down the hillside through weed-choked fields; the setting sun was at her back. The feet of the pilgrims raised a dust that caught in Alissende's throat and stung her eyes.

Far below, the lake was a sheet of scarlet. Towards the nearer shore a mountain reared out of the water, a mountain that was island and city and shrine, all at once. Roazon.

Its buildings were bathed in rosy light, like a city in a dream. Towers and rooftops rose against the sky, rushing upwards as if they would invade Heaven, until at its topmost level the mountain ended in the spires of the cathedral.

Beside this island city, as if tethered to it like a ship's boat, or the droplet from a pendant, lay another isle, the Pearl of Arvorig — the centre of the world. Alissende had not thought it would look so small.

The road ahead levelled out as the hills descended into the meadows surrounding the lake, and it marched thence-forth between two lines of standing stones, heading arrow-straight towards the city. By the time that Alissende, and the group of pilgrims she had travelled with, reached the lake shore, the sun had disappeared, leaving a crimson sky barred with cloud.

Along the last hundred yards of the road makeshift booths had been erected, selling food and drink and gim-crack keepsakes. Stallholders cried out their wares in raucous voices. Alissende felt as if the smell of all that food and cooking grease was settling like a film over her skin. Torches began to flare on poles, making the gathering twilight seem already night.

At the lakeside the road Alissende followed converged with two others, running north and south, at a wide open space in front of a line of buildings. These were stables, where grooms took the mounts of travellers on horseback, and an inn, where Alissende considered asking for a bed for the night, but the blaze of light and discordant singing from its taproom discouraged her. Besides, she should not pause now until she had crossed into Roazon itself.

The bridge between the shore and the city gate was already crammed with pilgrims. Alissende joined the crowd and shuffled forward, step by tedious step. To her left was a beggar in rags, hobbling along on a crutch, his face seamed with hideous scars, while on her right a young nobleman strutted in a gold-laced tunic. On either side of the arch a Knight was stationed, wearing the armour of the Legion. Staring expressionlessly ahead as the pilgrims moved between them, they might have been statues.

Once through the gate, Alissende let the same crowd carry her down a narrow street leading to the right. On one side of it was the city wall; on the other tall houses of honey-coloured stone, with heavy doors tight shut and high windows.

The street clung to the wall until it reached another gate. As Alissende stepped beneath its arch, the press of bodies around her suddenly melted away.

She stood on a flat, paved hythe, so extensive that even this crowd had room to move freely. It lay at the southern tip of the main island, and all along its sides, lamps, as yet unlit, hung from iron posts. Steps led down to the lake and the mooring poles for boats, but no boats were moored there now. Cool air moved against Alissende's face, and she wiped the sweat and dust away with a corner of her mantle.

The air held the scent of roses. Down the spine of the open space were mounds and banks of them, white and pale yellow and saffron, and the scarlet of blood. Already some of the pilgrims were carrying wreaths of them. Alissende could not help wondering that, in a land where crops failed, where drought succeeded storm, where pestilence thrived, the roses of Roazon should go on flourishing.

She watched carefully. Having never been here before, she did not know the details of the ritual. Acolytes were distributing the flowers, and once Alissende had seen what others did she attached herself to the end of a line, and eventually received her own cluster of half opened buds. The leaves felt cool on the palms of her hands. The scent was dizzying.

As she hesitated, wondering what to do next, she felt a hand on her arm. She turned, and saw a woman standing beside her, looking into Alissende's face with a friendly smile.

'Is this your first time? Do you need any guidance?'

'No, I...' Alissende would have drawn away from her then. She did not want advice, or companionship.

But the other woman did not notice her reluctance. 'There are candles over there, in those baskets by the waterside. But we have to wait until Duke Joscelin arrives from the chapel. The Duke of Roazon always lights the first candle . . .'

Alissende studied the woman covertly as she chattered. She was young – about Alissende's own age – small and plump, with bright brown hair drawn back into a single braid. The hand that still rested on Alissende's arm had paint ingrained around the fingernails. In her other hand she held a wreath of crimson roses.

'I think they're coming now,' she said. 'Stand over here, you'll see better.'

She drew Alissende towards the farthest tip of the island, where another bridge, a delicate arch, tethered the Pearl of Arvorig to it. The crowd was already thickening there, so Alissende gave in and went along with her. She felt secure, unobtrusive in this mêlée of beggars and noblemen and priests, where respectable matrons rubbed shoulders with women of the streets, and even with the blue-robed votaresses of the Matriarchy. Arguing would only draw attention to herself.

Where Roazon rose like a spear of stone, piercing the heavens, the Pearl of Arvorig was gently rounded, covered in trees and shrubs right down to the water's edge. Just visible through screening foliage were the grey walls of the chapel, older by far than the great city which dwarfed it: the place where God had first manifested himself in the world.

A winding path led from the chapel itself to the bridge; along it a small group of people were approaching. A tall, white-haired man in a golden mitre, wearing the embroidered vestments of the Church. Another, not so tall, but broader, in the silver armour and white surcoat of the Legion. His iron-grey hair was swept back from a high forehead, and he looked around arrogantly from deep-set eyes.

'That's Father Mathurin, the Archbishop,' Alissende's companion said. 'And then Father Reynaud, the Grand Master of the Legion. And *there* is Duke Joscelin.'

Alissende's eyes were drawn to a slighter figure in the midst of this group, a younger man with loosely curling golden hair. His white linen robe was perfectly plain, and he wore no adornment of circlet or rings.

'*No one* ever expected Joscelin to become Duke of Roazon,' the woman added, with a little gurgle of laughter. 'Duke Govrian had sent him off to be a holy brother.' Her laughter died; for a moment her gaze was rapt. 'It was all so strange . . .'

Alissende nodded. She knew the story; probably everyone in the whole of Arvorig knew it. Years ago, Duke Govrian's nephew had been arraigned for treason — real or imaginary — and after his execution Govrian had sent his infant son to the monastery at Brociel.

But the year after, Govrian's only son Primel died in a tournament accident, which left the young Joscelin as Govrian's nearest male heir. But Govrian refused to recall the boy, at first in the hope of fathering another son, and then, as he slid into debauched senility, out of a delight in tormenting his advisers, or perhaps a crazy hope of cheating death.

This winter past, still with no heir of his body, or none he cared to acknowledge, Duke Govrian had felt the touch of death. A dozen or more provincial lords were ready to go to war over the right to rule in Roazon. Dying in hatred of them all, and in terror — well deserved, so gossip had it — of the life to come, Govrian had been forced to recall his great-nephew.

Was it to be, after all, his last, twisted joke, to give the rule of the holiest city in the world into the hands of a man of God?

Watching the Duke Joscelin now pacing slowly over the bridge, listening to the words of the Grand Master of the Legion with a sweet and gentle gravity, Alissende could not help wondering whether he had welcomed the news of his inheritance.

'Duke Joscelin's induction takes place tomorrow,' Alissende's companion informed her. 'Will you stay to see it?'

Alissende's instincts told her to say no, but that might sound harsh. 'I . . . don't know.'

The procession had reached the waterside, where an acolyte handed Duke Joscelin a wreath of white roses with a single candle in its centre. A second acolyte stepped up with a lighted taper, and lit the candle.

With the wreath supported on the palms of his hands, Duke Joscelin stood a moment, gazing into the flame. The crowd around him had hushed, and his voice rang out clearly. 'Govrian, go with God; may this light shine in your memory.'

Stooping, he laid the wreath of roses on the surface of the lake.

That was the signal for the rest of the pilgrims. They began pressing forward, fixing candles into their own wreaths, and launching the tiny flames out onto the lake, until the whole waterside was edged with light.

Alissende's companion guided her towards one of the candle baskets, and they waited for their turn to come.

'My name is Morwenna,' the woman said.

She did not ask the question, but it was there in the bright, inquiring look she gave Alissende.

Alissende spoke her name reluctantly. She had imagined

coming and going here without making herself known to anyone. She felt there was nothing that she could offer in return for this woman's friendliness.

'That's a northern name,' Morwenna said. 'Do you come from Brogall?'

'No, from the east.' Thinking that she sounded too abrupt, Alissende added, 'It was my grandmother's name.'

'I live here, in the city,' Morwenna said. 'I'm an icon painter.'

Not wanting to share anything more of herself, Alissende murmured something, but at that moment they reached the baskets heaped with slender, white candles.

Morwenna fitted one among the stems of her own wreath. 'My mother died last winter,' she said, her bright look fading for a moment. 'She was old, and tired, and now she is at rest.'

Alissende said nothing, but she could not help a wave of bitterness sweeping over her. Morwenna was an icon painter; she must have painted God as Warrior, or as Judge, the militant and the austere. What place there for an old, tired woman? Or for a child too young to know anything but laughter and kindliness?

She was roused from this moment's abstraction by an acolyte touching her sleeve. 'Take your candles, mistress,' he said. 'One for each of those who died this past year.'

Embarrassed, and aware of the crowds waiting behind her, Alissende fumbled in the basket.

'Dear God, three!' Morwenna whispered, beside her.

As they moved away, Alissende struggling to set the candles in place with hands that were suddenly shaking, Morwenna asked her, 'Who were they?'

'My parents,' Alissende said. 'And my little brother. There was plague in our village.'

Morwenna touched her arm comfortingly. 'And you survived?'

'I was not there.' Alissende's voice was hard. The tight knot inside her, tied there on the day the tragic news reached her, was threatening to work loose – and she dared not let it. Her eyes blurred with treacherous tears.

She felt the cool touch of Morwenna's hands on hers, helping her to fix the candles, and then her companion led her to the edge of the water, where an acolyte lit their candles with a taper.

Morwenna held up her wreath. 'Ivona, go with God. May this light shine in your memory.' She crouched to let the roses, the glimmering candle, float out onto the darkening waters of the lake.

For a moment Alissende thought her voice would fail her. Appalled at her own weakness, she snatched at the last remnants of self-control, enough to speak their names and the ritual words, before she set her own wreath down beside Morwenna's, among countless other flames burning in memory of the beloved dead.

The light began stretching far out into the lake, as currents took the wreaths, spun them in a complex eddying around the hythe, and drew them away into the gathering darkness. Alissende stood watching as her own flames merged into the shimmer, and were lost.

She found herself weeping quietly and unrestrainedly, and without embarrassment now because she knew she was not alone. She could feel Morwenna's arm around her, and see tears on the other's face too.

At last Alissende drew back. 'I must go.'

Morwenna asked, 'Have you a place to stay?'

Alissende shook her head.

'Then you must come home with me.'

'No, I can't. You're kind, but—'

'Nonsense!' Morwenna took her arm. 'All the inns and lodging houses will be packed, and a lot of them are no place for a woman alone – even here in Roazon. You'll come with me.'

Alissende found she could not go on resisting. So, silently, not knowing where each step was taking her, she followed the woman who had become her unexpected friend across the hythe and back through the gate of the city.

3

The sky was darkening, the light in the west almost gone, as Aurel reached the waterside. As the acolyte with a long taper lit the single candle in his wreath of golden rosebuds, Aurel looked at the flame, not at him, and yet he was aware of the young man's expression of contempt. It troubled him very little; he was used to it, and he would not hide what he was from the Church that had cast him out.

When the candle was burning steadily, he spoke the words, then knelt at the water's edge and carefully lowered the wreath into the lake, giving it a little push so that it slid out and nudged its way into a cluster of others, its flame blending into the shimmer of so many, many more.

Aurel rose to his feet, and took a deep breath. His father was dead, and he had performed the ceremony as a dutiful son would have done. Now he was free.

Brushing the dust of the ground from the folds of his silken robe, he turned back towards the city gate. The crowds were thinning now. Most of the rose wreaths were

gone from the tables lining the centre of the hythe. Someone began lighting the lamps along the water's edge. It was
time to go.

As he climbed up towards the higher levels of the city,
Aurel's breath grew short, not from the steepness but from
the thought of what lay at the end of his journey. Five years
since he had last set foot in Roazon, but it might have been
yesterday. As far as he was concerned, it *was* yesterday – for
all that had passed between was waste and desolation. The
jewel-encrusted collar of his robe felt too tight around his
throat.

By now it was fully dark. On the lower levels, near the
city gates, taverns spilled out light and music, and the noise
of revelry. Aurel left them behind as he climbed into wider
streets where light leaked out through closed shutters, and
the sounds of supper parties in the houses behind them
were more muted. Little disturbed the quiet except for a
distant watchman's bell, and closer by the squalling of cats
in a courtyard garden.

He had carefully, discreetly, inquired earlier for the
house he was seeking, and eventually he found it. A torch
burnt over the archway and the outer gates were open. His
hands clenched among the folds of his silks, Aurel went in.

Light from an upper window illuminated the courtyard.
Roses scrambled over the walls and released their scent into
the night. A fountain played its soft, murmurous music in
the centre of the paved area.

On a bench beside the inner door a porter was seated,
and rose to his feet as he spotted Aurel.

Nervously Aurel said, 'Good evening. I wish to see Sir
Nicolas de Cotin. Tell him Aurel de Montfaucon is here.'

Wooden-faced, the porter looked him up and down. 'I'll
see if he's at home, sir,' he said at last. 'Wait here.'

Not the most courteous welcome, Aurel told himself as the man disappeared into the house. Trying to believe that it did not matter, he seated himself in a tiny rose arbour, whose leaves cast moving shadows over his hands as he waited, and the scent of the pale blossoms assailed him like the fumes of wine. A fire flickered in the depths of the emerald on the only ring he wore.

After a seeming eternity, the door of the house opened again, and the porter emerged. Following him, a tall, lithe figure paused silhouetted against the light. Aurel did not need to see his features to know him. He sprang to his feet and held out his hands. 'Nicolas!'

Nicolas de Cotin stepped slowly out into the courtyard, so that light from the window fell on his face and his bright golden hair. He was fastening a heavy silver brooch at the neck of his tunic, and made no move to take Aurel's hands.

As Aurel saw the man's blank expression, shading gradually to appalled recognition, he realized that he had made the most disastrous mistake of his life.

More hesitantly he repeated, 'Nicolas . . .'

Nicolas spun round and snapped at the porter, 'Go inside!'

The man went back into the house and the door thumped shut behind him.

Nicolas finished fastening the brooch. 'What are you doing here, Aurel?' he said. 'What do you want?'

Aurel fought down hysterical laughter. 'You know what I want, Nicolas. You always knew I would come back, as soon as I was free.'

A pause, silent but for the incessant tinkling of the fountain.

Then Nicolas said, 'Aurel, that was five years ago.'

'And does that matter? Does that change anything?'

Nicolas let out a sharp bark of laughter. 'Of course, it changes everything! Aurel, we were children. We didn't know what we were doing.'

'*I* knew.'

'I don't wonder.' Nicolas turned, paced rapidly across the courtyard, and paced back. 'Look at you! Do you have to go round dressed like a tavern whore? I've heard rumours about you, even here in Roazon. I know the sort of life you've been leading. Maybe you can get away with that sort of thing down in Kemper, but here in Roazon we—'

'Nicolas,' Aurel managed to interrupt him, 'all of that, it's not—'

'I don't want to know. Just get out. I don't want you here.'

Aurel stared at him. He could feel something cold and heavy in his chest, stifling his heart. 'Nicolas, you don't mean that?'

'Did anyone see you come in? I have a reputation to keep up. Thank God you didn't go to my mother's house! As it is, I'll have to pay the damn' porter here to keep his mouth shut.'

'But I—' Aurel made a desperate effort to keep his voice steady. 'I came to stay with you, Nicolas. I thought that's what you wanted.'

Nicolas drew a deep breath. 'Aurel, I'm betrothed now. I shall marry at the Feast of All Angels.'

'But Nicolas, we vowed to each other. We exchanged rings . . .'

'I told you, we were stupid children, playing a game. Now we're old enough to know that it was mortal sin.' He touched the brooches at his throat, and for the first time Aurel noticed that the twisted design incorporated the threefold Holy Knot. 'Aurel, she's a de Bellière. Have you any idea how many of that family are princes of the Church? She's Father Reynaud's niece, for God's sake!'

'Who is Father Reynaud?' Aurel asked, bewildered.

'Grand Master of the Legion. Where have you been, Aurel? They say they're a godless lot down in Kemper, and I can well believe it. If Father Reynaud received the least idea that you've been here, that you've even spoken with me, let alone ... Do you think he would allow me to marry his niece?'

The savage tone battered Aurel into stunned comprehension. 'You don't want me?'

Again a bark of laughter, a world of scorn in it. 'At last. No, I don't want you. Get out of here — *now*.'

Aurel took a step forward, and held out one hand, beseeching. 'Nicolas, please don't do this. I love you.'

'Haven't you heard a word I've said? I don't want you here. Now go.'

Aurel felt his tears spill over. Slowly he drew off the emerald and held it out.

'What's that?'

'Your ring, Nicolas.'

'Why do you think I want it?'

He made no move to take it, and at length Aurel let it drop. It tinkled on the flagstones and rolled out of sight.

Aurel turned away. The house door banged shut behind him as he left the courtyard.

He walked back, through the gates and down steep streets and stairways until he came back to the hythe. It was empty now, except for a few scattered roses. The votive candles out in the lake were winking out one by one.

Down yet more steps where, on every other night but this, boats would normally be tied to their mooring rings, then out into the lake. Cool water enfolded him like a garment. As he felt its touch he could not help flinching, but that did not stop him, and when the bottom of the lake shelved away from under his feet and left him floundering, he did not cry out.

Two

The long table in Regine de Vaux's dining hall was covered in snowy linen, and shone with silver and crystal. Master Pernet, the old steward, was lighting tapers.

Val paused in the doorway with a hand on his cousin's shoulder. 'It's only a supper party.'

Bertrand shrugged his hand away. His expression was gloomy. 'My mother will find something to criticize in me. She always does.'

Privately, Val had to admit that his cousin was right. He could also understand why Bertrand was a severe disappointment to a woman whose beauty had once been on the lips of every troubadour in Arvorig.

In a deep-red velvet tunic, over a blindingly white shirt, his face scrubbed, hair neatly trimmed and combed, Bertrand finally looked like what he was, the son of a noble house. Yet Val had no doubt that none of that would be enough for Jeanne d'Acquin. She would perceive nothing but her son's ugliness.

Bertrand never spoke about his early life on his father's estates at Acquin, or what had driven him away from home to seek refuge with his aunt in Roazon.

He had arrived wearing the coarse clothes of a peasant, already in rags. He had been riding a plough horse stolen from his father's fields. Even his voice, though beautiful and low-pitched, carried the accents of a peasant. He had stood there shaking in the entrance hall of Regine's house, refusing to plead, but convinced that his elegant aunt would send him straight back where he came from.

When Regine provided food, he attacked it wolfishly, ravenous, as if with no knowledge of the manners a man of his birth should use at table. It seemed no one had taught him what he needed to know.

Teaching Bertrand the civilized arts had driven Regine to distraction; he was certainly willing, but the neglect of many years could not be remedied in a few weeks. Val privately wondered whether Bertrand's newly acquired polish would stand up to the strain of a formal supper party under the cold eyes of his mother.

The deep-toned bell of the house door sounded. Master Pernet finished lighting the last taper, then turned and went out into the hall. Val could hear his mother's quick footsteps descending the stairs.

Bertrand followed Val out into the hall to greet their guests.

Holding the street door wide, Master Pernet gave a deep, respectful bow as the boy's parents entered.

Jeanne d'Acquin always reminded Val of a silver-gilt monstrance holding the relic of her former beauty. She was a tall, slender woman, as fair as her sister Regine was dark. Her pale blonde hair was drawn up sleekly to the top of her head and captured in a fashionable headdress, all gauze and pearls. Her gown was silver tissue, cut low to expose a white bosom on which she displayed a magnificent collar of opals. More gems glittered on her hands, while her eyes, like sapphires, glittered just as bright and cold as any of her jewels.

Bertrand's father, Robert d'Acquin, followed just behind her. He was scarcely as tall as his wife, with the broad shoulders and slim hips of a fighting man, though his chestnut hair was beginning to thin and the muscles of his face to sag. Whatever qualities of his had captured the famous beauty twenty years ago were not visible now. He was totally eclipsed by her, and might just as well have been one of the escort of servants who followed their master and mistress into the hall.

Jeanne paused just inside the door, her icy gaze travelling from side to side. Regine stepped forward, her hands outstretched. 'Sister, welcome. Have you – ?'

'I see you still give shelter to that worthless creature,' Jeanne interrupted, her voice thin and venomous. 'I wonder he has not disgusted you completely before now.'

Val felt her hostility like a slap of icy rain in his face. What Bertrand himself must feel was beyond him. He glanced at his cousin, prepared for an outburst, but Bertrand was silently staring at his boots, only his reddening face betraying him. Regine's careful instructions about how to welcome his parents courteously had obviously gone right out of his head.

'I have no complaints of Bertrand,' Regine replied calmly. She took no notice of Jeanne's contemptuous sniff, merely taking her hand to draw her further into the hall.

Val stepped forward and bowed. 'Good evening, Aunt. Uncle. You're very welcome to our house.'

Jeanne smiled graciously at him, and Robert responded with bluff good humour. 'Captain now, I hear. Well done, lad.'

'In a celibate order,' Jeanne added with a touch of malice, as Val murmured his thanks, and wondered how, even in rumour-ridden Roazon, the news of his promotion had reached his uncle so quickly. 'Regine, that means you'll have no grandchildren.'

'What matters is that Valery follows his heart.' Regine remained calm.

Val lost all stomach for this conversation, so despatched Master Pernet to bring water for the guests to wash their hands, and dismissed the d'Acquin servants to the kitchen where a meal would be waiting for them, too.

As Regine escorted her guests to the dining room, Bertrand at last remembered to execute a clumsy bow, and mumbled something inaudible towards the floor. Not the courteous welcome Regine had drilled into him earlier, but a great deal better than nothing.

Jeanne's gaze flicked over her son. 'Really, Bertrand,' she said, her voice high-pitched, mocking. 'At this rate you'll be a courtier in no time.'

At table, Val was seated beside his aunt, and devoted himself assiduously to her needs, if only to divert her attention from Bertrand placed on her other side. He sensed that Jeanne d'Acquin was well pleased to have a young man dancing attendance on her, even if he was her nephew — and celibate.

At the other side of the table Regine engaged Robert d'Acquin in conversation about his estates, crops, forests, the needs of his tenants — matters that even Bertrand would find familiar and easy to talk about.

But Bertrand said little, keeping his head down and his eyes fixed on his plate. It was possible that they might all get through this appalling meal without incident, and then Val could plead his duties in the citadel, and take Bertrand along with him.

But as the first course drew to a close, Jeanne seemed to

tire of Val's conversation, and turned sharply to her son. 'Bertrand, do you have to slouch like that?'

He gave her a flickering glance, and straightened self-consciously.

'You're very finely dressed tonight,' his mother continued. 'Regine, you show him more kindness than he deserves.'

'Not at all,' Regine replied, still keeping her voice even, though Val could see that a spark had woken in her eyes. 'Val and I have both become very fond of Bertrand. We're enjoying his visit.'

'Visit!' Jeanne's laugh tinkled out. 'After he came here and thrust himself on you . . .'

Because he could not bear his own home any longer. Val would have loved to speak the words aloud, but he knew how angry his mother would be if they quarrelled at her table.

He glanced over at Bertrand's father, but Robert d'Acquin's nose was buried in his cup of wine. His florid face looked more flushed than ever, and he was paying no attention to either his wife or son.

'And are you grateful to your aunt?' Jeanne rounded on her son again. 'Of course you are not! You sit there like an oaf, stuffing your face with food.' She waved a hand dismissively. 'You have the manners of a peasant.'

And whose fault is that? Val asked himself silently. Jeanne probably knew that she was being illogical. But logic did not matter here, only the impulse to hurt.

'Yes, a peasant,' Jeanne repeated, and an increased touch of malice had crept into her voice. 'Peasant you are, and peasant you will remain.' She dabbed her lips delicately with her napkin. 'Regine, you have not asked what brings us to Roazon.'

Val shot a puzzled glance at his mother. He himself had

never wondered about that, either. So many people came to the city for the Day of Memories, and yet as far as he knew none of the d'Acquin family had died in the past year. Yet certainly Jeanne would not have embarked on such a long journey just for the sake of visiting her sister — or her son.

Regine simply held out one hand, as an invitation to her sister to explain.

Jeanne cast a sidelong look, beneath her lashes, at her husband. 'We have come to make our confession to the Archbishop, and be absolved of our sin,' she said. 'And then we intend to petition Duke Joscelin, to put our affairs straight.'

This explanation was no explanation at all. Val grew even more puzzled, beginning to feel that he did not want to hear any more. Yet good manners kept him tied to the table, no matter what his aunt was about to reveal.

Looking mystified, Bertrand had flashed one glance at his mother, and then applied himself to his plate again.

'What do you mean?' Regine sounded as though thrown off balance by what her sister had just told her. 'What sin are you talking about?'

Again that knowing, sidelong look. 'Robert and I ... we did not wait to complete our marriage vows,' Jeanne confessed. 'When we were wed, I was already with child.'

Her voice was hesitant, and yet there was no blush of shame on her perfect skin. She was playing a part, Val realized in disgust; the part of a virtuous woman confessing to a single lapse.

'Really, Jeanne,' Regine said irritably, 'is there any need to make such a fuss over something that happened twenty years ago?'

Jeanne d'Acquin's eyes widened in a parody of shock. 'Sin

is sin, Sister, however long ago. How can I forget it, when the fruit of that sin sits here at table with us now?'

With a tiny movement of a gold-tipped finger she indicated Bertrand.

Bertrand's head came up again, turning to face his mother. Val felt suddenly afraid for him.

'My lady . . .' Robert finally stumbled into speech, putting a hand on his wife's arm. 'Maybe not here.'

Jeanne shook the hand off. 'Here,' she said with cold clarity. 'Now, you should all know,' she went on, 'that Holy Church tells us a child conceived out of wedlock is illegitimate, even if his parents marry. So he cannot inherit.'

Bertrand suddenly grew pale, something kindling in the depths of his eyes. Val was suddenly reminded that his cousin had already proved himself a formidable fighter, if only among the youth of the town.

'Jeanne!' There was nothing artificial about Regine's shock. 'Disinherit Bertrand? You cannot!'

'It was a sin,' Jeanne replied. 'And how can I doubt that the Judge is angry with us, when I see that . . . changeling, that goblin child, seated here? Why should Robert and I have made such an ugly creature together, unless it's punishment for our sin?'

'Mother.' Bertrand's voice was low, as if dredged up out of the depths of him. 'Acquin *should* be mine. I have—'

'Do you sit there and already lay claim to your father's lands?' Jeanne flashed back at him with poisonous malice. 'Can you not even wait until he lies in his grave?'

'You raised the question of inheritance, Aunt,' Val pointed out.

Jeanne ignored him.

Bertrand took in a long breath, then sighed it out. 'I will cross-petition.'

'You?' his mother sneered. '*You* speak before Duke Joscelin? You would be laughed out of court.'

'I will do it!' Bertrand's voice rose to a shout. He sprang to his feet, knocking the edge of the table. It rocked sideways and resettled with a jolt, tipping over his mother's full wine cup. Wine poured out of it, all over the tablecloth – and Jeanne's silver gown.

She jumped up with a screech, gazing down at the spreading red stain, the trickles of wine running down to her feet, the sopping breadth of silk beginning to cling to her.

Val saw his own mother close her eyes briefly and then reach out to Bertrand, who was unaware of her gesture. Robert, jerked out of an alcoholic haze, gazed stupidly at his wife.

Bertrand flushed deeply. For a brief moment Val had seen the man he could be, focused and formidable; now he was a shamefaced boy again. 'Mother, I'm sorry. I—'

'You clumsy oaf,' Jeanne snapped. 'This gown is ruined. But what could I expect? A hog in a sty would show more noble breeding.'

Val heard Bertrand's sudden gasp as he took a step back from the table, and the chair behind him crashed over.

Jeanne winced at the noise. 'Clod. Will you now break up your aunt's house, too?'

But before she had finished speaking, Bertrand had turned and blundered out of the room. Val heard him stumbling across the hall. The outer door opened and then crashed shut again.

Regine turned a furious look on her sister. 'Jeanne, how could you? Val, go after him and bring him home.'

Val was already on his feet. As he left the dining room he heard Jeanne d'Acquin's high, cold laughter.

Val ran out of the house, slamming the door behind him. The street was empty in both directions. On the opposite side, between two houses, a narrow flight of steps that led down towards the lake was wreathed in darkness.

As Val hesitated, he heard a crash from somewhere below. He began to hurry down the steps, barely slowing as the steep gables cut off the moonlight and left him totally in shadow. 'Bertrand, wait!'

Reaching the level ground of a cross alley, he almost stumbled over the remains of a shattered stone urn, the soil and flowers it contained spilling across the cobbles. Above his head a shutter creaked open. Ignoring the irate householder, Val dashed across the alley and flung himself down a second flight of steps.

Water glimmered through a gap between the walls as Val emerged into a small courtyard garden. Stone benches stood around a fountain, and roses scrambled over the boundary wall.

He saw Bertrand standing there, gripping the coping of the wall and leaning outwards. For one horrible minute, Val thought that he would throw himself over. He flung himself across the open space and grabbed his cousin by the shoulder.

Bertrand twisted round to shake him off, tears glittering on his face. 'Go away! I don't want you.'

'Mother sent me,' Val said peaceably. 'She—'

'Tell her everything's all right,' Bertrand broke in. 'I'll pack up and leave tomorrow.'

Realizing Bertrand had no intention of destroying himself, Val relaxed slightly. 'Where will you go?' he asked.

Bertrand shuddered, and his voice was thickened with rage. 'I'll sleep on the streets. I'll work for food. Until I can see Duke Joscelin himself and make my claim for Acquin.' He slammed both fists down hard on the rough stone wall. 'Acquin is *mine*,' he growled.

'I know it is,' Val said. 'But why can't you stay with us until your case comes to trial?'

'Aunt Regine won't want me now,' said Bertrand. He seemed to be veering wildly between a man's fury at the threat to his inheritance, and a boy's helpless misery in the face of his mother's hatred and his own clumsiness. 'I can't do anything right. I spoilt her party.'

'Rubbish,' said Val. '*Your mother* spoilt the party, by her nagging and criticizing, and then telling us that − that . . .' Val couldn't finish. He put a hand on Bertrand's shoulder, sympathetically this time. 'Come on, I'll buy you a cup of wine at the Plume of Feathers. We won't go back home until it's all over.'

Bertrand wiped a hand across his face. 'It won't ever be over,' he said thickly. 'I'd do anything − anything − if she would only *see* the real me, not this . . .' He gestured wildly to encompass his squat body, his flat, coarse features and bristly hair.

'I know,' said Val. Even though his imagination baulked at the idea of anyone seeking approval from a gilded bitch like Jeanne d'Acquin, he could feel Bertrand's hurt. 'Let's go and drink.'

'All right.' His cousin breathed out a long sigh.

Val looked tactfully away while Bertrand dragged out a handkerchief and mopped at his damp face. Gazing out across the lake, he caught sight of a golden glint, a turbulence in the water, near the steps to the hythe, where a few candles still cast light on the lake's dark surface.

He watched it for several seconds before he realized what he was seeing. Far below them, someone was struggling for his life.

2

Morwenna led Alissende to a street not far from the city wall, and paused in front of the door of a shop. The shop itself was shuttered, and there was not enough light for Alissende to read the sign, but a lamp was burning in the hallway and revealed a staircase leading upwards. A warm smell of cooking drifted down from above.

'Donan said he would get supper ready.' Morwenna closed the street door behind them and dropped a bar into place. 'Go on up. You must be worn out.'

Until Morwenna said that, Alissende had been unaware of her own weariness. Now it seemed an effort to mount each separate stair, but at last she stood on the upper landing. Morwenna pushed open a door and gestured for her to go in.

Blinking in lamp and firelight, Alissende saw a large, cluttered room whose walls were covered by painted panels, and the floor strewn with bright woven rugs. A table near the fire was set with earthenware cups and plates, while at the far end of the room another table, half in shadow, was scattered with painting equipment.

A young man was pacing up and down the room, a baby sleeping on his shoulder. As Alissende and Morwenna came in, he made a sign for silence. 'I've just got her off to sleep,' he whispered.

'There's a tooth coming through,' Morwenna said. 'This is my husband Donan. And this is Alissende, whom I met at the ceremony. She's going to stay here tonight. Go and lay Ivona down, and then we can eat.'

She took Alissende's cloak and hung it with her own behind the door. Donan disappeared with the baby, and came back a few moments later on his own. Morwenna fetched another cup and plate from a dresser.

Alissende felt herself in the centre of a whirl of quiet, purposeful activity. 'Can I help?' she asked.

'No, just sit here and I'll fetch the supper in. Donan, have we wine?'

He nodded and smiled, and ambled out again. As Morwenna followed him more quickly, Alissende went over to the table, but before she could sit down her eye was caught by the nearest wall panel. She moved closer to inspect it.

It depicted Roazon and the hills beyond. Angels thronged the sky around the topmost pinnacles of the city, while others danced above the rippling surface of the lake. Alissende could not remember ever seeing anything so beautiful.

At the sound of footsteps she half turned as Morwenna came back into the room with an earthenware pot in her hands, followed by Donan with a skin of wine and a basket of rolls.

'Did you paint this?' their guest asked. 'It's wonderful.'

Morwenna shrugged. 'We can't afford to buy tapestries.'

She took her place at the table and began to serve out fish stew from the pot. After thinking she would never want to eat again, Alissende discovered she was hungry. She sat down and ate the savoury food, growing drowsy from the warmth of the fire, barely listening as Morwenna and Donan discussed the events of the day.

When Morwenna asked her husband what he thought of

the latest icon she had painted, Donan got up to fetch it from the work table at the other end of the room. Alissende roused herself as Morwenna reached over and touched her on the wrist.

'I want to show you this,' her new friend said.

Donan set the icon down beside Alissende's plate, and she examined it curiously. She had expected another depiction of either the Warrior or the Judge – a skilful one, for she had already seen that Morwenna had rare talent – or perhaps an angel, one of the protectors of the city or of some great family who would be prepared to buy the icon so as to honour their guardian.

This was none of these. It was on an oval piece of board, small enough to nest in the palm of one hand. The background was the dull gold of all icons, and the figure painted there was a golden haired young man in a white robe. His face was ardent and in one hand he held a branch of juniper, while the other was raised in a gesture of blessing.

It occurred to Alissende, even while she gazed, that the young man bore more than a passing resemblance to Duke Joscelin.

She looked up from the icon to meet Morwenna's eyes. Her friend's bright cheerfulness had given way to uncertainty.

'He came to me in a dream,' she said. 'He announced himself as God the Healer. He told me to paint him.'

Alissende barely restrained herself from making the sign of the Knot as a proof against such blasphemy. Instead she clasped her hands tight. Those holy gestures that not so long ago had been second nature were nothing to her now – any more than the cruel God they honoured.

But *this* – a God of Healing? He represented something

she had never contemplated until now. And now, if ever, when pestilence walked in Arvorig and famine lay like a cloud on the horizon, when even the precious bloodline of the lords of Roazon had dwindled almost to nothing – perhaps the Warrior and the Judge were not enough any longer.

For Alissende herself, a Healer might be her only refuge. Or a mockery more cruel than anything endured before.

Was it possible that he had shown something of himself to Morwenna – an ordinary woman, not rich, or powerful, or learned? Yet, Alissende reminded herself, Morwenna was not so ordinary. Her painter's skill showed that, and the warmth in her that had reached out to Alissende's own need. Perhaps she was as worthy as any of the great ones of the city.

'You know, love,' Donan said thoughtfully, 'quite a lot of important people are going to be very unhappy about this icon.'

'Of course I know.' Morwenna frowned. 'But I had to paint it.'

'Will you show it?' Alissende asked, at the same moment as Donan almost echoed her question. 'Who would you show it to?'

Morwenna reached out and picked up the icon, with that same look of frowning uncertainty. Then her face cleared, became decisive. 'To Duke Joscelin – I shall give it to him tomorrow, as an induction gift.'

3

Tiphaine de Bellière scratched her nose with the end of her goosequill, blinking in the fading light. She considered

calling for tapers, but the crabbed writing on the pages of
the book she had borrowed was beginning to dance in front
of her eyes. Enough for one day. Besides, she was sure there
was something else she ought to be doing . . .

She sanded the ink on her notes, wiped the quill neatly
and closed the inkpot, and rose from her chair, unconsciously stretching to get rid of the cramps. As she turned
away from the window, her eyes fell on the bed, and the
new gown laid out across it. She clapped a hand over her
mouth. *Merciful God! Aunt Peronel will be furious!*

At the same moment the door was flung open. Peronel
de Cotin herself bustled in, silks billowing like a ship in
full sail. Once through the door, she halted and let out a
small shriek. 'Tiphaine!'

Tiphaine laced and unlaced her fingers. 'I'm sorry, Aunt.
I was . . .'

'Tiphaine, you know we're going to dine with your
Uncle Reynaud, so I expected you to be ready. And – oh,
sweet saints – look at your *hair*! And your inky *hands*! Mari,
go and fetch hot water *at once!*'

The maidservant, hovering outside in the passage, scurried off. Peronel darted at Tiphaine, grabbed her by the
shoulders and plumped her down in front of her mirror.
Snatching up the ivory comb, she plunged it into Tiphaine's
tangled hair.

'What Father Reynaud will think, I do not know,' she
said. 'And as for Nicolas . . . Tiphaine, young men expect
their wives to be pleasant, amiable, obedient. A few accom-
plishments, yes. A little music. A little fine embroidery. But
not an ink-stained scholar.' Tiphaine gasped as the comb
was tugged through a particularly obstinate snarl. 'They
really do *not* expect their wives to spend all day with their
nose in a book!'

Tiphaine thought it best not to say anything. She had lived a month now with her aunt, ever since her grandfather had died, and she found herself constantly being scolded. Aunt Peronel made everything seem so *complicated*. There were gowns for morning and gowns for evening, gowns to go walking and gowns to wear to the Offering ceremony; not forgetting elaborate gowns for evening parties. When she had lived at her grandfather's manor, she would wear linen in summer and wool in winter, and there was an end of it.

At this thought of her grandfather, she felt her throat tighten, and tears prick her eyes. They had lived so happily together! He would ride out daily to inspect his estates and converse with his tenants, while Tiphaine had the run of his library. And if she uncovered something difficult, her grandfather could always explain it to her.

But now she had scarcely any books, not being able to carry any more than could be loaded on the single pack mule Peronel had provided when she fetched her here to her new home in Roazon. Tiphaine wondered what would befall the books she and her grandfather had loved so much, abandoned now to mould and mice in his empty castle.

Resolutely Tiphaine put these thoughts away. Soon Mari brought in a basin of hot water so that Tiphaine could scrub the ink from her fingers, and then helped her get into the new gown, made of white silk, with silver embroidery and tiny pearls.

'No time to do *anything* more with your hair!' her aunt grumbled. 'Mari, that silver lace...' Rapidly the older woman drew Tiphaine's dark curls up on top of her head, and bound them with the silver fillet. 'There ... yes, I fancy that will do. Simple, but quite suitable for a young girl.

You know, Tiphaine, you could be quite beautiful if you would only take time to bother with yourself.'

As Mari fitted on silver slippers, Tiphaine murmured, 'Holy Church teaches us to scorn finery.'

'Yes, yes,' her aunt said impatiently. 'That is all very well for common women, or those who vow themselves to the Matriarchy. But you are a de Bellière, and you have a position to keep up.' She smiled, fluffing out Tiphaine's skirts. 'Besides, you want to please Nicolas, do you not? Mari, run downstairs and see if Master Nicolas is here to escort us.'

The servant girl bobbed a curtsey and sped off.

Peronel gave a last tweak to Tiphaine's curls and clasped a tiny pearl droplet, on its golden chain, around her neck. 'There,' she said. 'You look quite ready. Let us go down.'

Tiphaine followed her along the passage, struggling to manage her skirts, until they came to the head of the stairs.

Lamps were burning in the hall below, and by their light Tiphaine could see Nicolas de Cotin lounging against the wall. He was very handsome, she supposed, tall and fair, but he always appeared so well dressed and courteous that Tiphaine wondered whether she had ever encountered the real Nicolas.

He straightened up when he saw them. 'How beautiful you both look!'

Tiphaine gave him a vague smile, and as she reached the foot of the stairs took the arm he offered to her. She was not quite sure how, in the single month that she had lived in Roazon, she had managed to become betrothed to her cousin Nicolas. She could not remember him ever asking her – or perhaps she had been thinking of something else at the time. Whatever the reason, suddenly it had become an understanding between them, then a priest had spoken the words over them in the cathedral itself, and Aunt Peronel was busy making wedding plans.

Of course, Tiphaine had not told Nicolas about those sudden flashes of insight that sometimes came upon her out of nowhere. She certainly had not told her aunt, since they were random, out of Tiphaine's control, and hard to understand. What worried her a little was that out of all the shadows of future events that slipped into her mind, she had never seen an image of herself as Nicolas's wife.

Tiphaine had never met her uncle, Father Reynaud, until she came to live in Roazon. Her father's elder brother, he had renounced his inheritance to embrace the holy poverty of the Legion. Even now, on the Night of Memories when everyone feasted, he ate nothing but bread and a little salt fish, and drank only water.

His guests were better served, however, with a greater variety of dishes than Tiphaine had ever seen, even at Aunt Peronel's table. The guests themselves were richly dressed; her aunt's magnificence seemed nothing out of the ordinary. Tiphaine herself could have sunk comfortably into silent obscurity, except that Father Reynaud had seated her in the place of honour, at his right-hand side.

Apart from members of her own family, the only other guest Tiphaine recognized was the Archbishop, Father Mathurin, seated diagonally opposite her. He looked strangely smaller than that magnificent, remote figure in a gold-embroidered cope who had presided at the Offering ceremony in the cathedral.

He and Father Reynaud soon launched into a discussion

of a book on the nature of God, recently purchased for the cathedral library. Tiphaine's interest quickened as they spoke, but Nicolas was seated at her other side, assiduously plying her with attention; offering her wine, water, sauces, or paying her compliments, while all Tiphaine wanted to do was listen to the learned conversation to her left. How could she possibly follow the thread of Father Reynaud's argument if her cousin would keep babbling on at her?

When she was his wife, she asked herself dismally, would she ever have a moment of quiet again?

Father Reynaud's discussion with the Archbishop came to an end just as the plates were cleared, and the next course was set on the table. Father Reynaud turned to Tiphaine. 'Well, my dear, and how do you like Roazon?'

'It's a magnificent city, Father.' Tiphaine could not feel comfortable addressing this man as 'Uncle'.

'And you have everything you need?'

'Aunt Peronel is very kind,' Tiphaine said, 'but there is one thing . . .'

Father Reynaud smiled, and Tiphaine realized that he was expecting her to ask for a new gown, a piece of jewellery, or maybe a little lapdog like her aunt's. But it was too late to back off now.

'I have so few books, Father,' she said. 'Would I be permitted to borrow some from the cathedral library? Like the one you were discussing just now . . .'

Her voice trailed off.

Aunt Peronel hissed, 'Tiphaine!'

Across the table, the Archbishop was staring at her, more intrigued than shocked, but he left the answering of her request to Father Reynaud.

The Grand Master's deep-set eyes had suddenly turned

chilly. 'My child, that would not be suitable. The cathedral library is intended for *scholars*. I hardly think that you would find the books there entertaining.'

Tiphaine began to protest, but broke off as Nicolas put a hand on her arm.

'You must forgive my betrothed, Father,' he said. 'She doesn't understand the ways of Roazon as yet.'

Shame flooded over her at his patronizing tones. If they had been alone she would have defended herself, but now she realized they had drawn everyone's attention. From somewhere down the table came a tinkle of laughter.

'I ... I beg your pardon, Father,' Tiphaine said. Feeling her face burn, she applied herself to the food in front of her.

Father Reynaud broke the embarrassed silence by turning to Aunt Peronel. 'Do you attend the tournament in two days' time?'

She replied with a touch of pride, 'Nicolas is to take part.'

'Of course.' Father Reynaud unbent enough to smile. 'Then you must sit with me in my stand.' With a slightly malicious edge to his voice, he continued, 'And perhaps Lady Tiphaine here will preside as Queen of Beauty. Then, my child, if your Nicolas wins the tournament prize, you may present it to him.'

Tiphaine blinked, not entirely certain what Father Reynaud was asking of her, but she noticed more than one of the ladies around the table were looking frankly envious.

She could see no way out of this, so she inclined her head. 'Thank you, Father.'

Even as she spoke, another of those disturbing flashes of image came to her. She saw herself in a tiny, bright picture, like a holy icon. She was seated beneath a silken canopy — the tournament stand? She wore a coronet, adorned with a silver swan, its wings extended as if rising from its nest. Somehow she realized that this adornment was the prize for the tournament.

But that's ridiculous! she said to herself as the image flicked back into nothingness. *I should be giving the prize, not wearing it myself.*

Three

I

Val ran along the edge of the hythe, Bertrand pounding along behind him. The lake stretched undisturbed, silvered by the moonlight. Most of the lamps had burnt out, and only a few candle flames still glimmered on the water.

At first Val thought they had arrived too late, then a dark turmoil shattered the lacquered surface. He glimpsed the pale smudge of a face, and an arm flung upwards.

Val hit the surface in a running dive and struck out strongly. The water was a cold shock after the warmth of the summer night, as he thrust his way through clusters of bobbing wreaths. The scent of roses was an incongruous counterpoint to his fear and urgency.

By the time he reached him, the drowning man was sinking again, thrashing feebly as if at the end of his strength.

Val grabbed him by the shoulders just as he sank again. The man twisted his head to look at him, his eyes wide and terrified, hair plastered over his face.

'You're safe,' Val yelled. 'Don't struggle.'

At first he did not think the man had heard him, for his body spasmed, almost as if he was fighting to get away from his rescuer. Val barely managed to hold on to him as his head dipped under.

As he came up again, spitting out lake water, Val saw Bertrand beside him, a hand fastened in the drowning man's hair. An arm came up, weighted by waterlogged silk, and white fingers clawed feebly at Bertrand's face. Bertrand let out a curse and cuffed him across the side of the head with his free hand.

The man's eyes rolled back and he went limp in Val's grasp.

Supporting him between them, they swam back to the steps and hauled him out. At first he lay inert on the paving stones, until Bertrand turned him over, and pressed down rhythmically on his back, when water gushed from his mouth and he began to cough.

'He'll survive,' Bertrand panted.

Val looked down at the gasping creature at his feet. He was young, and dressed in elaborate silks, as if to celebrate the Day of Memories. But how had he come from there to here? Val did not see how he could have fallen into the water accidentally. Was this some drunken game that had gone wrong? But then surely his companions would have helped him out, or raised the alarm. Val shrugged. He could make no sense of it.

'What are we going to do with him?' Bertrand asked.

'I don't know.' Val bent over the stranger and shook him gently by the shoulder. 'Who are you? Where are you staying?'

When there was no response, Val shook his head anxiously. 'I could take him home . . .'

'With my mother still there?' An unholy grin spread over Bertrand's face. 'They would never forgive you.'

Val was sure that his mother would sympathize. But it would give Jeanne d'Acquin yet another reason to criticize and intrude.

'He can stay in the captain's lodgings,' he decided at last. 'Sir Guy has already moved out, so there'll be no one there tonight.'

Still bending over the rescued man, he went on, 'You'll come with us for tonight. We'll find your friends in the morning.'

There was a choking and barely coherent reply. 'No. Leave me alone.'

'I can't do that,' Val said patiently. 'You can't stay out here like this.'

Bertrand stood staring down at the half drowned creature on the paving stones. His new tunic was pulpy with lake water, that puddled at his feet. His earlier fury had vanished; he now looked perfectly composed.

'We'd better move him, then,' he said. 'We can't stand here all night.'

He grasped the sprawling man by one arm and began hoisting him to his feet, while Val supported him on the other side. Briefly the stranger struggled against their grasp, but he was too exhausted to resist for more than a few seconds. He seemed barely conscious.

A narrow stairway, criss-crossing back and forth up the steepest face of the island, led directly up from the hythe to the citadel. As Val and Bertrand hauled the young man up it, he scarcely cooperated; they were forced almost to carry him, a sodden weight sagging between them, while a deep shuddering coursed occasionally through all his body.

At the foot of the final flight of steps, Val paused to ease the ache across his shoulders. 'It's not far now, Bertrand. Go and buy us some hot wine at the Plume of Feathers.' He gestured down the alleyway to where a torch burnt at the far end; the faint sound of singing was carried

towards them on the breeze. 'He could take a chill and die
if we don't get him warm soon.'

As his cousin hurried off, Val dragged the man's arm
back over his shoulder and staggered with him up the last
flight of steps. Once at the top, he was within sight of the
postern gate leading into the citadel. A minute or two more
brought them to the door to the captain's lodgings.

As he paused, panting and fumbling for the door handle,
a footstep sounded on the flagstones and a figure emerged
out of the darkness. Val recognized his fellow lieutenant,
Girec d'Evron, still dressed in his ceremonial armour and
white surcoat.

'De Vaux, what in God's name are you doing?'

Val cursed silently. He had hoped to achieve this
without anyone seeing him, and of all the people to have to
explain to, Girec d'Evron was the most unwelcome.

'What does it look like?' he said tiredly. 'And what affair
is it of yours?'

'None, I thank the Judge.' Val was aware of the other
Knight's cold eyes fixed on the man he had rescued, who
seemed vaguely aware of the scrutiny, and let out a faint
moan, then turned his face away to hide it against Val's
shoulder.

D'Evron's narrow, pallid features twitched in disapproval. 'What a . . . fascinating life you lead, de Vaux.'

Val did not respond, but to his relief d'Evron moved
on, his pale form dissolving back into the darkness, leaving
Val to wrestle the door open at last and haul his half-
conscious burden up the turret stairs to the bedchamber.

The narrow bunk was stripped to its horsehair mattress;
the woollen blankets had been folded and piled neatly at its
foot. Laying the stranger down there, Val struck a spark

from flint and tinder, and lit a pottery lamp on the windowsill.

Then, awkwardly, Val pulled off the young man's sodden silks and wrapped a blanket around him. 'There – rest for a while,' he said. 'You'll be safe now.'

The young man kept his face averted. He murmured, 'You should have left me. I want to die.'

Val was shocked into to silence, but he reached out and touched one thin shoulder.

Immediately the man shrank away. 'Don't touch me.'

'I'm sorry . . .'

The other whipped his head round to face him, half sitting up. 'Do you know who I am? If you did, you would never want to touch me – Sir Knight of the Legion of God!'

Val found himself looking down into a beautiful, death-pale face from which incredible violet eyes blazed at him with a mixture of terror and fury. The young man was visibly shaking as he clutched the blanket around himself.

'Who are you, then?' Val asked quietly.

'My name is Aurel de Montfaucon.' He spat the words out with a defiant jerk of the head. 'Have you not heard of me? Has the story of my debauchery not penetrated as far as Roazon? Did they not warn you about me?'

Val wasn't sure what his own face was revealing, but to his shame, his hand had begun to move in the sign of the Knot – the automatic warding against evil. He recalled that Father Reynaud had mentioned this Aurel de Montfaucon in one of his recent sermons, fulminating against sin in such graphic terms that Val had almost begun to believe the Grand Master was enjoying himself hugely.

Val had imagined someone old in evil, planning and executing his sins with careful pleasure, not this desperate, sodden creature.

'What will you do now? Throw me out in the street?'

'And let you take yourself back to the lake? No.'

'It's too late now. I wish you had left me there...'

On the last few words the energy faded from his voice; he sounded totally desolate. He lay down again, clutching the blanket around himself, his face turned away.

Val controlled an impulse to sit down on the bed beside him and try to comfort him. Instead, he asked, 'Is it something you can tell me?'

A long pause; Val could do nothing but wait. Then Aurel de Montfaucon began to speak again, his voice rasping like a twisted thread. 'My father was a merchant in Kemper. He brought me to Roazon five years ago, to light the candle for my mother. I ... met someone here.' He raised his head again and fixed lambent eyes on Val, his voice gathering a little force as he continued. 'I didn't know ... I didn't ask for it! But I'd never thought that there could be such happiness. I loved him, and I thought he loved me.'

He hesitated, as if expecting a response, but Val found nothing to say.

'Then my father found us together,' Aurel went on. 'He beat me, and took me straight home. I waited there for five years — five years when I swore every day to make my father regret he had not cast me off and left me in Roazon. Meanwhile I gathered that ... reputation you know so well.' Now there was bitter mockery in his tone. 'And then at last my father died and I was free to come back and find my lover.' A ripple of harsh laughter shook him. 'He didn't want me. I even think he'd forgotten me.' He brushed one hand over his eyes, as if forcing back tears. 'He's betrothed. It's over, and I want to die.'

Val knew he should be sickened by this revelation of Aurel's sin, but what sickened him most was the thought of the man's pain. He was not sure what to say or do. The silence between them was taut as a bowstring.

A heavy tread on the stair outside broke it. The door was shoved open and Bertrand came in, carrying a cup with aromatic steam rising from it.

'Sorry I took so long,' he said with a cheerful grin. 'I think half of Roazon is in the Plume of Feathers tonight.' He handed the cup to Aurel.

The young man's gaze flickered over him and away again. He murmured a word of thanks and took a sip of the spiced wine.

'Bertrand,' Val instructed, 'can you go to the bathhouse? Straight through the main door of the barracks, at the end of the passage. You'll find some towels there, to get yourself dry.'

Bertrand went off again. The interruption had taken no more than a minute, but the tension between Val and his guest had dissolved. Val knew there would be no more confidences that night.

'Where will you go, when you leave here?'

'I came from Kemper by barge. But it's anchored on the lakeshore.' He rubbed his forehead vaguely. 'I don't think I could walk so far.'

'No need. You can sleep here. By morning the boats will all be back at the hythe, and you'll find someone to carry you across.'

Aurel nodded. 'You're very kind.'

Val waited until Aurel had emptied the cup, then handed him a fresh blanket before he settled down to sleep. Once he had relinquished the last scraps of consciousness, Val picked up the lamp and went downstairs again. Bertrand's sodden garments were strewn over the floor, and he was pulling on one of the Knights' linen robes.

He grinned as his cousin came in. 'Behold the Knight Companion!' he said, spreading his arms.

Val couldn't help smiling. The robe was stretched tight across Bertrand's massive shoulders, but its hem trailed on the floor.

'Why, have you thoughts that way?' he said.

'And take a vow of celibacy?' Bertrand laughed. 'I'm not as virtuous as you, Cousin.'

Val stripped off his own wet robe and began towelling himself vigorously, casting an eye over a platter of hot meat pasties. After the interrupted dinner earlier, he was ravenously hungry.

Bertrand brought two cups of spiced wine to the table. Jerking his head upwards, he asked, 'What was all that about? Do you know him?'

Val shook his head. 'I've never met him before. His name is Aurel de Montfaucon.'

The name obviously meant nothing to Bertrand. 'What happened to him?'

'Crossed in love.' Val tried awkwardly for a light tone, not sure that he could explain to Bertrand all that Aurel had revealed.

'Poor fool.' Bertrand snorted as he bit into a pasty. 'With looks like that, he could have all the women he wants.'

Val fastened his own robe, and sat down at the table to make sure of his share of food. Weariness descended on him like a blanket; he could have fallen asleep where he sat.

'I'm on duty from midnight,' he said to Bertrand, wanting to change the subject. 'I'll need to go round and inspect the citadel guards. Do you want to stay here – or go home? They'll be gone by now, I should think.'

Bertrand didn't hesitate. 'I'll stay here. Maybe somebody

should make sure him upstairs doesn't go wandering off into the lake again.'

'True.' Val stifled a yawn. 'I'm on duty tomorrow night, too. Looks like I won't get any sleep before the tournament.'

'What tournament? Where?'

'It's traditional, two days after the Day of Memories. Didn't you know?'

'I wish...' Bertrand's dark eyes were gleaming. 'Val, could I fight in this tournament? Lance and sword are noble weapons.' His face twisted in disappointment. 'But I've no horse or armour.'

Val smiled, suddenly feeling a hundred years older and more experienced than his eager cousin. 'I can lend you what you need.'

Bertrand drew in his breath sharply. 'Would you?'

'Why not? You are trained, aren't you?'

'I won't disgrace you, Cousin.' Bertrand bared his teeth in a smile of unholy delight. 'Oh, no,' he breathed, 'you don't need to worry about that.'

2

Tancred de Kervel, Seneschal of Roazon, paused beside the main doors of the great hall as the servants replenished wine flagons and set dishes of sweetmeats and spiced cakes along the tables. The feast to mark the Day of Memories was drawing to an end. Soon the ladies present would take their leave, though their lords would no doubt sit drinking for hours yet. Tancred reflected that he would be lucky to see his bed this side of dawn.

At the high table Duke Joscelin sat with his chin resting on clasped hands, his head turned towards Count Fragan of

Gwened, who sat on his right. His plain linen robe stood out through its lack of ostentation, among so much silk and velvet and fur. Count Fragan seemed to have plenty to say to him; if Tancred guessed right, he would be pre-empting the discussions held in the Council meeting that would follow Duke Joscelin's induction on the following day. Count Fragan seemed to find it difficult to accept that, for all the size and wealth of Gwened, the true power in Arvorig lay in this self-effacing young man who was now listening to him with polite attention.

Tancred sighed at the thought of those induction cer-emonies. There were still a thousand and one preparations to be made if Roazon was not to be shamed before the visiting lords and ambassadors. Not to mention the tour-nament to be held on the day after, though at least Father Reynaud and the Legion took most of the responsibility for that.

Tancred's head was aching violently and his crippled leg seemed to throb in sympathy. Leaning on his ashwood staff, he limped slowly down the passage as far as the Council chamber, where the following day's meeting would take place. At least, everything there was in readiness. Long oak tables, arranged in a square, were polished to mirror bright-ness. Fresh candles had been placed by each seat, the reflections of their silver holders gleaming pale on the silken surface of the wood, where it was touched by the moonlight that poured through the window.

On the far wall, its silvery light washed over the new tapestries, specially commissioned for Duke Joscelin's induction; Tancred himself had supervised their hanging earlier that day. They told in sequence the story of the first Duke of Roazon, the establishing of the city, the raising of the cathedral, and victory over the powers of darkness.

Master Yves the weaver, and his myriad staff, had depicted the legendary city of Autrys — an island like Roazon, or so the stories had it — off the coast of Arvorig, not far from Kemper. Autrys, so the common folk said, had been the home of demons, and at the moment when the first Duke of Roazon placed the circlet of his rank on his head, the raging seas had risen, to drown Autrys and its evil for ever under the waves.

The weaver had obviously enjoyed depicting this cataclysm: the waves crashing against walls and towers, swirling up the streets, engulfing the upper slopes of the evil city, while demons clung in terror to the last uncovered pinnacles of rock to escape the smothering water, or shrieked as it swept them away to drown.

Demons, Tancred thought, might well be more resilient than this. He allowed himself a sour smile. It was a good story, though, and it did the lords of Roazon no harm at all. Even in these enlightened times, there were people who still believed that if Roazon was left without a lord of the true line, then Autrys would rise again, and spread its darkness over all of Arvorig.

With a satisfied nod — the new tapestries were spectacular enough to impress the visiting barons — Tancred limped across to a side table where jugs of wine had been placed in readiness, and poured half a cup for himself. Sipping it, he stood gazing out into the night. So high above the lake here, he could see nothing but the sky, moon-silvered, and his own reflection shadowed and distorted by the glass so that the scar which puckered the left side of his face, drawing his mouth into a constant sneer, almost faded into the darkness. He met his own eyes, deep and questioning, and then turned away with a faint snort of disgust, setting down his wine cup, scarcely tasted, in the window embrasure.

He could hear voices now, and movement from the great hall. The ladies were withdrawing, with a sudden tinkling of laughter and the rustle of silken gowns, as they passed the door of the Council chamber. Then he stiffened as the door opened and a woman came in.

Tancred bowed. 'Lady Marjolaine.'

Marjolaine de Roazon laughed in surprise. She was flushed, and her hair was dishevelled. The roses she wore in the bosom of her gown were drooping now, but they sent out a wave of musky perfume. Tancred closed his eyes briefly on the memory of her father, Sir Primel, laughing and golden, with a rose — his lady's favour — fixed to his helmet as he rode out onto the tournament field where he was fated to die.

'Tancred,' Marjolaine admonished, 'since when do you need to bow to me, when we're alone?'

'You are the grandchild of the last Duke of Roazon, lady,' Tancred said. 'And soon to be the wife of the next.'

'And your friend too?' Marjolaine went to him and gripped his hand between both her own. She was serious now. 'I shall need a friend.'

'You're resolved, then?'

'Yes. What else can I do? The betrothal is to take place tomorrow after Duke Joscelin's induction.' Her eyes were suddenly warm, and distant. As if she had tapped into his own memory, she went on, 'Do you remember the day we lit a candle for my father? I was only six years old. You were his squire, and you held my hand all the way down to the lakeside. You spoke the words and helped me lay the roses on the water. I felt very grown-up, but I didn't really understand what was happening until I saw you weeping.'

'Yes, I remember.' Tancred's voice was hoarse.

'Then don't bow to me, not after all we've shared.' A

single tear spilt, and she wiped it away with the palm of her hand. Her voice became brighter, brittle-sounding, as she moved away from him towards the far wall. 'I came to look at these new tapestries.'

The seneschal watched her in silence as she scanned their woven images, and then approached them to examine the workmanship more closely. 'Master Yves is very skilled,' she murmured. 'I believe he has apprenticed both his sons to the craft?'

Tancred ignored her small-talk. Harshly, he asked her, 'Do you want this marriage?'

'I . . . don't know.' Marjolaine let out a sigh and turned to face him again. 'It does make sense. For I am Duke Govrian's granddaughter, his only living descendent, and Joscelin is my second cousin. Our marriage will secure the inheritance.'

'That isn't what I asked,' Tancred pointed out dryly.

'No . . . But Tancred, you know very well that a woman born as I am can never expect to choose in matters of love. I should be thankful that I am to be married to a man as upright as Duke Joscelin, and not . . . oh, Geoffrey de Brieg or some other old lecher.'

She paused; Tancred said nothing, only raising his brows questioningly.

'But . . . Joscelin's just a boy, Tancred! And more than that – he did not choose the monastery at Brociel, but he took it to his heart. If Grandfather had lived another week, he would have taken his final vows there. Now he is Duke of Roazon, he must take a wife, but there is something . . . Tancred, I think that in the depths of himself he has never renounced his celibacy.'

Tancred nodded. 'And you can happily give yourself to this marriage?'

'I must.' Marjolaine drew herself up, pushing back a wisp of hair that strayed over her face. 'I am the last in the direct line of Roazon. It is my duty.'

3

Sunlight angling across the bed woke Aurel. For a moment he blinked crusted eyes at the unfamiliar room, as memory came seeping back. The wild despair of the night before when Nicolas had sent him away. The terror of drowning and the even greater terror of being rescued to face life again. The passionate anger with which he had met the pity of the young Knight.

All of it was faded now. The world was grey, and he could feel nothing.

Stifling a groan as pain shot through his abused muscles, he crawled out of the cocoon of blankets and sat on the edge of the bed. His silken robe lay across the foot of it, dry now but with a stiff, sticky feel to it. The touch repelled him, but hearing movement in the room below he pulled the robe on, in case the Knight should come in and find him naked.

Moments later there were footsteps on the stairs and the door opened to admit his rescuer. Aurel saw him properly for the first time: the finely cut features, the dark hair curling loosely into the nape of his neck, the dark eyes regarding him without disgust or judgement.

'You're awake,' the Knight said. 'There's breakfast downstairs. Or do you need some water to wash with first?'

Aurel shook his head. He felt tongue-tied and stupid, as though his mind would not send the right messages to his lips.

'No – I only want to go.' He had hardly spoken when he realized the monstrous ingratitude of that, and added, stumbling over the words. 'I'm thankful – for my life, for your kindness, but I can't stay here.'

The young Knight nodded. 'If that's what you want.'

Aurel rose from the bed, swaying, but managed to recover himself before the other could move across the room to support him.

'I'm sorry, I don't know your name,' he said.

'Valery de Vaux,' the Knight replied. He turned and led the way down the stairs. The room below was full of the smell of warm bread, and at the table sat the other man Aurel vaguely remembered from the night before. His mouth was full, but he nodded cheerfully to the visitor.

'I'll walk down to the harbour with you,' Val said, 'and make sure you find a ferry to take you across to your barge.'

The city was only just rousing itself, though more people were out on the streets than Aurel would have expected. At the peak, near the citadel, the sun was shining brightly, but mist curled up the lower levels and lay in wisps over the lake and the hythe. Boats were now tied up where on the night before the mourners had launched their memories into the water; a few tattered wreaths bobbed at the edge of the steps. Further out in the lake fishermen were gathering a greater debris of roses and candles into their nets.

Val hailed a ferry boat, and its navigator began to hoist his sail. Aurel saw Val toss him a coin and briefly he felt embarrassed, until he realized how trivial that was in the face of everything else.

'Go safely,' Val said to him. Aurel had to meet the man's dark eyes, a serious, unaccusing gaze piercing him through. 'I will pray for you.'

As Aurel looked for words to thank him, the ferryman's impatient cry interrupted his stammering efforts. The boatman cast off. A breeze stiffened the sail, beginning to dissipate the last shreds of mist, and the boat slid out into the lake.

Aurel looked back to spot Val's tall figure still standing on the hythe, until it was lost in the dazzle of sunlight on the water.

Four

I

The sun had not yet climbed above the citadel wall when Alissende and Morwenna reached the square in front of the main gates, but already the crowds were gathering to see Duke Joscelin walk in procession to the cathedral for his ritual induction as Duke of Roazon. Some people squatting on the flagstones, wrapped in cloaks and blankets, had obviously been waiting there all night. Hawkers were moving among them, trays of warm rolls slung round their necks, the spicy scent of them tickling Alissende's nostrils as she followed Morwenna across the square. In the lee of the wall, someone had set up a brazier with a huge copper pot of ale upon it, and his customers huddled nearby with their hands clasped round horn beakers, shivering in the dawn chill.

Morwenna was carrying the new icon, her induction gift to Duke Joscelin, while Alissende held the baby Ivona drowsing against her shoulder. Briefly Alissende wished it could have been Donan who escorted his wife to the citadel to present her icon, but Donan had already gone off to join the other councillors of the silversmiths' guild, who had been assigned places in the cathedral itself to witness the imminent ceremony. Alissende felt not at all sure that she wanted to be involved, but Morwenna had made it clear that she did not want to go alone, and she had already shown Alissende so much kindness ... Stoically Alissende drew her mantle around herself and the baby; a few minutes more, and it would be over.

The citadel gates stood wide open, flanked on either side by an array of Knights Legionaries in their silver armour, their faces expressionless beneath plumed helmets. Morwenna paused beside the nearest one, and bobbed a curtsey.

'I have brought a gift for Duke Joscelin, sir,' she said, holding up the bundle wrapped in saffron-coloured silk. 'Where should I take it?'

The Knight unstiffened so far as to gesture through the gate towards a door standing open at the far side of a cobbled courtyard. 'Through there, mistress. Someone should be there to receive your gift.'

Morwenna curtseyed again, thanking him, and passed on through the gate. Alissende wondered briefly if she would be permitted to follow her friend, but no one tried to stop her.

Beyond the door was a large hall, its walls covered with tapestries, the vaulted ceiling hung with iron lamps. A short passageway led off to the right, with double doors open at the far end. Servants in the Roazon livery were passing up and down the corridor, carrying the gifts presented by townspeople like themselves.

Approaching the doors, Morwenna flashed a nervous glance at Alissende, and stepped into the room beyond. A pace or two behind, Alissende heard a harassed young voice exclaiming, 'Tancred, what are we going to do with it all?'

She paused on the threshold of the room beyond, almost believing herself transported from the real world into the treasure house of some legendary king. The sunlight, strengthening now, shone through narrow windows on to rows of trestle tables, heaped with all the opulent wealth of Roazon. Garments of silk and velvet, jewelled or crusted with embroidery. Vessels of gold and silver and porcelain. Caskets of carved and inlaid wood, spilling jewels, and flasks of perfume. Bowls of beaten copper heaped with spices, the air heavy with their scent. All the wealth of the numerous city guilds was represented.

In the midst of this opulence, Duke Joscelin, dressed in a plain robe of undyed linen, gazed around with a bewildered air, running his hands through dishevelled hair. 'We might sell it all and give the money to the poor?'

'My lord, these are gifts.' The speaker was a small man, robed in black velvet with a steward's chain of office across his shoulders. He bore a staff of pale, polished wood, shod with silver, and rapped it gently against the floor to emphasise his words. 'You must not seem to slight your people's love.'

Joscelin turned on him that look of gentle gravity that Alissende had witnessed before, during the ceremony on the hythe. 'As well slight them, then, by packing it all away in chests and clothes presses.' He shrugged and smiled faintly. 'But, Tancred, you know best. I'll leave everything in your hands.'

Tancred bowed his head. 'My lord, it's time for your robing.'

'So late already?' Joscelin looked startled. 'Tancred, you must—'

He broke off as he noticed the two young women standing by the door. Alissende suppressed a shiver as his gaze flicked over her in a rapid scrutiny, but as deep and intense as she had ever felt.

Morwenna looked flushed and more nervous than ever, as if she had not expected to meet Duke Joscelin himself, and already overwhelmed by the gifts bestowed on him.

'Come closer.' Joscelin waved one hand in a gesture of invitation. 'You wished to speak with us?'

As Morwenna moved forward between the tables, holding out her gift to him, the silken wrappings fell away. On the previous evening, Donan had fitted the icon into a silver frame. It even had a chain so that it could be worn like an ornament.

'I wished to give you this, my lord,' she said.

Joscelin came to meet her and inspected the icon, touching its frame lightly with the fingertips of one hand. 'Beautiful—' he breathed.

Morwenna flushed with pride and pleasure.

'Your own work, mistress?' Tancred had limped over to Joscelin's side, and was leaning heavily on his staff, so that he could examine the icon too. Facing him for the first time, Alissende saw the ugly scar stretching down the entire left side of his face.

Morwenna replied, 'The painting, sir. But the frame is my husband's – he is a silversmith.'

'I suspect that no one will much notice the frame,' Tancred said. 'You have rare talent, mistress. But the subject?' he went on. 'I don't recognize it.'

'I see it as God the Healer,' Morwenna said.

Alissende saw Tancred stiffen, though Joscelin himself – still apparently entranced by the beauty of the icon – did not react. Morwenna must have seen it too, for she added, 'I saw him in a dream, sir.'

Now the eyes of both men were turned on her, Tancred with something like shock and dismay, Joscelin quietly interested. Alissende wondered if either of them had noticed the portrait's resemblance to Joscelin himself, or what they thought that might mean.

'The Healer?' Joscelin murmured at last. 'Mistress, you have indeed been granted a great gift, and I thank you for allowing me to share it.'

He took the icon from her hands at last, raising it as if he would slip the chain over his head.

Tancred reached out a hand to stop him. 'No, my lord.'

Joscelin froze. 'No?'

As they measured each other, Alissende suddenly saw that Tancred – or anyone else – would be in error if they thought that Joscelin's youth and quiet demeanour were proof of weakness. The young lord was fully in command of himself.

After a few seconds, it was Tancred who looked away. 'My lord, you must get robed for the induction,' he said. 'You cannot wear that now.'

For an instant, Joscelin considered. 'You may be right.' Gathering icon and chain together, he laid them in Tancred's outstretched hand. 'Keep it for me, Tancred. It's not to be packed away and forgotten, do you understand?'

Tancred sighed. 'As you wish, my lord.'

Joscelin turned once more to the icon's creator. 'Your name, mistress?'

'Morwenna, my lord.'

Joscelin smiled at her, with genuine warmth and delight in his face. 'I shall remember.' As the steward shifted uneasily, he added, 'Yes, Tancred, I'm going now.'

He turned and strode swiftly down the length of the room to disappear through a door at its far end. Tancred meanwhile returned with a brooding look to the contemplation of the icon resting in his palm. Crippled and scarred as he was, Alissende thought, he might feel drawn to this concept of the Healer.

As the baby had begun to stir restlessly, Alissende edged

forward and touched Morwenna on the arm. It was time to go. Morwenna dropped another curtsey, murmuring, 'Your leave, sir,' and turned towards the door.

Harshly, Tancred demanded, 'Wait.'

Alissende's stomach lurched. Was he about to have them arrested for heresy? Yet his expression was not hostile. Behind that perpetual sneer was something closer to uncertainty.

'Mistress,' he asked, 'will you ever paint more of these?'

'Oh, yes, sir.' Morwenna's response was bright and open.

'Will you paint one for me, then?' He sounded nervous, stumbling over his words. 'But not with a chain like this . . .'

'Of course, sir,' Morwenna said. 'I can bring some other frames for you to choose.'

'Thank you. Tomorrow . . . no, tomorrow we have that damn' tournament. The next day, then. Ask for me at the gate.'

Morwenna withdrew, pulling Alissende after her, and giving way to a little bounce of joy as soon as they were safely into the passage.

'A new commission!' she said. 'Alissende, that man's the seneschal, Tancred de Kervel. If he likes my work, he might commission more of it, and other lords will see it too . . .'

She chattered on happily as they left the citadel, but Alissende wished that Tancred de Kervel's interest had been attracted by something else.

She could not help sharing Donan's view that the new icon was likely to cause a lot of trouble.

2

Valery de Vaux ran a comb through his hair, checked the pristine whiteness of his surcoat, and stepped out of the captain's lodgings, blinking in the bright sunlight. After escorting his unexpected guest down to the lake, he had snatched just a couple of hours' sleep, and now, forthcoming night duty or not, he had to muster the Knights Companions and with them attend Duke Joscelin during his induction.

Swiftly he threaded through the maze of courtyards at the rear of the citadel. Usually they were filled with the sound of hammering from armourers' workshops and smithies, and the reek of hot metal and burning horn. Today all was quiet, though, since the master craftsmen were already gone to take their privileged places in the cathedral, the workmen being given leave to watch the procession.

In the largest courtyard, the Knights Companions were already forming up under the critical eye of Girec d'Evron. Val murmured a word of thanks to him, receiving an unfriendly stare in reply. And there was something else, Val sensed, behind that hostility: a kind of repressed triumph as if d'Evron knew something that pleased him, and rejoiced in Val's ignorance.

Val's mouth tightened. He could expect nothing except resentment from d'Evron, when he must surely have expected the captaincy for himself. No hope of the easy working relationship Val had enjoyed with Sir Guy de Karenteg.

He motioned to Sulien de Plouzhel, bearing the banner of Roazon, to take his place at the head of the rank, and assumed his own place just behind him. The rest of the

Knights fell into a double column, and Girec d'Evron swung into place at the rear, bearing the banner of the Knights Companions.

As if someone had been watching — and clearly someone had — the main door into the citadel swung open and Duke Joscelin himself emerged. He dismissed the servants attending him before crossing the courtyard to join his knightly escort.

Bareheaded, his golden hair shone in the bright sunlight. His robe today was white silk, belted with pearl and silver, clasped at the throat with a diamond sunburst. Val had never seen him before in such magnificence, and yet somehow it suited Joscelin less than the plain linen he usually wore.

Val knelt to kiss his lord's hand: a thin hand still roughened from the manual work Joscelin had carried out as a novice in the monastery at Brociel, and still bare of his ring of office, that would be given to him during the ceremony.

At this physical touch, something sprang up in Val — a glittering fountain of hope. There had seemed no honour in serving Duke Govrian. What the previous lord had been as a young man Val did not know, but in his old age he had been cruel and self-indulgent, his appetites unrestrained by the sanctity of his office. Perhaps now they had a lord he could be proud to serve.

Joscelin smiled as Val rose and indicated where he should position himself. Sir Sulien raised the banner of Roazon, and a trumpet call rang out from the tower above the gateway. Guards pulled the gates open, and the procession moved off.

Cheering swelled from the crowds beyond as the Knights Companions marched slowly out through the gates, around their lord. The square outside was packed with people, except for a broad open swathe down the centre, kept clear with difficulty by men-at-arms. Val rested a hand on the hilt of his sword, and scanned the crowds. Just conceivably some lunatic assassin might be waiting there, but if he were the Knights Companions would be ready.

He relaxed slightly as they reached the main thorough-fare leading up to the cathedral. Here the entire street had been kept clear, though Val's gaze constantly raked upwards to where cheering and waving townspeople leant out of windows or over balconies, throwing down nothing more lethal than showers of rose petals.

A broad flight of steps led them up to the cathedral square. Outside the building itself the Archbishop stood, magnificent in gold-embroidered cope and mitre. The cathedral choir, grouped around him, broke into a welcoming anthem as the procession of Knights traversed the square. Val raised a hand to signal his Knights to halt, and let Duke Joscelin walk forward alone.

Within the narthex a thurifer was waiting, his censer swinging in majestic sweeps from side to side, who led the way into the cathedral nave. He was followed by the bearer of the Holy Knot, its golden symbol raised high on a wooden staff, flanked by two acolytes with lighted candles. The choir, still chanting, formed up behind them, and after them came Duke Joscelin himself with the Archbishop. Val signalled his Knights into motion again bringing up the rear.

The inside of the cathedral was a forest of pillars marching towards the distant sanctuary. Along the whole length of the nave, massive beams sprang upwards to support the roof. Each of them was carved into the likeness of an angel with outspread wings and hands folded on its breast, their robes painted in deep blues and crimsons, their hair gilded.

Representatives of all the noble houses of Arvorig stood beneath them on each side, along with honoured guests and ambassadors from the lands all around; then the councillors of the craft guilds of Roazon; high-ranking ministers of the Church; the Matriarch herself, appearing as a tiny figure in robes of white edged with blue, amid an escort of her holy sisters. Behind them all, crushed into every other available space within the cathedral, the ordinary people of Roazon had flocked, eager to see their lord assume his authority.

Ponderously the procession continued its way up the nave towards the sanctuary, clouds of incense billowing up from the thurible and wafting into a gossamer canopy of smoke far overhead.

Sunlight came angling though the tall, narrow windows, glinting off the upraised Knot, and flecking the congregation with dancing motes of coloured light, stippling the white surcoats of the Knights Companions as they proceeded slowly up the centre aisle towards the chancel.

When they reached the front rank of stalls reserved for the highest of the Arvorig nobility, the two files of Knights separated, heading off to each side. Val himself remained standing at the foot of the chancel steps, his official function there being to champion his lord in combat if anyone should challenge his right to rule. But for time out of mind this duty had been no more than ceremonial, and Val did not expect any challenges today – even though Count Fragan of Gwened, seated nearby in his ceremonial stall, wore a face that could have curdled milk. Duke Joscelin provided the only alternative to civil war in Arvorig, and everyone there knew it.

The ceremony began with another anthem from the

choir, followed by a sermon from the Archbishop himself. Val could not help his attention wandering to ask himself again just what Girec d'Evron had in mind. When they had been lieutenants together, d'Evron had not been above lying or cheating to present himself in a superior light, and Val could not imagine that had changed.

Soon the induction ceremony itself began, as acolytes brought a basin and water in a silver ewer for Joscelin's ritual wash. Then he turned to the congregation, speaking the same oath that all the Lords of Roazon had sworn, back through the generations until history vanished into legend.

'I swear in the strength of the Warrior, in the integrity of the Judge, that I will rule fairly in this place, and uphold the Church and protect the people, until I go myself to meet God face-to-face.'

His gaze was rapt, as if staring into a far distance beyond the walls of the cathedral, and his voice rang out with a clear certainty. How many previous lords, Val wondered, had sworn that oath with such obvious sincerity?

Then Master Eudon, the Head of the Guild Council, stepped forward and presented Joscelin with a bowl of fruit and grain to symbolize the people's pledge of support for their lord. An acolyte then relieved him of it, so that Joscelin could turn again and receive the ring of his office from Father Reynaud, representing the support of all the Church.

Once Joscelin had put the ring on his finger, the Archbishop gestured for him to kneel at the top of the sanctuary steps, facing towards the congregation. Standing behind him, the Archbishop raised the circlet, emblem of rule in Roazon, fashioned of silver as pale and clear as water, with no ornament but the threefold Knot.

As the Archbishop placed this on Joscelin's head, Val

caught a glimpse of something white, flitting above his head. He glanced up to see a dove fluttering among the carved angels of the rafters.

Joscelin had seen it too, for he rose to his feet, holding out a hand. The dove winged down to him, alighting on the outstretched hand, and Joscelin caressed its snowy feathers. For a moment the cathedral was so silent that its soft cooing could be clearly heard, and the smile on Duke Joscelin's face was so exalted that he might have been looking on Heaven itself.

3

Marjolaine de Roazon sat motionless in her stall as the Archbishop pronounced the words that drew the ceremony of induction to a close. As his words died away, into the silence came a sound like ripping silk. The young Captain of the Knights Companions, who had been standing motionless as a statue, had drawn his sword.

He raised it, flashing silver, over his head. 'Duke Joscelin!' he cried. His Knights raised their own swords, joining his acclamation, and then the rest of the congregation took up the cry, until the whole cathedral echoed.

Joscelin stepped forward and held his arms out to his people. Wave after wave of approbation crashed over him. Then, as the clamour continued, he turned to his cousin Marjolaine and reached out his hand.

A chill swept over her. She had known, of course, that Joscelin intended to solemnize their betrothal here today in the cathedral, while the nobility of all Arvorig was assembled, but she had managed to banish the thought. Now, as she rose from her place and went to join him at the head of the sanctuary steps, something at the back of her brain kept screaming at her that this was wrong.

Joscelin himself had barely escaped vows of perpetual poverty and chastity in the monastery at Brociel. Now he was lord of the holiest city in the world. What did he want with a wife?

Yet she dutifully stood beside him and took his hand, repeating the vows as the Archbishop directed her.

The chief cleric took a silken stole, embroidered with the Knot, and bound it around their clasped hands. As he spoke the words that united her to Joscelin, Marjolaine found she could not avoid the gaze of Tancred de Kervel.

While the congregation broke into a fresh clamour of approval, the seneschal remained silent, and the darkness in his eyes was deep enough to swallow the world.

Five

On the following morning, Marjolaine de Roazon took her place in the silk-draped stand overlooking the lists. Bright sunlight poured over the tournament field, around whose edge the competing knights had set up their pavilions, like clumps of huge, gaudy flowers. The knights themselves, with their squires and horses, were already gathered there.

The lists themselves were marked out by a double enclosure of whitewashed stakes. Black and silver banners, the ermines of the Legion, surmounted by the Knot, fluttered at the corners. The tilt running down the centre was painted in the same black and silver.

As she did every year, Marjolaine could not help remembering that tournament so long ago when her father had died. Or the tournament that had followed the next year's Day of Memories, when a newly knighted Tancred de Kervel, in what Marjolaine now recognized as desperate grief, had taken the field with the intention of getting himself killed, only incurring the injuries which meant he would never fight again.

Tournaments had not been kind to the House of Roazon, yet Marjolaine must sit here now, and smile and applaud, because that was the duty she was born to.

Duke Joscelin, having taken the seat beside her, was

gazing around himself with an air of bright interest. Clois-
tered as he had been for years, all this was new to him. The
Duke of Roazon wore his customary linen robe, with a holy
icon round his neck on a silver chain. Marjolaine could not
help but feel relieved that he would never become a fighting
man, though no doubt men like Fragan of Gwened would
find that cause for criticism. Yet for generations no Duke
of Roazon had been obliged to lead his army out to war,
and even in today's mock warfare Joscelin would be represented by his champion, the Captain of the Knights
Companions.

Joscelin turned to her. 'What will they expect of me
today?'

'Nothing very much. This is Father Reynaud's day.'
Marjolaine replied. 'Most of the combatants will be Knights
of the Legion or men from the retinues of visiting lords –
though anyone can issue a challenge. Father Reynaud and
Lord Tancred will act as judges. Then there's a prize for
the knight who contends most valiantly.'

Joscelin looked faintly alarmed. 'Should I have arranged
that?'

Marjolaine shook her head. 'No, as I told you, Father
Reynaud arranges everything. He will provide the prize, and
even choose the most beautiful lady here to present it.'

'And who will that be?'

'I don't know—' she began.

She broke off as Father Reynaud approached them,
escorting a young and very beautiful girl, with black curls
and huge dark eyes, and the most terrified expression
Marjolaine had ever seen. On her other side they were
accompanied by a young knight in a green and gold surcoat,
and beside him walked an older woman who shared his
rather overblown good looks.

Father Reynaud bowed. 'Duke Joscelin, Lady Marjolaine, I present the lady Tiphaine de Bellière, who will be Queen of Beauty here today.'

The young girl dropped a shy curtsey. She was truly lovely, Marjolaine thought, though clearly she had no idea how to behave in public.

Stretching out a hand to her, Marjolaine said, 'Come up here and sit by me.'

Tiphaine obeyed thankfully. The older woman, uninvited, followed her on to the stand, and kept twitching at the girl's skirts and her ribbons as she settled herself. Marjolaine stared at her, brows arched inquiringly.

Catching her glance, the older woman looked flustered, trying to bob a curtsey in the confines of the stand. 'I'm Peronel de Cotin, lady. I'm Tiphaine's aunt. My son Nicolas –' she gestured towards the young knight in green and gold – 'is betrothed to her.'

Noticing how Tiphaine was looking uncomfortable, Marjolaine wondered with interest if she too was unhappy about her betrothal.

'Then I'm sure I hope your Nicolas fights well for you,' Marjolaine said to Tiphaine, then gestured Peronel to a seat a little further along.

Lady Peronel babbled her thanks, and subsided there in a flutter of draperies. 'Tiphaine, child,' she murmured, 'you should give Nicolas a token to wear while he fights for you.'

The girl looked startled; then her fingers went to one of the knots of pearl and silver ribbon which adorned her gown, pulled it off, and leant over the stand to hand the knot of ribbon to her cousin. He pressed it to his lips, declaring, 'Lady, I fight in your name!'

How romantic, Marjolaine thought. *And how false.* She was beginning to feel quite sorry for this Tiphaine de Bellière.

2

Valery de Vaux stood near the end of the lists. He was armed, except for his helmet; instead of the plain white surcoat of the Legion he wore his own arms, a golden double chevron on a scarlet field. Behind him, his squire was walking his horse.

The stands for the noble spectators were filling up, and the edges of the field were already crowded with towns-people. Not far away, the Lord Seneschal was in deep conversation with one of the heralds. The tournament was about to begin.

Val had fought in tournaments before, but never until now as champion of the Duke of Roazon, an honour that came with his new captaincy. In that role, he would have to issue the first challenge, and he swallowed nervously. 'Lord Warrior,' he murmured, 'please don't let me make a fool of myself.'

Earlier that morning, he had provided his cousin Bertrand with armour from the general stock of the Knights Companions, and also a horse from their stables. The white surcoat of the Knights was suitable for Bertrand, being a novice in arms who was not yet knighted. Thinking of his cousin's delight as he rode onto the field, Val murmured a hasty addition to his prayer. 'And, Lord, please give him at least one victory.'

A line of trumpeters had swiftly formed up in front of the stands. Now they raised their instruments in a flash of gold, and sounded a fanfare. Val fixed on his helmet, took the reins from his squire, and mounted. Someone handed him a tilting lance, its point blunted by a coronal.

The horse was restive, side-stepping and throwing up its

head. Val leant forward and patted its glossy chestnut neck. 'Steady, Traveller. Steady.'

Collecting his mount, he nodded to the chief herald, then rode forward into the lists. The herald's voice, announcing Val's name and his challenge, echoed oddly in the confines of his padded helm. Val peered through the slit, curious who would appear at the other end of the tilt to answer him.

Not one of the younger knights; none of them would dare, so early in the day, and besides, Val had no wish to pitch himself against a novice. 'Not Bertrand,' he breathed. His erratic cousin might just decide it was a good idea.

He breathed a sigh of relief as a horseman emerged from the crowd at the other end of the lists, and he recognized the red lion of Count Fragan of Gwened. A worthy opponent; if Val defeated him, he would earn much honour for his own lord, and if he fell, it would not be so much shame to have lost against such a formidable combatant.

Then all such calculations fled out of his head as he set spurs to his horse, and Count Fragan came thundering down the tilt towards him.

Val crouched low over Traveller's neck, the coronal of his lance aimed fairly at the honour point of the Count's shield. He braced himself to strike, but at the last second Fragan swerved away; missing altogether, Val felt Fragan's lance clip the edge of his own shield.

He was rocked in the saddle, but kept his seat and rode on, panting hard. First honours to Fragan, then; he must watch out for that swerve as they rode the second course.

As he turned his horse at the far end of the lists Val had a confused impression of the crowd cheering. Then he needed to concentrate again as he and his opponent once again swept down the tilt towards each other.

This time Val kept the lance firmly poised as Count Fragan's red lion grew rapidly larger in his field of view. Ready for the same swerve this time, he swung his coronal across and let out a shout of triumph as it struck his opponent's shield squarely on the fess point.

The lance shattered. Count Fragan's horse reared. Then Val was past, the shouts of the crowd battering after him, until he could finally rein in Traveller at the end of the lists.

By some miracle, Count Fragan had stayed mounted. His horse under control again, he was trotting away from Val.

Val tossed aside the broken stump of his lance, and took another from his squire. He was not sure what to expect on this third and final course. The Count would surely never repeat a manoeuvre that had failed.

Again their thunderous dash down the tilt. This time Val tried swerving inwards, towards the barrier. His lance glanced off Count Fragan's shield; Count Fragan, taken by surprise, tried to swing his own weapon round. Val felt his opponent's coronal scrape his side, but his horse carried him on, and it was over.

At the far end he turned and raised a hand in salute to the Count, who returned the courtesy. *Honours about even*, Val thought, satisfied.

He dismounted and handed his horse and his helmet over to his squire, the animal to be walked for a while and rubbed down. Val himself would relax until it was time for him to fight again, strolling around the field. He could feel a twinge from his ribs, where Count Fragan's lance had struck, and knew he would have a magnificent bruise tomorrow.

Another challenger had appeared and was answered. Val

identified Count Fragan's son, Tariec, and Nicolas de Cotin, a knight of Roazon whom Val knew slightly.

Nicolas displayed the beginnings of a style, Val thought critically. Excessively showy, perhaps, but he was not too surprised to see him unhorse Tariec on the second course.

The crowd erupted into applause. A hand fell on Val's shoulder, distracting him. He turned to see Robert d'Acquin, also wearing armour, but with his helm tucked under one arm. He was smiling broadly. 'Well fought, nephew.'

'Thank you, sir.'

So Robert's contesting days were obviously not yet over. Bertrand had speculated earlier that his father would fight. He himself intended to take the field under a false name, for if he fought poorly he would hardly wish to bring shame on that of Acquin, especially with the threat of being disinherited.

'I wish you luck, sir,' Val went on.

Robert looked slightly embarrassed. 'I'll break a lance or two, but I'll not win the prize today. Not with all of Arvorig here. Once, maybe...' He shrugged. 'But those days are long gone.'

The older man looked more in command of himself here, Val thought, rather than dancing attendance on his imperious lady – as if this was where he really belonged. Val had a sudden glimpse of how splendid he must have appeared as a young man, jousting down all comers so as to bear off the prize in triumph to the ice-cold harridan he had married. A pang of sadness went through Val. Most men thought his own vow of celibacy must be hard to endure; when he looked at Robert d'Acquin, he could see that other choices might be ultimately harder.

'So, who do you wager will win?' Robert went on. 'You yourself, perhaps?'

'I doubt it, sir. Maybe d'Evron there,' said Val, watching the lists as Girec d'Evron rode out to challenge, for d'Evron was a fighter to be reckoned with. 'Or Count Fragan ... or maybe some unknown visiting knight none of us have ever heard of.'

Robert clapped him on the shoulder again. 'Maybe.' He whistled in admiration as Girec d'Evron neatly unhorsed his opponent on the first course. 'It's time I mounted myself,' he said. 'Time to see what you younger men are made of.'

Val watched him stride off and mount a leggy bay horse which a squire had been holding patiently. He himself began to weave his way through the crowd towards his own pavilion, all the while looking out for Bertrand. The morning was wearing on, yet so far he had seen nothing of his cousin.

Then Val spotted him, already mounted and walking his horse up and down just inside the inner fence. In fact, it was the horse Val noticed first of all; for Bertrand was helmeted and quite unrecognizable. He sat his horse well, Val thought.

He was just about to go across and wish his cousin good luck when the heralds announced a challenge from Count Fragan, and Bertrand trotted off to answer it. Val closed his eyes tight. Was Bertrand quite mad?

He took a step forward in a futile attempt to intercept his cousin, but too late; besides, Bertrand was not a child to be lessoned.

A moment later the herald called out, 'The Venturous Squire answers Count Fragan of Gwened.'

Val had to smile. The Venturous Squire! Bertrand had obviously listened to too many old tales of chivalry. Briefly he hoped that Count Fragan might withdraw, there being no need for any knight to accept challenge from a squire.

But Fragan merely set spurs to his mount, and seconds later both riders were hurtling towards each other down the tilt.

Val blinked. The best horse he had been able to find for Bertrand was past its first youth, so how was Bertrand managing to get such a speed out of it? He hunched over, almost flat along its neck, and his lance point never wavered.

The combatants clashed and splinters flew through the air as both lances shattered. Count Fragan's horse reared, then ran out wildly, leaving the Count himself spreadeagled on the turf. Bertrand galloped on, passing the end limit of the tilt. There was a moment's stunned silence, and then the whole crowd roared its appreciation.

'Oh, Cousin,' Val murmured to himself. 'It seems I've done you an injustice.'

'Who *is* that?' He turned to see the speaker was Sulien de Plouzhel. Val hesitated to reply, not wanting to lie, but Sulien did not wait for his answer and went trotting off towards the lists.

A moment later the heralds announced Sulien's own challenge to the Venturous Squire, and only minutes after that he had suffered the same fate as Count Fragan. He staggered to his feet and tramped away, as his squire ran to catch his master's horse. As he passed Val he exclaimed, 'Marvellous! A genius! Val, find out who he is.'

Val was beginning to relax and enjoy himself. Moving forward to get a better view, he found himself overhearing a group of knights who included Robert d'Acquin, Girec d'Evron and Nicolas de Cotin.

One of those unknown to Val was saying, 'I'll wager none of us could beat him!'

Nicolas turned and gave the speaker a disdainful look. 'He's no more than a squire. I'd not lower myself to challenge him.'

His companion roared with laughter. 'Well, that's a good excuse.'

Nicolas' face turned dusky red, then he muttered something and turned away, shouldering his way through the crowd towards the pavilions.

Girec d'Evron watched, sour-faced, as Bertrand neatly disposed of his next two opponents, and then beckoned for his horse. Pulling himself into the saddle, he snarled, 'De Cotin is right. Someone must teach the squire his place.'

Val closed his eyes. 'Oh, *please* . . .' Surely Bertrand's run of luck had to end sometime, and d'Evron was very skilled and vastly more experienced.

The first course was inconclusive, both riders successfully striking the other's shield, but without either lance breaking. Val felt his stomach churn. Already Girec had done better than any of the others who had so far ridden against Bertrand.

As the two contestants wheeled at the far limits of the lists, Robert d'Acquin came to stand beside Val. 'Unbelievable,' he murmured.

Val was afraid that he might start asking awkward questions, but they fell silent as the two combatants hurled themselves towards each other again. Val's colleague d'Evron was all polished technique, moving with smooth precision. There was nothing precise about Bertrand; he launched himself down the length of the tilt like a meteor.

Somehow, as d'Evron's lance came into play, Bertrand was not there in its path. But his own lance shattered on d'Evron's shield, lifting the Knight over the rump of his horse. As he fell, one foot caught in the stirrup, and the horse galloped away dragging him after it along the ground. Several men ran out onto the field to catch the animal.

Robert d'Acquin drove one mailed fist into the palm of his other hand. He was chuckling with as much pleasure as if he knew the victor was his own son. Urgently he, too, signed for his horse.

'I'll break a lance with him!' he said. 'He'll slaughter me, but what matter? I've never seen a fighter to rival him.'

Val opened his mouth to protest, but could not think what to say. In any case, Robert was already riding off speedily towards the heralds, who announced a moment later, 'Robert d'Acquin challenges the Venturous Squire!'

After the defeat of Girec d'Evron, Bertrand had controlled his mount, and was waiting at the far end of the lists. After this new challenge rang out he paused for a moment, then turned his horse and trotted away.

A sound rose from the crowd; a few jeering voices, but most simply puzzled. Robert d'Acquin waited until it was clear the mystery contestant had no intention of taking up his challenge, then turned and walked his horse back towards Val.

Dismounting, he tossed the reins to his squire and pulled off his helmet. His face was creased into a look of bewilderment. 'Why reject me? He's already beaten better men than I am. Why won't he fight with me?'

Val could have told him. Bertrand, with that unexpected streak of chivalry, would not take the risk of defeating his own father.

Robert stood shaking his head for a few seconds, and then said, 'Val, you challenge him. Try to get his helmet off. I want to know who he is.'

'Oh, no.' Val took a step backwards. 'He'll flatten me. I couldn't do it.'

His uncle snorted with disgust. 'Then I'll find someone who can.'

He strode off angrily and Val lost him in the crowd. But a few minutes later he saw Sir Guy de Karanteg riding up to the heralds.

'Sir Guy de Karanteg challenges the Venturous Squire!'

As Bertrand rode slowly back into the lists, d'Acquin came back to join his nephew. 'Now we'll see,' he muttered with satisfaction.

Val doubted it. Dishelming an opponent called for pinpoint accuracy, and so far Bertrand had allowed no one near enough to try. But unfortunately, he reflected, Sir Guy was the man to do so, if anyone could.

The lance, aimed higher than Bertrand's shield, seemed somehow to disconcert him. Besides, Val thought, he must be tiring after so many combats in rapid succession. Bertrand's own coronal struck de Karanteg's shield at an angle, while Sir Guy's lance tore into the side of his opponent's helmet.

The metal peeled back. The padding split and scattered. Val had a horrible vision of the coronal ploughing through Bertrand's skull.

And then his cousin was safely past, riding headlong towards them with the remains of his helmet falling away and his face finally revealed. It was reddened and sweating, his black hair plastered to his forehead.

Robert d'Acquin was staring. 'Bertrand,' he whispered, and then shouted aloud, 'My son, by the Warrior!' A broad smile spreading over his face, he ran towards Bertrand, dragged him from his horse, and folded him into a clumsy embrace.

Bertrand's face was a chaos of emotions. At first he had been half afraid that his father would be angry with him, but as he recognized the pride and approval blazing down on him he hung between laughter and tears.

'Boy, that was well fought.' Robert's voice was thick. 'Well fought indeed.'

'Father . . .' Bertrand bowed his head, and a moment later was being gripped once more tightly in his father's arms.

Val quietly withdrew to find his horse and prepare for another combat that could only prove an anticlimax now. He could not help wondering what Jeanne d'Acquin, watching beside his mother in the stands, was thinking about the triumph of her son.

3

Tiphaine de Bellière had never attended a tournament before, and was not enjoying it. The colour and the noise bewildered her and, as so often in this bewildering city, she longed for the quiet of her grandfather's estate.

Even though Lady Marjolaine had explained to her how the weapons were blunted, Tiphaine knew that it was possible that any of the knights could be seriously wounded. Lady Marjolaine's own father had died like that, and every time the combatants clashed, Tiphaine had to stop herself from visibly flinching.

Still, her own ordeal was not as bad as she had feared. Sitting upright at the front of the stand, she couldn't see whether anyone behind was staring at her. Lady Marjolaine and Duke Joscelin were being very kind, and if only Aunt Peronel would stop nagging at her to sit up straight and remember to smile, Tiphaine thought she could manage very well.

Idly her fingers traced the silver circlet in front of her,

which Father Reynaud had placed there as the prize for the
tournament. She had seen it before, in that brief, bright
vision at Father Reynaud's dinner table. It was just the
same: the decorative swan, with its wings raised for flight;
the pattern of the Knot repeated around the circlet itself.
Yet in her vision she herself had been wearing it, and she
could not understand how that might be.

As the sun began to go down, Father Reynaud finished
a discussion with the heralds and strode over to the stand,
mounting the steps so he could address Duke Joscelin.

'The clear winner is that young fellow in the white
surcoat,' he announced. 'The heralds will now—'

He broke off, gazing at the icon Duke Joscelin wore.
With a murmured, 'By your leave,' he lifted it and gave the
image a hard stare. 'My lord ... what is this?'

'It was an induction gift,' Duke Joscelin replied.

'This image!' There was a sharp edge to Reynaud's tone,
and even Tiphaine guessed that it was not the way he should
speak to his lord.

Joscelin's lifted brows suggested that he knew that too,
but he replied readily enough, 'It represents God the Healer.'

'My lord!' Father Reynaud sounded suddenly outraged.
'You cannot—'

'Father Reynaud.' Joscelin's tones grew firmer. 'Do you
presume to tell the Duke of Roazon what he may or may
not do?'

'My lord, Holy Church would tell you!'

Father Reynaud was still clutching the icon, but Joscelin
withdrew it from his hand. 'Father, this is not the place to
discuss such matters.'

'Then where do you suggest we discuss it?' Father
Reynaud stood his ground. 'You cannot simply—'

Duke Joscelin raised a hand to silence him. 'Father

Reynaud, go to the heralds and have them announce the winner. Then, if you wish, I will speak further with you.'

'My lord, with respect, that is not enough.' Father Reynaud's face had turned flint hard. 'This appears heresy, and it should be discussed by the Archbishop and with the other lords in full Council.'

'Very well.' Father Reynaud's strident tones had clearly failed to intimidate Joscelin. 'We will speak together first, and if there is then need we will call a Council.'

Father Reynaud hesitated, as if wanting to say more, then strode off again towards the group of heralds.

Tiphaine wondered what it all meant. Seeing that Lady Marjolaine was eyeing Joscelin with a faint frown between her brows, she leant over and touched her sleeve hesitantly. 'My lady, what does it signify?' she asked.

Marjolaine gave her a distracted smile. 'I don't know, but—'

She fell silent as the trumpets sounded, and Tiphaine herself sat back, resigned to enduring the final ceremonies of this interminable tournament. Now everyone would be gaping at her as she handed the silver circlet over to some sweating champion.

'The Venturous Squire, Bertrand d'Acquin, has won the day,' the herald announced.

A roar of applause went up from the crowd, which began to flow across the lists to see the winner receive his prize. Tiphaine swallowed nervously. She had never heard of Bertrand d'Acquin, though she supposed he must be well known to those who understood this sport. She was briefly anxious that Nicolas had not won, because he would surely be out of temper now, and then she realized that she had never expected him to.

Meanwhile, the victorious horseman was making his way

towards the stand she sat in, escorted by two knights on foot. One of the latter was Duke Joscelin's young champion, the other an older man who beamed with as much pride as though he had won the day himself.

As they drew closer, Tiphaine examined this Bertrand d'Acquin. His formerly white surcoat was filthy, and sweat streamed down his face, slicking his black hair into spikes. He looked terrified.

Tiphaine took up the silver circlet as he approached. 'Sir Bertrand—' she began.

'I – I'm no knight, my lady,' the young man interrupted, tripping over these few words in embarrassment.

As he fiddled with the horse's reins, from Nicolas' direction Tiphaine heard a muffled snigger. Bertrand obviously heard it, too, and his face reddened.

Stung, Tiphaine rose and leant over the edge of the stand, holding out the circlet in both hands. 'Knight or not,' she announced clearly, 'you have won the day and deserve this prize.'

She was about to set the circlet upon his head when he reached up and removed it from her hands.

'I'm unworthy to wear so . . . so fair a prize,' he declared. 'I will give it to you instead, to grace your beauty.' Then, standing up in the stirrups, he placed the silver circlet on Tiphaine's startled head.

Wonderingly, she looked up into his eyes and saw a tiny reflection of herself, the same image seen at Father Reynaud's dinner table. She smiled to have the puzzle explained, then heard Aunt Peronel hiss, 'Tiphaine!' from somewhere behind her.

Recovering herself, Tiphaine dropped a curtsey, unconsciously putting up a hand to steady the diadem's unaccustomed weight. 'Thank you,' she whispered, then impulsively she pulled off another of the knots of ribbon and pearl from her gown. Holding it out to him, she added, 'Please accept this token of my gratitude.'

Bertrand's soiled gauntlet folded round the scrap of filmy fabric as delicately as if clasping a butterfly. 'Lady, you do me too much honour,' he breathed.

He was now looking awkward, as if unsure of what to say or do next, when, to Tiphaine's relief, Lady Marjolaine stood up beside her. Lightly she laid a hand on Tiphaine's arm, and inclined her head towards Bertrand.

'You have our leave, sir,' she said. 'And we all wish you much joy in your victory.'

The young squire bowed to them both, and began to turn his horse around. The spectators fell back to give him passage, while Tiphaine noticed Nicolas standing just below her, his glare fixed hard on her and his mouth petulant. Tiphaine sighed ruefully. Between him and his mother, she might never hear the end of this.

Desperate to avoid the inevitable scolding, she looked round for some distraction, and saw one of the Knights Companions striding across the field towards them, flanked by a couple of men at arms. Duke Joscelin's champion and the newcomer were close enough for Tiphaine to overhear them.

'De Vaux.' His voice was high-pitched, peremptory. 'I've been looking for you.'

Sir Valery sounded weary as he replied. 'While on duty you address me as Captain.' He paused briefly for an apology, but it did not happen. 'Well, what is it, d'Evron? I need to get some fresh clothes.'

The other man smiled with a smug glance that chilled Tiphaine by its underlying triumph. 'Then you'll have to wait a while. You're under arrest.'

Sir Valery's head flew up in surprise. 'You're mad, d'Evron. Arrest? What for?'

D'Evron's smirk grew wider. 'On a charge of gross immorality.'

Six

Bertrand d'Acquin shuffled his feet and examined his finger-nails. He and his aunt Regine had been seated here since dawn in the Hall of Petitioners, waiting to speak to the Lord Seneschal and to discover what they could about Val's arrest.

When they first arrived, a servant had taken their names and disappeared through a door at the far end of the room. He had not yet returned, and Bertrand's patience was unravelling.

Regine sat quietly beside him, her hands folded in her lap and her eyes closed. From time to time her lips moved as though she prayed. She was deathly pale, and Bertrand knew she had not slept.

Unobtrusively, he slid a hand inside his tunic pocket and drew out the same knot of ribbon Tiphaine de Bellière had presented to him the day before. Then, almost guiltily, he replaced it, remembering that the lady was betrothed to someone else. Yet he desperately wanted to hold on to it. He would never show it to anyone, never disgrace her name or the brief kindness she had shown him. Just as some fair lady from an old tale of chivalry might have rewarded her knight.

He had heard they were marrying her to Nicolas de Cotin; no wonder the man's mother had thrown a fit. Even back in Acquin Bertrand had heard of the de Bellières and their wealth. While he, Bertrand d'Acquin, was not even knighted, his inheritance now in question, and on top of that he was the ugliest man in Arvorig. But it did no harm to dream.

He was jerked out of his musings by the sound of that distant door opening again. A servant's voice called out, 'Madame de Vaux?'

Hastily, Regine got to her feet.

'My Lord Seneschal will see you now.'

Bertrand took her arm and they followed the servant through the same door and down a passage. Regine pressed his hand, but did not speak.

The servant approached another door and threw it open. 'My lord Tancred, the petitioners are here.'

They entered to find themselves in a large room whose walls were all lined with shelves stuffed with books and scrolls. Yet more books were piled on benches and across the floor. Even the large table dominating the middle of the room was covered with papers.

Tancred de Kervel was seated on the other side of the table. Bertrand instantly recognized his harsh-looking face from the tournament – and half expected a reception to match. But Sir Tancred's gaze was mild and his voice quiet. 'Regine de Vaux and ... your nephew Bertrand d'Acquin, I believe. Please be seated. You're here to inquire about the charges made against Sir Valery?'

Regine sank into the seat Bertrand had placed for her. 'My lord, whatever they charge him with, my son is innocent, I know it!'

Tancred murmured something indistinct and flicked through the pile of papers nearest to him. 'The details of the accusation have not reached me yet. On an ecclesiastical matter like this, I would not necessarily be notified.'

Regine leant forward, twisting her hands together. 'But how can I help him if no one will say what he is accused of?'

Tancred spread his hands. 'If I knew, I would tell you.'

'If *you* can't help us, sir, who can?' Bertrand intervened.

'You might arrange to see Father Reynaud...' The seneschal paused thoughtfully. 'No, at this hour he will be at prayer. And the trial will begin shortly.'

'Then is there nothing we can do?' Regine asked, anguished.

'Madam, I fear not.' As Bertrand began to protest Tancred raised a hand. 'If Sir Valery is innocent, you have nothing to fear.'

Bertrand snorted, and the seneschal's eyes flicked in his direction, but it was to Regine he spoke. 'Madam, I promise you that your son will have been well treated.' His mouth twisted. 'It's quite some time since we strung prisoners up by their thumbs.'

'May I see him first?' Regine asked.

'No, but you may sit in the gallery and hear his trial.' Tancred turned to the servant still waiting by the door. 'Yann, take Madame de Vaux and her nephew to a guest room, and have some breakfast brought to them. Then ask Lady Marjolaine if she will attend them.' He smiled at Regine, and Bertrand caught a glimpse of the warmth that might lie behind his sardonic exterior. 'Lady Marjolaine will certainly make sure the officers of the court admit you.'

'That's gracious of her, sir.' Regine dropped a curtsey. 'And of you.'

Bertrand was escorting Regine out of the room when

Tancred called him back. 'You have a case of your own coming up this morning, I believe.'

'That's right, sir,' Bertrand mumbled.

Tancred's mouth resumed the sardonic twist. 'Then it looks as if we shall all have a very interesting time today.'

2

The Knot Chamber within the citadel of Roazon was a large, hexagonal room whose walls were noticeably bare of tapestries. All across one of its six sides extended a dais where the Duke of Roazon would sit in judgement; on the wall above hung a large icon of the divine Judge. The Duke's throne of polished granite was flanked by lesser seats for his advisers. Two officers of the court, with ceremonial rods, already stood there, waiting for the proceedings to begin.

The rest of the room was lined with seating for prisoners, petitioners and witnesses, while above was a gallery where the townspeople could come and observe the deliberations of the court. Across the floor of the open space in the centre, the Holy Knot stood out in polished obsidian against the rough grey flagstones.

As men-at-arms escorted Val into the chamber, he blinked, after the dimness of the cells, against the brilliant sunlight pouring down from windows set high in the walls. He could hear rustling and murmuring from the gallery above, and could eventually discern that the seats were packed with spectators eager, he thought bitterly, to see one of the Knights Companions put to shame.

He still had no clear idea of what crime he was supposed to have committed. Either his gaolers did not themselves know or would not tell him. But he knew full well that he was innocent of anything that could be deemed 'gross immorality', nor could he imagine how anyone in the court would take that accusation seriously.

Hesitating in the doorway, he spotted his mother seated in the front row of the gallery. She leaned forward and smiled at him, raising one hand unobtrusively in greeting. He noticed to his surprise that Duke Joscelin's betrothed was seated beside her.

Lady Marjolaine? Val was puzzled and surprised, assuming that such a great lady would barely know they existed.

The men-at-arms then urged Val forward, leading him to a seat by the wall adjoining the judgment dais. Once seated, and suppressing the oppressive sense that everyone was staring at him, Val found leisure to look around himself.

His cousin Bertrand was seated right opposite, arms folded and booted feet stuck out in front of him. As his eyes met Val's, his face creased into a cheerful grin.

Not far from him sat his parents. Jeanne d'Acquin, demure in a high-necked gown, looked suspiciously like a cat anticipating cream. Val's Uncle Robert looked simply uneasy, and kept shifting in his seat.

A few places further on, Val recognized Girec d'Evron. His smug expression was to be anticipated. But Val had scarcely time to brood on his adversary when the door at the back of the dais swung open.

As Duke Joscelin entered, all in the chamber rose to their feet. As usual, he wore a plain linen robe, and again the icon Val had first noticed at the tournament the day before. The two men following him had also opted for simplicity: for the Archbishop a black cassock, for Father Reynaud the plain robe of the Legion.

Duke Joscelin bowed once to the assembly and took his
seat, looking young and diffident against the monumental
granite throne. The Archbishop and Father Reynaud sat
down on either side of him. Finally, Tancred de Kervel
entered the chamber and limped across to a seat at one side
of the dais. On reaching it, he tapped a gavel on the reading
desk in front of him, raked the courtroom with his disdainful dark eyes, and began, 'The court may sit.'

Amidst the shuffling as everyone settled themselves,
Lord Tancred selected one of the several documents lying
on the desk, and proclaimed, 'Sir Robert d'Acquin deposes
that due to his and his lady's sin through anticipating their
marriage vows, his elder son Bertrand is therefore illegitimate. In consequence, he petitions this court to have the
said Bertrand set aside, and his younger son Oliver declared
heir to all his estates of Acquin.'

As Tancred read out the deposition, there was an
increase of murmuring from the gallery above. He directed
a freezing glance upwards, and the sound died abruptly.

Duke Joscelin had been listening gravely, and now turned
to the Archbishop. 'Your Grace?'

The Archbishop got to his feet. 'By ecclesiastical law,
my lord—'

He broke off as Robert d'Acquin suddenly rose to his
feet on the other side of the courtroom. His face was
infused with the dull red of acute embarrassment. Clearing
his throat loudly, he began, 'With Your Grace's pardon—'

Tancred interrupted him. 'Sir Robert, you are in breach
of court procedure.'

In spite of his anxiety about his own position, Val was
becoming interested. What was going on here? His aunt
Jeanne d'Acquin's head had whipped round to stare at her
husband, her brows snapping upwards in a look of shock

and disapproval. Whatever Robert intended to say, Val felt sure his lady had known nothing about it.

Sir Robert stood shuffling his feet at the seneschal's rebuke, but he did not sit down. Tancred signalled to the officers of the court but before they could move Duke Joscelin held out a hand to check them, exchanged a glance with the Archbishop, and then nodded to Tancred.

Tancred sighed in resignation, and said, 'The court recognizes Robert d'Acquin.'

Sir Robert raised his head, took a breath, and spoke out solidly. 'My lords, I request your leave to withdraw the petition.'

His wife's furious *'What?'* was lost amid the exclamations of surprise from the gallery above. Val met Bertrand's gaze again, and caught a look of triumph on his cousin's face.

'Please explain to the court,' Tancred demanded.

'My lords, you yourselves were all present at the tournament yesterday,' Robert said, 'where my son here fought with courage and won the prize with courtesy.' Clearing his throat again, he went on, voice thick with emotion. 'He is truly my son, and I ask for no better heir to my lands of Acquin.'

Despite all his own troubles, Val could not help a smile of pure delight.

The three judges then conferred briefly. Being close to the dais, he heard Father Reynaud whisper, 'My lord, you may create a dangerous precedent.' But the Archbishop replied, 'The Church has always looked leniently on such affairs.'

Duke Joscelin murmured something to each of them in turn and rose to his feet. The rumble in the courtroom died.

'Sir Robert,' Joscelin said, 'I must ask, have you any doubt that this Bertrand is your son?'

'None whatsoever, my lord.'

'Then your request is granted. Seneschal, please note that the petition has been withdrawn.'

Tancred picked up his pen and made an annotation. The gallery broke out into applause, which this time no one bothered to quell. Val saw his mother smiling proudly down at her nephew.

Robert d'Acquin meanwhile strode across the chamber, pulled Bertrand to his feet and enveloped him in a bear hug. His wife had also risen to her feet. 'My lord!' she exclaimed, outraged. 'You cannot do this!'

Tancred brought his gavel down with a crash. 'The court does not recognize you, madam.'

'I insist! I—'

'Be silent, madam, or you will be removed.'

Jeanne's face went white with fury, her fists clenched. She threw a final scorching glance at her husband and son, and then turned her back on them, and swept out of the courtroom.

Evntually Robert clapped his son on the shoulder and followed her out. As the hubbub died down, Bertrand took his seat again.

As the court settled back into silence, a heavy weight of apprehension gathered in Val's stomach. His own case must be next.

The seneschal seemed to take an eternity to rearrange his documents, but finally Tancred found the one he wanted, and read aloud from it. 'Sir Valery de Vaux is hereby accused of gross immorality, in that he spent the Night of Memories with a certain notorious Aurel de Montfaucon, against the edicts of the Judge and his vows of celibacy as a Knight Companion. The court calls—'

Val leapt white-faced to his feet in the midst of shocked

gasps and exclamations from the gallery. 'Who has told this lie?' he demanded.

The seneschal rapped twice with his gavel. 'Sir Valery, the court does not recognize you.' His voice was firm but not hostile. 'You will have the opportunity to speak when—'

'A moment, Seneschal.' Duke Joscelin interrupted in his turn. 'Sir Valery,' he asked, 'did you not know the charge against you before now?'

Val bowed towards him. 'No, my lord.'

Joscelin's brows drew together in a faint frown. 'Father Reynaud, why was no explanation given to the accused?'

Father Reynaud grunted. 'The facts seem clear enough.'

Joscelin seemed to give that some thought. 'Sir Valery, have you been offered the opportunity to call witnesses to absolve you of this charge?'

'Not yet, my lord.'

The frown again, more pronounced now. 'If this represents the justice of Roazon, then it shames us all.'

Clearing his throat, the Archbishop leant forward. 'My lord, in an ecclesiastical matter such as this—'

Joscelin silenced him with a gesture. 'Lord Seneschal.' He turned to Tancred. 'These faults must be put right.'

'Yes, my lord.' Spots of colour burned on Tancred's cheekbones as he scribbled notes.

In these few moments' respite Val had a chance to think about what they accused him of. True, he had spent part of the Night of Memories with Aurel de Montfaucon in his lodging. But there had been no sin between them, and besides, surely no one but Bertrand knew of it.

Except ... Girec d'Evron was present here in the court. Their brief meeting outside the captain's lodgings had slipped from Val's mind until now. But surely not even d'Evron could have suspected carnal desires in either of the two men, soaking wet from the lake and with Aurel barely conscious.

Of course not. Inwardly Val sneered at his own naivety. But if Girec d'Evron could make the charge stick, it would be an effective way to get rid of Val and leave clear his own route to the captaincy.

Oh, d'Evron, Val realized with a sudden pulse of feral delight. *You have given yourself into my hands.*

Tancred had finished writing now, so Duke Joscelin gave him a nod of approval and turned back to Val. 'Sir Valery, do you wish to request an adjournment to prepare your defence and call your witnesses?'

'No my lord.' Val glanced at Bertrand, whose face was fixed in gleeful anticipation. 'The only witness I need is already here in court.'

He bowed and resumed his seat. Lord Seneschal Tancred, still flustered from the unexpected interruption, called out, 'The court summons Sir Girec d'Evron.'

D'Evron rose smugly to his feet. 'My lords,' he began, 'on the Night of Memories, while all decent folk were about their devotions, I saw with my own eyes Sir Valery sneak into the captain's lodgings with a certain Aurel de Montfaucon.'

'A moment, Sir Girec.' It was Duke Joscelin who interrupted again. 'How did you recognize this Aurel de Montfaucon? I am told he comes from Kemper. Have you encountered him before?'

For a moment d'Evron looked disconcerted, as if he would have preferred to deny all connection with such a notorious libertine. Then he said, 'Yes, my lord. Two years ago now, I was sent with letters to the Commander of the Legion garrison in Kemper. Aurel de Montfaucon's father –

a man of exceptional piety, my lord, unlike his son – hosted a dinner for the Knights on behalf of the merchants of Kemper. The son was present.'

Duke Joscelin waved a hand. 'Very well, Sir Girec. Go on.'

D'Evron cleared his throat. 'Clearly de Vaux and de Montfaucon spent the night together in the captain's lodgings. They were seen leaving the place together early the next morning.'

Duke Joscelin leant forward in his seat, examining d'Evron wide-eyed, as if he was some strange creature the duke had never seen before.

'But you did not yourself see them leave?' he inquired.

'No, my lord,' D'Evron sounded shocked. 'At that hour, I was at prayer. But I can call witnesses – the boatman, and a baker, opening his shop – who saw the two men together.'

'You *have* been diligent,' said Duke Joscelin.

D'Evron smirked and bowed, though to Val the words had not sounded much like a compliment.

'I think we have no need of them for the present,' Joscelin decided. 'Sir Valery, have you questions for this witness?'

'Yes, my lord.' Val pulled himself to his feet again. 'Sir Girec, have you checked the duty rosters for the Night of Memories?'

D'Evron's smile vanished abruptly. 'No.'

'Then it escaped your ... diligence ... that I was on duty that night?'

Girec d'Evron relaxed, shrugging. 'It did, but what of it? You still would have plenty of time for your ... filthy concourse with that libertine. Are you denying that you spent the night with him?'

'I don't deny that de Montfaucon spent the night in the

captain's lodgings. As you say, you saw us there yourself. Tell me, d'Evron, did you notice anything strange about our appearance?'

'Yes.' D'Evron sounded puzzled. 'You were both wet.'

As concisely as he could, Val turned to explain to the court how he had spotted Aurel struggling in the lake and gone to help him, though he said nothing yet of Bertrand's involvement. *Let d'Evron hang himself.* 'I took Aurel to the captain's lodgings,' he finished, 'because there was nowhere else.'

D'Evron broke in. 'You expect us to believe that on your unsupported word?' he asked contemptuously.

'No,' said Val. 'My lords, I ask leave to call a witness – Bertrand d'Acquin.'

Bertrand was already on his feet, pacing eagerly towards the dais and planting himself in the centre of the Holy Knot.

'The court recognizes Bertrand d'Acquin,' Tancred said.

Bertrand did not even wait for Val to question him as he proceeded to confirm Val's account of that night.

'Of course you would speak up for your cousin,' d'Evron said dismissively. 'How is it I did not see you there?'

'I was buying food and wine in the Plume of Feathers,' Bertrand explained. 'I'm sure they'll remember me there.'

Joscelin nodded. 'So no sin occurred. Indeed, it seems to me that there was no opportunity for sin to occur. Father Reynaud, why was this charge brought at all?'

Father Reynaud's face had turned a dusky purple. 'Your pardon, my lord. I trusted what d'Evron here told me.'

'Without even allowing Sir Valery to give an explanation, or investigating the facts that would have come to light immediately if you had bothered to look for them.' Joscelin's voice had turned steely, and Val had a sudden

insight into how formidable the new young duke could be.
'Father Reynaud, I feel inclined to arraign both you and Sir
Girec d'Evron for negligence and deliberate perjury—'

'My lord!' Father Reynaud sounded appalled.

'I shall not do so. This court, and the Legion, have
today been brought into sufficient disrepute already. You
will discipline your Knight, Father, and report to me this
evening on what steps you have taken.'

Father Reynaud bowed his head. 'Yes, my lord.'

Applause erupted from the gallery, and Val caught sight
of his mother rising to her feet and making her way towards
the doors, relief and joy in her face.

Then Bertrand was over beside him, clapping him on the
shoulder so that Val almost staggered under the blow. They
stood side by side as Duke Joscelin led the Archbishop and
the seneschal out of the courtroom.

Val found his gaze briefly meeting d'Evron's, and he
almost flinched at the intensity of venom in his eyes. He
had not imagined that anyone could hate him as much as
that.

Before he gave way to Bertrand's urging for them to go and
get a drink, Val waited at the foot of the stairs leading
down from the gallery. His mother and Lady Marjolaine
appeared almost at once, the others on the stairs having
drawn back in deference to Duke Joscelin's betrothed.

'My lady.' Val bowed and bent over her hand. 'Thank
you.'

'I could do very little to help,' Marjolaine apologized.

As she stood smiling at Val, suddenly he became aware
of her warm, golden beauty, and the rose perfume she wore
– and realized that he still clasped her hand. He released it

immediately, and felt himself flushing. 'We are still grateful, my lady,' he said.

As the two women continued down the corridor that led to the citadel garden, Val stood looking after her, bemused.

Bertrand clapped him on the shoulder. 'That drink, Cousin? Unless you want to stand there all day like a love-sick sheep.'

Val let his cousin pilot him towards the citadel's outer door. 'Don't be ridiculous!'

Bertrand let out a cynical chuckle. 'She's Duke Joscelin's betrothed, Cousin – and you're a vowed celibate.'

'I think your triumph in the trial's turned your brain,' Val retorted peevishly.

But as he stepped out into the courtyard, the noon sunlight seemed suddenly garish, sending a pang of dismay right through him. He was sure of his vocation. He had always been sure. So were beauty and kindness enough to turn him away from his sworn service?

As he followed Bertrand down the street to the Plume of Feathers, to his horror Val realized that he could no longer confidently answer that question.

3

Father Reynaud's rooms were located in the central keep of the citadel, not in the Legion barracks, but apart from that they shared the bare austerity in which all the Knights Legionaries lived. In the anteroom, where he waited to receive Girec d'Evron, the only furnishings were a table and a couple of plain wooden chairs, a shelf of scrolls and books, and a storage chest under the window.

Father Reynaud was pacing the room impatiently, his

heavy features still dark with anger. He paused when he heard a knock at the door. 'Come in.'

Girec d'Evron entered and closed the door behind him. Without waiting for his superior to speak, he went down on one knee and said, 'Your pardon, Father.'

'Oh, get up,' Father Reynaud growled irritably. He went to sit himself behind the table, but he did not offer the younger man the other chair. 'Well? What's your excuse?'

'Father?'

'How do you justify that ... appalling public exhibition?'

D'Evron's face turned the colour of cold porridge. His mouth worked in silence for a moment. 'Father, I truly believed ...' he said at last. 'I only wished to root out sin.'

'Don't lie to me!' Father Reynaud brought his hand down hard on the table. 'You wanted to root out de Vaux from his captaincy.' He leant forward threateningly. 'Listen to me, d'Evron. You wanted the captaincy yourself. The whole of the Legion knows it. And I think no worse of you for that. If the decision had been mine ...' He shrugged. 'But by tradition, the retiring captain has the right to nominate his successor, unless his choice is clearly unsuitable, and Sir Guy de Karanteg chose de Vaux. Tell me, d'Evron, what *should* your reaction to that have been?'

D'Evron looked at his feet. 'I should have submitted myself humbly to the will of the Judge, Father.'

'Exactly. Instead of which you came to me with this cock and bull story about the new captain ... and I was fool enough to believe you.' Father Reynaud exhaled heavily. 'And because of your mistake I have been publicly reprimanded by the Duke of Roazon, and the good name of the Legion has been held up to ridicule.'

He paused, but Girec d'Evron had no more to say. 'Very

well,' Father Reynaud continued. 'At the Offering tomorrow morning, you will make your public confession before your fellow Knights, and accept the penance decided by Holy Church.'

D'Evron straightened up, looking faintly relieved. 'Of course, Father.'

'In addition,' Father Reynaud went on, 'from now on you must be stripped of your lieutenancy, and of your place in the Knights Companions.'

D'Evron's mouth dropped open. 'Father . . .'

'Do you imagine that you have any scrap of authority left to you in this place?' Father Reynaud said scathingly. 'Or that Duke Joscelin would tolerate you in attendance on him?'

'The words were forced out of him. 'Then . . . am I no longer a Knight of the Legion?'

'Don't tempt me. But no, only God can release you from your vows. You will accompany Sir Guy de Karanteg, and take your place in the detachment of the Legion which serves Count Fragan of Gwened.' Some of the grimness went from Father Reynaud's voice as he added, 'With diligence, you may rise in esteem again.'

'Father, I will strive to do so.'

D'Evron's tones seemed all humility now, his head bowed submissively. Father Reynaud wished he could see the younger man's eyes.

'Very well, you may go and find Sir Guy, to report to him. You are henceforth relieved of all duties with the Knights Companions.'

D'Evron left the room in silence, while Father Reynaud promised himself a word with Sir Guy before the ex-captain left for Gwened.

4

Val took supper with his mother that evening. They sat alone at table, for Sir Robert d'Acquin had borne Bertrand away to his own inn, and Val assumed that his cousin would go home now with his father.

'He'll come to say goodbye,' Regine said intuitively.

She was just getting up from the table when they heard the outer door opening, and a moment later Bertrand himself strode into the dining room. He looked flushed and dishevelled, as if he had been drinking, but his new air of triumph and self-confidence had vanished.

'What's the matter, my dear?' Regine asked anxiously.

Bertrand shrugged uncomfortably, and then burst out, 'Aunt Regine, it's my mother! She wouldn't speak to me. At supper, she wouldn't sit at table with us. I can't go home with them,' he finished miserably. 'Father can't handle her either in such a mood.'

Val's opinion was that Robert d'Acquin should have made himself master in his own house long ago, but it was probably too late for that now. 'What will you do?' he asked.

Bertrand shrugged again. The self-assured young man who had recently appeared so briefly had now utterly vanished.

'You can stay here with me for as long as you want,' Regine suggested.

Bertrand shook his head. Slowly, and with clear reluctance, he said, 'I have had an offer. Count Fragan sent a man to give me this letter.'

He pulled a crumpled scrap of paper out of his belt pouch and handed it to Val; it looked as if it had been crushed into a ball and straightened out again.

Val read a letter that was short and businesslike, offering Bertrand, hero of the tournament, a place in Count Fragan's retinue, to train his men-at-arms. It promised a wage of six crowns a month. Silently he passed it across to his mother.

'I shall probably accept it,' Bertrand said gloomily. 'What else is there for me? I can't go home now, and however kind you are, Aunt, I can't stay here for ever.'

'Accept this offer?' Regine looked up from reading the letter. Val had rarely seen his mother in a passion of anger. 'To offer you such a trivial post, and for pay! I wonder you can even contemplate agreeing.'

'What else is there?' Bertrand repeated, laughing uncomfortably. 'I may have unhorsed him on the tournament field,' he added, 'but he is still Count of all Gwened, and Acquin no more than a manor.'

'Your birth is every bit as good as his,' said Regine. 'Sit down now, Bertrand, and write him a refusal. Master Pernet shall see it delivered first thing in the morning.'

As Bertrand hesitated, Val called for the steward to fetch pen, ink and paper. But when they were set on the table in front of him Bertrand made no move to write.

'Do you know,' he began with an unsteady laugh. 'a year or so ago, a sister of the Matriarchy stayed overnight with us at Acquin. She looked in the scrying bowl for each of us, and prophesied greatness would come my way.' Bitter with self-contempt, he added, 'Very likely indeed!'

'Nothing more so,' protested Regine with glowing eyes. 'The sisters of the Matriarchy see true.'

But Bertrand moved on. 'Aunt, I can't stay here with you, and this isn't what I wanted, but it's decent employment. And maybe if I please the count, he . . .' His voice trailed into silence under Regine's fierce gaze.

'Remember, Bertrand, how you recently made me a

promise,' she said, 'never to engage in fighting except with a noble weapon. To sell your sword for pay – is that noble?'

'Mother's right. Write it.' Val pushed the pen closer to Bertrand's hand. 'There'll be a better offer eventually, knighthood, and service with a lord who will really value you.'

'Knighthood . . .' Bertrand sounded wistful, as if the very idea was unattainable. 'Maybe . . .' He picked up the pen and dipped it and then held it out to Val in embarrassment. 'Write it for me, will you? I . . . I don't know what words to use.'

Val accepted the pen and pulled the sheet of paper towards him. Did Bertrand even know how to write, he wondered; maybe no one at Acquin had ever taught him. But he did not press the question; his cousin had been hurt enough for one day.

And as Val went off to find Master Pernet and arrange for the letter's delivery, he could not suppress a rising tide of sadness, reflecting that the triumph of the tournament, the subsequent vindication when Robert d'Acquin had acknowledged Bertrand as his son – how it had all trickled away like water in the sand, and left Bertrand still without a home or a firm purpose.

Later that evening Val took his leave of them and climbed the hill towards the citadel. Roazon was very quiet at that hour, a few windows still showing lights, a few torches still burning outside taverns, but by now most of the towns-people were in their beds.

Moonlight blanched the rooftops and the cathedral spire soaring over all the city. Val paused at the head of a narrow stairway and, looking back between the clustering houses, could catch a glimpse of the dark lake and the road that led away from the city to the north. He had never even dreamed of following that road. He loved Roazon too much, and everything he had ever wanted was here around him. But now he could not help wondering what would it be like to ride abroad, to see new places, to learn new customs, to meet men and women who honoured strange gods – or no god at all.

To be other than you are, he thought to himself.

Suddenly impatient, he swung away. As his shoulder brushed a climbing rose spilling over the wall, it dislodged a shower of pale petals and a heavy fragrance surged around him.

At the smell, he was once again in the citadel, looking into the eyes of the Lady Marjolaine. Hazel eyes, he was sure of that, and he could still feel her fingers, warm within his own.

And also he could hear Bertrand's voice: 'A lovesick sheep? She's Duke Joscelin's, and you're vowed to celibacy.'

Irritably, Val shook his head. This was all nonsense. Tomorrow he would rise and go about his duties as usual, and such fancies would be gone. He would serve his master, Duke Joscelin, as he had vowed to do, and life would go on peacefully, as it always had in Roazon, under divine protection.

But, running up the last steep street towards the captain's lodgings, he could not quite escape from that scent of roses.

PART TWO

Prison Walls

Seven

'Lord Tancred seemed pleased with his icon,' Morwenna said happily. 'I think I must paint more of them.'

She sat at her work table, laying out her colours, while Alissende unpacked the market basket. Donan was in his silversmith's shop below, and the baby Ivona gurgled contentedly in a cradle next to her mother.

Somehow, in the days that followed Duke Joscelin's induction ritual, Alissende had settled down easily in the little household. She had no pressing demands on her, and the thoughts of destroying herself which she had once briefly entertained had dissipated after the candle-lit ceremony on the Day of Memories.

Here she could make herself useful by taking on the household tasks, thus giving Morwenna more time for her icon painting.

'Will the Church accept this new idea?' Alissende asked uneasily. 'Did Lord Tancred tell you anything else?'

'Not much.' Morwenna's answer was cheerful; clearly she had not picked up her new friend's apprehension. 'I only spoke with him for a few minutes.' Carefully she began to mix her colours.

Alissende paused in storing apples on the shelf, and then decided not to give further voice to her worries. Morwenna now believed she had a divine commission to paint the Healer, and nothing would turn her away from it.

All the same, Alissende was not sure that things could be dismissed so lightly. When she had gone out to market early that morning, there had been some talk of Duke Joscelin's new icon. The citizens of Roazon, she discovered, were prone to discuss Church doctrine as readily as most people dissected their neighbours or the latest scandals.

Many had noticed Duke Joscelin wearing an icon to the tournament, but had no clear understanding of what it signified.

'It's all going to lead to trouble,' muttered the apple woman to her friend at the neighbouring stall as she packed Alissende's basket.

Now, as Alissende settled herself by the window with Morwenna's mending basket, she could not help feeling tempted to look in the scrying bowl, to see what it would reveal of the future. She had renounced this practice, along with so much else she had never regretted, but now, sensing trouble gathering around her new friends, she could not silence a tiny voice teasing at her mind. *Only once. To help them. What harm can it do?*

No, she replied. Firmly she took up her needle and began to repair the lace trim on one of Ivona's gowns.

2

Sunlight shone through the trees in the citadel's garden, dappling Lady Marjolaine's elaborate skirts as she sat beside the pool. The sweet trickling of the fountain was the only sound she could hear.

Stitching pearls along the edge of an embroidered sleeve, she realized that she liked what she had seen of that young Knight who had faced the false accusations at his trial with such courage and honour. She would like to know him better. The image of that beautiful, austere face framed by black curls came between her and her needlework, and she blinked it away firmly. She would not moon over him like some silly girl. She was Lady of Roazon – and Duke Joscelin's betrothed.

Joscelin himself was also seated by the edge of the pool, one hand extended into the spray of the fountain. He looked totally relaxed, as if nothing was on his mind but enjoying the sunlight and the cool spill of water.

Marjolaine noticed that he still wore that unusual icon.

In the days that followed the tournament, the noble visitors had begun to take their leave. Few still remained – Count Fragan chief among them – and soon they too would be gone from the city. Roazon would return to its peaceful but busy routine. There could be no more excitement until the Feast of All Angels, when the whole of Arvorig would gather again, to see Marjolaine and Joscelin married.

She concentrated, setting in the stitches with rapid skill, her impending marriage being something that for most of the time she succeeded in putting to the back of her mind.

A murmur from her betrothed made her suddenly look up. He was gazing in the direction of the garden gate, and Marjolaine turned to see Count Fragan himself striding towards them.

'What does *he* want?' she murmured, low enough for not even Joscelin to hear her.

He rose as the count approached. 'Count Fragan. How can I help you?'

'I've come to take my leave of you, my lord,' Fragan explained. 'My attendants and I will ride for Gwened tomorrow.'

'Then I wish you a pleasant journey,' said his host.

As Marjolaine listened to the two men exchange courtesies, she had to admit that she would be well relieved to see Fragan go. His only son Tariec — now a whey-faced youth of sixteen — could trace the Roazon lineage through his mother, and it was well known that during Duke Govrian's last illness Fragan had nourished hopes of seeing his boy named as next Duke of Roazon.

Despite his having swiftly offered allegiance to Joscelin, she could not feel wholly at ease in this man's presence, or disguise from herself a wariness of his ambition.

Count Fragan bowed once more, preparing to withdraw, when the sound of other voices reached them. This time it was Father Reynaud and the Archbishop approaching through the trees.

A faint chill crept over her. Their expressions told her that this was no courtesy call.

Count Fragan stepped away, ready to depart, but Father Reynaud put out a hand to stop him. 'Stay a moment, my lord count. What we have to say may well concern you.'

That was a breach of courtesy here, in Duke Joscelin's private garden. Marjolaine opened her lips to deliver a stinging rebuke, but before she could speak, Joscelin himself replied amiably, 'By all means, my lord. Please, sit. Shall I call for wine?'

'No, my lord.' Father Reynaud seated himself ponderously on one end of a stone bench. 'We are here to discuss a very serious matter.'

The Archbishop sat down beside him, while Count Fragan took up his stance nearby, hands clasped behind his back. To Marjolaine's eyes, all three looked uncomfortably like judges presiding at a trial.

But Joscelin's expression of sunny good humour did not change. Sitting down by the pool again, he held out a hand to Father Reynaud. 'Please.'

'You must know why we are here.' When Duke Joscelin did not respond, Father Reynaud added harshly, 'That heretical image, my lord – perhaps you would explain to us why you wear it.'

'Of course.' Joscelin still seemed untroubled.

Something cold clutched at Marjolaine's heart. *He doesn't understand.*

'As you can see, it's an icon,' Duke Joscelin went on. 'The painter experienced a vision of the divinity as Healer, and felt compelled to paint his likeness.'

'My lord,' Father Reynaud began with a weighty approach to courtesy, 'there is no Healer in our creed. We worship the divine in only two aspects, as Warrior and as Judge.'

'And there can be no further revelation?' Joscelin asked mildly.

'To the holy men of the Church, perhaps,' Father Reynaud said. 'But to a mere painter – and you have told me a woman, too!'

'She should be questioned about this vision,' the Archbishop suggested.

'Yes indeed, before she does more damage,' said Father Reynaud. 'Have others been painted?'

'Lord Tancred possesses one, I believe,' said Joscelin. He had taken the icon into one hand, and was gazing down meditatively at its painted image. 'And I expect she will paint many more.'

'I should like one,' Marjolaine intervened. To tell the

truth, she had barely given it a thought, but could think of no other way of showing her support for Joscelin.

The surprise in Father Reynaud's sideways gaze was a tiny satisfaction to her. 'Nonsense,' he said. 'The production of such pernicious images must be stopped at once.'

Marjolaine began to protest, but the Archbishop spoke over her. 'Yes, certainly, at least until the Church has had proper time to consider the matter.'

Father Reynaud's only response was an ill-tempered snort.

'My lords,' Joscelin began. 'As men of authority—' he took in both churchmen and Count Fragan with a tiny gesture of his hand – 'you rest your hearts in the Warrior or the Judge. But for others – the poor, the weak, children? Where shall they find peace and comfort?'

'In obedience to their betters,' Father Reynaud snapped.

'Not by inventing some new aspect of the divine,' the Archbishop added.

'Aye, Your Grace.' Count Fragan, after listening all this while with needle-sharp concentration, now joined in the discussion for the first time. 'And that's the crux of this argument, as far as I can see. Is this new aspect an invention, or is it not?'

The Archbishop nodded. 'You speak true, my lord. The woman must be summoned for questioning, and meanwhile we must all pray for enlightenment.'

'But Father...' Lady Marjolaine leaned forward earnestly. 'There may be other signs to guide us. Have you ever wondered why the Holy Knot itself has *three* branches?'

Father Reynaud made a typically dismissive gesture, and only the Archbishop deigned to give her an answer. 'Indeed, my lady. Holy Church teaches that the one divinity reaches down to us in two aspects – Warrior and Judge. *That* is what those three branches of the Holy Knot mean. To add a fourth is heresy.'

'But are you so sure that Holy Church interprets correctly?' Marjolaine asked.

Father Reynaud shot to his feet, glaring down at her. 'It is not for a woman — not even the Lady of Roazon — to question the teachings of Holy Church.'

Marjolaine took a deep breath, ready to defend herself, but Joscelin interrupted her.

'Then it is decided,' he said. 'Father Reynaud, Your Grace, you will seek guidance by study and prayer. Meanwhile we will send for the painter so that she may be questioned further about her vision. And then—'

'And you, my lord duke?' Father Reynaud challenged him. 'Will you take off that heretical image you wear until a decision has been made?'

Duke Joscelin gazed back at him, with blue eyes cool and tranquil. 'No, Father,' he said. 'I don't believe I shall.'

'You'll recall that you swore an oath at your induction,' the Grand Master went on angrily, 'promising to uphold the Church. Is this how you keep it?'

The young duke kept that bright gaze fixed on him, but before he could reply, Count Fragan noisily cleared his throat. 'Take thought, my lord,' he said. 'You may soon find that not even the Duke of Roazon can defy the Church and get away with it.'

3

Alissende was just folding her work away, beginning to think about preparing the midday meal, when she heard knocking at the street door below. Morwenna, engrossed by now in her painting, seemed not to notice until heavy footsteps sounded on the stairs.

She looked up, her brush poised in one hand. 'Who can that be?'

Alissende rose to her feet as the door swung open. A Knight in the armour of the Legion stood there, flanked by a couple of men-at-arms. Donan stood behind them on the landing, looking worried.

'Yes?' Morwenna said, sounding puzzled but not alarmed.

The Knight stepped forward. 'The Grand Master summons you to the citadel.'

Donan pushed his way past the men-at-arms and into the room. 'What's this all about?'

The Knight said flatly, 'Father Reynaud commands her presence. He must question her about her icon.'

'Give me a moment to wash.' Smiling confidently, Morwenna wiped her brush on a rag and stood up.

The soldiers stepped back to let her go from the room, leaving Alissende and Donan to stare at each other.

'How long will she be needed?' Donan asked, sounding uneasy.

'Until Father Reynaud is satisfied,' the Knight replied. 'If she gives him honest answers, she should return soon.'

Alissende could not help wondering whether *soon* would mean a few hours or a few days. The Knight went over to Morwenna's table and examined the images she had been working on.

He picked up a half finished icon in one mailed hand. 'This must go to the Grand Master, too,' he said. 'Are there any more?'

'No,' Alissende replied quickly, while Donan asked, 'What does Father Reynaud want with it?'

The Knight did not answer, but continued checking the equipment on the work table, then searched through the cupboard which stood open beside it, where Morwenna stored her materials.

Beginning to get angry, Donan strode across the room. 'What do you think you're doing?'

'All of this is now placed under the Grand Master's jurisdiction,' the Knight said. 'Nothing here must be touched until he gives leave.'

'And by what right—' Donan began, breaking off as Morwenna returned.

She had obviously heard the last few words. 'Don't worry, Donan.' She took down her cloak from the back of the door. 'Everything will be all right once I explain to the Grand Master.'

'I still don't like this,' Donan said, with a hostile glare at the intruder. 'Shall I come with you?'

'No, love, you've got too much work to do.' Morwenna fastened her cloak and turned to the Knight. 'There, I'm ready now.'

'Then I'll come,' offered Alissende.

Morwenna clasped her hand briefly. 'I'd rather you stayed to look after Ivona.' Glancing from Alissende to her husband, she seemed to divine something of their apprehension. 'Don't worry!' she repeated cheerfully. 'I'll be back home before you know it.'

Listening to her go down the stairs surrounded by her escort, Alissende could not feel so sure. The temptation of the scrying bowl returned forcefully.

Perhaps tonight, she promised herself. *If she doesn't come home, perhaps tonight.*

Eight

Aurel de Montfaucon stepped across the gangplank from the barge to the quayside. The moon rode high above the rooftops of Kemper, where the river Rinvier met the sea, a soft sea breeze driving wisps of cloud across its face. Opposite him, torches flared above tavern doors; from somewhere close by, jangling music drowned out the sound of the waves breaking against the harbour wall.

The barge which had brought him from Roazon was now berthed in its usual place, beside others belonging to House Montfaucon. With a tiny shock, Aurel realized that now they all belonged to him.

Since his father's death, he had never really thought about his inheritance. At first his whole mind and heart had been filled with the faithless Nicolas. Then had come despair, and after that a dull acceptance. On the journey downriver he had made no plans for what he would do when he reached home.

Now, with the familiar warehouses and taverns of the Kemper waterfront before him, and with the warm salty air playing around him, his mind began to reawaken. There would be affairs to settle, decisions to be made. In spite of his previous self-indulgent way of life, he was not entirely stupid, and he knew the demands that House Montfaucon would make on him.

His mouth twisted. Now that there was no hope any longer of life with his erstwhile lover, he would accept his fate and become a merchant. More than that, he could give up the life he had been leading; with his father dead, there was no need for it any more as a means of rebellion. Perhaps he would even achieve respectability. Perhaps somewhere his father, even now, was rejoicing in his late, hard-won, unexpected victory.

A crewman, leaving the barge with a knapsack over his shoulder, paused and touched his forehead respectfully. 'Shall I call you a chair, sir?'

'What?' The man's words roused Aurel from contemplating his future. 'Oh – no, thank you. I shall walk.'

The man saluted again and crossed the quayside to the lighted windows of the nearest tavern. Aurel watched him go, and then turned for home.

At first the street led steeply upwards, and Aurel could not help remembering Roazon at the end of the Day of Memories, when he had climbed its slopes so eagerly to meet Nicolas again. But soon he reached a broad paved road, winding lazily up the side of the hill to the quarter where the mansions of the wealthy merchants and nobles of Kemper lay enclosed in leafy gardens, far from the bustle and smells of the harbour.

It was the supper hour, and everything was quiet; the air was warm with the scent of hidden flowers. Aurel encountered few people as he climbed the hill, and no one stopped to speak to him.

When he reached his father's house, its courtyard gate was firmly closed. Aurel lifted the great brass knocker and let it fall. After a moment someone slid back the shutter of the peephole. A light was burning beyond in the courtyard, but shadow fell across the porter's face.

The voice that spoke to Aurel came out of darkness. 'I'm sorry, sir, the master's not at home to visitors.'

Aurel's mind spun. *The master?* For a minute he fought with the sickening fancy that his father was not dead after all.

'Can't you see who I am?' he said sharply, stepping back into a patch of moonlight so the man could get a good look at him.

There was another long moment until the shutter snapped back across the peephole, then Aurel waited for the porter to finally open the door, but it stayed closed. Veering between anger and apprehension, he was about to grasp the knocker again when he heard footsteps and voices in the courtyard. A moment later the door swung open.

His younger brother, Cado, was standing there. To Aurel's surprise, he looked almost pleased to see him – as far as Cado's sanctimonious features could look pleased about anything.

'Well, Brother Aurel . . .' he said, a smile spreading slowly over his well-scrubbed face. 'We expected you some days past.'

Aurel shrugged. 'The bargemaster seemed in no hurry.'

'And was your journey a pleasant one?'

'Not in the least,' Aurel said impatiently. 'And must we stand here discussing it in the street? It grows late, and—'

As he spoke he stepped forward to enter the court-yard but, instead of standing back to admit him, Cado planted a hand on his chest and pushed him back into the roadway.

'Just a minute, Brother,' Cado said. As he turned, over his shoulder Aurel could see the house steward, looking uncomfortable. Cado twitched a document out of the man's hand, and thrust it at Aurel. 'Read that.'

Aurel straightened out the document; it was his father's will. The strong black script was easily legible in the moonlight, and it did not take long for Aurel to extract its gist, or find the reason for Cado's air of smug satisfaction. Apart from the usual bequests to charities and remembrances to friends, there was only one provision. Aurel himself was disinherited; Cado was to be their father's only heir.

'You may keep that,' Cado said smoothly. 'It is a copy.' He began to close the door again.

Aurel stepped forward. 'Wait, you can't just . . .'

'Can't? Aurel, for five years you mocked the laws of the Judge and drove Father to despair by your licentious living. No doubt you drove him into an early grave. Can you wonder that he found me a fitter heir for House Montfaucon?'

No, Aurel thought bitterly. *No wonder at all.* He only wondered that he had been such a fool as never to have expected this.

Cado was closing the gate again.

Aurel reached out to stop him. 'Where shall I go? What—?'

'Do you expect me to bother answering that?'

Aurel wanted to claw the smirk from his brother's face. He wished that he had turned away, with dignity at least, but rising panic made him clutch at the gate, trying to force his way inside.

His brother stoutly barred his way, pushing his face up close to Aurel's. 'Get out of here,' he said, 'or I'll have you thrown out.'

Another hard shove sent Aurel staggering back into the road, where he fell sprawling on the paving stones, the breath driven out of him.

'Go to your decadent friends,' Cado sneered. 'Or if all else fails, try this house's back door. I'm sure you can persuade the cook to find you some scraps.'

The gate slammed shut with a hollow crash, leaving Aurel to pull himself painfully to his feet. In his fall, he had scraped one hand, and beads of blood oozed darkly in the blanched light. His robe was covered with the dust from the road.

Aurel stared at the gate, wanting to fling himself at it. But there was nothing between himself and his brother, no shared liking or respect to make Cado take pity on him now.

Aurel's head went up and his mouth hardened. He would not ask again for pity, even if there might be any hope of it. He turned away, and began to walk slowly back down the hill.

His first impulse was to head back to the barge. He had left some clothes there, jewels that he could sell ... But before he reached the waterside he knew that he would only meet further humiliation if he tried to reclaim his possessions. Cado must have had servants waiting ready to warn him as soon as the barge docked, and by now someone would certainly have informed the returning barge crew who their new master was.

Aurel possessed only the clothes he was wearing, and a small amount of money in the purse at his belt – enough, perhaps, for two or three days at a decent inn. He was just that far away from destitution.

Certainly there were houses where he might expect some sort of welcome, but there would be a price attached to that, and it was not one that Aurel felt like paying. The resolve to put his old life behind him, which he had made less than an hour ago, was difficult to forget. There must be another way.

Without conscious plan, he found himself wandering downwards through a series of terraced gardens overlooking the sea. Moonlight rippled peacefully on the water below. Pausing, Aurel leant one hand against the trunk of a frangipani, breathing the scent of its waxy blooms. He would find an inn now. Next day he would consult his father's lawyer – not to question his father's will, for he was very sure that Cado would not have dared drive him away unless his title to the property was secure – but to ask what work he might find. He could write a neat hand; he understood accounts and trade. Perhaps one of the other great mercantile Houses would employ him as a clerk.

Then he asked himself: who would employ Aurel de Montfaucon, with the tarnished reputation he had spent so long and so much diligence acquiring? Who would care whether he starved or not? Realizing for the first time how exhausted he felt, he slumped to rest against the tree and sighed. There was no one, not in the whole of Arvorig, who cared whether he lived or died.

A voice behind him spoke softly, 'Good evening, Aurel.'

Aurel swung round, looking up into a familiar face.

Vissarion was not a native of Kemper, or even of Arvorig. The gentle sibilance the language assumed on his lips was unfamiliar. Rumour said he came from the East, but no one was sure – though there were stories enough.

'Messire Vissarion,' Aurel replied nervously. 'Good evening.'

Vissarion smiled down at him. His hair was longer than the usual fashion, curling thickly on his shoulders, and black against his pale skin. He wore a velvet tunic whose folds rippled like ink at every slight movement. Its hanging sleeves were lined with silk the colour of dried blood, out of which emerged hands unnaturally long and slender, and exquisitely manicured.

His dark eyes continued appraising Aurel. 'You're newly returned, I take it?' he murmured. 'This is a cold homecoming for you.'

For a second Aurel wondered how he could know, but even as he asked himself the question he realized how stupid it was. Cado would have taken great satisfaction in spreading the story of his brother's ruin through the whole of Kemper.

Now he was not sure how to reply. In the old days, when his only thought had been to wreak revenge on his father for parting him from his lover, when every black smear on his reputation had been another blow struck in their battle, he had yet stayed well away from Vissarion. Though certain hints had assured him he would be welcome in Vissarion's circle, he had made no attempt to penetrate that spacious mansion overlooking the harbour. No one knew what really went on there, and speculation usually died in a flurry of uncomfortable laughter. Frankly, this man terrified Aurel.

In the face of Aurel's awkward silence, Vissarion's smile deepened. 'What will you do now?' he asked.

'I . . . don't really know. I have money for an inn, but—'

'And when that is gone?' There was a cutting edge beneath the velvet softness.

That was the question Aurel had so far failed to answer. With no hope of respectable employment, he had only one remaining asset, and that was easily come by in Kemper, from the courtesans who summoned their lovers to pretty bowers on the hillside, to the wretches who sold themselves for coppers in waterfront taverns. Aurel shrank from discovering where in that hierarchy he might find himself, or what he might now be forced to do for survival.

He wanted to escape from this moment, but he could not tear himself away from those compelling eyes, which certainly discerned everything he had not put into words.

His gaze still fixed on Aurel's face, Vissarion reached for his hand and clasped it. 'You had far better come home with me,' he said softly.

Pure fear lanced suddenly through Aurel. He wanted to tear his hand away, but those long, delicate fingers enmeshed it in steel chains. He could feel himself shaking.

The other man's dark eyes narrowed in amusement. 'Come, my dear Aurel — supper and a bed for the night. No more than that. What do you say?'

Aurel was still instinctively reluctant. Common sense told him to give courteous thanks, and leave to find an inn. But stronger than common sense was the anger that had been swelling within him ever since his own brother had slammed the door in his face. His family had disinherited him. The Church had cast him out. If no one else wanted him, he would go with this man who did.

Vissarion must have noticed a change in his expression. 'That's better,' he sighed, and his fingers reached out to touch Aurel's hair, tiptoed over his face, then tilted up his chin so that he had to gaze into his benefactor's eyes. Vissarion's hand bore a fugitive, musky perfume that mingled with the pervasive scent of the frangipani.

'Oh, please . . .' Aurel whispered.

'There's nothing to fear.' A hint of laughter in that velvet voice. 'You will come with me, won't you?'

Aurel bowed his head in resignation. He was helpless,

a prisoner, like a fly trapped in a honeyed web. 'Yes,' he murmured, in a voice scarcely audible, 'I'll come with you.'

2

Aymon, King of Brogall, was dressing for the night's banquet when a servant announced the arrival of a courier from Arvorig with an urgent message. The king paused in the act of buckling on a gold-embossed belt. Arvorig, that damnably irritating southern peninsula, which should rationally be a province of his own Brogall . . .

Its people even spoke the same language, though with a barbarous accent. They filched the names to give their children, they worshipped the same God, often with a tedious intensity. Surely it must be logical that Brogall should rule them.

When Duke Govrian seemed likely to die without an heir, Aymon had nourished hopes, but the old fool had unearthed some monkish great-nephew, or third cousin, or such, and that rich and desirable, impossibly pious land was as unattainable as ever.

Unless this courier carried better news? Sir Baudet de la Roche, Aymon's ambassador in Arvorig, was an old fox with half a lifetime of diplomacy behind him, and he did not use words like 'urgent' lightly.

The king finished buckling the belt, settling it comfortably over folds of russet velvet. 'Send him up,' he told the servant.

He selected a brooch from the coffer presented to him by his groom of the chamber. While the man went off to fetch a mirror, he weighed the brooch, a topaz set in gold, in one hand, and smiled slightly.

'Good news, my lord?' the groom inquired, as he held up the sheet of polished silver.

Aymon pinned the brooch in place at his throat. 'Yes,' he said. 'Something tells me *very* good news.'

He ran impatient hands through his leonine hair, waved away a pot of unguent his groom was offering, and strode off through his suite of rooms towards the antechamber in time to meet the courier just as the servant ushered him in.

The courier sank to his knees, holding out a letter on which Aymon recognized de la Roche's seal. 'Very well,' he said to the courier. 'You may go now. But hold yourself ready; I may send for you again.'

He broke open the seal and flung himself into a chair, unfolding the crackling parchment. The servant lit a lamp and placed it on the table at his elbow, before withdrawing.

Through narrowed eyes Aymon scanned the letter, hesitated, then read it again. The first part described Duke Joscelin's ceremonial induction. It was the second half of the letter that interested Aymon. Duke Joscelin, it seemed, had taken to wearing an icon representing the Healer, much to the disapproval of the Grand Master and the Archbishop. In Sir Baudet's opinion, the action put the new duke in breach of the oath he had sworn to uphold the Church at his induction. He had also intervened in the case of an ecclesiastical prisoner, an unprecedented move which the Church considered an unwarranted intrusion into its territory.

The dukes of Roazon, as Sir Baudet pointed out, might lie, steal, murder and fornicate to their heart's content – as the late, unlamented Duke Govrian had so flamboyantly proved – provided that they let the Church conduct its own affairs without interference. Whereas Duke Joscelin, who seemed ready to flirt with heresy and attempt to limit the authority of the Church, was likely to find himself soon in serious trouble.

Though aware that by now his court would be assembled below, waiting for him to appear before supper could start, the king made no move to hurry, but instead, he called for a servant. 'Send Maugis to me.'

Even King Aymon himself would have struggled to explain exactly what position Maugis occupied in his entourage. A versatile and very useful man, he appeared scant moments after he had been summoned, almost as if he had been waiting – which, for all Aymon knew, he probably had.

Aymon handed over the parchment. 'Read this.'

Maugis bent his head over it. A small man, with receding dark hair and an amiable face that concealed a razor-sharp mind, he carried no weapon save for a knife at his belt, and his clothes were plain, even shabby. He was a man you would not look at twice, which was a great asset in the kind of work Aymon employed him for.

Maugis scanned the letter rapidly and looked up. 'Interesting, my lord.'

Aymon agreed. 'What do you suggest?'

Maugis smiled and tapped the folded parchment thoughtfully against his other hand. 'A border raid, my lord? Incursions from Arvorig over to your side of the mountains? Providing a good excuse for you to move your troops into the area, to protect your loyal peasantry from those Arvorig bandits.'

'Excellent!' Aymon slammed a fist down on the table.

'And if I might suggest, my lord...? I could make myself useful to you in Roazon. A riot against this new heresy would seriously inconvenience Duke Joscelin.'

A broad grin spread over the king's face. This was indeed a man after his own heart. 'You may leave tomorrow,' he said. 'Draw on the treasury for whatever you need. And Maugis . . .'

'Yes, my lord?'

'No need to report yourself to Sir Baudet de la Roche when you get there.'

The other inclined his head. 'Of course not, my lord.'

He swiftly withdrew, leaving the folded parchment on the table. As Aymon stowed it in the pouch at his belt, he found himself in a better temper than for months. Expansively, he even looked forward to sitting down at table with a pack of fawning courtiers who usually bored him to screaming pitch, and even with the appallingly tedious woman he had married for reasons of state.

Arvorig might at last be within his grasp. Play the game right – and he trusted Maugis for that – he might even grasp it with the Church's blessing. What more could a divinely appointed monarch ask?

Late but in no hurry, Aymon was still smiling as he went down to supper.

3

Vissarion led Aurel through a gate of iron scrollwork which he locked behind them; there was no sign of a porter. Ahead a path wound through shrubs with broad, pale flowers, glimmering in the moonlight. Their scent hung heavy in the warm air.

The house itself was of white marble, a long and low building, fronted by a colonnade. As Vissarion led him up the steps and into the entrance hall, where a fountain played in a grotto of ferns, Aurel's fear increased. He wanted to retreat, but it was too late now.

Bracing himself, he began, 'Messire Vissarion, it grows late, and I'm tired—'

Vissarion chuckled, low in his throat. 'Nonsense, we shall dine soon, but first you must bathe. Your appearance — forgive me — is a disaster.'

Aurel had to admit that he was right. He felt grubby; his hair was dishevelled and his robe creased and filthy from his scuffle with Cado.

'No more argument,' Vissarion said firmly. He led the way down a passage to one side of the entrance hall and threw open the door at the far end. 'Through here. Take as much time as you need.' As Aurel passed him, he tapped his shoulder. 'And my name is Vissarion. Use it.'

Beyond the door was a magnificent bathing suite, the bath itself a deep pool surrounded by intricate mosaic. Steps led gently down into warm, perfumed water. Though he might have expected attendants, the whole place was empty, and Aurel's movements set up a faint echo.

He stripped off his soiled clothes and lowered himself into the bath. His mind was still a turmoil of fear and uncertainty, but he could not prevent his body from relaxing, responding treacherously to the luxury that surrounded it.

On returning to the changing room, he found that someone had left a set of fresh clothes there, an ivory comb, and several alabaster pots of perfume. Anxiety, which had almost retreated, thudded back into his throat again. He had heard no one, and he shrank from the thought that someone had crept into the suite, observing him naked, perhaps, when he thought he was alone.

He felt dizzy, and his head spun with apprehension of what he imagined was to come. Struggling to stay calm, he dressed himself in the new attire. The robe was made of heavy, rustling silk, a pale aquamarine with silver embroidery like the foam cresting a wave. There were silken slippers to match it, and a belt of fine silver mesh.

Aurel combed his hair, but ignored the pots of perfume, and examined himself in the full-length mirror of polished silver as if he was a stranger. No doubt of what he himself was, he thought with a hint of bitterness — or of what Vissarion intended him to become. Yet the wide, watchful eyes contradicted that assumption; something about all this — about Vissarion himself — was not straightforward at all.

Trying to shrug off his apprehension, Aurel went out into the passage. His host was lounging in a window alcove near the door. Had he been there all along, Aurel wondered. Had he, perhaps, been watching?

Vissarion was smiling as he turned to Aurel and held out a hand. 'What a transformation! Come now, supper is ready.'

He led Aurel back along the passage and towards a pair of doors at the rear of the entrance hall. These were painted with vines and serpents and strange winged creatures, but Aurel had no more than a glimpse of them before Vissarion flung them apart and ushered him through.

Beyond lay a large room whose floor was an intricate mosaic of green and scarlet and white. The walls were plain white, neither decorated nor covered with tapestries, though here and there was displayed a piece of fine embroidery. Light came from a forest of tapers on silver stands, arranged in a circle around the low dining table. Couches covered in sea-green velvet provided seating places for a dozen guests, but he and Vissarion were alone.

Vissarion gestured him to a seat on one of the couches

and sat down beside him. As the soft cushions folded around him, Aurel met his host's eyes uncertainly and caught a look of amusement. Vissarion said nothing, however, only ringing a small silver bell that stood on a side table.

Servants suddenly appeared through a door at the far end of the huge room, and within the next few minutes, passing to and fro, had loaded the table with salvers of food and crystal jugs of wine, before retreating in silence.

Relief welled over Aurel. He had been ready to believe that their supper would appear by magic, like something from an exotic tale, and the discovery that Vissarion employed servants made his household seem almost ordinary. Perhaps Vissarion did not deserve the stories told about him, any more than Aurel himself had deserved the worst of his own reputation. The thought sparked a fellow-feeling within him, almost a friendliness, so that he was gradually able to smile and relax in front of his host.

The food was unfamiliar to him: cuts of exotic meats and vegetables in spicy sauce; fish served with some kind of pickle that seared the back of his throat; rice coloured with saffron; flat cakes of bread sprinkled with poppy seeds.

Aurel realized he had not eaten since midday, on the barge, back in what seemed like another world. Warmth crept through him as he ate, and he began to feel drowsy.

'My dear.' Vissarion touched his wrist, speaking softly. 'You're exhausted, but you shall sleep soon, I promise.'

Aurel smiled back at Vissarion as he reached out and refilled his wine cup. The wine was pale and flowery, and so cold it misted the outside of the goblet. Aurel sipped, letting the fragrant liquid trickle over his tongue. He could have curled up there and then on the couch and slept, if it would not have been so appallingly discourteous.

He looked into the other's eyes; he could still see amusement there, but also something like appreciation, as if Vissarion was pleased with him.

Aurel reached out to him, and began to say, 'You're being so good to me . . .' when he was interrupted by another touch on his hand.

'A moment more,' Vissarion said. 'Then there is something I must ask you.'

Aurel sank back among the cushions bemused as Vissarion rang the bell again. The servants reappeared, cleared away the dishes, leaving plates of sweetmeats and a bowl of rosewater and a linen towel for them to wash their hands.

When all this activity was finished, and the servants had retreated, Vissarion said, 'So you are newly returned from Roazon. Did you witness the new duke's induction ceremony?'

Aurel shook his head. 'I left earlier that morning.' A glint of something like annoyance flashed in Vissarion's eyes, and Aurel was thrown into desperate disappointment, as if he had failed a new friend.

'No matter.' The voice was still soft. 'I had a . . . servant there. He came back more speedily, telling me of a white dove appearing in the cathedral. Some say it's a sign of divine favour.'

Aurel stared. 'Surely—'

'Oh, you and I are not so superstitious.' Yet Vissarion looked frustrated, drumming his long fingers on the table edge. 'But if the people of Roazon believe that Heaven is smiling on their duke, it will make him all the more difficult to get rid of.'

'Get rid of?' Aurel, bewildered, tried to struggle up from the smothering cushions. 'No one can get rid of the appointed Duke of Roazon!'

Vissarion flashed him a look of definite annoyance, and

Aurel shrank back. Then the smile returned. 'What do you know of Autrys?'

Aurel felt more confused than ever. 'Autrys?' He remembered, years ago, his old nurse telling him and his brother stories of Autrys, the island of demons, which had been destroyed after the first Duke of Roazon had assumed his office. It was said to lie off the coast, not far from Kemper, and when the wind blew in the right direction, you could sometimes hear the bells of its black cathedral tolling beneath the waves. 'But, Vissarion, that's just an old tale,' he said.

'It has pleased the Church to have everyone believe that,' Vissarion said. 'But no, the existence of Autrys is true history. My servants and I have spent a long time in ... research. We can be sure of that.'

'But why,' Aurel asked, 'if it was so evil?'

Vissarion shrugged. 'Do you really believe that only the Church has the right to decide what is and is not evil? Once Autrys was gone, the Church vilified it, yes ... because they dared not risk its power rising again.'

'Rising again?' Aurel felt a sudden stab of fear. 'But Autrys was totally destroyed.'

Vissarion's eyes narrowed in amusement. 'Don't be absurd, my dear. These things are never truly gone. Autrys was a place of real power,' he went on, while Aurel's mind spun with the implications of what he was saying. 'Because that power challenged the Church, the Church destroyed it and denounced it as evil. Because Autrys offered a freedom – the freedom to speak, and think, and be anything we wish, instead of parroting the rigid doctrines of the Church. Would you call that evil, Aurel?'

Aurel gazed at him. Vissarion's eyes seemed to promise everything: acceptance, respect, a world where Aurel would be no longer an outcast. Slowly, he shook his head.

'Well done.' Vissarion filled Aurel's wine cup again, and Aurel ducked his head and drank hastily, suddenly embarrassed by the approbation in his host's eyes.

Catching his breath, he asked, 'But what has Duke Joscelin to do with all that?'

'You surely know the old story,' Vissarion replied, 'that if there remains no duke of the true line in Roazon, Autrys will rise again. When Duke Govrian died and the direct line failed, we had hopes that Autrys might be free to resurrect itself. But then Duke Govrian named Joscelin as his heir, and—' his mouth became a hard line '—Autrys is prisoned still.'

'Then ... you want to depose the new duke?' Aurel's breath fluttered in his chest. This was no longer a pleasant supper party; Vissarion had made him into a conspirator, and was speaking treason. He should have been afraid; he was afraid, a little, and yet far stronger was the vision of personal freedom that Vissarion had shown him.

'But why?' he continued, when Vissarion did not reply.

His words faded into a gasp as Vissarion shot out a hand and tangled his fingers in Aurel's hair, forcing his head round until they faced each other fully. The man's eyes burned; Aurel half expected to receive his kiss – and did not know whether he quivered from delight or trepidation.

'My mother was a woman of Arvorig,' Vissarion said finally. His voice kept level, contradicting the flame in his eyes. 'She was seized by pirates and sold as a concubine in the east, in a land where my father was a great lord.' His mouth twisted. 'Of course he did not acknowledge me. Instead, he had me taught the arts of pleasing, and sold me in his turn. My new master was ... interesting, and in his service I learnt much more.'

He broke off and refilled the wine cups. Though his

head was already spinning, Aurel let its cold, delicious drops trickle down his throat.

'My new master believed he had total control of me,' Vissarion went on, 'and so he grew careless. One night I killed him, rifled what wealth I could carry, and fled the city. And at last I came to Arvorig, to this house where my mother once worked in the kitchens. Only one thing matters to me now: that no one should again be enslaved as she and I were, should need to fear as we feared.' He leant towards Aurel, and folded tapering fingers around his hand. 'And so you will help me, Aurel, to bring this about? To free the world of such oppression?'

'Oh, yes, Vissarion,' Aurel whispered. 'I'll do anything you tell me.'

'Good.' Vissarion's grip tightened on Aurel's hand, and he rose to his feet, drawing his guest up with him. 'Come with me.'

The floor felt uneven under Aurel's feet and to his shame he stumbled. 'I'm sorry,' he murmured.

In the soft shimmer of the tapers he saw the other smiling into his eyes. 'No matter, take my arm. We're not going far.'

Out in the hall, a servant was waiting, holding a dark lantern, which he handed to Vissarion. Another pulled open the outer door, and Aurel was drawn out into the night.

A narrow pathway led around one side of the house, winding among the shrubs of the garden towards the gentle slopes of the hill beyond. The cool, scented air thankfully cleared Aurel's head a little. The moon had set, but by the lantern light he could see when the trimmed elegance of the garden gave way to wilder woodland. The smooth paving of the path became uneven stones, trees crowded closer, and overhanging ferns brushed his robe as he went by.

Gradually the path sloped upwards, and then reached a flight of rough steps cut into the hillside. Moss-covered stones, the height of a man, lined the ascent on either side.

At the top of the stairway Vissarion paused, holding the lantern high, so Aurel could see that the path was split in two by another standing stone whose surface was incised with spiral patterns made more distinct by some kind of reddish pigment that had been rubbed into the grooves. Behind the decorated stone, a passage led into the hill itself.

Vissarion urged him gently forward. 'There's nothing to be afraid of,' he murmured. 'In a little while, you will belong to me.'

Docilely, Aurel let Vissarion lead him on, right into the passage beyond. The tunnel curved gently, so that the entrance was soon lost behind them. The lantern's yellow light seemed sickly and feeble as they headed deeper into the hill, but Aurel caught glimpses of yet more carvings on the stones on either side. Grit and debris crackled under his feet, moisture soaking through his light slippers. Though it was cold here, the air felt thick, and soon he felt himself gasping for breath. The soft rustle of robes was all that he could hear.

Just as Aurel was beginning to think that this passage had no end, the walls fell away on either side and he realized he was now standing in a large circular chamber. Vissarion set the lantern in a niche; by its flickering light Aurel could see walls of interlocked stone, with slabs of rock laid over them, to form a roof rising no more than a few inches above their heads. Aurel had a sudden, oppressive sense of the sheer weight of earth above him, of all that separated him from the safe, familiar world above ground.

At the far side of the chamber, where the lantern light fell brightest, a shape was cut into the rock. At first Aurel thought that it was the Holy Knot, though the branches seemed too short and stumpy. Then he almost thought that he could make out a face there, wedge-shaped like a serpent's. Somehow the thing seemed to be shifting, though, or perhaps that was due to the uneven flame of the lantern ... or his own weariness and all the wine he had drunk. Aurel blinked, and the shape had changed again, became a claw stretched out to grasp him.

He turned questioningly, but Vissarion raised his hand and laid a finger on Aurel's lips for silence. So they waited; Aurel could *feel* the waiting, and see the eagerness glinting in his companion's eyes.

After what seemed like an uncounted time, Aurel felt hands pressing lightly on his shoulders, encouraging him to kneel. Vissarion himself remained standing behind him; looking up with raised arms, palms held outward, towards the shape on the opposite wall.

At the same moment Aurel sensed a return to that weight of oppression that had assailed him when he first came into the chamber, yet heavier, thicker now, as if the roof had fallen in and he was buried under tons of earth, the last breath forced out of him.

Yet the chamber had not changed, unless it had grown subtly darker. The shape in the rock had begun to resemble a face again. Could those be eyes he saw — or no more than a reflection of the lantern light on angled planes of rock?

Somehow he felt that others were now entering the chamber, but he could see no sign of them, and when he tried to turn his head it was as if he was frozen in place, his gaze fixed on the shifting thing on the chamber wall.

'Master,' Vissarion said suddenly — and Aurel did not know whom he addressed — 'Master, regard your servant, Aurel de Montfaucon.'

The shifting light of the lantern again seemed to change the face – if it *was* a face – through an additional gleam of interest in its eyes.

'He now dedicates himself to you,' Vissarion continued, 'to fight for the resurrection of Autrys and the freedom of the world. Aurel de Montfaucon, do you consent?'

Aurel hesitated, feeling torn between hope and fear.

Vissarion's voice sharpened. 'You must give your consent.'

In the end, Aurel realized he had no choice. It was too late now for retreat or escape. He already belonged to Vissarion – and to the mysterious, half-present 'Master' he served.

'Yes, I consent,' his words sighed out.

Vissarion lowered his arms, and reached out a hand to help Aurel stand. 'Very good.'

As he felt the arm supporting him, Aurel felt somehow the sense of oppression in the chamber had lifted. The mesmerizing shape on the wall looked no more than some random cracks in the surrounding rock.

As he drew a long, shaky breath of relief, Vissarion said firmly, 'Now you are one of us, there is a task for you to do.'

'What is it?' Aurel asked nervously.

Vissarion smiled down at him. 'To assassinate Duke Joscelin.'

As he lifted the lantern from its niche, its shutter clattered down, and the chamber was plunged into impenetrable darkness.

Nine

I

Morning sunlight poured through the window of Tiphaine de Bellière's bedchamber, wakening jewel colours in the embroidery threads scattered over the table. But Tiphaine gazed at them with intense dislike, and similarly at the breadth of yellow silk she was supposed to be ornamenting.

The silk was to become a sleeve for Nicolas to wear as a favour at the next tournament. *A sleeve?* Tiphaine thought contemptuously. Had the ladies of old romance ever really given their sleeves to their lovers? What did that do to the rest of the gown? *Making* a sleeve, that no one would ever wear, seemed to her the height of madness. Sighing, Tiphaine raised her needle and set in another stitch. It was crooked and ugly, she knew, nothing like the tiny, exquisite stitches that Aunt Peronel herself achieved.

'Heavens, child!' Aunt Peronel had said, on seeing Tiphaine's first attempt at embroidery. 'Have you learnt *nothing* in that house of your grandfather's?'

But then, Tiphaine thought, no one would notice her inadequate stitchery when the sleeve was tied round Nicolas' helmet. Crossly, she thrust the needle through the fabric again and started as it penetrated her own finger. A few spots of blood beaded bright on the yellow silk, soaking in before Tiphaine could dab at it with her handkerchief.

She was going to be scolded again, she could see.

As she was sucking her injured finger, she heard hurried footsteps on the stairs, and again began stitching assiduously, folding the silk over so the blood-spots did not show.

A moment later Aunt Peronel was in the room. 'Leave that, child, and come right away to my solar! Nicolas is here.'

Tiphaine was sure that any lady in an old romance would feel a flutter of excitement when she heard that her betrothed had come to visit. But all she herself felt was relief that she need not go on with this wretched stitching. Laying the silk aside, she followed her aunt obediently downstairs to the solar.

Nicolas was pacing restlessly between window and hearth, a cup of wine in his hand. Aunt Peronel dismissed the servant and went to sit in her favourite chair beside the hearth, taking up her own embroidery.

'Do settle down, Nicolas,' she said. 'You make my head ache with your pacing.'

Nicolas had paused politely to kiss Tiphaine's hand, but she could see that he had other things on his mind.

'Mother, what have you heard of this new heresy?' he asked finally.

Aunt Peronel flapped a hand in front of her face. 'Mercy, Nicolas, what do I know about heresy? That sort of thing is for priests and scholars. What has it to do with me?'

Her son began to pace again.

Tiphaine sat down in the window seat and arranged her skirts. 'Do you mean Duke Joscelin's supposed heresy?' she asked.

Nicolas stared at her, looking as startled as if his mother's sewing casket had sat up and spoken to him. He folded his arms portentously, but when he replied, it was to his mother that he spoke.

'Yes, they say Duke Joscelin has begun to worship some deity he calls the Healer,' he announced.

'I still don't see what that has to do with us,' Aunt Peronel said fretfully.

'What it has to do with us,' Nicolas told her, 'is that if he's not careful, Duke Joscelin will get himself deposed.'

Aunt Peronel looked at him with open mouth. 'Nonsense!'

'Not nonsense at all, Mother. Duke Joscelin rules only with the consent of the Church. If he persists in a heresy, the Church will remove him. It's as simple as that.'

'Well, I'm sure I don't know,' said Aunt Peronel, flustered.

'And if the Church does remove him,' Tiphaine broke in, 'who will be Duke of Roazon in his place?'

Nicolas gave her a wary look, as if reluctant to concede that she had asked him an intelligent question. 'The only other man in the direct Roazon bloodline,' he said, 'is Tariec, Count Fragan's son. He could claim through his mother, who was Govrian's niece.'

He glanced from Tiphaine to his mother and back again, as if he expected them to understand something he had not actually said.

'Well?' Aunt Peronel asked querulously.

'Consider this. Our manors of Cotin and Bellière both lie in Gwened, so we all owe service to Fragan as our liege lord.'

'Who is a vassal of the Duke of Roazon,' Tiphaine said, feeling uneasy. She could see the way Nicolas' mind was working, and she did not like it.

'And if we must choose between a Duke of Roazon who

is a self-proclaimed heretic, and the son and heir of our own liege lord . . .?' Nicolas said.

Aunt Peronel responded with an exclamation of annoyance. 'There! I've stitched this whole petal in the wrong colour. Nicolas, you distract me with all this talk of heresy.'

She spread out the offending silk and examined it with a vexed expression.

Tiphaine got up. 'Here, Aunt, give it to me,' she said. 'I'll soon take out the stitches for you.'

'Thank you, Tiphaine.' Aunt Peronel handed over the silk with a gusty sigh. 'You're growing very considerate.'

Throughout all this, Nicolas stood in front of the hearth, gulping the wine he had not tasted until now. He then poured himself another cupful. He would be drunk before midday, if he went on like this, Tiphaine thought, as she took her aunt's scissors and excised the offending blue petal from an otherwise red rose. Glancing up, she surveyed his reddening face and protuberant eyes with what she realized was mild dislike.

This is the man I must marry, she thought.

'What we need to consider,' Nicolas went on, 'is what our attitude should be. If I were to go now to Count Fragan and pledge him the future support of Cotin and Bellière, there's bound to be great rewards for us when Tariec becomes Duke of Roazon.'

'But if Duke Joscelin is not deposed, and learns how you have plotted against him—' Tiphaine began.

'Plotting? I said nothing of plotting,' said Nicolas.

Tiphaine shrugged. She was feeling reckless. 'Call it what you please,' she said. 'But what will Duke Joscelin call it, if he finds you offered your support to the man who wants to unseat him?'

'Tiphaine!' The usual outraged squawk from Aunt Peronel. 'Tiphaine, this is a matter for men.'

'It is a matter for me too, Aunt, if Nicolas is to speak for my lands of Bellière.'

'But he is your betrothed!'

Nicolas went over to Tiphaine, taking her hand and patting it comfortingly. It was all she could do not to jab him with her scissors.

'Don't worry. I will arrange everything,' he said. 'There's no need to be afraid.'

Tiphaine withdrew her hand from his. 'I'm *not* afraid,' she said. 'Except of being called traitor.'

She rose and handed her aunt's work back with a little curtsey. 'Excuse me, Aunt, Nicolas,' she said, and slipped out of the room.

I have now as good as quarrelled with Nicolas, she thought, as she mounted the stairs to her own chamber. I have spoken my mind openly in front of him and Aunt Peronel.

She felt, just a little, as if the bars of the cage surrounding her might be ready to gape open and set her free.

2

Daylight through the open door of the captain's lodgings was cut off briefly as Sulien de Plouzhel came inside. Sketching a salute, he threw himself down on to the bench under the window.

'You wanted to see me, Captain, sir?'

Val looked up from the table, where he was compiling

the duty rosters. 'Yes, I've been thinking about those two lieutenancies. It's not good to have both posts vacant — so who do you suggest for the other one?'

'The other one?' Sulien sat upright.

'Yes.' Val grinned. 'You've been ready for this promotion for a year at least.'

'I know we're good friends, Val, but . . .' Sulien shrugged uneasily.

'Friendship has nothing to do with it. You're the best man for the job.'

Sulien was a tall, lanky young man, with bright red hair and pale skin that flushed easily — as it did now. His outward carelessness masked, as Val knew, a real commitment to his vocation as a Knight of the Legion. And as senior lieutenant he would be unquestionably easier for Val to work with than the recently departed Girec d'Evron.

Sitting upright, both hands on his knees, Sulien seriously considered the question Val had asked him. But for the second vacant lieutenancy there was no obvious choice.

In the end Val pushed the nearly empty sheet of paper away, and poured a mug of wine for himself and Sulien — the same harsh stuff sent up from the Plume of Feathers. 'I'll have to go on thinking about it. Here, let's drink a toast to absent friends.'

Sulien took the cup and grinned. 'You don't mean d'Evron, surely? Gladly — so long as he *stays* absent.'

'I spotted him in the market yesterday,' Val said, pushing his chair back from the table so he could stretch his legs. 'I'll be glad when Count Fragan returns home and takes d'Evron with him.'

'Hmm . . .' Sulien gazed into his wine cup. 'I notice how

all the other provincial lords go home, but Fragan stays. He got himself ready to depart, and then he changed his mind. What is he up to, I wonder?'

'Does he have to be up to anything?'

'Fragan's well known to be a devious bastard,' Sulien said. 'He doesn't do anything without a good reason.'

Their eyes met. Val could not help thinking of all the gossip he had heard over the last few days about the icon of the Healer that Duke Joscelin insisted on wearing. Heresy, it was muttered.

'This icon . . .' he began uneasily. It might seem such a small thing, but every time the duke wore it he was throwing down a public challenge to the ecclesiastical power in Roazon.

Sulien broke in. 'Joscelin is my liege lord,' he said. 'I ask for none better. But he's an innocent if he thinks he can wear an image offensive to the Church and get away with it.'

'He *is* an innocent,' said Val.

'And if Count Fragan sees signs of Duke Joscelin about to lose his office . . . even the merest chance of it,' Sulien went on, holding up a hand, 'he'll wait here indefinitely to claim the title in his son's name.'

Val was disgusted. 'All Tariec cares about is getting drunk every night and chasing chambermaids. *That* imbecile to be Duke of Roazon!'

'But if he makes the right pious noises, the Church will soon back him against a self-confessed heretic. They put up with his kinsman Govrian for thirty years, so what's the problem with Tariec?'

'And where will that leave us?' Val asked. 'What about the Knights Companions themselves, if the Duke of Roazon is deposed? Where do our loyalties lie?'

Sulien drained the cup of wine and banged it down on the bench beside him. 'That, my friend Captain, is something you will soon have to decide.'

3

Aurel opened his eyes. He lay in bed, in a spacious room lit by cool light pouring through silken mesh at the window. Outside he could hear birdsong and, at a distance, the sea. His mouth was dry and his head ached.

Struggling among soft pillows and silken coverings, he managed to sit up, wincing as an even sharper pain stabbed through his head. Had he really drunk so much the night before? Groping for memory, he recalled the underground chamber, and that shape in the rock that looked so much like a face. He had then known fear enough to sober anyone, so why should he feel so ill now?

After all that had happened before, he had expected to have to spend the night with Vissarion, but, on their return to the house, his host had despatched a servant to escort him to this room. Aurel had the sense of being laid aside, to be taken up again when Vissarion needed him.

A low side table held a jug of water and a cup. His hand shaking so much that he spilt more than he swallowed, he managed to take a sip or two. Then he looked round the room.

Like the dining hall it was only sparsely furnished: not much beyond the bed, a clothes press against one wall, and a low couch below the window. The aquamarine robe from the night before had been tossed over the arm of the couch, with one trailing sleeve puddled on the floor. Against the far wall was a washstand with basin and ewer.

Slowly, uncertainly, Aurel got out of bed and stumbled over. The water contained in the ewer was warm, so it must have been placed there not long before. He washed quickly, alert for any sound outside his room. He dreaded that Vissarion would return and find him naked, and for want of any other garment he went to pick up the robe draped over the couch.

Its silk was crumpled, with a faint, fugitive perfume in the folds — something sweet and heavy, like incense. Suddenly the thought of putting it on again revolted him, so he went to investigate the clothes press. Inside it he found a white linen tunic, so modest and respectable that not even his father could have complained.

He had scarcely time to dress — was fastening the tunic at his shoulder with a silver pin — when he heard a footstep in the passage outside. Vissarion's appearance was so timely that Aurel could not help wondering once again whether his host had some way of watching him when he thought he was alone. He shivered at the thought.

'Feeling cold, my dear?' Vissarion inquired, smiling as he came into the room and closed the door behind him. 'Outside the sun is shining. The morning grows late — you must make ready.'

'Ready? For what?' Aurel asked.

Vissarion was carrying a silver ring and a knife in a leather sheath that was worked with silver. He laid both the objects down on the table by the bed before he replied. 'Your barge to Roazon leaves on the afternoon tide.'

'To Roazon?' Aurel knew he sounded stupid, and could only hope that the recovering memories of the night before were no more than evil dreams.

'You are still resolved, surely?' Vissarion asked, with a

sudden hauteur that made Aurel feel as exposed as if naked. 'To kill the heretic Joscelin? For Autrys?' He strode over and caught Aurel by the shoulders. 'For freedom?'

Aurel tried to back away. 'I – I don't think I can,' he stammered.

Vissarion smiled. 'There's nothing to fear.'

'But – they know me there. They won't let me anywhere near Duke Joscelin.'

The teasing smile still touched Vissarion's lips. 'You worry about nothing – see.'

He took up the silver ring; it had a flat, dark stone, like a signet ring, though the stone bore no device. Vissarion slid it onto Aurel's finger, and turned him towards the mirror.

Aurel gasped as the image of himself blurred. He blinked, thinking that a mist had covered his eyes. When it cleared, he found he was looking at a stranger, yet as he half raised a hand in rejection of what he saw, he realized that it was indeed himself.

Height and build had not changed, and he still wore the same white tunic with its shoulder pin, but his golden hair had faded to a light brown and the curls which he had worn defiantly longer than respectability dictated were now shorn to a feathery cap that clung to his head. His eyes were grey, his features longer and thinner, looking a year or two older.

Vissarion's reflection, standing behind the image, showed amusement at his confusion. 'Will they know you now?' he asked.

Still unable to drag his eyes away from his own changed appearance, Aurel shook his head.

Vissarion spun him round, away from the mirror. 'You must go forthwith to the citadel in Roazon, and find

yourself a place in Joscelin's household. A humble position
– as clerk, or someone's body servant will do. When you are
there . . .'

He fetched the knife and drew it halfway from its
sheath. The hilt, too, was silver, set with a sapphire winking
like an eye. Light rippled down the slim blade whose metal
was dark and silky. It lay in Vissarion's palm like a sleeping
serpent.

'Take care, my dear,' Vissarion said. 'One scratch brings
death.'

Aurel met his eyes, fear crowding upon fear. 'I can't,' he
whispered. 'I'm sorry.'

'Nonsense,' Vissarion argued. 'You will do very well.
And once Duke Joscelin is dead, you will be rewarded with
all you have ever wanted.' He slid the knife back into the
sheath and clipped it to the belt of Aurel's tunic. 'Now
come, there's time for us to enjoy a meal before your barge
leaves.'

Following him down the marble staircase, Aurel realized
that he was now hopelessly enthralled to Vissarion – or to
the darkness he served. There was no escape, no choice but
to carry out the deed laid on him.

Desperately he clung to his new-found belief that the
return of Autrys would bring freedom not just for himself,
but for the whole of Arvorig. Desperately – for if that were
not true, then how could he contemplate killing a man who
had as yet done no wrong to anyone?

4

That same day, after a midday meal during which Aunt
Peronel had left her in no doubt about her displeasure,

Tiphaine paid a visit to Father Reynaud himself. Aunt Peronel made no objection, for once, only insisting that she take a servant as escort. 'You can't run around in Roazon as your grandfather allowed you out in the fields at Bellière.'

As she trod demurely in the steps of the servant, Tiphaine found herself remembering Bertrand d'Acquin, the brilliance of his black eyes – and wondering what his kisses would feel like. He was not as handsome as Nicolas, certainly, but he was alive, he was *real*, and he had looked at her as if she was real, too, not just the obedient doll that Nicolas would doubtless make her.

It was no good, Tiphaine realized, to dwell on that. And probably this Bertrand had never given her another thought since their encounter at the tournament.

She was interrupted in her musings by their arrival at the citadel. On asking for Father Reynaud, she and her servant were shown into a small room overlooking the garden, and left to wait. Soon, the Grand Master joined them.

He wore a simple black cassock and a silver pectoral Knot, but his austerity dissolved into a small smile when he saw her.

'Welcome, Niece,' he said. 'How may I help you?'

Tiphaine glanced at her aunt's servant, who still stood by the door. If he stayed, every word she said would find its way back to Peronel.

'I should like to speak to you alone, Uncle.'

Father Reynaud frowned. 'I am a Knight of the Legion, child. I should never be alone with a woman, not even my own niece.'

Tiphaine bit her lip. 'But on a spiritual matter, Father . . .?'

For a moment she saw uncertainty in Father Reynaud's

eyes, and, to her astonishment, something like longing there. In his Order dedicated, as it was, to war, and with all the cares of its administration on his shoulders, perhaps no one consulted him on spiritual matters any more. Perhaps the priest was losing himself in the Grand Master.

'Please, Father . . .' she persevered.

'Very well.' He waved a hand at the servant. 'Go and wait for us in the entrance hall. I shall bring Lady Tiphaine to you as soon as we have finished.'

He waited for the servant to go out, his footsteps dying away down the outside corridor, before he seated himself and spoke again. 'You wish to make confession, child?'

'No, Father, but I'm sorely in need of guidance.' She glanced away from him, down into the garden where a solitary woman in a servant's woollen gown was gathering roses. Tiphaine interlaced her fingers in her lap. 'Father, you know that I'm betrothed to my cousin, Nicolas de Cotin.'

'Yes.'

'Do you approve of this marriage, Father?'

At a muffled snort of amusement from Father Reynaud, she looked at him to see his mouth quirking again into a smile. 'It's a little late to be consulting me about that, child.'

Tiphaine felt herself reddening. 'I know, Father . . .'

He moved a hand dismissively. 'The de Cotins were ever looking to advance themselves, and I'm sometimes sorry our family ever became connected with them.' He hesitated, and then went on, 'If I had not renounced my inheritance for the Church, I myself would be Lord of Bellière now, and you would have needed my consent for your marriage.'

'Would you have given it, Father?'

Father Reynaud shrugged. 'I know of no harm in Nicolas. No money either, of course, as with all the de Cotins. But he's handsome enough, and no doubt that draws you to him?'

Tiphaine felt her flush deepening. 'No, Father, it does not.'

Father Reynaud leant forward till they were almost touching. 'What are you saying, child? Do you not want to marry your cousin?'

'No, Father, I don't. Is there a way – any way – of setting our betrothal aside?'

She waited tensely as Father Reynaud thought over his reply.

'Difficult,' he said at last. '*He* could set it aside, of course, without giving any reason. But he's unlikely to do that, when he would lose all the de Bellière estates.'

Strange, Tiphaine thought, that it was accepted without question between them that Nicolas did not love her. *I should have known my uncle better*, she realized. *He and I can talk together.*

'Suppose I did something to make him really angry,' she suggested, realizing that should be easy enough. 'Something *indecent*?' she added, choosing one of Aunt Peronel's favourite words of rebuke.

Father Reynaud coughed and glanced aside. 'I think not, child. Even if Nicolas did not make your shame public, once he repudiated you no decent man would marry you afterwards.'

'And can I repudiate him?' she asked.

'Have you quarrelled with him?' Father Reynaud gave her a keen glance.

'Not – not really, Father.' She did not dare repeat her

conversation with Nicolas that morning. She would be
repeating treason, or as good as, and she could not imagine
the consequences.

'Well, then . . . ?'

'I don't feel ready for marriage, Father.' True enough.

'Natural modesty? It becomes you, child.' Father Reynaud had begun to relax, shifting in his seat as if about to
draw their conversation to a close.

Panicky, Tiphaine repeated her question. '*Can* I repudiate him, Father?'

'It is a weighty thing,' he began, 'to dissolve a betrothal
blessed by the Church. You might do it, if Nicolas was
guilty of some great dishonour.'

Such as treason? Tiphaine thought. But Nicolas might do
or say nothing drastic right away, she knew. *Waiting to see
which way the cat would jump*, as her old nurse put it.

'Or if he did something . . .' Father Reynaud searched
for a word, 'something *indecent.*'

'If he made love to another woman?' Tiphaine asked
frankly. 'Or visited those taverns on the lakeside road?' She
added, 'I know about them.'

Father Reynaud looked away again. 'Child, however
much we may regret it, many young men do such things,
and still make good husbands to their wives.'

'Then he would have to do something *really* dreadful?'

'So dreadful that I think – I hope – you could not
conceive of it.'

'That's a pity,' said Tiphaine.

She knew very well that Nicolas would never do anything
quite like that. For one thing – she surprised herself by her
insight – he was too much of a coward. He might like to
go peacocking around on the tournament field in a bright
surcoat, with a lady's favour on his helm, but he had not

dared to challenge Bertrand, even though he had grudged him his victory.

'Child.' Father Reynaud leant forward to pat her hand. 'You are worrying about nothing. Many young girls fear marriage, and it is right and proper that they should. But they turn into happy wives and mothers in the end.'

Despairing, Tiphaine realized that she would get no more from him, and her fugitive visions had as usual deserted her when she had real need of them. She rose and dropped a deep curtsey. 'Thank you, Father. You have given me much to think about.'

More than enough, she thought, as she returned to her aunt's house.

Ten

I

Alissende had just finished feeding baby Ivona when she heard the slam of the street door below. Ivona, already drowsy, whimpered as Alissende settled her in her cradle, but was already asleep by the time Donan came into the room.

Alissende straightened up and turned to him 'Well?'

Donan shook his head, looking tired and discouraged. 'They won't let me see her. No one will tell me what's going on. Alissende, it's been five days now!'

Alissende hooked the kettle off the fire and poured some hot water into a mug, an aromatic smell drifting into the room.

'You look worn out. Sit down and drink this. Supper will be ready soon.'

Donan wrapped his hands round the mug and took a sip. 'Alissende, you're wonderful,' he said, trying to smile and failing miserably. 'What are we going to do?'

Alissende made her own drink and sat down beside the fire, opposite him. 'What about your family? Is there anyone who could help?'

Donan shook his head with a faint sound of disgust. 'None of us have any influence. Besides, my parents and sister never much liked Morwenna. They wanted me to wed some nice girl who would keep house for me like a good

Guildsman's wife. But a painter . . .' He shrugged and added, 'Morwenna's family live in Kervrest, and her father and her brothers are all sailors. I can write them a letter, but God knows when they'll get it.'

Alissende nodded. 'Then *we* must do something.'

'But what?'

'We must petition Duke Joscelin himself.' Donan's eyes lit up with the beginnings of interest, and Alissende added eagerly, 'I heard in the market today that Duke Joscelin doesn't care for the way the Church treats its prisoners.' And, remembering, she added, 'Lord Tancred possesses one of Morwenna's icons. He could help us, Donan. He could get us in to see Duke Joscelin.'

She rose and went over to Morwenna's work table. Gathering paper, pen and ink, she sat down to write.

After watching her for a few moments, Donan got to his feet, letting out a long sigh. 'I'll see to our supper.'

Later that evening, after the letter was written and sealed, Donan set off to visit some of the other Guild councillors, to see if they could exert any pressure on the Church. He did not have much hope – and nor did Alissende – but she encouraged him because she wanted the house to herself for a while.

With Donan out, and the baby sleeping, she would finally have leisure to look in the scrying bowl. So far she had resisted this temptation, assuring herself that Morwenna would soon be home again, but she could not go on pretending. What she was *now* – a wandering drifter without home or purpose – could be little help to her new friend. What she had once been was a very different matter.

She first went to the kitchen and returned with an earthenware bowl filled with water. Checking that little Ivona still slept, she set the bowl on Morwenna's work

table and seated herself in front of it. Closing her eyes,
she folded her hands and sought for the centring – the
meditation technique that once had been second nature to
her.

'Grant me your vision,' she spoke silently inside her
head. 'Show me what you would have me see.'

She opened her eyes to see the water still clear in its
bowl, reflecting only the light of the tapers. Firmly she
fought down a pang of disappointment, refusing to let it
disturb her focus, refusing to entertain the thought that
somehow, in her months of rejection, she might have lost
her former powers.

Then suddenly the surface of the water became ridged
like a wind-tossed lake. Once it stilled again, Alissende bent
forward and gazed down into the depths beneath.

The reflected light from the tapers had vanished now.
For a moment all she could see was roiling cloud. When
that thinned away, she found herself looking down at the
citadel of Roazon, as if she were a bird hovering above the
square that fronted its main gates.

As on the day she had watched Duke Joscelin's induction
procession, the open space was crowded again, with a
heaving mob pressed up against the gates. Though her
current vision was silent, she could see their yelling faces
were distorted by anger and fear.

As she watched, a Knight of the Legion appeared
through the gates, carrying a parchment. He tried to read
aloud from it but could not make himself heard above the
noise of the crowd. When a stone struck him on the
shoulder, he made one more vain effort to be heard, and
then retreated.

As Alissende pondered when this would happen, and
what might have provoked such a riot, the water in the

basin swirled and that vision was lost. More rapid images succeeded it: a young girl half turned towards her, her face lit with a look of surprise and welcome; a man on horseback, riding hard, with a sword in his hand; the blue and gold banner of Brogall, fluttering in the wind; Duke Joscelin walking towards her along a lakeshore, a sprig of juniper in his hand.

Alissende had not realized, until then, how dependent she had once been upon her sisters in the Order – on how they would patiently piece together their individual scraps of vision until they could make sense of the whole. For up till now, she had never tried this alone.

The water clear again, she thought that her visions were over. Then a last image formed, and Alissende drew back in shock.

Here was Morwenna, but not as she had last seen her. For now her friend looked thin and pale, and where her eyes had once been were ragged holes leaking blood.

Then the water went dark, and Alissende saw nothing at all.

2

Three days out of Kemper, Aurel's despair began to recede. Away from the sinister Vissarion, that sense of being in thrall to him was weakening. Aurel felt free to ask himself what he really wanted to do.

It was a question hard to answer, but he knew what he did *not* want. He was no assassin, and if the return of Autrys could only be accomplished by a good man's death, then it must truly be an evil place. Aurel realized he wanted nothing more to do with Vissarion's plots.

As the sun began to go down on that third day of travelling, Aurel stood by the rail as they pulled into the landing-stage at Maravou. This was a small town surrounded by vineyards, where his father had regularly traded for wine. Its houses crowded up the hillside, their white walls now painted a glowing honey colour by the westering sun. A church bell was already ringing the summons to the evening Offering.

Coming to a sudden decision, Aurel returned to his cabin, rolled up a couple of changes of clothing, and thrust deep inside this bundle the pouch of money which Vissarion had provided.

Standing in front of the cabin's tiny mirror, he tried to tug off the ring. For a few minutes he struggled with it, surprised that it slid quite comfortably around his finger, but he could not remove it whatever he tried. That unfamiliar face in the mirror still looked out at him, though his own fear was alive in the stranger's grey eyes.

Very well, he said to himself at last, panting. *I'll keep this face. I'll be Aurel de Montfaucon no longer. Then all the more easily I can start again.*

He discovered there was even a kind of excitement in the thought that he could begin again, without the burden of his reputation. Tucking the bundle under one arm, he headed casually across the deck and, as he crossed the gangplank, he unclipped the assassin's knife from his belt and let it fall into the river beneath him.

Climbing the steep main street, he found a small tavern where he could order a meal of fresh-caught river fish and a flagon of the local wine. The tap-room he sat in was small and clean; a harper was tuning his instrument at one end.

As Aurel finished eating, the landlord came up to him.

'Excellent, thank you,' Aurel replied to his inquiry. 'Do you know of any good lodgings? Clean, and not too expensive?'

The landlord grinned. 'You couldn't do better than with my sister, sir. Turn right out of here, and it's up at the top of this street.' He gestured. 'The house with the red door. And ask for Mistress Loiza.'

Aurel slowly savoured his last cupful of wine, and left the tavern. He was certain he turned right, as instructed, but somehow he soon found himself descending a flight of steps which brought him out onto the quayside, opposite the same barge he had disembarked from.

Murmuring in irritation, Aurel climbed all the way up the main street again, passing the tavern where he had recently eaten, but this time turned off into a narrow alley which led steadily downwards in a series of serpentine windings . . . until he emerged on the quayside again.

The first cold fingers of fear began to trail down his spine. Once could easily be a newcomer's mistake. But twice . . .?

He tried again, a third attempt. By now night was falling, and it was harder to see where he was heading. Each time he felt himself beginning to descend again, he would turn to climb the hill, until in his exhaustion he was not sure where he was at all.

The sound of raucous laughter through the open door of another inn seemed to mock him. The darkness of the streets seemed to shroud narrow, triangular faces with gleaming eyes. Sometimes he even thought he could hear footsteps following him.

After more than an hour of this, his concentration wavered. Then he found himself on a street which led on to the quayside once again.

Totally defeated, Aurel climbed back onto the barge.
Tomorrow, he promised himself — knowing that this promise
was empty. Something purposeful was watching him, holding him here, and would not allow him to leave.

When he entered his cabin, he was not even surprised to
see the serpent knife, in its sheath, lying neatly on his
pillow.

3

The seneschal was privileged to enter Duke Joscelin's private
rooms with the minimum of formality. He held out a paper.
'Read that, my lord,' he said.

Joscelin himself was seated in the window alcove, facing
his betrothed, Lady Marjolaine, over a chessboard. One of
her attendants was seated in a far corner, mending linen.
Joscelin waited for a moment, moved a knight to threaten
her bishop, then looked up inquiringly.

'It's addressed to you,' Tancred said, 'though it came by
my office. I think you should read it at once, my lord.'

Joscelin took the paper and unfolded it, while, Tancred
met Lady Marjolaine's eyes.

'You're troubled?' she said thoughtfully.

He nodded, forbearing to explain. She would know soon
enough.

When Joscelin had finished reading, he passed the paper
across to his betrothed. 'Lord Tancred,' he said, 'I thought
I made it clear that I could not tolerate the Church keeping
unconvicted prisoners shut away like this.'

'You did, my lord.'

'Yet here is Mistress Morwenna, being arrested for

heresy, and her husband writes that he is prevented from seeing her.'

'Not arrested for heresy, my lord,' the seneschal corrected. 'Held merely for questioning.'

Joscelin made a dismissive gesture, that almost scattered the chess pieces. 'It comes to the same.'

Lady Marjolaine looked up from the letter. 'We must do something.'

'Unfortunately,' said Tancred, 'the Church is within its rights.'

Joscelin frowned, his normally open, candid countenance constricted in thought. *Is this what he will become?* Tancred wondered. *Is that what we are doing to him, making him Duke of Roazon?*

'My lord...' Tancred continued, a headache beginning to throb behind his eyes. 'My lord, there is Church law and state law. Though you have power over Roazon and the whole of Arvorig, you do not command the Church. Indeed, there's a sense in which the Church commands you, for the lords of Roazon have always held their power under the authority of the Church.'

'Then how to proceed?'

'Begin by tabling a motion for the next full Council?'

'But that's months away, at the Feast of All Angels!' Marjolaine interrupted indignantly. 'Is that poor woman to be cut off from her family until then?'

'This affair may be concluded by then,' suggested Tancred.

Joscelin remained deep in thought for a moment longer, then clapped his hands for a servant. When the man appeared, he instructed, 'Go to Father Reynaud, and ask him to attend me as soon as he can.'

As the servant was withdrawing, Marjolaine added, 'And have someone send in wine, and spices – whatever's ready. Seneschal,' she said when the servant had gone, 'come and sit over here, in the shade. You look weary.'

She had noticed, Tancred reflected as he took the seat she pointed to, out of the glare of the sun, and yet he felt unreasonably irritated. Did she think he was senile?

The chess game now forgotten, Joscelin paced the room restlessly until two maidservants arrived. Tancred waved away the sweetmeats, but accepted a cup of pale golden wine.

Next a heavy tread sounded in the anteroom, and the guard on the door announced Father Reynaud.

'My lord.' He bowed to Joscelin. 'How may I serve you?'

Joscelin went back to the chess table and snapped up Master Donan's petition. Without a word he handed it over.

Tancred watched the Grand Master narrowly as he read it. The man's heavy features gave little away, and when he spoke it was with little expression. 'Well, my lord?'

'Well?' Joscelin, for his part, sounded agitated, and Tancred wanted to warn him to keep calm, for letting his feelings run away with him would get him nowhere with Father Reynaud. But naturally he said nothing; it was not his place to speak.

'Father,' Marjolaine broke in, before the Grand Master could reply, 'please be seated. Will you take wine with us?'

'No, lady,' Father Reynaud replied austerely. 'Today I am fasting.'

He did, however, consent to seat himself, still holding Donan's petition. Gesturing with it, he said, 'What would you have me do, my lord?'

'What, you can ask that?' Joscelin's voice was sharp. 'Have this poor woman returned to her family, of course.'

Tancred caught an anxious glance from Marjolaine. Joscelin was handling this all wrong, and she knew it, too. He should remain calm, talk round the problem, defer to Father Reynaud's judgement. Instead, he had shot out an impassioned demand straight away, leaving himself open to the inevitable refusal.

'Impossible,' said Father Reynaud.

'Impossible, why?'

'The Church has not yet finished its examination.'

'Then what is taking so long?' Joscelin sounded genuinely puzzled. 'Mistress Morwenna claims to have had a vision, that inspired what she painted...' He touched his own icon. 'Anyone could have learned these facts from her in less than half an hour. Why has the Church seen fit to keep her imprisoned for the best part of a week?'

'A week is not so long,' Father Reynaud suggested.

'Then how long do you expect to keep her? What are they doing to her?'

'The woman is well treated,' Father Reynaud replied, his cold calm contrasting sharply with Joscelin's increasing disquiet. 'She has food and clean linen, and the services of a confessor. What more could she want?'

'Her husband and baby,' Marjolaine murmured, though Tancred thought no one but he himself had heard her.

'I still want to know why you detain her so long,' Joscelin said.

'My lord.' Father Reynaud leant forward, his hands on his knees, as if he was lessoning a recalcitrant novice. 'This is not some simple matter. It is the Church's duty to be sure of what is right. The woman must be questioned repeatedly, to make sure that her story is consistent.'

Joscelin opened his mouth to protest, and then closed it tightly. Tancred hoped he was learning wisdom, but it might be too late.

'Our best scholars and our holiest men must all have their chance to speak with her,' Father Reynaud went on. 'They must have the opportunity to consult their books, and discuss this unusual matter with each other.'

'And could they not do all this while allowing Mistress Morwenna to live at home with her family?'

'My lord!' Father Reynaud sounded exasperated now. 'And have her spread this heresy further?'

'This *heresy*?' There was a note of challenge in Joscelin's voice as he drew himself up and faced Father Reynaud. 'It sounds, Father, as if your mind is already made up – for all your talk of books and holy men.'

Father Reynaud nodded. 'True, my lord. There is no doubt in *my* mind that this is heresy. Yet,' he added, 'if Holy Church should eventually pronounce it true doctrine, I am ready to be lessoned.'

Strangely, Tancred believed him. It was too easy, he knew, to dismiss Father Reynaud as someone seeking only to augment his own power; there was more to the man than that.

'Father,' said Joscelin, 'I demand that you release Mistress Morwenna.'

'And I regret, my lord, that I must refuse. She is not my prisoner, but the prisoner of Holy Church, and due process must be observed.' He rose and bowed. 'Now, my lord, if you will excuse me ...'

Joscelin hesitated, as if he would argue further, then dismissed him curtly. The Grand Master withdrew with that same ponderous calm that he had shown throughout.

'And now what do we do?' Marjolaine asked.

Tancred suspected that she did not expect an answer,

but Joscelin gave her one. 'I shall go down to the dungeons, and order her release myself.'

Alarmed, the seneschal struggled to his feet. 'My lord, you must not!'

'*Must* not?' There was new authority in Joscelin's voice.

'She won't be watched by the mere citadel guards,' Tancred explained. 'There'll be a Church guard on her – perhaps even Knights of the Legion. Think what will happen if you give them an order and they disobey it.'

'What, disobey the Duke of Roazon?' Joscelin sounded puzzled again; for a moment, shocking himself, Tancred half wished to have Duke Govrian back. The man had been a libertine, but he had understood how power worked, and how far he could go.

'Mistress Morwenna's guards will be under the direct authority of the Church,' Tancred said. 'So if you command and they disobey, what happens to your authority then?'

Joscelin stared at him, baffled. 'Then am I to do nothing?'

Marjolaine went to him and took his hand. 'There's nothing you can do – but I can. I will go to her.'

'Lady . . .' The seneschal was suddenly anxious. He did not want to see her involved in this.

As she turned a brilliant smile on him, her golden beauty almost eclipsed the sunlight. 'Think, Tancred! I have no power to release her, so they will let me in to see her. I can make sure she is being genuinely well treated – not just as Father Reynaud thinks is sufficient!'

She was right, Tancred realized, and that was a great deal better than nothing. Mistress Morwenna would discover she had friends, that she was not completely forgotten.

'Are you sure the guards will admit you?' Joscelin asked uncertainly.

Marjolaine laughed. 'I'm a woman, so what harm can I possibly do? Besides, if they do refuse me, it doesn't matter significantly. What would signify humiliation for you is nothing for me.'

And she was unlikely to be refused, Tancred reflected. The Lady of Roazon, Duke Govrian's granddaughter, last of the direct ruling line, represented an authority, however unspoken, that perhaps even Joscelin did not own. And what guard, even a celibate Knight of the Legion, could resist such determined beauty?

Joscelin nodded, recovering his self-possession. 'Yes, go. Take her what comfort you may.' To the seneschal he added, 'We *will* raise this at the next Council. However long it takes, I will end such injustice.'

But visions of Mistress Morwenna in a dank and comfortless dungeon were dispelled when Marjolaine went in search of her. Instead, she was kept in a room near the top of the White Tower, that part of the citadel which the Legion claimed for its own.

It was a small room, and austere, though no worse than those which the Knights themselves occupied, either up here or down in the barracks. The walls and floor were bare, except for a Holy Knot emblem hanging on the wall opposite the door; there was a bed beneath the narrow window, besides a chair and a table where the remains of the midday meal lay on a tray.

When the guard admitted Lady Marjolaine – as she had predicted, there was little question of her right to visit there – Morwenna had been seated on the bed, her head bowed, but as the door swung open she sprang to her feet.

'Lady!' she exclaimed, sinking into a deep curtsey.

The guard closed the door behind her and Marjolaine heard the key turn in the lock and the bolts slide home. Going over to Morwenna, she took her hands to raise her up. 'Now tell me how I can help you,' she said.

Sitting Morwenna down on the bed again, she thought the painter looked drawn and anxious, but not broken by her imprisonment. Her hair was drawn back neatly into a single braid; her gown though plain was clean.

'Lady, have you word of my husband and my baby?' she asked.

Marjolaine moved the chair so she could sit opposite her. 'Your husband has petitioned Duke Joscelin himself for your release. He would have granted it, but the Church will not allow it.'

Hope flared briefly in Morwenna's eyes. 'Lady, do you know what it means?' she asked. 'They question me, but they tell me nothing.'

'The Grand Master says that Holy Church must have time to study what you tell them, and carefully consider what their decision must be.'

'They have decided already.' Morwenna sounded scornful. 'They quote their books of scripture at me, and say that I cannot possibly understand. And truly, lady,' she added, her scorn replaced by a desperate eagerness, 'I am no scholar, but I – I have seen . . .'

'Tell me,' said Marjolaine, 'what did you see?'

'I felt myself standing on the Pearl of Arvorig, in the woodland surrounding the chapel.' Morwenna's eyes widened, her voice sounded breathless, as though even now she relived her vision. 'I saw him walk towards me across the lake. He wore a white robe, his hair shining like the sun, and he carried a branch of juniper. And when he reached the shore where I was standing, he laid his hand on my head and instructed me to paint him. And then I woke up in my own bed, with the sun coming up and little Ivona grizzling to be fed.'

'But you're sure it wasn't just a dream?' Marjolaine pressed gently.

Morwenna looked at her, smiling faintly. 'It was as different from a dream as this clear daylight.'

Marjolaine was impressed by her conviction. Until now, she had thought little of the whole issue, except as to how it affected Joscelin. Now she began to wonder. Could this be a true vision? Morwenna herself believed so, that was clear.

'What does Father Reynaud himself say about this?' she asked.

A trace of scorn returned. 'He tells me I am just a woman, and so should not meddle with holy things, but stay at home and care for my family. Which I would do, and gladly, if he would only let me go to them!' Her voice quavered as she added, 'Lady, is there nothing to be done?'

Marjolaine shook her head sadly. 'The Church is not ready to release you yet. But I may be able to help a little. You shall have pen and paper, and if you write a letter to your husband I will see that he receives it.'

The renewed light in Morwenna's face made her feel suddenly humble, that she could bring such joy for such a trivial thing. 'Oh, lady, that would mean so much! Today, you mean?'

'As soon as I can lay hands on what you need,' Marjolaine promised.

She got up, and Morwenna attempted a curtsey, but Marjolaine prevented her by drawing her into an embrace. 'Don't be afraid,' she said. 'You are not forgotten.'

She called for the guard to unlock the door. At the head

of the stairs she saw Sir Valery de Vaux talking to one of the two guards on duty, no doubt in the midst of his tour of inspection.

'Sir Valery,' she greeted him.

'Lady.' He bowed quickly to her, though she did not miss the flicker of surprise – and some deeper uneasiness? – that he covered up almost at once. 'How may I serve you?'

She was about to pass on when she remembered her promise to Morwenna. 'There is one thing you could do for me, Sir Valery.'

His eyes lit up, for a moment reminding her of Morwenna. 'I am at your command, lady.'

Marjolaine put out her hand, drawing him out of earshot of the guard. She was surprised to feel a tingle of excitement at that simple contact. Instantly she released him – she was Lady of Roazon.

She took a breath to calm herself. 'You know that Mistress Morwenna, the icon painter, is imprisoned here?' Sir Valery was nodding before she had finished. 'I have promised to get a letter delivered to her husband. Would you take it for me – or find a man to do it?'

'I'll do it myself.' He hesitated. 'Has Father Reynaud given leave for this?'

Marjolaine smiled. 'Father Reynaud knows nothing about it. And between you and me, Sir Valery, what he doesn't know won't hurt him.'

She was half prepared for him to refuse then, and to insist on seeking permission. Instead, he said, unsmiling, 'I'm sure Father Reynaud has many more important things to see to.'

'Then we shall relieve him of this one,' said Marjolaine, delighted. 'And if Morwenna's husband should write her a letter in reply, please bring it to me, and I will see it delivered.'

They had come to the foot of the stairs, where Sir Valery bowed again. 'Have her letter sent to the captain's lodgings, lady. It will find me there.'

Marjolaine thanked him and took her leave. But at the outer door of the tower, she could not stop herself from glancing back. Sir Valery still stood where she had left him, staring after her. She caught a glimpse of his face, so open yet somehow vulnerable, and filled with that same uneasiness she had noticed earlier.

4

Two nights after stopping at Maravou, Aurel's barge berthed itself beside the wharf at Loudec, just another of the little towns strung along the banks of the Rinvier like beads on a necklace.

Aurel's fears were increasing as the days of his journey slipped past, and when he had eaten in one of the riverside taverns, he made a final attempt to escape and lose himself. All to no purpose. Just as they had done in Maravou, all the streets he followed looped back on themselves, until he was returned once more to his starting point.

'Very well.' He spoke aloud, trying to gain courage from hearing his own voice raised in defiance, though he could not disguise a betraying quaver. A fisherman, walking past with his silver catch in a rush creel, shot him a suspicious look, and he fell silent.

Very well, he repeated in his mind. *If I cannot escape, suppose I just stay here?*

He could take a room in a tavern — lock himself in, if

necessary — and in the morning the barge would leave without him. And after that, surely it would be possible to take passage on another, heading downriver again, away from Roazon and the innocent man he was meant to kill.

But as soon as he turned towards the tavern where he had eaten earlier, a sharp pain stabbed through his left hand. Glancing at it, he saw that the silver ring Vissarion had given him had begun to glow with a white light.

As he stared at it, the pain intensified, like white-hot metal flowing through his veins. A cry forced out of him, he fell to his knees, writhing, to the ground, clutching his afflicted hand against him. The air around him seemed suddenly on fire, and every breath increased his agony.

Hearing footsteps and voices, he raised his head and to see a group of dark figures, walking along the wharf towards him.

'Help me . . .' Aurel gasped. 'Please!'

The men paused; then one said loudly, 'Drunk as a drowned mouse.' The group passed on, leaving him sobbing with pain and terror. He rolled over on the ground, grinding his hand against the gritty flagstones of the wharf, as if that could abate the torment.

Then, sounding very quiet and close, he heard Vissarion's voice. 'Aurel, look at the ring.'

As Aurel did so, the fiery glow sank to a glimmer, and the pain gradually ebbed until it was bearable. Trembling, Aurel limply dragged himself upright to sit with his back against a bollard.

A reddish light had woken in the flat dark stone adorning the ring, and within it Aurel could see a tiny image of Vissarion's face. Tiny, but exquisitely clear, so that Aurel could read his features: no approval there now, not even amusement, only a cold contempt.

'You failed to take the hint I delivered to you in Maravou,' Vissarion said. 'So it's been necessary to teach you a sharper lesson. Have you learnt it yet?'

The question was accompanied by another knife-thrust of agony.

'Please . . .' Aurel whispered.

'It's under your control, my dear,' the voice continued. 'Remember how you pledged yourself to me — and to our Master. Keep your pledge, and you will have no more trouble.'

Before Aurel could frame a reply, the light died. The pain retreating, Aurel was left alone outside the golden circle of light cast by the torches from the nearby tavern. Beside him the river, black with a glint of silver, plashed softly against the wharf. He began to weep.

After a while, he dragged himself to his feet and went back to the barge.

Eleven

In the days that followed the tournament, Bertrand d'Acquin had got used to spending most evenings in the Plume of Feathers. It was noisy and cheerful, and that suited him. Sometimes he would meet his cousin Val there, but more often he would get into casual conversation, or a game of dice with the craftsmen who frequented the tavern or the visiting merchants who stayed there.

Walking along the street one evening, Bertrand saw the tavern doors open, and light spilling out onto the cobbles. The music of hurdy-gurdy or cittern, which usually greeted him as he turned the corner, was absent. Instead he could hear the murmur of voices; now and again one of them was raised in a shout. They sounded hostile.

Bertrand quickened his pace. He suspected something more than the usual tavern brawl; he could break heads with the best of them, but he didn't like the sound of this.

The tavern itself was packed. It took Bertrand some time to squeeze in through the door, then more until he managed to push his way over to a bench and stand on it so that he could see over the heads of the crowd. He could hear a single voice raised above the murmuring, speaking from the other end of the taproom.

'. . . displeasing to the Judge. And what then, my friends? Will this city still enjoy divine protection, do you think?'

At length he reached a bench set up against the wall, and climbed on it.

The speaker was also standing on a bench, head and shoulders above the rest of the crowd. No priest, Bertrand saw, he looked like a minor craftsman, or maybe a clerk, a small man with receding hair and shabby clothes.

'Our harvests are bad,' he went on. 'A murrain strikes our cattle. There are no fish in our nets.'

'That's nothing new,' a voice shouted.

'Too true, my friend,' the speaker replied. 'The Judge already turned his face away from Duke Govrian, but if this new duke persists in heresy, he will be angrier still. He will strike this city! He will rain down fire from heaven!'

Somebody yelled out, 'Rubbish!' but more voices were raised to drown him out.

'And what will we do then?' the man continued. 'Our businesses, even our wives and children will be consumed...'

Bertrand scanned the crowd. Usually there were a few Knights Companions relaxing off duty in the Plume, but he noticed none tonight. By the door into the kitchen, fat Mistress Kannaig, the landlady, stood wringing her hands, her gaze fixed on the speaker.

Bertrand cupped his hands around his mouth. 'Hey, Kannaig!' he shouted. 'Do you want him out?'

Mistress Kannaig started, looked round and saw him. 'That I do, Master Bertrand!' she cried.

'Consider it done!'

'We must speak our mind to Duke Joscelin! We must warn him...'

Bertrand lost the rest of the man's speech as he launched himself joyfully into the crowd. Within seconds the audience, relatively quiet until then, became a heaving mob. Some of the men were still yelling for quiet so that they could listen, some of them yelling for the speaker to get out of there, and others just yelling now that the fun seemed to have started.

Bertrand's fist crunched into a face that was unfortunately in his way, and he briefly wondered what his Aunt Regine might say if she heard about this. But a fist could be a noble weapon when employed in a noble cause, and getting rid of this seditious little rat was noble enough, for sure.

At last he had fought his way across the room, and grabbed the speaker by one arm, hauling him down from the bench. The man writhed vainly in his grasp.

'The Judge will punish you...' he gasped out.

'I'm terrified,' said Bertrand.

He got a firm grip on the protesting man's collar and propelled him towards the kitchen door, which Mistress Kannaig was holding open ready. Once through, she slammed it behind them, the racket from the taproom abruptly diminishing.

'We might douse him in an ale barrel.' Bertrand examined his prisoner, still struggling in a hopeless attempt to free himself. 'Waste of good ale, though.'

'Just get him out of here, Master Bertrand.' Mistress Kannaig grabbed an iron skillet and brandished it in front of the man's nose. 'And if you set foot in my tavern again, you ... you louse, I'll have the guard take you up for treason.'

She opened the back door that led into an alley behind the Plume, and Bertrand heaved the man through it. He vanished rapidly into the darkness. For a moment, Bertrand heard scrabbling sounds, and waited for the threats that usually manifested at this point in a struggle, but none came. Everything grew quiet, and he realized that the trouble-maker was gone.

He stepped back into the taproom; Mistress Kannaig followed, to draw a mug of ale and thrust it into his hand. By now the room was clearing, the dispute having surged out into the street, while those who remained were setting tables and benches upright again.

Val and the lanky red-headed Knight – Sulien was his name, Bertrand remembered – were just then walking in, looking around in bewilderment. Bertrand called out a greeting and went over to join them.

'What happened here?' Val asked. He grinned slowly as he noticed Bertrand's tunic was torn and his shirt smeared with blood. 'Having fun?'

'Just a bit of exercise,' Bertrand joked. More seriously, he gave them a brief account of what had happened there.

'A man preaching sedition?' Val looked disturbed. 'Who was he, do you know?'

'Never seen him before,' Mistress Kannaig said, as she came up with wine for the two newcomers. 'And if I never see him again, it'll be too soon.'

'You might have done better to hold on to him,' Val said. 'He could cause more trouble somewhere else.' As Bertrand drained his tankard thirstily, his cousin added, 'I'd dearly love to know how much Count Fragan has to do with this.'

2

Aurel stood once again upon the hythe, beneath the tower-ing bulk of Roazon. Sunlight shimmered on the lake, and

the Holy Knot emblem on the topmost pinnacle of the
cathedral burned gold against a blue sky.

When he had left from this place, after the disastrous Night of Memories, the hythe had been almost
deserted. Now the everyday bustle went on all around him,
fishermen unloading their scanty catches and barge crews
transporting their cargo to warehouses within the walls. No
one seemed to notice him as he stood near the bridge leading to the Pearl of Arvorig, feeling almost as if he was
invisible.

Aurel could not help thinking that his devious purpose
must be written in blazing letters across his forehead. He
was surprised that the Legion had not already turned out to
arrest him.

He wore a decent tunic of blue linen, with a dark blue
mantle over it, unobtrusive garments and suitable for the
summer heat. Underneath the tunic, belted tight against his
skin, was the serpent knife.

Aurel did not want to think about the weapon, but he
was constantly aware of it. On the barge he had carried it
openly, but had hidden it before he stepped onto the hythe.
Now he kept wanting to check that the shape of it was not
visible under the fine linen of his tunic.

Blinking against the bright sunlight, he began to walk
towards the city gates. He must climb up to the citadel and
seek employment there, as Vissarion had instructed, until
he found a chance to get near to Duke Joscelin, and strike
the blow. He was like a spear specially fashioned and
directed by Vissarion. In war, no one is concerned about
the spent weapon, and Aurel did not know what would
happen to him once his task was done.

Inwardly he was howling in terror, yet he was irrevocably
in thrall to Vissarion, or Vissarion's Master — that presence

barely manifest in this world, yet exuding its power into those ready to receive it.

Vissarion had promised him that this was the way, to freedom, to acceptance. Aurel wanted to believe that, and yet could not, any longer. For Vissarion had spoken of detesting slavery, yet he had enslaved Aurel beyond all hope or help. All the old tales must be true: Autrys was evil. *Better starving in Kemper than this*, Aurel thought, bitterly regretting that he had ever thought of trusting Vissarion. Yet his last scrap of independence seemed too weak now, himself too much afraid, to spur him to another attempt at escape.

As he climbed towards the citadel, he could not help noticing the knots of people standing on street corners, the raised voices. Passing through the Armourers' Quarter, he noticed a man haranguing the crowd from a balcony above one of the workshops. The belligerent mood of his audience penetrated even Aurel's blanketed perceptions, and he wondered what was happening there, but could not summon the will to stop and ask someone. He merely skirted the crowd and moved on.

There were crowds too in the square facing the gate of the citadel, jostling against Aurel as he tried to slip through them. Occasionally he caught scraps of conversation: '... divine punishment ...'; 'No duke has the power ...' Aurel could not work out what any of it meant.

The citadel gates stood open, with men-at-arms stationed on either side, and more of them visible in the courtyard beyond. As Aurel approached, fear pulsed in his throat. He would likely be arrested, searched, the knife discovered ... Yet his thrall to Vissarion was so strong that he kept moving, unhesitatingly, and approached the nearest soldier.

'Sir ...' he began nervously, and then wondered if he

should be sounding so respectful. 'I have business with the seneschal, Lord Tancred.'

The man's gaze flicked over him, but his face remained expressionless, with no shadow of suspicion. 'Through there.' He pointed towards a door on the far side of the courtyard. 'Speak to one of the servants.'

Aurel nodded in acknowledgement, and passed on through the gates. Though he had never entered the citadel of Roazon before, there were more guards in evidence than he had expected – reaction to the unrest outside, he supposed. None of them paid any attention to him as he went in through the door the guard had indicated.

Aurel was passed from one servant to another, until he was shown to a seat in a narrow, vaulted hallway and left to wait.

Eventually another servant appeared and conducted him down another passage, to a room at the far end. 'Lord Tancred, a petitioner,' he said, and left Aurel hovering on the threshold, looking around with mingled curiosity and awe.

The large room was lined from floor to ceiling with shelves of books and scrolls. More books were piled on the floor, and dust floated in a shaft of sunlight slanting in through the window.

The sunlight reached a table in the middle of the room, the mess of papers that covered it, and the neatly clasped hands of the man Aurel had come to visit.

Lord Tancred was dark and harsh-featured, with a disfiguring scar. 'Well?' he said, while Aurel still stood in the doorway. 'Come in and close the door. I haven't got all day.'

At Tancred's invitation Aurel took the seat on the opposite side of the table.

'My lord,' he began hesitantly, 'I have come to ask ... if you will give me employment here in the citadel.'

Tancred's brows snapped up. 'What employment? If you're a craftsman or a mason you should approach one of the under-stewards.'

'No, my lord, I ...' Aurel cleared his throat and tried again. 'I can read and write a good hand. I can cast accounts.' He began to speak more easily as what he had to say hovered somewhere near the truth. 'I know about merchandise, how to tell good from bad, and what a fair price should be for most commodities.'

Lord Tancred set his elbows on the table and rested his chin on his clasped hands. 'Indeed,' he said. 'What's your name, and who are you?'

'My name is Melin,' said Aurel, giving the alias he had settled on. 'My father's a merchant, but I'm a younger son, and there'll be no inheritance for me. I decided to make my own way and see the world.'

'Admirable,' Tancred murmured, with a slightly sour note that told Aurel he remained unimpressed. 'We are somewhat short of clerks here,' he admitted, 'as *they* all want to get out and see the world, too.'

He reached across the table to find a clean piece of paper and pushed it over towards Aurel. As he did so, he presented his undamaged profile. With that disfiguring scar hidden, Aurel suddenly glimpsed beyond the harshness, saw instead fine-cut features that should radiate hope and purpose, not be twisted into ill-humour. He did not know how Lord Tancred had come by his scar, but he found himself suddenly confronted by an image of the man the seneschal should have been.

Only a moment, and then that image was gone, but it

left Aurel feeling agitated, embarrassed, almost, as if he had seen something he was not intended to see.

'Write,' Tancred directed, pushing a pen and inkwell within Aurel's reach.

He began to dictate a letter, some formal nonsense that might be intended for one of the provincial lords. Aurel kept up easily; still wondering what the real man might be like, behind the authority of the seneschal's office.

Eventually Tancred stopped dictating, held out his hand for the sheet of paper, and examined it. 'Legible,' he said, the faint tone of surprise robbing the comment of any sense of approval. 'Very well, Master Melin, I will give you a trial. Waste your time here, or gossip about your work to others in the taverns, and your career will be a short one.'

Thanking him, Aurel wished that he could genuinely fulfil this task, that he could stay here indefinitely in the citadel, safe and unobtrusive – and that he had never set eyes on Vissarion or heard the name of Autrys.

3

As soon as Alissende left the house, she could feel a different mood in the city. People were everywhere, gathered into anxious groups. Those protesting against the new duke's supposed heresy had stirred up the turmoil rapidly. Most of the craftsmen's shops were closed and shuttered, for safety perhaps, and the stalls in Cornmarket Square were bare and deserted.

As she turned into the main street approaching the citadel, she was unwillingly caught up in a crowd, all heading in the same direction. She almost gave way to panic; she did not like crowds. Most of her life had been spent in a country village or in the cool seclusion of her Order, where once her robes would have guaranteed respect. Now she was alone and vulnerable.

Briefly she wondered whether she should hurry back to the house and ask Donan to accompany her. But he had something to do and, besides, she had meant not to tell him what she had resolved, in case she should be refused, and give him hope to no purpose.

She let the crowd carry her along, until she came to the citadel square. The street emerged right opposite its gates, but at first Alissende could see nothing over the heads of the crowds packed tightly in front of her. There was no hope of fighting her way through them, so instead she began working her way around the periphery.

Climbing a flight of steps that approached the Guildhall, she could now see clearly over the sea of heads, surging back and forth. The angry shouting of the mob sounded like the roaring impact of waves on rocks.

Men-at-arms were in the act of thrusting the gates closed, forcing back those citizens who were trying to push their way inside. As Alissende gazed, she recalled the scene of her vision in the scrying bowl: the appearance of the Knight of the Legion, attempting to read out a proclamation, the casting of a stone which forced him back inside.

She had known in advance, but nothing she could do would have prevented it. Still trying to stay clear of the main mob, she hurried on around the edge of the square, feeling icy cold despite the morning sunlight. Was that other vision also true — that grim image she had seen of Morwenna? Would she fail there, too? Perhaps it was already too late to save her friend's sight.

At last Alissende reached the side street she had been

heading for, and tugged the bell set into a high wall beside
a wrought iron gate. Like someone who falls into a river
in spate, she had struggled against the current, yet it had
borne her inexorably on, and thrown her up against this
gate, the last place in Roazon she had intended to come to.

She heard the bell sound as if at a distance. Looking
through the scrolled iron, she could discern the green of a
garden, and caught the fresh smell of herbs cutting through
the odours of the dusty street. Grey-paved paths wound
through the shrubbery. Soon a blue-robed sister of the
Matriarchy approached along one of them, key in hand, and
unlocked the outer gate.

Beckoning Alissende inside, she closed the gate instantly
behind her and locked it again, after a brief glance up the
street towards the citadel square from where the hubbub
still sounded.

'Yes?' she said, as she turned away. 'How may I serve
you?'

Alissende dropped a curtsey, restraining herself from the
formal gesture with which one sister usually greeted
another. She had renounced the right to that — as to so
much else. 'Sister, I beg for a few moments of the Matriarch's time.'

'The Matriarch?' The sister was tall, with iron grey hair
and severe features which turned more severe still after
Alissende made her request. 'She sees very few people. But I
am almoner here, so if it's a question of—'

'No, no, Sister,' Alissende said hurriedly. 'I'm in no need
of alms. This is a much weightier matter, a grave injustice
which the Matriarch might help to set right.'

The almoner looked her over with cool grey eyes, then
nodded abruptly. 'I will see if the Matriarch will speak with
you. What is your name, mistress?'

'Alissende.' The words wrenched out of her, she added, 'Once I was Sister Alissende of Kareiz.'

At that she was ready for more questions, or even a sudden rejection, but the almoner made no response to her revelation, saying only, 'Come.'

She turned and led Alissende down a path, where sweet herbs gave up their fuller scent as her robes brushed against them, and through a door in the white-walled building flanking the other side of the garden. Gesturing to an alcove with a wooden settle in the hallway, she said, 'Wait here,' and continued down the passage.

Alissende seated herself, and kept her eyes downcast, conscious of floorboards silky with beeswax polish, of whitewashed walls, and the Holy Knot emblem hanging opposite her. Occasionally she could hear footsteps at a distance, or the murmur of voices, but she saw no one else until the almoner reappeared and gestured for her to follow.

'The Matriarch will see you.' Her severity seemed to relax as she continued, 'She is old, but tends to exert herself more than is wise. I beg of you not to tire her needlessly.' She swung open a door.

Alissende nodded her understanding and went on in, the door closing behind her. The sunlit floorboards seemed to stretch in front of her for an eternity, as far as the window where a woman was seated in a carved wooden chair, gazing out at another part of the garden.

Alissende's first thought was how tiny the Matriarch was. She looked almost like a child in that great chair, her feet resting on a footstool. Her snowy-white hair was soft and wispy like a child's, and she wore robes of the same snowy white, edged with the Matriarchal blue.

Smiling, she held out a thin, veined hand to Alissende. 'Come, my dear, but tread quietly.'

As Alissende drew nearer she realized that the Matriarch held a plate, with a few scraps of bread, on her lap, and sparrows were pecking at crumbs on the sill. They fluttered up in alarm at Alissende's approach, only to settle again a moment later.

The Matriarch drew her feet off the footstool and gestured for Alissende to sit herself there. She then crumbled more of the bread to toss to the birds, before saying 'Sister, tell me why you left Kareiz.'

An ache gathered in Alissende's chest. This was not what she had come here to speak about. 'You know about me, Mother?' she asked.

The Matriarch inclined her head. 'A report of your flight reached me, of course.' Gently but determinedly, she repeated, 'Now, tell me why.'

Alissende thought for a moment that she would be unable to give voice without weeping, and yet somehow the words were there and she found she could speak them, her gaze fixed on the floor under the blue-edged hem of the Matriarch's robe.

'My parents and my young brother died when plague attacked our village. If I had been there with them, my healing skills might have saved them all.'

'Child, we never know what *might* have been. The plague has defeated even the most skilled healers in Arvorig.'

'But I could have tried! Instead, I devoted my life to God, and so *I* was safe—' in her agitation she spat the word out – 'safe there in Kareiz, and not where I was really needed. What kind of God would accept my gift and make such cruel use of it?' She fought for breath as the ache of remorse in her chest grew almost intolerable. 'A God who countenances evil? Or maybe no God at all – and the whole of life a mockery?'

'Child, do you truly believe that?'

Alissende's tears finally spilled over. 'There is such pain in living, Mother, such pain.' As she covered her face with her mantle, she felt a hand touch her on the head as she released her grief.

At last the tears were spent and she looked up to meet the Matriarch's eyes. They were the milky blue of extreme old age, but filled with kindliness and compassion.

'And so then you fled from Kareiz,' she said. 'And after that?'

'Then I came *here*, Mother — to light candles for them on the Day of Memories. And during the ceremony . . .' It took an effort for Alissende to bring herself back to the reason for her visit. 'I met an icon painter, a woman named Morwenna.'

The Matriarch nodded. 'I know her work.'

She gestured towards the opposite wall, where Alissende noticed for the first time an icon hanging. It represented the First Matriarch, surrounded by angels, as she blessed the rising towers that would become the cathedral of Roazon, and was filled with the glowing light and energy that Alissende had come to recognize as Morwenna's signature.

'Beautiful . . .' she whispered, almost distracted again from what she had come to say. She continued, 'Morwenna befriended me when I desperately needed a friend. Since then I have stayed with her and her husband. And now — oh, Mother, she is in such great trouble!'

'What has happened?'

Alissende explained how Morwenna had received a vision of the divine Healer, and then painted the icon which she subsequently gave to Duke Joscelin as an induction gift. 'But the Church is antagonistic, Mother,' she finished. 'They took Morwenna away to question her about the vision she experienced. That was almost two weeks ago, and she hasn't come home yet. Her husband has been trying to get to see her, but they will not admit him. We wrote a petition to Duke Joscelin – who did what he could – and Lady Marjolaine herself has taken messages for us, but even they cannot get Morwenna released. Mother, she has a young baby at home, and—'

The Matriarch raised a hand to silence her. For a moment Alissende wondered if all this had been in vain. The Matriarch might believe, like the rest of the Church authorities, that this icon was heretical; she might refuse to help.

Alissende wanted to plead further, but she was rapidly falling back into old habits of obedience. It seemed imposs-ible to speak until the Matriarch gave her leave.

'Is your friend being ill-treated?' the Matriarch asked at length.

'Lady Marjolaine says she has all she needs, but . . .' She broke off, uncertain now what she wanted to say.

'Yes, child?'

'Mother, I looked in the scrying bowl.' Alissende glanced up to see how the Matriarch would react to this, learning that Alissende had returned to an old discipline which should be forbidden to her since abandoning her Order. 'I did not wish to, but—'

'And did you receive a true vision?' the old woman asked.

Alissende swallowed. 'I saw a riot in the square,' she said. 'And . . . and I saw Morwenna blinded. Mother, if they deprive her of sight, how will she ever paint again?'

The Matriarch fell silent again, her expression troubled. At last she said, 'The Church may occasionally shelter evil men; we would be foolish to deny that. But truly I believe

that there are none such here in Roazon.' Her mouth
quirked almost in amusement. 'If Father Reynaud has a
fault, it is too strict an adherence to the law. And there is
no law that would allow him to blind any of his prisoners.'
The trace of amusement faded, leaving only seriousness
behind. 'What would you have me do?' she asked.

'Mother, could you speak to the Grand Master and the
Archbishop? They will surely listen to you.'

Relief flooded over her as the Matriarch scarcely hesitated. 'True, this supposed heresy must be examined,' she
said, 'but I see no reason to keep a young woman away from
her husband and her child. She would, I assume, agree not
to paint any more such icons until the Church gave her
leave?'

Alissende was not so sure of that. Morwenna appeared
certain of the validity of her vision, and of what she had to
do. And yet, to be allowed to go home to Donan and Ivona
... 'I think she could be persuaded,' she suggested.

The Matriarch nodded again. 'Then I will do as you ask.'

'Oh, Mother, thank you!' She reached out to clasp the
hand the Matriarch extended to her.

'As for the blinding, that may never happen,' the Matriarch said. 'Child, you know as well as I do that the visions
of the scrying bowl need interpretation. Do you wish to
return to our order and then you can look in the bowl again
with your sisters here, so you can share their counsel?'

Something inside Alissende longed to do exactly that,
but she drew back, releasing the Matriarch's hand. 'No,
Mother, I am not worthy to do that, now.'

The Matriarch smiled. 'God finds you still worthy, my
dear, or he would have granted you no visions at all.'

To return to them, Alissende thought, to belong again,

to practise her former skills along with her sisters, amid the quiet routines of prayer and praise and the sharing of wisdom ... No. She had already made her decision. That life was not for her, not any longer.

'Donan and the baby need me,' she decided.

The Matriarch dipped her head in acceptance. 'Then go safely, child. I hope you may see your friend come home again soon.'

Alissende thanked her, and dared to make the ritual obeisance of kissing the hem of the Matriarch's robe. As she withdrew, the old woman scattered the last of the crumbs for the sparrows, leaving Alissende with a final image of her, robed in white and seated in the spill of sunlight from the window, surrounded by birdsong and the fluttering of wings.

4

Count Fragan of Gwened was lodged in the citadel, accompanied by his son Tariec and the immediate members of his retinue, while the rest of his entourage were camped in pavilions along the lakeshore, not far from the tournament field.

While the citadel fomented hysterical charges of heresy, Fragan preferred to have himself rowed gently across the lake, to enter the luxurious shelter of a pavilion and dine among his own people. He sat there now, the meal ended, and eyed Tariec with sour disapproval.

Almost two weeks had passed since his discussion in the citadel garden with Duke Joscelin and the two churchmen. On the strength of that, Fragan had delayed his own return to Gwened. If the Church saw fit to depose a potentially heretic duke, he wanted to remain on hand to support Tariec's right to succeed Joscelin as ruler of Roazon.

Count Fragan's wife was the daughter of Duke Govrian's younger brother. Though it was previously unknown for inheritance to pass through the female line, it was now not impossible, since there were no remaining male heirs of the Roazon bloodline. Fragan optimistically considered there should be little opposition to Tariec.

If only Tariec himself could be persuaded to take more of an interest in his own future ... There he sat, slumped in his chair, mechanically munching candied fruits alternated with mouthfuls of wine. The youth had already drunk more than was good for him, and even Fragan could not pretend that he looked like a future Duke of Roazon.

Irritated, Fragan moved the silver wine ewer out of reach as Tariec stretched for it again.

'Father ...' Tariec protested.

'You've drunk enough. Go off to bed half sober for once. I'll call the boatman for you.'

Fragan was rising from his seat when a servant ducked in through the open flap of the pavilion. 'My lord, a Knight of the Legion has come asking leave to speak with you.'

News from the citadel? Fragan was instantly alert. Had he been a fool to leave it, even for these few hours? 'Send him in,' he growled.

The servant retreated, and a moment later a Knight took his place. Tall and austere in his formal silver armour and white surcoat, he had a pale, narrow face framed in lank brown hair. He bowed on entering Fragan's presence.

'Well?' said Fragan brusquely.

'My lord count, I am Girec d'Evron. I have the honour to serve you now as a Knight of the Legion.'

Fragan relaxed slightly. Not from the citadel, then, but one of his own men — if they could truly be called his own, when their ultimate allegiance lay elsewhere. 'I don't know you,' he said.

'I have served you for only a few days, my lord,' d'Evron said. 'Before that I was stationed in the citadel.'

'Just a minute.' Fragan sat upright, pushing his plate away. 'You were involved in that damn' trial . . .'

D'Evron flushed, and Fragan half smiled with pleasure that the barb had gone home. D'Evron had made a fool of himself over that affair, and deservedly, if not for malice then for sheer stupidity. But Fragan guessed he would now have no cause to love Duke Joscelin, so he might prove useful.

The Count leaned forward encouragingly. 'Why did you request to see me?'

'My lord, I — and many others of the Legion — are deeply concerned about this new heresy that has arisen in Roazon. That a woman should presume to depict a new manifestation of the divine, and that the Duke of Roazon himself should encourage her sick fancies . . . can you conceive anything more shocking?'

'Some of us are more easily shocked than others,' Fragan replied dryly. 'However, I take your point. Proceed.'

'It's a matter of grave disappointment to us, my Lord Count,' d'Evron continued, as if choosing his words carefully, 'that the Church has not given a clear lead in condemning this new heresy.'

'Not yet,' Fragan suggested.

'As you say, my lord, not yet.' D'Evron looked slightly taken aback at this interruption. 'And yet to men of true religious zeal, can there be two views permitted about the matter? Even the common people now rise up in protest!'

'They do?' said Fragan. 'That's more than *I* know.'

'There is unrest, my lord,' said d'Evron. 'What we all need, my lord count, is a strong man to lead us back into the true faith.' When Fragan did not respond, he added more tentatively, 'And there is another heir of the true bloodline of Roazon, as well as Duke Joscelin.'

Fragan spared a glance for Tariec, still slumped in his seat, drawing patterns with one finger in the spilled wine. If d'Evron was seriously looking for his strong new leader there, he was even more of a fool than Fragan had thought.

'Your son is young,' d'Evron said, as if he guessed some of Fragan's thoughts. 'So there might be perhaps ... a Regency.'

Not so much of a fool then, Fragan admitted to himself. There was malice in d'Evron, that could pull Joscelin down in revenge for the Knight's own humiliation, and a certain cunning that would use the path of piety to achieve it.

'You speak treason?' he said neutrally.

D'Evron looked genuinely appalled. Was it possible, Fragan wondered, that he could deceive even himself?

'My lord count, I have prayed unceasingly,' he protested. 'And I feel that my true allegiance – and that of all Knights of the Legion – must be to our divine vocation.'

'Of course, of course.' Fragan waved a hand. 'So tell me what your vocation would have you do.'

D'Evron moistened his lips and moved a pace closer. 'My lord, you would be serving our faith if you yourself deposed this heretic.'

Fragan stared at him, genuinely astonished. 'Only the Church can decide that.'

'But if the Church will not act ... if the Church itself moves away from the divine will...? Then, my lord, you would be justified. And the Legion would help you do it.'

'Rubbish.' Fragan threw himself back in his chair. Clearly, this man was stupid after all, if not raving mad. 'They would have to turn against their own Grand Master.'

D'Evron's pale eyes fixed on the Count, not at all disconcerted. 'They will do so, my lord.'

'What proof have you?'

'I have spoken with many of them, my lord. And they would be with us. Not all, I admit, but enough.'

You would split the Legion itself, then, Fragan thought. *And bring down the Grand Master, who stripped you of your place in the Knights Companions and humilated you. Who do you imagine would replace him, I wonder?*

'What about Sir Guy de Karanteg? How does *he* feel?' Though the man had only recently been appointed Commander of the Legion in Gwened. Fragan had already been impressed by de Karanteg. 'What does he think about all this?'

D'Evron coughed. 'Sir Guy is not a pious man.'

So that means he has no part in this heresy witch-hunt, Fragan informed himself, promising himself to have a word with de Karanteg before this risky business proceeded much further.

'My lord count, there is more,' D'Evron said.

'More?'

'There are other men − loyal citizens of Roazon − who feel as I do. They are here to beg you to help their suffering city.'

'Loyal men who speak treason?' Fragan could not suppress a feral smile. 'This I must see, so bring them in.'

D'Evron bowed his way out of the pavilion. While he was away, Fragan grabbed Tariec's shoulder and gave him a shake.

'Sit up,' he snarled. 'This is your future we're discussing. At least try to look as if you're listening.'

Tariec pulled away from him, with an injured look, and sat back in his chair just as d'Evron came back, holding open the entrance flap for two other men to precede him.

The first was an elderly, balding man wearing a robe of fine damask with a gilded leather belt around his corpulent stomach. The second was younger, in fashionable tunic and hose, with bright gold hair and startlingly handsome features. He stepped forward quickly and knelt at Fragan's feet.

'My lord, I am Sir Nicolas de Cotin,' he said. 'The manor of my family lies within your lands, and I come to pledge you my allegiance.'

His voice shook slightly and there was fear in his eyes. The count guessed that, for all his apparent eagerness, he was not altogether confident about the step he was taking.

'And if your allegiance to Gwened conflicts with your allegiance to Roazon?' Fragan asked mildly.

De Cotin swallowed uncomfortably. 'My lord, I am truly loyal to Roazon and to the Church.'

'How admirable. That does not, however, answer my question.'

'If Duke Joscelin has become a heretic, then he must be the traitor, not I!' De Cotin had managed to assume a certain defiance. He hesitated briefly, but then plunged on. 'My lord, if you will defend our Church and the city, I can pledge you help from the fief of Cotin, and from Bellière too, which belongs to my betrothed wife.'

'My thanks.' Fragan waved him aside, already finding the man tedious. His motives were obvious enough: sheer self-advancement, if ever Tariec were to sit in Joscelin's place. 'And you, sir,' he continued to the other newcomer. 'Have you also come to pledge me your allegiance?'

As Nicolas retreated towards the silken wall of the

pavilion, the fat man stepped forward. He was sweating freely, but Fragan guessed that his agitation was less from anxiety and more from standing in the presence of one of the greatest lords of Arvorig.

He bowed clumsily. 'My lord, I am Master Eudon, Guildsmaster of the Jewellers and Head of the Guild Council here in Roazon. I have not come to pledge allegiance for we are craftsmen, my lord, not soldiers, and we have little to offer you—'

'Get to the point, man.'

'I come to beg your help, my lord! Our city's in turmoil – like an ants' nest stirred with a stick. There's robbery ... looting ... Our Guildsmen cannot work. These insane quarrels *must* end!'

'And what do you think I can do?'

'My lord count, you're a man of the world. You must have seen what's been happening in Arvorig these last few years. We had hoped that Duke Joscelin would set us on the road to prosperity again, but you know there can be no prosperity without order. Duke Joscelin is young and inexperienced. What can he possibly know?' Panting, the corpulent Guildsmaster pulled a silken kerchief from his robe and mopped his forehead. 'We only want a quiet life, my lord, no more than that – and we'd do a lot to support the man who can give it to us.'

His eyes were fixed imploringly on Fragan himself; no one was even trying to pretend any longer that Tariec would be more than a figurehead. And, in fact, that suited Fragan very well. Let the boy do as he was told, and he might one day sit in the seat of the Duke of Roazon, but as to where the real power lay ... that was a different matter.

'Unrest in Roazon ...?' Fragan mused. Briefly he wondered whether that was entirely a natural eruption. Foment-

ing disorder was a good way of loosening Joscelin's hold on
the city; Fragan might have thought of it himself, if he had
yet fully decided to seize power on his son's behalf. But
then, he reflected, the citizens of Roazon were always
strangely volatile when it came to matters of faith. Alongside all the usual worldly ambitions, they prided themselves
on living in the holiest city of the world. Disturbances
would arise here without anyone trying to stir them up.

That did not mean, however, that someone prudent
might not give them a helping hand.

'I will think of this,' he said decisively. 'For now, leave
us. Sir Girec, attend me tomorrow.'

When all three had gone, he left his son to snort and
snore in a hoggish half-sleep, and took a walk along the
lakeshore under the stars. Fragan scarcely took his eyes
from the mountainous silhouette of the city that reared
dark across the glinting water.

At length he stooped to pick up a stone from the water's
edge, and let it nestle in his palm. It was smoothly rounded
from being tumbled for long ages in lake and river, of a
comfortable weight with a faint glitter of quartz diapering
its grey surface.

'Mine,' Count Fragan said softly, and clenched his
fingers around it.

Twelve

As the days went by, Aurel settled into his new life. He was allotted a small room in the West Tower, which housed the rest of Lord Tancred's staff, and ate daily at a table in the great hall with the other clerks, the heralds, the archivists. He soon learnt to answer easily to his new name of Melin.

He had never worked so hard in his life, crawling into bed each night with letters and figures still dancing in front of his eyes. He carefully learnt the routines, and the way Lord Tancred liked things done. His fingers began to form calluses from continually holding a pen.

Yet somehow he found this work satisfying. Partly it may have been because Lord Tancred himself worked harder than anyone, yet he was not incapable of being pleased, and generous enough to show it. Partly it was that for the first time in years Aurel had broken out of a destructive, exhausting cycle of sin and guilt that had become his only way of taking revenge on his father.

The sole shadow on his horizon was the thought of his real purpose here in Roazon – and that darkened everything. Vissarion had not used the ring to communicate with him again, but Aurel learnt to endure a perpetual nagging ache in the hand that bore it, punctuated by an occasional vicious stab of pain. As if he could ever be in danger of forgetting why Vissarion had sent him to Roazon . . .

Sometimes he just wanted it over, whatever the consequences; sometimes he looked only for ways to postpone his task, but in the end, he had little choice. The Duke of Roazon could not seem to take a step out of his own apartments without an escort of friends, servants and guards around him; he appeared never alone. Besides, Aurel's own work occupied him so fully that he had little leisure to give an opportunity of reaching the city's ruler, and so day slipped into day while the serpent knife remained snugly belted to his side, like the perpetual touch of a cold hand.

One morning, Aurel reported to Tancred's workroom to collect the task assigned to him for that day, to find the seneschal studying a parchment ornately secured with a heavy seal and ties of twisted gold.

Seeing Aurel, he tossed the document across the table towards him. 'Read that.'

Aurel studied it and realized it was a letter, from King Aymon of Brogall, a kingdom in the north, complaining of some border raid. Bandits from Arvorig, he said, had burnt and looted several farms within his territory, and driven off cattle. Aymon warned of his intention of taking serious steps to secure his own border.

'His Majesty hasn't lost any time,' Tancred commented drily.

Bewildered, Aurel shot a questioning look at him.

Tancred shrugged. 'There may indeed have been a border raid. These incidents happen, even within Arvorig, but I doubt it here. Aymon has heard of this dissent over the icon, I'd guess, and he wants to be ready if further trouble erupts.'

'He would invade us?'

'Aymon has had his eye on Arvorig for years, like his father before him.' Tancred snorted contemptuously. 'But they're such good sons of the Church — officially — that they would try nothing while Church and state move together in harmony.'

Aurel began to understand. 'But if the Church declares the new duke a heretic . . .'

'Then Aymon would be given the excuse he needs.' Tancred paused, his face tightening with anxiety. 'Brogall could crush Arvorig in an afternoon.'

Shaking off the brief abstraction, he stood up. 'Duke Joscelin must be warned of this development immediately. Come with me, Melin. We may need someone to draft the words of our response.' He thrust a few sheets of fresh paper and an inkhorn towards Aurel. 'You write a neat hand, and you seem to know how to keep your mouth shut.'

From Tancred, that was high praise indeed; as he followed obediently, Aurel felt warmed by it.

Yet when they reached Duke Joscelin's apartments, the ruler of Roazon was not there.

2

When the arrival of the Grand Master was announced to her, the Matriarch was well aware that this visit would be a difficult one. She did not suppose for one moment that Father Reynaud had welcomed her request for an audience with him.

She received him in the same sparse room where she had talked with Alissende on another sunlit day. How much more agreeable, she thought, to continue watching the birds in the garden, and perhaps meditate on a verse from her book of devotion, than to exert herself in handling this stern and uncompromising man.

Sister Levenes, the almoner, ushered him in, and he came straight to the point.

'Well, Mother,' he said, 'how may I help you?'

The Matriarch folded her hands in front of her. 'This young woman – the icon painter – you have detained...'

Father Reynaud straightened up suddenly in his seat. 'I suppose there's no way of keeping anything from you, Mother.'

'Tell me more about her.'

'She claims she has holy visions ... she paints a new aspect of the divine.' He paused, cold grey eyes boring into her. 'I myself have spoken with the woman. She seems honest. I'd swear she sincerely believes what she tells me. If she was not so sincere – if she was merely a fool, or deceitful, or hysterical, I would know better how to deal with her. As it is ... she's become the most dangerous woman in Roazon.'

'And is her vision true?'

Father Reynaud reacted to her gentle question as if it was the prelude to the torturer's rack. 'I don't know. The Judge forgive me, I don't know. But true or not, we *cannot* afford to accept it.'

'True or not?' The Matriarch hinted a faint rebuke.

'Mother, you know as well as I do how the people fear heresy. They fear that the famine and pestilence we suffer is a divine punishment for sin. Already we have had rioting ... the other day a mob tried to break into the citadel. Duke Joscelin doesn't help, by insisting on wearing that damned icon she painted. And in the north King Aymon is just waiting for an excuse to move against Arvorig. We must maintain peace and stability, at all costs.'

'At *all* costs, Father?' He did not rise to that question,

so the Matriarch continued, 'If the Church should accept the icon painter's vision, would the people themselves not accept it too?'

'Some would but I think not all ... and besides, the Archbishop and his scholars have been searching the scriptures diligently, yet found no reason to redefine the nature of our faith. None of this would have signified if our ruler had not embraced the woman's interpretation.'

'And meanwhile all this time Mistress Morwenna stays in prison,' the Matriarch said crisply. 'Could she not be sent home under house arrest?'

'That is not normal procedure.'

'And normal procedure must be followed, no matter what?'

'Mother, she would find no protection at home. There's fighting out in the streets almost every day. At least she's safe from the mob where she is.'

'Are you so sure of that?' the Matriarch asked. 'The sister who spoke to me of her had already looked into the scrying bowl and seen the painter blinded.'

Father Reynaud turned white. There was no mistaking his outrage. 'And you thought that I – or the Church – would countenance such a thing?'

'No.' The Matriarch reached out her hand in a gentle, placatory gesture. 'And so I told the sister.'

'But if the mob do get their hands on her ... dear God!' Father Reynaud breathed out. 'They might well try to stamp out the heresy by blinding the painter who began it. I am decided, Mother. She stays in the citadel. No one will harm her there.'

The Matriarch sighed. She had not intended to find the Grand Master such a valid reason to continue Morwenna's imprisonment. Yet what he said was true enough. Anything they did to alleviate her position might plunge her into worse danger.

The Matriarch sighed. 'Then I will leave Morwenna to your compassion, Father.' Turning in her chair, she pointed to the icon of the First Matriarch, hanging on her wall. 'Have you seen her other work?'

Father Reynaud got to his feet, seeming relieved for the distraction, and went to contemplate the icon more closely. The Matriarch was pleased to witness the wonder and stillness settling over his face. There was a chink, maybe, in the armour of his severity.

'She is skilled indeed . . .' he murmured.

'And her skill must not be lost to us,' the Matriarch warned.

He blinked as if a strong light had suddenly shone into his eyes, and turned away from the image. 'Mother, you know how evil takes pride in destroying what is best and brightest. If Mistress Morwenna's vision was not a divine gift, then it may be demonic in origin. That also we must consider.'

The Matriarch caught her breath in consternation. 'I had not thought of that.'

'Roazon is revered as the holiest city in the world,' said Father Reynaud. 'You think that evil would not rejoice to bring it down?'

'Mistress Morwenna would not surrender herself to demons,' insisted the Matriarch.

'She is a good woman, true.' Father Reynaud spoke decisively. 'But some evil may be using her without her knowledge.' He laid a hand on his breast and bowed to her. 'Mother, I will think on all you have said.'

As he took his leave, the Matriarch wished she could

think of more arguments to offer him. She had summoned him here in the hope of convincing him; instead, he had almost convinced her.

When Sister Levenes re-entered, the Matriarch was once more gazing out into her garden. 'Sister,' she said, 'I will speak to all the sisters assembled before Compline this evening. We must all of us look into our scrying bowls, and learn what we can. I feel a darkness falling over Roazon, and I do not know how we can hold it back.'

3

'This is madness,' Sulien de Plouzhel said, as he hoisted the banner of Roazon into its harness and steadied it with one hand, while the rest of Duke Joscelin's escort formed up around him.

Val shrugged as well as he could inside the heavy ceremonial armour. 'Duke Joscelin wishes to pray.'

'Then what's wrong with his private chapel? Why does he have to go on foot through the city, when some of the people we meet might like to see him burnt at the stake as a heretic?'

'Are you saying that the Duke of Roazon can't go where he likes?'

Sulien raised his eyes, but did not reply. Val let his gaze travel over the rest of the escort: shining armour, dazzling white surcoats, the proper austerity for the Knights Companions of the Legion. And swords ready to hand – weapons which Val hoped fervently would not be needed.

In the privacy of his own mind, he shared Sulien's uneasiness. Although the full-scale riot of a few days before had settled down at last, every day brought reports of new trouble. There was an outbreak of plague in Maravou, cattle in Tregor were miscarrying their calves, and a sudden storm had wrecked a grain ship on its way to the harbour at Kervrest. The alarmed populace saw every new disaster as proof of divine anger. It was not the time for the Duke of Roazon to walk through the city without good reason.

But, for Joscelin, as Val well knew, the need to pray was good reason enough, and the Pearl of Arvorig was the place he had chosen.

Val had wondered whether Lady Marjolaine would accompany him, but when Joscelin appeared he was alone, leaving Val torn between relief and disappointment. When carrying messages between the icon painter and her family, he had seen his master's betrothed several times, and each time provided delight so intense that it became a torment. Yet he could not bring himself to delegate the task to one of the younger Knights.

He had made his vows of celibacy without a backward glance, and felt warned by the destructive thrall in which Robert d'Acquin lay to his beautiful, heartless wife. Besides, there was the knowledge that he had solemnly dedicated his life to his faith.

But he had never known desire before. Never felt the delight that pierced him so utterly in Marjolaine's presence. Never until now.

One night he had even dreamed of lying naked beside her, and woke in an agony of shame, to huddle wakeful until dawn for fear of dreaming again.

He had not confessed to anyone, but he had prayed fervently to be released from such fantasies. So far, his prayer remained unanswered.

Duke Joscelin greeted his escort with his usual courtesy, and took his place in their midst. As always, he wore just a plain linen robe, with no other ornament except for the icon. It seemed to announce his supposed heresy like a trumpet call, but Val knew very well it was futile to ask Joscelin to remove it.

Signalling to the guards to open the gates, he himself led the small group out into the city, preceded by Sulien who bore the precious banner of Roazon.

As the armed escort marched out through the citadel gates, the square appeared quiet, and the shallow stairway leading down from it was almost deserted. In the terrace garden below the roses were now overblown, their petals scattering the grass, though their heavy scent still filled the air. Cloying, Val thought, and his skin felt sticky with it.

Then as they descended from the heights the crowds of onlookers began to gather. The morning was well advanced, and many townspeople were out to do their marketing, or visit a workshop, or simply to stand around in the streets and gossip. Some of them scarcely paused in what they were doing as their duke went by, but some of them stopped to call a greeting, or a hostile jeer.

Val kept a hand on the hilt of his sword, half expecting some of the crowd to block the street ahead of them, but all fell back as the escort advanced. Though fixing his eyes on the road ahead, he was peripherally aware of men and women appearing at windows, or leaning over balconies above.

He could not glance round to see how his ruler was taking it all. He found he was sweating in his elaborate armour, with an ache of tension across his shoulder blades. The banner of silver and black dipped and swayed just ahead of him as Sulien negotiated the last flight of stairs that would bring them down to the hythe.

Finally beginning to relax slightly, Val became conscious

of something that had already been niggling at his aware-
ness. Among the familiar faces of the ordinary citizens on
either side, were other faces that did not completely blend
in with them. All of them, he noticed, were men, alert and
watchful. Uneasily, Val remembered that brawl in the Plume
of Feathers, and the stranger Bertrand had thrown out. Was
he at work still, along with these others? Did someone from
outside want more rioting in Roazon?

He let these questions rest as the escort reached the
archway leading to the hythe itself and passed through it,
still unscathed, with Duke Joscelin safely among them. The
sounds of the crowd died away behind them, to be replaced
by the gentle plash of the lake water against the steps and
mooring posts.

Val studied the length of the hythe as far as the bridge
which linked it to the island. Knights of the Legion already
were drawn up beside it, and at the end of the bridge three
figures stood, waiting.

The first, a round and elderly man wearing a grey habit,
was the chaplain, Father Cornely. The second, Val recognized with surprise, was Count Fragan of Gwened. And the
third was his former colleague, Girec d'Evron.

Sulien's head went up, recognizing them too, but still
he did not break step. He inquired, without looking back,
'A welcoming committee?'

As they approached the bridge, Count Fragan stepped
forward, as if to bar their way.

Sulien hesitated, but Val moved up to face the count.
'Please clear the way, my lord,' he said. 'Duke Joscelin
intends to make his way to the chapel.'

'The Pearl of Arvorig is too holy for any heretic to tread
there,' Fragan snarled, with a grim set to his mouth.

Before Val could protest, Joscelin's calm voice spoke at his shoulder. 'Captain, stand aside for me.'

He could only obey, so Val motioned for the escort to fall back, though he himself remained close to his ruler, ready to draw his sword if needed.

A light sheen of sweat covered Joscelin's face, but his step was easy and his expression confident, as he moved up to face his declared adversary.

'My lord count, you do not have command here.'

'I do not in myself,' Fragan conceded. 'But I speak as the voice of the Church.'

'Indeed?' Joscelin smiled slightly. 'And has the Church no voice of her own, Father Cornely?'

The little chaplain wrung his hands in distress, his face turning pink under the wispy white fringe around his priestly tonsure.

'My lord, this island is the holiest place in all the world,' he said. 'We cannot allow a heretic to defile it.'

'But the Church has never declared me heretic,' said Joscelin. 'Where is the Archbishop? Or the Grand Master?'

A good question, Val thought.

'You must answer to them first,' said Count Fragan. 'Until then, you cannot enter here.'

For a second Val stood uncertain. Were they to go back through the jeering crowds, back to what amounted to imprisonment inside the citadel? What other choice was there?

But then Count Fragan stepped forward and laid a heavy hand on Joscelin's arm. 'Joscelin, called Duke of Roazon, I now arrest you in the name of the Church.'

And Val found his choice laid out for him. He drew his sword swiftly from the scabbard.

'You exceed your authority, my lord. Release him.'

Fragan obeyed, and moved back, but only to draw his own sword. Val could hear the silken chorus as Girec d'Evron and the Knights of the Legion drew theirs. Where was Sir Guy de Karanteg, Val wondered. He would never have allowed this; the count must have somehow got rid of him.

But there was no time to think of that now. The sparse escort of the Knights Companions gathered instinctively in a ring around Duke Joscelin, all facing outwards, to protect him.

'Fall back to the city gate!' Val cried out.

But then Count Fragan's blade shivered against his own, and the Knights Legionaries closed in. A few of them stumbled in their advance as Sulien bravely swept the banner round to crack them at knee height. Then one of them hacked through the staff, so that the sacred banner itself fell to the ground and was trampled underfoot.

Val spared a glance for his master. Blue eyes blazing, Duke Joscelin's hands were closed tight around the icon, his lips moving as though he prayed. For a man without armour, without weapons, he looked entirely unafraid.

Very slowly Duke Joscelin's Knights were winning their way back to the gate, where Val now planned to barricade themselves in the gatehouse, and wait for reinforcements down from the citadel.

Knight fighting Knight, he thought. *We vowed ourselves, and now we turn on each other.*

There was a choking cry from the man beside him as d'Evron's sword found a chink in the armour and slid home. The fallen Knight rolled over in agony.

'Damn you, d'Evron!' Val snarled, stepping into the gap to tighten the protective circle.

'Look, sir!'

At Sulien's voice, Val spared a glance over his shoulder towards the gate. Through it was marching another column of the Legion, their swords drawn.

Within moments, Joscelin and escort would be utterly overwhelmed.

Then Val noticed someone else. A small figure was pounding down the length of the hythe towards them. *'Bertrand!'*

His cousin hurtled into the fray, hooked the feet from under a Knight Legionary, and grabbed away his sword as he crashed to the ground. Slashing a blow at d'Evron, who backed away in astonishment at this unexpected onslaught, he thrust himself next to Val.

'A boat!' he yelled. 'You need a boat!'

Val gaped. 'Leave Roazon?'

But Bertrand was already driving his way forward across the hythe towards the nearest fishing boat. Caught up in his determination, Val urged his men to follow, cutting through the circling opponents before the new arrivals could reach them.

Bertrand leapt into the boat and snatched up the mooring rope. Sulien scrambled down after him, still clutching the tattered banner, and took hold of the tiller. Val pushed Duke Joscelin ahead of him, turned to aim one last blow at Girec d'Evron, and then followed. Two more of the escort made it into the boat, before Bertrand pushed off and started hoisting the sail.

As Val gazed back towards the hythe, separated from them now by a widening expanse of glittering water, he saw that the remaining Knights Companions were making a last, hopeless stand, trying to hold back the Knights Legionaries, who were already heading for a second moored boat.

'Where did you spring from?' Val asked Bertrand. 'And what do we do now?'

Bertrand pulled the rope taut and cleated it, staring up to watch the sail fill with wind. 'I saw what was happening, and it seemed you could do with some help.'

The boat lifted, skimming over the lake. Behind them, the Knights Legionaries were putting out.

'Where do you want to go?' Sulien called from the tiller.

It was Bertrand who replied. 'The Legion stables. We need horses.'

'And after that?'

'To Acquin, of course,' said Bertrand. 'Where else? I know Duke Joscelin will find loyal followers there.'

The Duke of Roazon was seated near the stern, wind blowing through his hair. His head was turned towards the towering shape of his city, and his face was rapt as he made his way into exile.

PART THREE

Spears from the North

Thirteen

Aurel was seated at his desk in the clerks' room, writing letters from Lord Tancred's scribbled notes, and hoping he was correct in deciphering the seneschal's vile hand. He heard running footsteps outside in the passage, a shout in the distance, and the banging of a door.

He raised his head. 'What's that?

None of the other clerks, heads still bent over their pages, answered him. Uneasy as he had been all morning, since reading that letter from King Aymon, Aurel got up, went to the door, and looked up and down the passage.

He was in time to see Lord Tancred limping hastily towards him, a servant in his wake, babbling something about Count Fragan that Aurel could make no sense of.

'My lord, what is it?' Aurel asked.

'That's what *I* want to know.' Tancred was abrupt. He turned to the servant. 'Pull yourself together, man. Tell this to the Lady Marjolaine, and say I will attend her presently.' As the servant sped off, he nodded to Aurel. 'Come with me, if you wish.'

Aurel hurried after him, through the door which led to the Hall of Petitioners. The outside door crashed open just as they arrived. Count Fragan of Gwened stood there, a sword in his hand, Knights of the Legion filing past him on either side, clearly under his orders, to vanish in several different directions. Escorted by two of them, Count Fragan paced forward into the hall.

Tancred went to meet him. 'My lord count, why do you come here with drawn sword?'

Fragan gave him a grim smile, and sheathed his weapon. 'It was drawn in a holy cause, sir seneschal. With the help of the Legion, I have driven out the heretic Duke from Roazon.'

Aurel saw Tancred's face grow pale, its scar all the more prominent. 'Duke Joscelin driven out?' he said.

'He was last seen riding for the forest with a rabble of his Knights Companions.' Fragan smiled grimly. 'They won't get far.'

'And your reason for this?' Tancred recovered his authority. 'Has the Church decreed Duke Joscelin a heretic?'

'Not yet. But their decree will not be long in coming.'

Tancred thumped his staff on the floor. 'Count Fragan, you had no right to do this.'

Fragan shrugged. 'It is done. Now stand aside, Seneschal, and let me—'

He broke off as another door was flung open and Father Reynaud strode into the hall. During his short time working in the citadel, Aurel had known him to be a formidable man, but he had never understood how potent his anger could be. Now it was gathered round him like a thundercloud. Though unarmed, he faced squarely up to Count Fragan, and Aurel could not have said which appeared the more dangerous.

'Fragan.' Father Reynaud's voice was charged with fury. 'Explain yourself. Why do you presume to give orders to my men?'

'I have nothing to explain.' Fragan's expression was bland. 'The Knights Legionaries could no longer endure

their allegiance to a heretic duke, so I answered their plea
to—'

'And you, d'Evron,' Father Reynaud went on as if Fragan
had not spoken. 'I might have known I'd find your hand in
this.'

'I seek only the will of God,' the young Knight replied
piously.

The Grand Master snorted his contempt. 'Fragan, you're
a traitor.'

An ugly look flashed across the count's face, and he
hung on to his calm with an effort. 'A traitor to the heretic?
I think not.'

'Duke Joscelin is not deemed a heretic until the Church
decrees it.'

'And the Church does nothing meanwhile but dither and
make pious noises,' Fragan retorted. 'While good men's
allegiance wavers, the city descends into riot.'

His gaze riveted to the quarrelling men, Aurel started at
the touch of Tancred's cool fingers fastening around his
wrist. The seneschal nodded towards the passageway, and
drew him back silently in the direction they had come. He
did not speak until they stood once more outside the clerks'
room.

'I want you to write a letter now,' Tancred murmured.
'A summary of what has happened – for all the other
provincial dukes and lords – and a request for shelter and
support for Duke Joscelin if he comes their way. Some of
them are undoubtedly loyal, and the whole pack of them
will likely band together to stop Fragan from seizing power.
Write out – oh, a dozen copies immediately, and bring them
to me in Lady Marjolaine's apartment. And say nothing to
the other clerks.'

Aurel nodded and slipped inside the room, where all the others were still busy at their tasks. One or two of them looked up as he reappeared, but none asked him any inconvenient questions.

As he crossed the room to the paper store, Aurel felt as if a heavy weight had been lifted from him. Duke Joscelin was gone, for the moment no one knew where. And if he was not here, Aurel could not attempt to kill him. He drew a long breath at the thought of being free.

But his euphoria lasted no more than a few seconds. As he stepped into the tiny store-room, with its sharp smell of ink, its shelves stacked with paper, parchment and quills, a sudden pain lanced down his hand from the silver ring he wore. He could not restrain a gasp, but managed to swing the door shut behind him and lean against it, praying that none of the other clerks would disturb him.

'No . . . not now,' he whispered.

But the pain intensified until Aurel could barely stand. He clawed at the ring, trying to wrench it off his finger, knowing the effort was futile. He felt as though his blood were turned to acid.

'Make it stop,' he pleaded. 'What do you want of me?'

Cradling his hand against his breast, he noticed once more a reddish light waken in the ring's flat stone, bathing the windowless room in a blood-like glow. Gradually, Vissarion's face formed there, staring at him with a look of venomous fury.

'You have delayed too long,' he snarled. 'And now Joscelin has escaped you.'

'Please . . . I did my best,' Aurel gasped.

'You achieved nothing.' Another stab of agony, more vicious still, leaving Aurel trembling helplessly and bathed in sweat.

'Let me go, please,' he begged. 'I can do no more. Duke Joscelin is gone – isn't that enough?'

'Gone from Roazon, but still its rightful duke,' Vissarion hissed. 'Autrys still awaits its time – and you still have your task to do. You must follow him.'

'How can I? I don't even know where he is going.'

'That you will find out.' Though the face was so tiny, Aurel could discern the malevolence in its eyes. 'And once you do know, go after him.'

'But—' This task seemed impossible.

'You will find a way.' The tones had turned silken, gentle, and were all the more terrifying for that. 'Or must I summon my Master to lesson you?'

Aurel recalled the half-seen, half-sensed presence beneath the hill in Kemper, and he shuddered. If that shape should manifest itself here, among the stacks of paper and jars of ink, he felt sure he would lose his reason.

'No ... I'll do as you say,' he whispered.

The light in the ring died away, and the pain with it, leaving Aurel shivering and weeping in the dark. He slowly pulled himself upright, and fumbled out his kerchief to wipe his tear-stained face.

For all his efforts, when he went back into the clerks' room, the man at the next desk looked up and stared curiously. 'What's the matter with you?'

Ignoring him, Aurel dipped the pen to begin his letters for Lord Tancred.

2

Under the trees, the darkness was almost complete. Val was about to call out to Bertrand, suggesting they make camp

for the night, when he realized that light was filtering
through from somewhere up ahead. The trees were thinning
out now, and a few moments later Val found himself on the
edge of the forest.

They were four days out from Roazon. Their escape had
begun as a frantic race, with the Knights of the Legion hard
behind them, until they reached the great forest of Brecilien.
Once into the trees, Bertrand had led them by narrow,
looping paths, along stream beds and up banks so steep
they had to dismount and lead their horses. Thus they
continued until Val was sure at last that they had thrown
off pursuit.

Streaks of red were fading in the west, while to the east
the sky was a cold, greenish arch, studded with the first
stars. Ahead, smooth turf sloped away to where a river
curled lazily along the valley bottom. On the far side lay a
dark huddle of buildings.

Bertrand raised a hand and pointed. 'Acquin.'

Behind Val, the rest of their little party was emerging
from the forest. Duke Joscelin looked tired but still alert,
gazing round him with bright interest. Sulien de Plouzhel
and the other Knights Companions – young Lucien de
Gwern and an older man, Hervé de Malestreg – seemed
wearier still. Their heavy ceremonial armour was never
meant for such a long journey, but to ride unarmed would
have been madness when Joscelin's enemies must still be
looking for them.

Living off the forest – woodcraft was another of Bertrand's unexpected skills – had not helped any of them, and
nor had a summer storm earlier that day, when rain and
wind had lashed the trees until it seemed that they were
about to take flight.

Bringing up the rear, Sulien guided his horse to Val's

side. He had pushed back his coif, revealing how sweat had darkened his red hair and plastered it to his head. 'Are we going to ride all night?' he asked. 'The horses—'

'No, don't worry,' Bertrand said cheerfully, overhearing. 'Down there is Acquin — and my father's lands. We'll all eat well and sleep dry tonight.'

'Thank God for that!' muttered Sulien.

Bertrand urged his horse into motion again, and the others followed him down into the valley. Occasionally they disturbed the pale shapes of sheep in the gathering dusk, which galloped away bleating, and once a rabbit started up right under the hooves of Val's horse, but Traveller was too weary even to shy.

Before they reached the river they encountered a road, unpaved but well used, its surface beaten down hard. Bertrand turned onto it, leading them towards a stone bridge ahead.

By now it was almost completely dark, and the only sound was the secret murmur of the river as it ran through rushes lining its banks, while its central channel lay quietly black and glittering in starshine. On the opposite bank, lights were beginning to appear, lamps burning yellow in the windows of the snug houses of the village. Smoke rose from hearthfires, and its sharp tang reached Val on the night air.

As Bertrand led them on to the bridge, a voice rang out from the far side. 'Who rides into Acquin?'

'Hoel!' Bertrand shouted back. He slid from his horse and bounded across.

From a rough wooden shelter at the side of the road emerged a huge young countryman with a thatch of straw-coloured hair, carrying a pike in one hand. Val reached for his sword, but then the man dropped his pike and grabbed Bertrand into a rough embrace.

'Hoel . . .' Bertrand's voice was muffled against the young man's shoulder. 'Let me breathe!'

Hoel released him, a broad grin all over his face. 'Bertrand, my friend, it's good to see you back.'

Val knew a moment's astonishment that Robert d'Acquin's serfs should address his son so familiarly, until he remembered that, denied the upbringing his rank and birth deserved, Bertrand had made his friends among them. For some reason the thought heartened him, and he smiled as he rode across the bridge.

Bertrand turned to him, a wide grin on his face. 'Hoel, this is my cousin Val. Is my father at home?'

'Aye, Sir Robert's home,' said Hoel. 'He'll be glad to see you, belike. He told us all about how you won that tournament, and opened a cask of ale for us.'

Val felt relieved to hear that Robert's new-found pride in his son had survived the journey back here to Acquin — and the disapproval of his lady. Maybe they would be welcome in Bertrand's home now.

The village's single winding street was quiet. The company rode past a mill, its wheel still at this hour, past a forge where a scrawny yellow dog dashed out in front of them, barking fiercely, and on past the houses on the other side, where the road wound upwards to the gate of the fortified manor house.

A single lamp burned above the gateway, where Bertrand jerked a loop of rope, and a bell jangled somewhere above his head. A shutter in the gatehouse snapped open and a voice called, 'Who knocks?'

'Loik, it's me,' Bertrand said pleasantly. 'Get down here and open the gate.'

A muffled exclamation was cut off as the shutter was pulled closed. After a pause, during which Val could hear running footsteps and a voice shouting orders, one of the iron-bound gates was pulled open, wide enough for the whole company to ride through.

'Bertrand! Is it you?' The porter was staring. 'Never did I think to see ... I've sent word up to your father, sir,' he added.

Bertrand dismounted and tossed his reins to a groom who came running up. Turning towards the others, he spread his arms and said, 'Friends, welcome to Acquin.'

As Val also dismounted, that was the signal for the others to do the same. More grooms appeared to lead their mounts away.

A shout of 'Bertrand!' and Sir Robert d'Acquin himself was striding across the courtyard, his arms extended to embrace his son.

Bertrand hugged his father and then drew back, letting Robert see that he was not alone. Robert's gaze travelled over his companions, and then his eyes widened as he saw Duke Joscelin.

'My lord!' he exclaimed. 'You do my house honour ...'

His voice died away as he realized that something was amiss. The Duke of Roazon did not normally travel with a rag-tag escort such as this, with no advance word of his coming.

'I am Duke of Roazon no longer.' Joscelin spoke with a quiet gravity that stilled Bertrand's protest, and his father's exclamation of surprise. 'I have no home, no power, and no friends but these. There may be an enemy force behind us right now. If you turned us from your gates I could not blame you.'

Bertrand let out an irritated hiss through his teeth. Did Joscelin have to be quite so honest, before they had even the chance for food and rest?

'Turn you from our gates!' Sir Robert sounded outraged. 'With respect, my lord, what nonsense! Come in,
come in, and you can tell me everything over supper.'

By the time Val and the others reached the great hall of
the manor house, some servants were fixing torches in
sconces around the walls, while others set up trestle tables.
A fire burnt brightly in the hearth at one end, where a
couple of hunting dogs sprawled blissfully in the warmth.

Robert called to an elderly man – his steward, Val
guessed – who was supervising these operations. 'Graelent,
have rooms made ready for our guests, and fetch fresh
clothes.'

'All will be ready soon,' the steward said calmly. 'Meanwhile, my lords,' he added, 'why not sit by the fire and drink
a cup of wine.'

As they moved down the length of the hall, a door at its
far end crashed open. A boy of about sixteen stood there,
tall and slender, with Jeanne d'Acquin's lint-fair hair. Seeing
his startling good looks, Val realized that this must be
Jeanne's younger son Oliver, the brother she had wished to
usurp Bertrand's place as heir of Acquin.

Val expected him to show hostility; instead, the boy
hurled himself down the hall and grabbed his brother.
'Bertrand, you're home! Tell me about Roazon ... Tell me
about the tournament!'

'Later,' Bertrand said, laughing.

'Offer welcome to Duke Joscelin, boy,' said Robert.

Oliver turned at his father's bidding, and knelt before
their duke. He pressed Joscelin's hand to his forehead, and
then stared up at him, in young and ardent innocence. 'My
lord, be welcome here,' he said. 'I am Oliver d'Acquin. My
sword is yours.'

Smiling, Joscelin raised him up. 'Thank you for your

loyalty,' he said. 'But I don't know yet whether I will need your sword.' He made a little gesture towards his tiny band of followers. 'We don't have the strength to fight.'

'We can discuss all that in the morning,' said Sir Robert. 'In the meantime, my lord, tell me what brings you here like this. Then I will know better what help Acquin can give you.'

He herded everyone towards the benches arranged by the fire, where a servant was already pouring wine for them. Val waited till his men were served, and only then took a cup for himself. He was beginning to feel relaxed, grateful for this warmth and shelter, when the door at the far end of the hall opened again.

Jeanne d'Acquin stood there, her gown glittering in the firelight, and she looked thoroughly furious. Bertrand broke off a conversation with his brother as he noticed her.

'Husband,' she said icily, 'will you tell me what this means?'

3

Nicolas de Cotin was feeling justifiably pleased with himself as he mounted the stair inside the citadel, leading to Count Fragan's apartments. He had laid his wager on the right cock; Joscelin was gone, and Fragan was Duke of Roazon, in fact if not in law. Soon the Church would have no choice but to declare Duke Joscelin a heretic, and institute Tariec in his place. Fragan would still rule, however, and he was not a man to forget his friends.

When the guard ushered Nicolas into the anteroom, he found Count Fragan seated at a table with paper and writing materials scattered over its surface. He was pressing his seal ring on a folded sheet which he handed to a man in riding dress who stood beside him. The courier saluted and left.

'Nicolas.' Count Fragan's greeting was genial, but his visitor knew what respect was due. He laid a hand on his breast and sank to one knee. 'My lord count.'

'Get up, man. I've no time for this.' Fragan left the table. 'There's a task for you.'

'Command me, lord,' Nicolas said.

Fragan clapped him on the shoulder with a smile of satisfaction, but beneath the benign surface was something else that Nicolas could not quite fathom, and did not want to see. He shook off the sensation and waited for his orders.

'I want you to ride to Gwened,' Count Fragan said. 'Take the best horse from our stables, and make what speed you may.' Returning to the table he folded a letter, dropped wax on it and sealed it with his ring. 'Carry this to my steward. He is instructed to gather provisions and load them on supply wagons for transportation here to Roazon.'

'Do we lack supplies, my lord?' Nicolas asked, puzzled.

Fragan gave him a narrow look, and Nicolas realized, though he was not sure why, that his question had been a foolish one.

'Storehouses are dwindling all over Arvorig,' Fragan said, as if lessoning a small child, 'and Roazon is a populous city. Its wealth is in craft work, in learning, and—' a slight sneer '—in holiness. It relies on a constant supply of food. I do not propose to wait and see whether the lords who have regularly sent tribute to Roazon will deny it now. We're in the time of harvest, such as it is, and I will stock our barns and granaries as best I may, in case winter comes and finds us wanting.'

As he finished he cocked a brow at Nicolas as if asking him whether that had been clear enough.

Nicolas felt himself flushing. 'I understand, my lord.'

'Wonderful.' Fragan pushed the first letter across the table towards him, and began to fold and seal a second one. 'This,' he went on, 'is addressed to the constable of my castle. He is to make sure that Gwened is properly fortified and secure – in case any other lord should think to attack it in my absence. That done, he is to provide you with as many men as he can spare to escort the baggage train on its way back here. You will be in command, is that clear?'

Nicolas straightened. 'Yes, my lord count.'

'Excellent. Serve me well and I will be grateful. Bungle this, and . . . but I'm sure you will not bungle it.'

Nicolas swallowed hard, and grabbed up the two letters from the table. 'No, my lord. You can rely on me.'

As he retreated down the stairs, he did not feel quite so pleased with himself as he had on the way up.

Fourteen

I

The stormy weather had cleared up, and the sun shone on Acquin. In the great hall, the tables had been dismantled except for one, where Joscelin and his followers now sat to take counsel over a breakfast of bread, cheese and ale.

Joscelin, Sulien, Bertrand and his father — Val looked round at their anxious faces, and wondered that the fate of all Arvorig might rest on so few.

'My lord,' Sir Robert began. 'My fief of Acquin is at your disposal. Ask of me what you will.'

Joscelin looked uncertain. 'I have prayed for guidance,' he said, 'yet I cannot discern God's will in this. Perhaps I should not try to regain rule in Roazon. Count Fragan's son—'

'That whey-faced brat!' Sir Robert exploded, slamming a hand down on the table so that the ale cups rattled. 'I'll die before I swear allegiance to him.'

'And so will many others,' said Val. 'My lord, you are the rightful Duke of Roazon. Many will refuse to accept Tariec, though some will try to make claims of their own. Without you, their rivalries will tear the whole of Arvorig apart.'

A tiny frown settled between Joscelin's brows. 'Yet how may I return there without war? And how may I fight without men?'

'There are men here,' said Sir Robert.

'The village lads will follow me,' Bertrand added comfortably.

'But how many are they?' Sulien asked. 'You can't fight a campaign with just half a dozen Knights and a few of your 'lads', Bertrand. What about our weapons and supplies?'

'Acquin can provide some,' said Sir Robert.

'We might hire mercenaries,' Bertrand suggested.

His father shook his head. 'Mercenaries need payment. I can give you a little money, but not enough for that.'

Bertrand scowled fiercely and thrust his fingers deep into his thatch of black hair. Val thought it best to leave him to brood.

'We need to decide where to go next,' he said, changing the subject. 'For all your goodwill, sir—' he nodded to their host '—we can't stay here at Acquin. It's not defensible enough. If Count Fragan's men find us here, they'll slaughter all of us and devastate the whole village. We need to find a base behind strong walls, somewhere an army can't reach easily.'

'I've been thinking about that.' Sulien flashed him a grin. 'I think I know just the place. A few miles downstream from my brother's manor at Plouzhel, you come to the de Bellière lands.' He leant forward and started to draw on the table top with a few splashes of spilt ale. 'The castle stands on a bluff where the Ster meets the Ruzel. The river runs swift and deep beneath the walls, and it's never been taken by siege or by assault.' Sitting back, he looked triumphantly round the table. 'That's where we need to go.'

'And what will the lord of Bellière think about that?' Robert asked. 'Whose side is he on?'

'Ah, that's the best of my plan,' Sulien said smugly. 'There is no lord of Bellière now. The old lord died last winter, and his only heir is a girl, his granddaughter.'

Bertrand looked up from his brooding. 'Tiphaine de Bellière?' he asked.

'That's her.' Sulien shrugged. 'The castle at Bellière is deserted, but for a steward and a few servants. It's my guess they'll welcome us.'

There was a stir of movement around the table as they looked at each other, encouraged by being able to plan ahead even a few days.

'How far?' Val asked Sulien. 'How many days' ride from here?'

'Three, maybe four,' Sulien replied. 'Here, look...' Again he dipped his finger in the spilt ale and began to extend his map.

Val leant forward, following so intently that he did not hear the hall door re-open, or the sound of anyone approaching until Jeanne d'Acquin's crystalline voice asked, 'How long, my lords, may we expect the honour of your presence here?'

On the evening before, after demanding an explanation, she had withdrawn, not deigning to sit in their company at supper. She had not, Val remembered, shown Joscelin much deference. Uneasily, he guessed that she might hate him, for giving that judgement against her in the Knot Chamber of Roazon.

'We'll ride off tomorrow,' Sir Robert said.

'We?' Jeanne's face was pinched with fury. The famous beauty was now in abeyance, and Val could imagine what she would look like when she was old. 'Robert, you will not join this ... crazy enterprise.'

It was an order, not a question, and Val found himself

intensely interested, to see whether his uncle would dare stand up to her. But it was Bertrand who replied, forestalling his father.

'Don't worry, Mother.' He rose, displaying a courtesy and self-possession that Val had never seen in him before – at least, not when he was facing this harpy. 'Father will stay here to guard Acquin, so there's nothing to be afraid of.'

'I am *not* afraid!' Jeanne was growing more furious by the second.

'Now just a minute,' her husband said. 'Neither my wife nor my son tells me what to do.' The look he shot Bertrand was not displeased, though he avoided looking at his wife at all. 'If my lord bids me ride with him, I shall ride.'

Joscelin looked bewildered. 'Sir Valery . . .?'

Val shrugged. 'If we're all going to wall ourselves up in Bellière, then better that Sir Robert stays where he is. To be free to send us provisions, to rouse men to our call . . .'

'I will do that gladly,' said his host.

'Men? Provisions?' Jeanne repeated. 'Where do you expect to find them? Will you drain Acquin for this fool's campaign?'

Sir Robert glared at her then. 'To the last grain of corn,' he said.

'Nonsense!' Jeanne's silks swirled round her as she turned away. 'You have taken leave of your senses.'

As she began to walk away, for the first time Val noticed that young Oliver was behind her, hovering uneasily between her and the door.

'Father,' he said nervously, 'I want to ride with Bertrand.'

'*What?*' Jeanne whirled on him. 'Don't be absurd. You're just a boy.'

Oliver reddened.

Grinning faintly, Bertrand said, 'Ride with us and welcome.'

'I forbid it!' said Jeanne.

'It's Father's leave I need, not yours,' Oliver blurted out, and then looked terrified at what he had said.

'He will not give it.' Jeanne spat out each word, her eyes fixed on her husband. 'He will not take my only son away from me.'

At those cruel words, Val could not help glancing at Bertrand, and saw him flinch. 'Mother . . .' he began.

'Silence!' Jeanne hissed at him.

'We'll discuss this.' Robert was trying to be diplomatic.

'We will *not* discuss it,' his wife retorted. 'He stays with me. Come, Oliver.'

She motioned the boy to follow her, as peremptorily as she might have summoned a junior servant. Miserably Oliver was moving to obey, when suddenly Duke Joscelin rose from the table. He went over to Jeanne d'Acquin, his hands held out to her.

'My lady, I see you are in great pain,' he said. 'Let it go. Your husband and your sons love you. Just set them free, and they will come back to honour you.'

Jeanne stared at him. She did not take his hands; her own hands, holding up her skirts, as she prepared to sweep out of the hall, were clenched on the silk, crushing it.

'How dare you!' Her voice, no more than a whisper, seemed to echo round the hall. 'How dare you speak so to me?'

Val did not know how she could resist the candour and warmth in Joscelin's face, but her eyes remained hard. She turned her back on him, and stalked out of the hall.

Oliver gave his father an apologetic look, then followed her.

Joscelin stood looking after her until the door had closed behind her, then sighed and returned to the table.

The rest of that day was filled with preparations. Sir Robert, and Graelent the steward, saw to the loading of baggage carts and packs for mules with sacks of corn and flour and dried pulses, flasks of wine and oil, dried meat and fish parcelled in layers of coarse linen. Val was afraid, with the poor harvests the whole of Arvorig had been suffering, that the manor could not spare so much, but Robert's renewed pride in Bertrand was spurring him to generosity.

While Bertrand went out into the village to assemble his 'lads', Val and Sulien went over the armoury, collecting what weapons they could, finding mail shirts to replace their ceremonial plate armour. Lucien and Hervé rode out in separate directions, returning that evening to report no sign yet of Fragan's men or the Knights of the Legion.

On the following morning, Val emerged into the court-yard to see mules being loaded and horses harnessed to the baggage carts. The gates stood open. Beside them Bertrand stood with a gaggle of about twenty village lads, dressed in an odd collection of leather armour and mail, with weapons ranging from swords and bows to quarter-staffs and scythes. As Bertrand was addressing them, he clapped one on the shoulder and the whole group erupted into loud laughter.

What are we doing? Val asked himself, suddenly chilled. *This is no army to face Count Fragan.*

As soon as Bertrand saw him, he came striding across the courtyard. Dressed in mail, and wearing a surcoat with the black eagle of the house of Acquin, he looked focused, formidable. But the cheerfulness in his face soon faded, and by the time he reached Val he was looking cold and grim. 'Come with me,' he said.

He strode on into the house, not even looking to see if his cousin would follow.

Val caught him up. 'What's the matter?'

'We need money for this campaign,' Bertrand said. 'And I know where I can get it. Trouble is—' he gave Val a lopsided grin '—I'm not sure I dare.'

He led the way up a spiral stair, into a part of the manor where Val had never set foot before. Mystified, he followed, not realising, until Bertrand rapped smartly on a door and swung it open, that Bertrand was taking him into Jeanne d'Acquin's solar.

She was seated beside a brightly blazing fire, her embroidery in her lap, while two small girls – Bertrand had young sisters, Val remembered – sat on stools at her feet. The elder was bent diligently over her own stitching, while the younger was sorting and tidying a rainbow of silken threads and laying them out in a basket.

In the window alcove was seated Oliver d'Acquin, his head bent over a lute. He struck a false note, then put the instrument aside, as Bertrand came in.

'My lady.' Bertrand bowed, stiffly formal.

Jeanne looked up at him, her needle poised. 'Well?'

'My lady,' said Bertrand, 'you know that I ride on campaign to set Duke Joscelin back in his rightful place. We cannot pay men, feed them or arm them, without money.'

'And what have I to give you?' Jeanne asked indifferently.

Bertrand cleared his throat – not as self-possessed, Val could see, as he wanted to pretend. 'Your jewels,' he said.

'What?' Jeanne was finally startled out of her icy uncon-cern. 'Bertrand, you're out of your mind.'

Bertrand flashed a look at Val. If he fell to pleading, Jeanne would have already won. After that second's hesitation, Bertrand seemed to realize it, and strode across the chamber to where a wooden coffer, bound with iron, stood on top of a chest against the wall.

As he took it up, his mother sprang to her feet, spilling the silk she was embroidering to the floor. 'No! Leave it!'

But her son tucked the coffer under one arm. Val could guess the value of the contents from the gems that sparkled on Jeanne's fingers and at her throat.

'I'm sorry,' Bertrand said, and took a step towards the door.

'No!' The little girls looked on, round-eyed, as their mother swept across the room to confront him. Her cold gaze had turned to fire. 'You dare not,' she said, in a tone of scorching contempt.

'Yes, Mother, I do dare.' Bertrand's voice began to shake. 'Our need is great. No one will ever say that Acquin was not loyal to its suzerain.'

'To that pious fool?' his mother sneered.

'To our rightful duke – and I will serve him while my life lasts, by any means I may.' His voice cracked, suddenly sounding young and desperate. 'Mother, we'll drive out Count Fragan. Then I'll bring you even *better* jewels...'

Val put a hand on his cousin's arm and nodded towards the stairway outside. Bertrand met his eyes briefly, a world of love and pain in that glance, and began to move for the door. Jeanne reached out as if she would wrestle with him for possession of her casket, then seemed to realize how much dignity she would lose.

She drew herself up. 'Go, then,' the words spat out. 'Go, and never return to Acquin so long as I live.'

'That is as necessity may drive me,' Bertrand said, but Val caught the glint of tears on his face.

Bertrand paused a moment more and spoke to Oliver. 'If you want to ride with us, come now.'

'He will not,' said Jeanne.

'He may choose for himself.' Still a quiver in his voice betrayed Bertrand's hard-won independence. 'If he comes with us, I swear I will bring him home safe, or die trying.'

He paused a moment longer. Oliver had risen from his seat but stood as if paralysed, darting glances from his brother to his mother.

Bertrand said, 'Choose, Oliver.' Without waiting any longer for a reply, he turned and almost ran down the stairs. Val took one look at Jeanne's frozen countenance, and followed.

By the time he reached the foot of the stairs, his cousin was out in the courtyard. Val was in time to see him toss the jewel coffer into one of the baggage carts, then mount the horse one of his lads was holding ready for him.

A scream erupted from the room above, then another, spiralling up into hysterical shrieking. Running footsteps sounded on the stairs, and a moment later Oliver appeared. Flushed and dishevelled, his face streaked red from where his mother's nails had scored across it, he was still clutching his lute.

'I'll ride with you, Bertrand,' he said. 'Don't forbid it, Father. I *will* go.'

Robert d'Acquin put a hand on his younger son's shoulder, talking to him quietly, till the boy's agitation visibly calmed.

Meanwhile the cavalcade was forming up, ready to move out of the gates. Sulien took the lead, with the banner of Roazon mounted on a new staff, and Bertrand followed just a pace behind. The 'lads', some mounted on mules or hill ponies, others on foot, formed up around the baggage carts.

Val pulled himself into the saddle of his horse, and he and Oliver rode together at the tail end of the file, urging their mounts into a trot to catch up by the time the slowly moving wagons reached the outskirts of the village.

As far as Val could see, his cousin Bertrand did not once turn to look back at the walls of Acquin.

2

Tiphaine de Bellière was seated at her window. Her gaze fixed, she did not see the rooftops and gardens of Roazon. Instead, another of her bright mental pictures had flicked before her eyes.

She saw an upland stretching towards hills. Out of a rocky defile, a troop of horsemen came riding, their armour shining in the sunlight. The foremost carried a banner; as its blue silk rippled out in the wind, Tiphaine discerned the golden lilies of Brogall.

The first riders began to pick up speed as they reached the smoother turf. Behind, more and more of them appeared from the cleft in the hills, as if the line of them would never end.

The blue and gold banner swelled until it filled all Tiphaine's vision. Then the picture winked out, leaving her shivering in the morning sun.

She sprang to her feet, letting fall Nicolas' embroidered sleeve, treading on it in her haste to find someone, and tell them what she had seen.

At the door she paused. She had never before told anyone of her visions – not even her grandfather, or Father

Patern, the kindly chaplain at Bellière. Prophecy was an art of the Matriarchy; Tiphaine did not know how the holy sisters practised their skill, but she was sure it must amount to something more than the fugitive glimpses that came to her, unheralded and enigmatic. Besides, she was afraid that if others knew of this they would send her off to the nearest convent to become a holy sister herself; Tiphaine knew herself totally unfitted for such a life of pious discipline.

But this was different. Troops riding? And could that cleft in the hills be one of the passes that led from Brogall into Arvorig? If it was — even a bare possibility — Tiphaine could not keep this warning to herself. She left her room and hurried downstairs to find her aunt.

The door to Aunt Peronel's solar was open. Standing outside, Tiphaine could hear Nicolas' voice.

'I'm leaving at once, Mother. Count Fragan has entrusted me with a vital mission to Gwened.'

As Tiphaine went in, her aunt was seated as usual by the fire with her stitchery spread around her; Nicolas stood in front of her, looking very fine in his riding dress, slapping a pair of gloves into the palm of his hand.

'Nicolas—?'

He swung round to meet her, smiling. 'Little Tiphaine, I've come to take my leave. Count Fragan is sending me to Gwened.'

It had worked, then, Tiphaine thought sourly. The cat had finally jumped, and Nicolas was on the right side after all — or at least the winning side, as far as anyone could tell. Count Fragan's hand was firm on Roazon, and no one yet knew what had happened to Duke Joscelin.

But now she had little leisure to think of that. 'Nicolas,' she began. 'I have seen . . .' How to explain to him? 'The

Warrior has sent me a vision,' she went on, trying to steady her voice, carefully choosing words that she thought might make him listen. 'I saw troops from Brogall riding into Roazon.'

'Child, whatever are you saying?' Aunt Peronel asked fretfully. 'You must be ill. The air of Roazon can be pernicious in the summer. Come over here and let me feel your forehead.'

'I'm not ill, Aunt,' Tiphaine said. 'Nicolas, it's true, I saw it. We must do something – tell someone . . .'

Nicolas came over to her and put his hands on her shoulders. He was still smiling indulgently, as if dealing with a small child.

'Tiphaine, dearest, you're imagining things. You mustn't bother your pretty head with such nonsense'

'It's not nonsense!' Tiphaine said desperately. 'I must—'

'It certainly is!' her aunt interrupted, turning from querulous to angry. 'Visions, indeed! Why should *you* receive a vision, may I ask?'

Tiphaine knew that was a good question. She did not understand it herself; she only knew what she had seen.

'Come, give me a kiss before I go,' Nicolas said, before she could find a reply. 'I must ride for Gwened. And you must leave all these matters of war to the men who understand them. Just make yourself even more beautiful for my return!'

He kissed her on the forehead and then the lips. *I would rather be kissed by a toad*, Tiphaine suddenly thought, despairingly. She said nothing as Nicolas bade farewell to his mother; she knew there was nothing more she could say.

*

That same afternoon, when Aunt Peronel, her feet up on a footstool, was dozing over her embroidery, Tiphaine slipped out and climbed the steep streets leading to the citadel.

The citadel gates, which had always stood open before, were closed now. Count Fragan was taking no chances, Tiphaine could see. She stood by the metal bars until she managed to attract the attention of a bored guard standing inside.

'Yes, pretty one?' he said, strolling over to her.

Tiphaine drew herself up. 'Please let me in. I am Tiphaine de Bellière, and I wish to see my uncle, the Grand Master.'

The guard's lascivious grin abruptly vanished. 'I'm sorry, lady, but Father Reynaud is seeing no one. He's indisposed.'

'Indisposed?' Tiphaine repeated. 'Have the healers been with him? If you let me in,' she added, 'I can see what needs to be done for him.'

The guard shook his head, and a ghost of the grin reappeared. 'No, lady, you can't get in like that. I'm sure everything's been done proper for Father Reynaud, but he's not seeing anyone.'

'In that case . . .' Tiphaine was even more on her dignity. 'In that case, please ask Lady Marjolaine if she will see me.'

3

Marjolaine de Roazon had withdrawn to the seclusion of her garden, as she did so often in these days since her betrothed had fled the city. She felt she could breathe there, in the open; whereas inside the lowering walls of the citadel she felt suffocated. Perhaps in this garden, she thought wryly, she had some illusion of freedom. She did not deceive herself that she was truly free, not since Count Fragan had taken up rule in Roazon.

Her workbasket lay disregarded at her feet, and she clasped her hands together to keep herself from fidgeting as she watched the seneschal pacing the path in front of her.

'Is that girl mad?' he asked abruptly.

'Certainly not,' said Marjolaine. 'She seemed distressed, but perfectly rational. And she believed what she told me, I'm sure of that. Whether it was a true vision...' She shrugged.

'Vision or no vision, the suggestion is sound,' said Tancred, pausing briefly beside the fountain before limping rapidly back towards the bench where Marjolaine sat. 'The time is ripe for Aymon to invade. I warned Count Fragan as much, but will he listen?'

'I have sent for Count Fragan,' Marjolaine told him. 'Perhaps he'll listen to this new warning.'

Tancred stopped and stared at her, amusement trying to break through his anxiety. He had grown older, Marjolaine thought, in the days since Joscelin's departure. The lines of pain on his face had deepened, and silver frosted more thickly in his hair. It was becoming harder to remember that he was still a comparatively young man.

'Sent for the count?' he said. 'Will he come, do you think?'

'I'm certain of it,' Marjolaine said composedly. 'He's here now.'

The seneschal swung round to see where Count Fragan had just appeared on the path which led down to the door from the citadel. He bowed slightly as the count approached, but his expression was frigid.

Count Fragan ignored him, though he bowed to Lady Marjolaine. 'Lady, how may I serve you?'

As Marjolaine launched into a description of Tiphaine de Bellière's revelation, Fragan, without invitation, sat down on the bench at her side, and listened in silence until she had finished.

'And you believed this?' he asked. 'Lady, there's no need to worry. The city is full of hysterical women just now, but it's safe in my hands, believe me.'

'The young woman was not hysterical,' Marjolaine protested.

Fragan merely looked amused. 'Prophecy!' he said. 'Women's nonsense. I've even had the Matriarch pestering me with messages too.'

'I've spoken of this before, my lord,' Tancred broke in. 'You wouldn't need a vision to know that Aymon is looking for any chance to invade us. I showed you his letter about a so-called border raid.'

Fragan sighed, and looked from one to the other of them, resting his hands on his knees. 'You'll give me no peace, will you? What do you expect me to do — send out an army to meet King Aymon? He'd interpret that as a declaration of war — not to mention the fact that I haven't the troops to do it.'

'You might at least send a few men out to watch the passes,' Tancred said.

Fragan considered for a moment. 'Very well. If it makes you happy and will stop you nagging at me, Seneschal. And for your part,' he added, 'you might see that the weapons in our armoury are furbished up.'

Tancred gave a disdainful sniff. 'Already done, my lord.'

Fragan pulled himself to his feet, as if to leave. But, instead, he remained staring down at Lady Marjolaine. There was a gleam in his eyes that she did not care for.

'Now, my lady, to more important matters,' he said. 'Since your future husband is now a fugitive, you may consider your betrothal at an end.'

Marjolaine felt an unpleasant jolt at her heart, but she schooled herself to keep a surface of calm in front of Fragan. 'My lord, only the Church can dissolve my betrothal, unless Duke Joscelin or I should have cause to repudiate the other.'

'You could find such cause on the grounds of his heresy,' said Fragan.

'His heresy is still not proven.' A bubble of anger was beginning to swell inside Marjolaine, and she added, 'Besides, even if it were, I should not repudiate him.'

Fragan let out a bark of laughter. 'Lady, you don't mean to tell me you really want to marry that ... monk?'

She rose to face him; he was not a tall man, and she could see herself reflected in his bold, contemptuous eyes. 'Count Fragan, what I wish is none of your business. I shall continue to do my duty as Lady of Roazon.'

Her freezing dignity might have crushed a lesser man, but Fragan showed no signs of that. Instead, he smiled. 'You will indeed do your duty, my lady. You will marry the new Duke of Roazon, as was always your destiny. You will marry my son Tariec.'

Marjolaine could not repress an inarticulate cry of protest, and hated her own vulnerability as she noticed the glint of satisfaction in Fragan's eyes.

'*What?*' Tancred sounded outraged. 'That ... boy? He's barely left his wetnurse!'

'Keep out of this, Seneschal.' Fragan did not bother to look at him; his gaze was still fixed intently on Marjolaine.

A chill crept through her; for a moment she could

understand those women who would throw weeping fits to get their way, or use wiles of beauty and desire to bend men to their will. But she had always despised such weakness, and she would not give way to it now.

'I will not marry Tariec,' she said, pleased that her voice was still calm. 'The Church will not permit it, if I am unwilling.'

'Don't believe that, lady.' Fragan was still smiling, with the confidence of a man who knows he has won. 'The Church will do as it's damn' well told — and so will you.'

Fifteen

King Aymon knelt in his private chapel while the priest intoned the words of the Offering. His hands, folded in the attitude of prayer, itched to be fingering the letter which had just arrived from Roazon – from his creature Maugis.

When the courier had put it into his hands the Angelus bell was already ringing. Aymon had barely time to break the seal and give the letter one swift perusal before he had to escort his wife to the chapel. She was a meticulously pious woman, and all the more so when, as now, she was bearing a child. Another strong son, Aymon hoped, who might one day hold his new fief of Arvorig.

If only he could study that letter now, for Maugis's news was remarkable. Instead of the expected denunciation and trial of Duke Joscelin for heresy, the man had escaped, vanished into the forest of Brecilien. Meanwhile, Count Fragan, with the backing of the Legion, had claimed Roazon in the name of his son and heir, Tariec.

Behind his clasped hands Aymon could barely restrain a grin. Even better than saving Arvorig from heresy, he could be seen to save it from this upstart count. He would ride for Roazon in support of Joscelin, vanquish that fool Fragan and re-take the city in the name of its rightful duke.

Handing it over to that same rightful duke would be another matter altogether. If Joscelin ever came out of Brecilien – and there were things in there that no rational man questioned – he would scarcely be fit to rule. Ill health, or a convenient fit of piety, would send him back to the monastery he came from, with no questions asked.

Or if he should prove at all recalcitrant, Aymon might well allow the Church to enlighten him further, and declare Duke Joscelin a heretic after all. Aymon doubted he would need to use the assassin's dagger – a crude method at best.

The choir broke into an anthem of thankfulness, pure treble voices soaring to the chapel roof. Aymon's heart soared with them. Truly, he had much to be thankful for.

2

Baby Ivona took a single unsteady step and sat down abruptly with a look of surprise. Smiling gently, where she knelt before the fire, Alissende held out her hands. 'Come, Ivona. Good girl, come.'

The afternoon sun cast long shafts of light on the floor of the kitchen in Morwenna's house. Warm smells came from a pot on the fire and the loaves baking in the bread oven. Soon Donan would come up from his workshop and they would eat.

She might almost be wed to Donan, Alissende reflected, as Ivona struggled to her feet again and investigated further this new method of moving. She cared for his child. She cooked and cleaned and marketed while he worked at his craft. There was an easy friendship between them, and except for married love, they could have been husband and wife.

In truth, as Alissende knew, Donan wanted no woman but Morwenna. Though he attempted to remain resolutely cheerful, there was a look of bewildered loss in his eyes when he thought Alissende did not notice. He lived from one message with news of his wife to the next.

Even so, some of their neighbours gossiped about them. Alissende had overheard scraps of conversation, and caught sideways glances as she came and went. She shrugged the slurs off; there was no sin between her and Donan.

Besides, she thought, *what choice have I? How can I leave them now?*

Ivona tottered forward to fall gurgling in Alissende's lap. She swept the child up and sat with an arm around her, while Ivona babbled earnestly to her own fingers. She was a happy child, and after only a few days of grizzling when Morwenna left she had settled down.

But it should have been Morwenna, guiding her first steps, listening to this babble, not Alissende or any other friend. Morwenna was her mother, and should not be missing all these precious stages of her child's early life.

Alissende heard the street door shut below, and Donan driving the bolts home as the workshop was closed for the day. Soon he would be climbing the stairs to join them.

'Daddy's coming home,' she said to Ivona.

Ivona looked up, her face breaking into a smile. She grabbed at a strand of Alissende's chestnut hair and tugged it. 'Mama,' she said clearly. 'Mama.'

Alissende stared at her, horrified, then swept the child up into a tight embrace, against her shoulder. 'Oh, no, sweetheart, no,' she whispered. 'Not me. Your mama will come home soon, I promise.'

3

The cathedral stall of the Duke of Roazon remained vacant. Count Fragan sat in the place of honour on its right, with his son Tariec on its other side. The boy had fidgeted throughout the Offering, Tancred noted sourly, and seemed to show about as much understanding of the solemn ritual as one of the cathedral cats. Probably less, since the cats were well-conducted animals.

As the choir processed out, the pure notes of the recessional dying away, the seneschal left his own seat and slipped through a side door into the vestry. It was a dusty room lined with clothes presses and with cupboards for the cathedral plate.

Minutes later, the Archbishop and the lesser clergy arrived there in a swirl of gold-embroidered vestments. Tancred stepped forward. 'You asked to see me, my lord.'

'Seneschal.' The Archbishop let out a gusty sigh. He took off his mitre and handed it to an acolyte, while a second acolyte stood behind him, ready to ease off the heavy brocade cope. Shrugging out of this finery, the Archbishop looked suddenly diminished: no great prince of the Church, but an old and tired man in a simple white cassock. He waved the acolytes away and drew Tancred into a quiet corner, away from the sacristan and his servers who were clearing the silver and linen brought in from the altar. 'What's happening, do you know? Where is Duke Joscelin? Count Fragan badgers me day and night to declare him heretic, but no one will tell me anything definite.'

'There's little to tell,' said Tancred. 'No one knows exactly where Duke Joscelin is.' He permitted himself a sardonic smile. 'Though we can assume he is still alive and free, or Fragan would be in a better temper.'

'True.' The Archbishop signed himself with the Holy Knot. 'May the Warrior and the Judge protect him.'

Tancred cocked a brow. 'You have decided, perhaps, that he is *not* a heretic?'

'I have decided nothing.' The old man drew himself up with a flash of authority. 'The Church's time is its own, and I take orders from none but God ... certainly not from Count Fragan.'

Fingering his pectoral Knot, he paced across the rapidly clearing vestry, then turned back. 'And Father Reynaud?' he asked. 'I haven't seen him in many days. When I sent word that I wished to speak with him, they told me he was ill.'

Tancred shook his head. 'He's not ill — not unless fury has driven him into fits. He's kept under guard in his own quarters, since Count Fragan has taken command of the Legion into his own hands — with the connivance of Girec d'Evron.'

'This cannot be!' The old man was appalled. 'I must speak with Count Fragan...'

'Speak all you like, my lord. It won't make any difference. Besides, most of the Knights Legionaries had already been persuaded that Duke Joscelin is a heretic. That helped give Fragan his chance. And what of the Lady Marjolaine, my lord?' Tancred added. 'Has Fragan spoken to you of this new marriage?'

'To his son ... the idea is grotesque, and so I told him. A betrothal is not to be lightly set aside,' the Archbishop continued. 'Lady Marjolaine belongs to Duke Joscelin — at least until the question of his heresy is decided. For her to marry another would be a grievous sin.'

'You can be sure that Lady Marjolaine knows that,' said
Tancred. 'Whether Fragan understands it, of course, is quite
another matter.' Urgently, he went on, 'Stand firm, my lord.
If you give way now, what stands between us and Fragan's
naked ambition?'

The Archbishop shook his head, sighing. He looked
bewildered, his air of authority vanished, and Tancred felt a
sharp stab of anxiety. He respected, as everyone did, the
Archbishop's holiness and learning. But he doubted that
the old man had the courage to go on defying Fragan, in the
face of such threats as the count was quite capable of
carrying out.

Once again the Archbishop made the sign of the Holy
Knot. 'The Judge help us all, for without him, Roazon will
go down into the night.'

Leaving the Archbishop to his prayers, Tancred walked out
into the square fronting the cathedral. The sun was high,
beating down from a pale sky, the day uncomfortably hot
and heavy, as if a storm was brewing. Tancred's robe of
stiff, figured silk weighed like mail on his shoulders.

On the stairway that led down from the cathedral square,
the roses that twined among the balustrades were drooping,
their blooms withered or gone. Tancred made a mental note
to remind the gardeners about watering and dead-heading
them. There would be another flush of blossom in autumn,
but for now their flowering was over.

Then he noticed one late, half-opened bud, golden with
a flush of carmine at the centre. Tancred plucked it, stifling
a curse as a thorn speared his finger. He would give it to
Lady Marjolaine, and even so tiny a gesture might please
her in the midst of her troubles.

Count Fragan already behaved as if her marriage to Tariec was a certainty, and though Marjolaine was steadfast in refusing, Tancred could see anxiety had settled on her like a cloak. If he had ever wished for power, more than the practical authority of the seneschal's office, it would have been to lift the cloak from her and lead her out into joy.

Pausing on the stairway, oblivious to the startled glances of passers-by, Tancred gazed down into the crimson heart of the rose. Once he had tried to throw away his life in grief over Marjolaine's father. Now he regretted that youthful stupidity — not that he denied his grief, but he would have given much to have his youthful strength restored, so that it might serve her better. At least his life remained, and might still be spent for her.

'Primel,' he murmured, 'forgive me. Forgive me all I could never tell you. If anything in me can sustain her, she shall have it, even to my death.'

This pledge spoken — it had been made, long ago, in his heart — Tancred felt a surge of new resolve. Still carrying the flower carefully, he continued on his way to the citadel.

Later that day, the seneschal was in his workroom, checking the linen inventory, when the newest young clerk, Melin, tapped on the door and entered.

'Letters to sign and seal, sir,' he said, gently depositing the bundle on the table in front of Tancred.

Tancred gave him a sideways glance as he reached for a pen. He could never get out of his head the instinct that there was more to this Melin than met the eye. In the early days, he had even considered the possibility that he was a spy, but, after testing him with a couple of confidential tasks, had come to the conclusion that he was trustworthy. There was still, however, something odd about him.

'Any news?' he asked.

Melin shook his head; Tancred expected nothing else. His letters to the various provincial lords had clearly been intercepted by Count Fragan's men, and now the count made sure that all despatches arriving from outside were delivered to him in person.

Tancred paused in the act of sealing a final letter, intended for the wine merchant who supplied the court. It occurred to him that the man's warehouses were situated on the lowest level of the city, near the hythe gate. If this merchant could be persuaded to smuggle out a message ... Tancred sighed as he dripped the wax on to the paper and pressed his seal ring to it. He was not even sure of the merchant's loyalties, much less his courage.

He was handing the letters back to Melin for distribution when he heard footsteps pounding along the passage outside, then someone hammering on the door. It flew open before he could respond.

A man in dusty riding boots staggered in, panting. 'Lord Tancred! It's King Aymon, sir ... he's crossed the border with his army. He's riding down towards Roazon!'

Sixteen

Val stood by the window of the gatehouse at Bellière and looked out. The castle was set high on a bluff above the confluence of the Ster and the Ruzel rivers. On one side trees massed into a dark barrier; on the other the ground fell away into a steep ravine with the water chattering along below.

As Sulien had foretold, the manor of Bellière was almost deserted. The old housekeeper Nolwen remained, as did the chaplain Father Patern, and a handful of servants. There were no fighting men to guard its walls, none but those Val and Bertrand had brought with them.

Behind Val, Bertrand was seated at the table, having set up his headquarters here in the gatehouse. Though he always deferred to his cousin, he had somehow drifted into command.

From this same room, with its rough stone walls and narrow windows, messages were going out regularly as a call to arms in Duke Joscelin's cause. Not signed and sealed on parchment addressed to provincial counts and lords, these travelled by word of mouth through a succession of people who slid in and out again, without leaving their names: foresters and charcoal-burners, farmers and pig-women and pedlars. Val could picture word of Joscelin's presence here spreading through Arvorig like a spider's web. Count

Fragan might command the roads and rivers that radiated from Roazon itself, but the forests and uplands were Bertrand's.

Soon, Val hoped, sufficient forces would gather at Bellière to challenge Fragan and drive him out for good.

The table was spread with maps, and Bertrand was calculating the various distances to the seats of each provincial ruler. 'All of them must have heard what has happened by now,' he said, tugging at his stubbly black hair. 'But they don't do anything. Why don't they make a move?'

Val shrugged. 'They're wondering which side to support, I'd guess. None of them will really want to help Fragan, but they won't risk running foul of the Church while there's still a chance Duke Joscelin will be named heretic.'

Bertrand gave a low growl, deep in his throat. 'What about loyalty? Honour?'

He was interrupted by the sound of footsteps, running along the wall-walk. The door burst open. His brother Oliver stood there, his face alive with excitement.

'There are men coming on the road from Gwened!'

Bertrand rose, his chair grating backwards on the flagged floor. 'How many?'

'Twenty or more, with baggage carts. Some look like Knights Legionaries.'

'Ours — or Fragan's?' Bertrand wondered aloud. He grinned at Val. 'Let's go and take a look.'

Val followed him out along the wall-walk towards the east tower. From there they could see clearly the junction of the two rivers that enclosed Bellière like a pair of tongs, and the road which ran along the northern bank, beyond their confluence.

Some way down the road, still partly obscured by the cloud of dust thrown up by their horses' hooves, a group of riders was approaching. Sunlight glanced off armour, and the black and silver banner of the Legion fluttered in the wind.

Behind them, stretching into the distance, followed a line of baggage wagons drawn by mules, with more horsemen riding on either side as escort. Then Val could just make out a second banner beyond, and recognized the red and gold of Gwened.

'Not ours, then,' he said, pointing.

'Not yet.' Bertrand grabbed his younger brother, who was leaning out eagerly between two merlons, and pulled him back. 'Don't advertise our presence, lad,' he said. 'There's a good chance they may think Bellière is deserted, so they won't be expecting trouble here.'

'We're going to give them trouble?' Val asked, with a pulse of excitement.

'I think so, Cousin, don't you? We could use that baggage train.'

Though he did not want to sound reluctant, Val couldn't help warning, 'Those are trained knights down there, and we're badly outnumbered.'

'But we're fresh, and they're tired from the road,' replied Bertrand. 'And besides, they're not expecting us.' He clapped his cousin on the shoulder. 'Come on.' Then he ran down the steps to the courtyard, calling for horses.

The next few minutes went past in such a flurry that Val's mind seemed to become detached from his body, intent on arming himself with whatever equipment came to hand, rather than reflecting that before the hour was out he might be dead. This was not the elaborate ritual of a tournament; this was real.

For a few dizzying moments the outer courtyard seemed full of plunging horses and men running about, but the chaos quickly resolved itself. Soon they were all mounted and drawn up at the main gate. Bertrand's horse was waiting for him, Hoel holding its bridle, but Bertrand himself was still up on the wall-walk with his village lads. Bows ready, they knelt behind the arrow-slits in the merlons, while Bertrand stood at the end of the line, peering out at the baggage train.

Beside Val, Sulien murmured, 'He's quite mad.' Then he chuckled. 'He makes us mad along with him.'

Up on the wall-walk, Bertrand yelled out, 'Now!'

The bows sang. From the other side of the walls rose shouts of alarm, and the sound of trampling and neighing horses. Bertrand remained there a moment longer, staring down, then turned and ran back down the steps, his face lit up with satisfaction.

Mounting, he nodded for Hoel to pull open the gate. Just as he was ready to set spurs to his horse, he suddenly froze, staring at Oliver.

'What are you doing? I didn't give you leave.'

'Please, Brother!' Oliver's face was still starry with excitement. 'I can fight.'

'You've had no training,' Bertrand snapped at him. 'You stay here.'

The boy's excitement faded to sulkiness as he pulled his horse away from their group. Bertrand gave him a nod and led the others out through the gate at a brisk trot.

Nudging up beside him on the road leading to the bridge over the Ster, Val studied the baggage train again. The enemy riders had reached a stretch of road close to the castle, before coming to a halt.

Some of the knights were still mounted but a few had taken cover behind the carts. One cart had overturned, the mules drawing it it floundering in the dust of the road with a high-pitched squealing. A couple of horses were careering around loose, with one man lying motionless upon the road, and another fallen to the rocks at the side of the river.

Val took that in as they raced for the bridge, Bertrand picking up the pace until by the time they reached it they were at full gallop. The mounted knights escorting the baggage train wheeled to face this new threat.

Val had just time to reflect that once again he was raising his sword against brother Knights, then was headlong into the midst of battle and there was no more time for thought.

Nothing mattered now except the clash of weapons. Dust billowed from the ground to choke him and the world beyond his visor blurred. Harsh shouting, and the scream of horses.

As he hacked downwards at an enemy knight Val felt the other's chain-mail give way beneath his blade. The sword sinking home, bright blood flowered over the wounded man's surcoat. He lost his grip on the reins and fell to the ground, to be trampled by his own horse as it careered wildly away.

Then Bertrand was yelling something in Val's ear, thrusting himself between him and another knight, parrying with his shield the stroke meant for Val. Val brought up his sword again and plunged back into the attack.

At once he realized that they were being gradually forced back towards the bridge. Of course they were too few; the whole idea had been madness. The storm of arrows from the battlements had ceased, once Bertrand's lads risked shooting at their own side, allowing Fragan's knights to recover ground.

Glancing wildly round, while fighting off the attack of a

knight in green and gold, Val caught sight of Sulien being hard-pressed on two sides, Bertrand himself in the thick of the combat, and over there was Oliver—

Oliver! Val realized, with a shock.

Bertrand's young brother was managing well, darting around the edges of the skirmish, and harrying the enemy with strokes from unexpected angles. There was blood on his surcoat, but Val guessed it was not his own. The boy let out a series of excited war-whoops.

Bertrand will kill him, Val thought – then realized that Fragan's men would probably do that job first.

More shouting from the castle. Glancing behind, Val saw Bertrand's village lads break out through the gate and speed down towards the bridge, brandishing whatever weapons they could snatch up.

The enemy would massacre them! 'Bertrand!' Val yelled desperately. 'Bertrand, retreat!'

If they could not reach the gates, and close them against the enemy, then Bellière would fall. Duke Joscelin would be left unprotected in the hands of Count Fragan's men.

A distant horn blast sounded above the shouting. Peering through dust and sweat, Val discerned a bright blur approaching on the road beyond the baggage train – which rapidly resolved itself into another group of Knights, in gleaming armour with white surcoats, racing up to join the battle.

Val groaned in despair. Their last hope, even of retreat, had vanished. Piercing him like an arrow shaft came the thought that he would never see the Lady Marjolaine again, nor hear her voice nor see her smile.

Then he stared again in disbelief as the newcomers fell upon the knights escorting the baggage train and began to drive them back.

The assault on Bertrand's men wavered. Taking heart, Val pressed forward again to reach his cousin's side. Their enemy in between were breaking and fleeing, spurring their exhausted mounts up the road towards Roazon, abandoning their dead and wounded behind them.

The press of battle had broken up into individual combats, with a few of the enemy still trying to stand their ground, but in no time at all Val and Bertrand had pressed their way back to the abandoned wagons – and came face to face with the leader of their rescuers.

'I thought we would meet again, sooner or later.' He pulled off his helmet, and held out a hand to Val.

Val was too stupefied even to take the hand offered. The grinning man was Sir Guy de Karanteg.

'But, sir, I thought . . .' he stammered.

He broke off as Bertrand's hand fell on his arm, and his cousin pointed grimly.

Val turned, and a cold hand closed over his heart. Further up the road, he could see Oliver's chestnut gelding running free. Of the boy himself, there was no sign.

'I told him to stay back!' Bertrand slammed a fist down on the table.

Duke Joscelin, seated beside the fire, turned a face illumined by reassurance. 'Your brother is not dead.'

The day of the battle was reaching an end; the remains of their supper were strewn over the table in Duke Joscelin's ante-room, but no one had much appetite for Nolwen's excellent cooking, even though the contents of the supply carts – sacks of flour and dried peas, kegs of salted fish, barrels of wine, even one load of spare weapons – were now safely locked in the Bellière store rooms. No one could put the fate of Oliver d'Acquin out of their mind, or forget his cheerful chatter and the sweet sound of his lute.

They had scoured the field of battle for his body, in vain, and Val had even sent a couple of his men downriver to see if somehow young Oliver had been toppled into the current and swept away. They too had returned empty-handed. Meanwhile Sir Guy had led his troops in pursuit of Fragan's followers, in case they had taken the boy prisoner. But their enemies had enjoyed too good a start, and Sir Guy also had returned without news.

'He's as good as dead,' Bertrand said thickly. 'If he's Fragan's prisoner ... Will he torture Oliver, do you think, to find out where Duke Joscelin is?'

Val tightened his hand on Bertrand's shoulder. 'Fragan won't know who he is,' he said, trying to convince himself too. 'He wasn't wearing the Acquin arms, and nor were you. And the lad's not stupid. If he keeps his mouth shut, Fragan will have no reason to associate our attack with Duke Joscelin.'

'If they think he's a common bandit, they'll hang him,' Bertrand said.

'You can see Oliver is of noble birth, just by looking at him,' intervened Sulien.

'They'll ransom him, sooner or later.' Sir Guy reached for the wine jug and tipped wine into his cup. 'That's how things are always done.'

That's how things were done, Val reflected, back in the days which now seemed almost remote as legend. War in Arvorig was only a distant memory, even occasional disputes between provincial lords being settled peaceably by the laws of the holy city.

We can break a lance with exquisite courtesy, he thought. *We joust to entertain ladies. What has that to do with war?*

'Will Fragan guess where we are?' he whispered to Sir Guy. 'Do you think we should move out?'

Sir Guy took another gulp of wine. 'Not unless you can find a more secure position somewhere else, and I doubt it. Bellière's defences are superb, provided you stay inside them,' he added, flicking a glance of mingled reproof and approval at Bertrand. 'So no more death or glory sorties. Where would you have been if my Knights hadn't turned up?'

'How did you come here, sir?' Val asked, his mood lightening a little when he remembered the glorious moment when Sir Guy had led his men to their aid, and turned defeat into victory.

'I've broken with Fragan,' Sir Guy said. 'I'll not serve a traitor. I took all the loyal men with me, and set out for Roazon.'

'But you'll stay here now?' Val said. 'With Duke Joscelin?'

'Aye, lad.' Sir Guy pushed a hand through his thinning hair. 'But I'll not be taking command, I warn you. It's easy to see who the men follow here.'

Bertrand was still sitting, with head bowed, staring wretchedly at the table. Val filled a cup with wine and nudged it towards him.

His cousin sighed, scrubbing his hands over his face. 'I gave my word to my mother that I would bring Oliver home safe, or die trying.' His voice was unsteady. 'Oh, God, what shall I do if I'm forsworn?'

2

From Lady Marjolaine's solar, a peephole, concealed by a
carving, provided a view of the great hall. She stood there
now, watching the scene that unfolded below.

At the far end, on the dais, Count Fragan was seated on
a massive carved throne, his booted feet planted in front of
him. Lord Tancred stood beside him, wearing the seneschal's formal robes, his staff of office in his hand.

From the main doors, right below her viewpoint, came
a trumpet call, and a voice announced, 'The herald of King
Aymon of Brogall requests an audience.'

Fragan gestured an invitation to approach, and the
herald proceeded up the length of the hall, at last coming
into Marjolaine's sight.

Marjolaine could not yet see his face, but he was a
tall man, his movements brisk, wearing a blue tabard
strewn with the golden lilies of Brogall, and a sword at his
side.

Advancing right up to the dais he bowed to Count
Fragan – a bow nicely calculated, Marjolaine noticed, to
avoid any charge of discourtesy without conveying real
respect. 'My master sends greetings to you, my lord count,'
he said, holding out the sealed scroll he carried.

Fragan did not reply, merely waved a hand at Tancred
to go and accept the message.

Tancred broke the seal, scanned what was written on the
parchment, then handed it over to the count.

As Fragan also read it, his brows snapped together in
annoyance. 'King Aymon here accuses me of usurping the
rightful Duke of Roazon,' he snarled. 'He is mistaken.'

'Indeed, my lord?' The herald managed to sound bored.

'Duke Joscelin forfeited his right to rule here by embracing a grievous heresy,' Fragan said. 'I have not myself usurped his place, but claimed it rightfully on behalf of my son, who bears the true blood of Roazon through his mother.'

'King Aymon insists that the Church has not pronounced Duke Joscelin a heretic,' said the herald. 'That being the case, he has no choice but to march on Arvorig to reinstate Duke Joscelin on his rightful throne.'

Fragan snorted in disgust. 'If I could believe that, I'd believe anything.'

'I am bidden to ask you, my lord, whether you will now retreat, give up your place here, and let Duke Joscelin be recalled.'

For a moment Fragan stared at him with eyes narrowed, as if not deigning to reply at all. Then he said, firmly, 'No, I will not. And you may tell your King Aymon that he possesses no authority over the affairs of Arvorig.'

Though sunlight lay in heavy slabs across the floor below, to Marjolaine, it seemed as if a cold wind had begun to blow. *War,* she thought. *Nothing can stop it now.*

Echoing her thought, the herald continued, 'I will report your words as instructed, my lord. But this is a sad day for Arvorig.'

'Sad indeed,' said Fragan, rising suddenly to his feet. 'Tell your master that unless he retreats within his own borders, we will meet him in the field.'

As the herald bowed and withdrew, Fragan stood and watched him go — crumpling the rejected parchment into a ball between his hands. As the sound of the closing doors echoed through the great hall, he let out a curse, and swung round on the seneschal. 'Have that damn' ambassador thrown into a cell,' he ordered.

Flinging the crumpled document from him, he stalked off through the private door behind the dais.

By the time Marjolaine had descended to the hall, the guards had gone. Only Tancred remained. He had retrieved the parchment and was smoothing it out, reading the message once again as if he could make it yield up something other than utter disaster.

Glancing up at her, he said, 'You overheard that?'

Marjolaine nodded; he knew about her peephole. 'Can we resist King Aymon?' she asked.

'Oh, we can *resist* him.' Tancred's tone was bitter. 'But beating him off is a different matter. Aymon has all the resources of Brogall at his command. Arvorig is small in comparison, and we haven't fought a real battle for generations.'

'Then Fragan must treat with him, surely?' said Marjolaine.

The seneschal let out a snort of disgust. 'Try telling Count Fragan that. He is already mobilizing the citadel guard, and his own followers, and the Legion. He'll soon put a force into the field.'

'They'll be cut to pieces,' Marjolaine whispered. 'Why does he not prepare for a siege ... while sending word for help from the provincial lords ...?'

'Roazon is poorly stocked for a siege,' Tancred replied. 'And Fragan places no faith at all in the provincial rulers. But you're right – he can't win a battle against the strength of Aymon.'

'And who will guard Roazon, if Fragan strips it of its few fighting men?'

Tancred refolded the parchment. Marjolaine noticed – a

tiny detail perceived as the knowledge of disaster swirled around her – that his hands were quite steady.

'Those of us who are left,' he said.

'We will, dear friend,' said Marjolaine, reaching out to touch his arm, 'and more than that. When Count Fragan leads his army out through the gates, we must close them behind him. Whatever else may happen, he will never enter Roazon again.'

Cold light seeped into the citadel courtyard as Count Fragan assembled his men. The sun had not yet burnt away the morning mist; swathes of it enveloped them as they drew up into lines, almost, Marjolaine thought, as if they were already being folded into their shrouds.

Even the shouted orders, and the sound of armoured feet on stone, were deadened, suffocated in that pervading white blanket.

Marjolaine stood long at a window above the courtyard, watching as Fragan finally ordered the gates to be opened, and led his men out. The banners of Gwened, of Roazon and the Legion accompanied them, their colours muted in the grey morning light.

'Where is Duke Joscelin?' she murmured, half to herself.

'No one knows,' the seneschal replied. 'Or even if he lives.'

'He lives,' Marjolaine repeated with certainty. 'Sir Valery de Vaux was with him – and that strange cousin of his who triumphed in the tournament.'

'Bertrand d'Acquin.' Tancred grunted approval, his eyes still fixed on the departing columns of men. 'Trustworthy, both of them.'

'I know.' Marjolaine thought how in recent days she had

come to rely on Sir Valery de Vaux. He would prove himself faithful in greater things, she was sure. Faithful to his calling as a Knight of the Legion ... Then she shook her head impatiently, driving the persistent thought of him from her mind.

Side by side, she and the seneschal watched until the last of Fragan's doomed army had marched away, and two of the few remaining citadel guards had closed the gates behind them.

Marjolaine could imagine those lines of warriors, still threading their way down through the city's hushed streets and stairways, until they reached and crossed the causeway. Horses would be waiting ready for them by the huge stables on the lakeside road – and then they would ride north to meet King Aymon.

Her imagination failed her to accompany them on that ride, but not to envisage the pitiful few of them who would ever ride back again.

'Very well,' she said evenly, when the gates were finally shut. 'Tancred, summon the Guildsmasters to meet with us here. Beg the Archbishop and the Matriarch to join us too, or send us their representatives. Call the captain of all the guards who remain. Let us see what we can plan in Council to save our city.'

The seneschal bowed to her, a glint in his dark eyes.

'And meanwhile,' said Marjolaine, 'I shall see if my authority suffices now to arrange release for Father Reynaud.'

She rested her hands on the long table, interlaced her fingers, and looked inquiringly around the Council chamber, gathering the attention of the men and women before her.

The Archbishop; the Matriarch herself, with her almoner, Sister Levenes; Master Eudon, the Head of the Guild Council; Guildsmasters of most of the city's crafts guilds were there; Lord Tancred, of course; lastly, Father Reynaud himself, newly released from being confined to his quarters, and obviously nursing considerable resentment against the man who had put him there.

It was just past midday, and only a narrow slice of sunlight penetrated the room, leaving it cool and quiet. Murmured conversations fell into silence as Lady Marjolaine prepared to speak.

Though having rehearsed in her mind what she intended to say, she knew a moment's misgiving. Roazon had never before known the rule of a woman. The lot of a great noblewoman like herself was to look beautiful, to please her husband, and to bear him sons. She was not expected to wield authority.

Yet out in the city there were many women who worked at a craft as well as bringing up their families. One or two of them even sat before her now, heads of their guilds, and well respected. Under their gaze, Marjolaine knew she could not fail in her duty. She had not asked for this burden, but there was no one else.

'Friends,' she began, 'you all know that Count Fragan has led his men off to war. It is left for us who remain here to provide for the safety of our city.'

'But we are not fighting men,' Master Eudon quavered, his face the colour of unbaked dough. 'What can we do?'

'Listen, to begin with,' the seneschal snapped at him.

Master Eudon threw him an affronted look, but said no more.

'I have given this much thought,' Marjolaine went on, 'and I have already taken the advice of Lord Tancred and

Father Reynaud.' The seneschal's primarily, she added to
herself, for Father Reynaud's contribution had consisted
mostly of ranting against Count Fragan who had imprisoned him and led his Knights out to die, though he seemed
calmer now. 'First we must place a guard on our gates and
on our walls, and it is there, Master Eudon, that you can
help us.' Not giving the Guildsmaster the chance to protest,
she went on quickly to explain. 'All able-bodied guildsmen
must agree to take a tour of duty. You will draw up a roster
and present it to us by tomorrow morning. Your fellow
Guildsmasters here will help you.'

Master Eudon looked faintly relieved to be given a task
within his capacity. He nodded pompously. 'It will be done,
my lady.' As the other Guildsmasters at the table murmured
agreement, Marjolaine found herself relaxing too. These
measures were only sensible, and there was no reason for
anyone to oppose her.

'Second,' she said, 'we must accept that King Aymon
will win his contest with Count Fragan, and besiege our
city. That means we have just a few days – no more. In that
time, all women and children who wish to leave for safer
places must do so. I will have this news cried in the streets.'

'Where are they to go?' one Guildsmaster asked.

'Wherever they want,' the seneschal replied. 'Most surely
have friends or families living elsewhere. They'll be safer
away from a city under siege.'

'They will need food and money for their journey,'
Marjolaine added. 'So if they are in need, they may come
here to the citadel and ask for help.'

That provoked a further stir of approval, and encouraged
Marjolaine on to her next, less popular decree.

'Our storehouses are not so full as I would like,' she
said, 'so we must begin as we mean to go on. All surplus

stocks of food in the city must be brought here to the citadel, where Father Reynaud has agreed to organize a daily distribution once the siege is set.'

She waited for a protest, and the heads of the brewers' and bakers' guilds, who would be deeply affected by such an edict, glanced at each other, seeming about to argue. When the Grand Master glared at them, both Guildsmasters responded with reluctant nods of assent.

'Thank you for your cooperation,' said Marjolaine. 'Meanwhile, Lord Tancred has already sent word out to the surrounding farms, to send us their surplus also for storage against the siege.'

If she stood up and looked out of the window, across the city and down as far as the lakeshore, she would see reapers in the fields, gathering their scanty harvest. It would never provide enough to sustain the population of Roazon through several weeks, if not months of siege. *And what end to that suffering?* Marjolaine wondered, with a chill in her heart. *What use is all this planning, if no one will help us against King Aymon?*

'Lady Marjolaine,' the Matriarch broke in on her thoughts, speaking to her as an equal, with the exquisite authority of her office. 'There will be many wounded men, fleeing from the battle, and once the siege is set there will be injuries to our citizens. We of the Matriarchy gladly put our healing skills at your service.'

'But we need a separate place for a hospital,' Sister Levenes added practically. 'Laymen may never enter our House.'

'Lord Seneschal?' Marjolaine inquired.

It was Father Reynaud who replied. 'The Legion's barracks now lies almost empty. You may use that if it suits.' There was a heavy grief about him as he spoke, and

Marjolaine knew that he was wondering how many of his Knights would never ride home through the city gates again.

The Matriarch, seated beside him, reached out to touch his hand.

'I thank you both,' said Marjolaine. She had achieved what she had hoped, more easily than she thought possible. As she glanced around the table she saw renewed confidence, and felt a little spurt of hope to think that she had called it up. 'Friends,' she concluded, 'we must go now to our many urgent tasks.'

Seventeen

Many times on the road back to Roazon, Nicolas de Cotin wished he had never saddled himself with a prisoner. When he had seen the horse throw its rider, he had scarcely thought before dismounting, dragging the stunned boy across his own saddle-bow, and riding on.

Even when he and his remaining men halted a little way into the forest and regrouped, it seemed the obvious thing to bind the boy's hands and threaten him with a painful death if he gave trouble. He had caught a mount for the prisoner, its own rider fallen in the skirmish, and kept him on a leading rein thereafter.

At least, Nicolas had thought, he would have something useful to offer to Count Fragan in compensation for the disastrous loss of the baggage carts.

By nightfall, Nicolas and his remaining men had penetrated deeply into the forest. Once Nicolas was fairly certain they were not being pursued, he set the men to building a fire, and scouting for game to supplement their scanty rations. He and a sergeant at arms seated their prisoner roughly down with his back to a tree and bound his arms behind him.

'Now,' Nicolas said, drawing his dagger and stroking it. 'You can start by telling me who you are.'

The boy looked up at him. He was startlingly handsome,

Nicolas thought, with silver-gold hair and sapphire eyes. His glowing looks shone out through the filth and scratches he had acquired in the fight and the fall from his horse. It flitted through Nicolas's mind to wonder what he would look like naked, but immediately he banished the idea. That part of his life was over; he owed his love to Tiphaine – or at least he meant to wed her.

The boy stared up at him and said nothing, his eyes holding fear and defiance.

'You know I can easily kill you?' Nicolas asked sharply. 'So answer my question.'

His prisoner shook his head. 'I don't think you will,' he said. 'Otherwise you would have killed me back at Bellière.'

The boy's reasoning was good, Nicolas had to admit. He gripped the dagger threateningly. 'I may not kill you,' he said, 'but I can make you wish I had. I want to know who else was with you at Bellière.'

The boy's direct gaze never wavered but he said nothing more. Nicolas, assailed by rising fury, was tempted to spoil that beauty with a few slashes from his dagger, but he did not quite dare do it. The word 'ransom' was in the forefront of his mind. He was always in debt, and if this boy was of noble blood – as clearly he was – there could be profit in it.

Nicolas thrust his dagger back into its sheath. 'I'll give you time to think it over,' he said, but a faintly mocking defiance in the boy's eyes told him that his threats were empty.

As he turned away, he could feel the sergeant's eyes also boring into his back, honed by contempt.

By the time he and his party were a day's ride away from Roazon, Nicolas was thoroughly sick of the boy. He rode with such a blithe confidence now, that Nicolas found himself constantly glancing backwards along the road in case the youth knew that a rescue party would soon be upon them.

Sometimes, too, the boy would burst into song, and had the men of Gwened singing with him. Nicolas found it all intensely irritating.

Worse still, the men who supposedly were under his command more or less ignored him now, as if they blamed him for their defeat in the skirmish. The men from Gwened looked to their sergeant for orders, and the Legion to their own senior officer.

During the course of the next day, Nicolas and his men began to encounter little groups of refugees on the road, mostly women and children, all journeying away from Roazon.

At first he took little notice, but by the fourth or fifth such encounter he was getting curious, and pulled his horse over across the road to block their way.

'Where are you going?' he demanded.

The group shuffled to a halt, an older woman in the lead. She set down her bundle, folded her arms across her chest and glared up at him. 'The roads are free for anyone. Who wants to know?'

'The banner should tell you,' Nicolas snarled, pointing at the Gwened standard. 'We are Count Fragan's men. You would do well not to scorn his authority.'

The woman's response was eloquent; she spat on the ground at his horse's feet. Picking up her bundle again, she gestured to her followers, and the whole group waded off through the bracken at the side of the road to avoid the horsemen.

Bringing up the rear, a young woman with a baby paused and looked up at Nicolas with a sunny smile. 'If you're riding to Roazon, sir, you might find that your banner's not welcome now. Count Fragan's authority doesn't run there any more.'

'What do you mean? Stop her!' he added to the sergeant.

Thrusting the banner he held at the nearest of his men, the sergeant dismounted and faced the young woman. 'Tell us what you know, mistress.'

The woman pulled her baby closer to her, but showed no other sign of fear. 'Count Fragan has ridden out to meet King Aymon's army. The Lady Marjolaine rules in Roazon now.'

'King Aymon's army — what army?' Nicolas cried.

'King Aymon has crossed the border,' she explained. 'He's campaigning to bring back Duke Joscelin.'

Nicolas' brain was whirling. He had known none of this, and he could make no sense of it, nor decide what he ought to do next. While he sat silent in consternation, the sergeant gestured the woman on her way, and mounted his horse again.

'Well, sir,' he said, 'that changes things, and no mistake.'

The sun was going down as Nicolas and his men came to the edge of the forest and had their first sight of Roazon. The lake was dyed red by the setting sun; the city itself was a spear of extravagant rose. Nicolas thought longingly of depositing his prisoner in the citadel dungeons, and seeing how this pestilential boy liked that. After that would come a decent meal in his favourite inn, and a good night's sleep in his own bed.

He tried to ignore the worm of unease the woman's news had called up in him. If there was any truth in it, any more than the vapourings of a hysterical female, then surely Count Fragan would drive out Aymon. Anything else was unthinkable.

More unthinkable still was the memory of what Tiphaine had told him on the day he left Roazon. More vapouring, to be sure, for Nicolas refused even to consider that his betrothed might have experienced a true vision.

If Lady Marjolaine had truly sought to usurp Fragan's authority, then she must be lessoned. And Count Fragan might be more than grateful, Nicolas reflected, to the man who gave her that lesson.

Before he could set spurs to his horse to begin the last stage of their journey, he heard the sound of singing – not the boy this time, but many voices together, hushed and sweet in the evening air.

Riding through the outermost fringe of the forest, he skirted a hazel brake and came upon the largest group of travellers he had seen yet – twenty or more seated around a wayside shrine where a young priest was conducting the evening Offering.

Nicolas would have ridden past, but the men of the Legion were already dismounting to join in the prayers, and so he halted, signing to the men of Gwened to do the same, and reluctantly bowed his head.

By the time the service was over the sun had gone and darkness was swiftly gathering. The travellers moved off to spread blankets under the trees, while some began to collect fallen branches for a fire. Nicolas beckoned to the priest. 'What's going on here?' he snapped.

The fresh-faced young man blinked in surprise at his tone, but answered readily. 'These people come from Roazon, sir, and are fleeing from the war.'

'Fleeing – to where?' Nicolas felt more irritated by the second. 'Do they expect to live in the forest? Or beg for their bread in the country villages?'

'No indeed, sir,' the priest said, with a joyful smile. 'Some of them have families in other cities, and will go to join them. For the rest – all of them can work, and all have enough for the journey. Lady Marjolaine has seen to that.'

'Lady Marjolaine?' Nicolas tried to inject chilly disapproval into his voice. 'Can it be true, then, that a woman rules in Roazon?'

'Through the grace of God, yes,' the young priest said, apparently oblivious of Nicolas's hostility.

'Tell us of this war.' The sergeant had come to stand beside Nicolas.

Nicolas barely listened to the priest's reply. In any case, he said little that they had not already heard. Count Fragan had led his army out to meet King Aymon somewhere in the hills to the north, but no word had come as yet to tell of victory or defeat.

'Meanwhile,' the priest finished, 'Lady Marjolaine and the Lord Seneschal guard the safety of our city.'

Lord Tancred, too! Nicolas thought in disgust. *That twisted scrap of a man!* Certainly it was time he returned to Roazon and straightened things out for Count Fragan's return.

'We must ride on,' he said to the sergeant.

'No need, sir,' the priest said warmly. 'Stay and share supper with us. The gates of Roazon are now locked at sunset, and no one will be admitted until the morning.'

'What nonsense is this?' Nicolas demanded roughly. 'They will admit us, being on Count Fragan's business.'

'Then you least of all,' the priest argued, his radiant goodwill faltering for the first time. 'Lady Marjolaine has ordered that none of Fragan's men are to be admitted.'

Nicolas felt as if he had taken a blow in the stomach. Could this really be true? The count out in the field, and the city gates closed to him — and Nicolas had openly declared himself Fragan's man! Forcing his scattered wits to work, he realized that this was indeed not the best moment to ride down to Roazon and start hammering on the gates for admittance. He needed time to think what his next move should be.

'In that case,' he said, forcing a gracious tone, 'we will stay with you for the night, and guard you from danger.'

Firelight had sprung up in the travellers' camp spread under the trees. A whiff of cooking tickled Nicolas's nostrils. The sound of happy voices reached him, one voice in particular raised in song.

Staring across, Nicolas made out his own wretched prisoner settled comfortably by the nearest camp fire. Someone had given him a lute, and his music pealed out merrily.

Danger seemed far off.

'Come, sir,' the priest said, with a wide gesture towards the fires.

Following him reluctantly, Nicolas murmured to the sergeant, 'Tomorrow I'll get all this sorted out.'

In the darkness he could not be sure if the sergeant's answering glance held respect or mockery.

2

'Alissende! Alissende!' Donan was shouting up from the workshop below. His heavy footsteps on the stairs roused Ivona from her sleep. Alissende looked up from cleaning the breakfast dishes as the door burst open.

For a moment she was alarmed, until she saw his face was flushed with delight. 'What is it?'

'Alissende, there's a servant here from the citadel. He says we can go and visit Morwenna!'

'How wonderful! When – now?'

'Yes, right away. I'm shutting up shop, so get Ivona ready.'

Leaving the dishes, Alissende put on her cloak, and swirled a shawl around the baby. Ivona made just a brief protest at being scooped up from her cradle, then settled against Alissende's shoulder, dozing again with her thumb in her mouth.

Alissende was down the stairs before Donan's apprentice had finished bolting the shop shutters. Donan gave the lad the rest of the day off, and led them to where the servant from the citadel was waiting in the street.

On the way up there, they found most of the shops were shuttered and few people on the streets. The citadel gate too was firmly closed, though a guard opened it promptly when the servant announced them.

Then it was only moments before they began climbing the stairs to Morwenna's tower room.

Alissende hung back to let Donan enter first and greet his wife. She glimpsed him catching Morwenna into a tight embrace, and turned her face aside discreetly, only going into the room herself when she heard Morwenna ask shakily, 'Where is Ivona?'

Donan steered his wife round by the shoulder. Morwenna held out her arms longingly and Alissende handed her child to her.

Let Ivona recognize her mother, she prayed silently, and knew her prayer was answered when the baby gave a delighted gurgle.

Then their excitement overflowed, and there was news to be exchanged.

Morwenna had changed subtly, Alissende thought, in the weeks of her imprisonment: no signs of ill-treatment, but her bright confidence was gone. She was thinner, looked older, and wore an unfamiliar gravity.

Her anxiety emerged as she sat down on her bed with Ivona in her lap. 'Lady Marjolaine tells me that many women and children are leaving the city, before King Aymon's soldiers arrive. Alissende, I want you to go, too, and take Ivona to safety.'

'But we can't just leave you here!' Alissende's protest was instinctive. 'You'll be allowed other visits from us.'

Morwenna dabbed at her tears with a kerchief. 'I know. But think, if Aymon takes the city ... you know what soldiers do to women and children. Do you think I would prefer that?'

'Then let's persuade them to release you, so all of you can go,' said Donan.

Morwenna shook her head. 'I already know they will not. But *I'm* safe here!' she cried. 'As a prisoner of the Legion, I'm probably the safest person in this whole city.'

Yet I had that vision of you blinded, Alissende recalled.

'Go.' Morwenna choked back tears. 'Go while you can. I have family in Kervrest who'll take you in and care for you.'

'It's best,' Donan agreed, looking as distressed as his wife. 'I must stay to help defend the city. As soon as I can, I'll send word.'

'It might not be for too long,' Morwenna added, with a pitiful attempt at bravery.

Staring at them both, Alissende could not find further words to protest. But the rapping of the guard on the door interrupted what else she might have said.

Morwenna sprang to her feet and thrust Ivona into Alissende's arms. 'Take her and go!'

Alissende stared down at the baby, who was beginning to whimper in bewilderment at all the noise. A moment later she felt Donan's hand on her shoulder, guiding her firmly out of the room.

'I'll take care of her,' Alissende promised. 'Her life before mine, I swear it.'

Then the door closed and there was nothing more to be said.

3

'You wear no weapon, not even a belt knife?' observed the Lord Seneschal.

Aurel was aware of the cold touch of the serpent knife, bound close to his side beneath his tunic. 'No, my lord,' he replied.

Tancred was standing at the window of his workroom, looking out over the deserted courtyard. He had spoken the words over his shoulder as Aurel entered the room. As he turned to face him, Aurel saw that he held a short sword in a battered leather scabbard.

'I used this myself, long ago.' He offered it to Aurel. 'It's yours, for your own safety, if you want it.'

Aurel made no move to take it. 'My lord, I'm not trained in using one.'

'Listen, lad, if King Aymon breaks in here we'll all need to resist: guildsmen, cooks, clerks ... Unless you prefer to be butchered without putting up a fight. So take it.'

He stepped closer and thrust the sword into Aurel's hands, then gripped his shoulder. 'You came to Roazon at

the wrong time. There's still time to get out, if you prefer.
I could arrange it.'

'I've nowhere else to go.' Aurel's response was automatic,
and he did not consider until after he had spoken that the
words were true.

He almost expected another warning stab of pain, but
Vissarion was always careful to communicate when Aurel
was alone. The ring remained quiescent.

The seneschal's dark eyes, so close to his own, were
unreadable. His grip on Aurel's shoulder tightened for an
instant before he released him. 'Stay, then, but protect
yourself.'

He moved back to the table and began to sort through
the documents strewn across its surface. As Aurel watched
him, he felt surprised at a surge of amused affection. He
could not understand how anyone as untidy as his employer
could manage to be so efficient.

'I've some papers here for Guildsmaster Eudon,' the
seneschal muttered, finally gathering half a dozen sheets
together. 'I want you to take them yourself – into his hands
and no other's. Then the old fool can't pretend he never
received them.'

'Yes, my lord.'

Just then the door swung open and a servant inquired,
'My lord, will you see Sir Nicolas de Cotin?'

Aurel's start of surprise went unnoticed as his former
lover pushed past the servant and entered the room without
invitation. He strode across to lean over Tancred's table,
planting his hands on it aggressively.

'Why were my men refused entry to the city?' His face
was reddened with fury. 'Why am I refused audience with
the Lady Marjolaine?'

The Lord Seneschal stiffened at this belligerent tone,

gazing at the intruder as if at something vile found squirming beneath a stone. He slid back in his seat and folded his hands in front of him. 'Your men?' he said coolly.

'The escort I brought with me from Gwened.'

'Ah.' Tancred relaxed slightly. 'Well, that explains it. No one from Gwened is admitted into Roazon.'

'Why not? That's lunacy!' Nicolas's head thrust forward aggressively; he was barely holding on to his temper. 'Count Fragan rules here now, in his son's name.'

'Not any longer.' The seneschal's tone was bland. 'By driving out our rightful duke, Count Fragan gave Aymon of Brogall the excuse he was looking for to invade us. Now your count has led out the city guard and the Legion to die needlessly in battle. He is therefore not popular in Roazon, and — forgive me — if you continue to announce your allegiance here, you're a braver man than I ever took you for.'

Nicolas's voice spiralled up out of control. 'What would you know of bravery, you undersized cripple!'

He lunged forward across the table at Tancred. But the seneschal, on reflex, had flung his chair back. Without thinking, Aurel thrust himself between them, drawing the battered sword he still held in his hands.

As he confronted Nicolas, the blade gleaming between them, his heart was hammering in his chest; he could not believe that Nicolas would not see beyond the unobtrusive mask of Melin the clerk and recognize him as Aurel.

Nicolas, meanwhile, looked pop-eyed with astonishment, almost as if part of the furniture had reared up against him. His hand went to the hilt of his own weapon, then surprisingly he took a step backwards, spitting a curse.

The seneschal had risen to his feet, white-faced, with a

hectic spot of colour on each cheek-bone. 'All is well, Melin. Stand aside.'

Reluctantly, Aurel obeyed him.

Tancred drew his seat forward and sat down again. His voice even but chilly, he began, 'Sir Nicolas, what is your purpose in coming here?'

Nicolas seemed calmer. 'I told you. I want to know what is going on here,' he said sulkily. 'They told me the city has shut out Count Fragan, and that the Lady Marjolaine is now in charge. A woman? How can that be true?'

'A great and valiant lady,' said Lord Tancred. 'And the last of the Roazon bloodline, until Duke Joscelin himself returns.'

'Lord Joscelin has proven himself a heretic!'

The seneschal waved a hand impatiently. 'We will not revive that argument now. Sir Nicolas, forgive me. I'm a busy man, so if you have no more to say than this, I have no time to listen. If you are a loyal subject of Arvorig, then—'

'Of course I'm loyal!'

'To whom, I wonder,' Tancred murmured, but did not pursue the matter. More briskly, he asked, 'You come here with men from Gwened?'

'Yes.' Nicolas still sounded sulky. 'And some Knights of the Legion.'

'Where are they now?'

'Outside the gates.'

'Excellent.' Tancred smiled approvingly. 'The Knights Legionaries may enter, as we need them to defend the city. The men of Gwened may not, but if you are ready to demonstrate your loyalty, they could do Arvorig great service.'

'What service?' Nicolas asked suspiciously.

'We are sending the woman and children away to safety,' Tancred said. 'If you agree, you could escort a party of Gwened families back there on your men's return.'

Nicolas looked taken aback, but then nodded. 'Very well.'

Tancred relaxed, some of the chill evaporating. 'You yourself have family here, do you not?' he said. 'They may wish to join the party. Can you have them waiting at the causeway gate in say ... three hours?'

Nicolas nodded, and took his leave with the belligerence leached out of him. As the door closed behind him, the seneschal exhaled deeply. 'Insolent young puppy!'

Aurel remained staring at the closed door. To *that* he had given his love? For *that* he had made an enemy of his father, and his own name a byword for profligacy throughout Arvorig? For *that* he would once have ended his own life? He tried to recall the rapture he had felt at Nicolas's touch, the pride of being loved by him ... and found it all gone.

Once more Tancred came and rested a hand on his shoulder. 'Put the sword away,' he said. 'Truly, Melin, I had no idea you could prove so formidable!'

Feeling himself flush, Aurel sheathed the weapon. His heart beat wildly again on remembering that impulse to defend his employer. He had felt no fear; was not sure what had prompted him.

Tancred's eyes regarded him warmly – he who always seemed so cold and abrupt – and he was even smiling faintly. He handed Aurel the documents he had gathered up before Nicolas de Cotin had interrupted.

'Here, take these quickly to the Guildsmaster. Come

straight back, and we'll collect a party of Gwened folk to go with Sir Nicolas.'

As Aurel took the papers and went out, he seemed to feel a tide of new loyalty rising within himself. If he had done all that for Nicolas, he asked himself, what would he do for Tancred?

Eudon was not to be found in the Guildhall, but Aurel eventually tracked him down to his jeweller's workshop. Returning to the citadel, he saw a crowd gathered in the street ahead of him. In its midst was a man in the tattered uniform of the city guard, his face filthy and sweat-stained, his left arm held in a sling whose linen was brown with dried blood.

'What news? What news?' the crowd were crying out to him.

'Let me through,' he replied. 'I must speak with my lady.'

He tried to struggle through, but they hemmed him round relentlessly. The man was almost exhausted.

'What news?' rose the cry again.

The guardsman swung round, his eyes wild. 'News?' he echoed. 'The battle is lost. Count Fragan and his son are dead. The Legion is cut to pieces. It's all over, and King Aymon is coming!'

'King Aymon is coming!' The cry was taken up, echoing through the streets, as the terrified crowd began to scatter.

Aurel heard the grim news spreading like ripples from a stone cast into a pool. He went up to the messenger, half fainting now from wounds and weariness, and gripped his arm to support him.

'King Aymon is coming,' the man repeated in a rasping whisper, and collapsed on the ground at his feet.

4

Tiphaine finished lacing up her old linen gown – never fine enough to wear in Roazon until now – and slipped her feet into her stoutest pair of leather slippers.

Beyond the door of her bedchamber she could hear other doors opening and closing, and the distant voice of her Aunt Peronel raised in complaint. Since Cousin Nicolas had banged his way into the house an hour ago, that shrill voice had hardly been silent.

Until now, Aunt Peronel had refused to believe that anything could disturb the settled complacency of her privileged life. An invading army was unthinkable; therefore she could not bring herself to think about it. The news Nicolas brought had driven her into a fit of the vapours, and when she recovered she was inclined to blame everybody else for what she saw as a personal misfortune.

From somewhere below came the crash of breaking crockery, and another shriek of fury. Tiphaine sighed, putting on her cloak, and picked up the travelling bundle she had already packed.

Then she paused. She had never given thought to her jewels, knowing that she would not need them on her journey, but now she realized that, when they arrived in Gwened, they would badly need money for food and lodgings.

Throwing open the chest at the foot of her bed she took out the leather pouch which held the rings and necklaces her aunt had bought for her – using Tiphaine's own money – since she had come to Roazon. None of them had meant anything to Tiphaine, except – as she thrust the pouch into the bundle among her underthings, she could feel its curved outline – the swan circlet Bertrand had given her on winning the tournament.

Not that, she thought. *I will never sell that.*

She picked up her bundle and went to the door. Pausing with her fingers on the handle, she looked back round the room that she had occupied for such a comparatively short time. It meant nothing to her either, and her only regret would be her grandfather's books, piled neatly on the table under the window.

She had studied so assiduously, trying to understand the world, and now she was forced to leave it all behind.

Consciously she straightened her back, holding her head high. Now she would leave other things too; not tangible objects like her books, but the naivety that had let Aunt Peronel mould her – and the mistake that had bound her to Cousin Nicolas.

Somehow, she promised herself, she would find a way to release herself from their betrothal. Tiphaine de Bellière would decide her own future.

Down in the entrance hall, her aunt was piling up bundles, boxes and corded bales, fluttering from solar to kitchen and back again, scolding the servants and lamenting their exodus.

'Mother!' Nicolas was exasperated. 'You can't take all of this stuff with you. I explained, just what you can carry.'

Aunt Peronel stopped and stared at him, wisps of hair straying around a face reddened from her exertions. 'Don't be absurd, Nicolas! How can I possibly carry everything I

shall be needing in Gwened? Count Fragan will be summoning us to court, and you cannot expect me to present myself
in my shift.'

A familiar shriek of outrage put an end to her flood of
words as Tiphaine, coming down the last few steps, stopped
in front of her aunt.

'Stupid girl, you look like a peasant in those old rags.
Go and change into something smarter *at once!*'

'Aunt, we've a long way to travel—'

'She's right,' Nicolas said curtly, before Tiphaine could
finish. 'We'll be days on the road and we won't find inns
every night. She is dressed just as she should be.' He spoke
as if at the end of his temper.

Tiphaine reflected, with some wonder, that she had just
heard perhaps the only true compliment he had ever paid
her.

Aunt Peronel stared, as if contrasting Tiphaine's worn
gown of dark blue linen with her own beribboned silks. She
opened her mouth as if to protest, but closed it again with
a disgusted snort.

'Nicolas,' Tiphaine said, 'is there a cart we could hire?'

'Of course, a cart,' Aunt Peronel said approvingly. 'And
some horses. Go and see to it, Nicolas.'

'Mother, there are no horses left,' Nicolas replied tiredly.
'I might manage a handcart, I suppose. But be ready to leave
as soon as I get back.'

He went out quickly before his mother could make any
more demands. Aunt Peronel sniffed disdainfully and vanished once more into her solar.

A maid appeared at the top of the stairs at that moment,
her arms filled with frothing silken petticoats.

'Leave those, Mari,' Tiphaine said. 'Go and find some
blankets instead.'

The girl rolled her eyes, and went back the way she had come. Tiphaine set down her own bundle and began investigating the mountain of baggage her aunt had assembled, wondering how much of it was really useful, and how much they would need to leave behind.

Just inside the causeway gate, a small crowd of women and children had already gathered, along with the men who had come to say goodbye to them. Nicolas pushed his way through them to the gate itself.

His mother's two menservants had manoeuvred a small handcart down the steep streets and stairways of Roazon, and put it down with sighs of relief. Aunt Peronel sank down on it at once, fanning herself with her hand. 'Where has my son gone?' she said loudly, and turned to the nearest servant. 'Go and find Sir Nicolas at once and tell him he must fetch horses for us. It's absurd to think of our walking all the way to Gwened.'

The servant she had addressed touched his forehead respectfully. 'I'm sorry, ma'am. We've been summoned to join the watch guarding the walls. We must leave you now.'

Aunt Peronel's voice again rose to a screech. 'Don't be absurd! I need you. Who will push the cart?'

Tiphaine swung away from her in embarrassment, and almost cannoned into a young woman with a baby in her arms.

'I'm sorry.' Tiphaine stepped back, briefly thinking that caught recognition in the woman's face. But Tiphaine felt she had never met her before, so she must have been mistaken.

'That's all right.' The young woman smiled at her.

'My aunt doesn't understand what all this is about,' said Tiphaine. 'Are you going to Gwened too?'

'Yes, to begin with.'

Tiphaine felt encouraged at the thought that she might have found someone to share the long road with, a relief from the constant demands that Aunt Peronel and Nicolas would doubtless make on her. 'I'm Tiphaine de Bellière,' she announced boldly.

'My name is Alissende.'

But before Tiphaine could say any more, her aunt called out, 'Tiphaine, go and find Nicolas at once.'

With an apologetic glance at her new friend, Tiphaine headed through the gates. Outside the city walls, away from the dusty street, the air seemed cooler, a faint breeze blowing over the gentle lap of lake water. Tiphaine caught sight of her cousin at once, standing at the far end of the causeway. She could tell from his stance that he was furious. He was addressing another young man, who was sitting on the grassy edge of the lake.

As Tiphaine crossed the causeway towards him, she heard Nicolas demanding, 'What do you mean, gone? Gone where?'

The young man shrugged. 'To Gwened, I suppose. More of the Gwened guard turned up, with news that Count Fragan had been defeated — killed, maybe. Then they tried to enter the city but the city guard prevented them. So they rode off towards Gwened. And all your lot, too.' He jerked his head towards the road leading south.

'And why are you still here, then?' Nicolas sounded disgusted.

The boy smiled up at him sunnily. 'I'm your prisoner, remember. Besides, they made off with all the horses.'

Nicolas let out a foul curse, then realized that Tiphaine was standing quietly beside him.

'Your mother wants you,' she explained.

'Then she'll have to wait.' Nicolas ran his hands through his hair in a wild gesture of frustration. 'How am I supposed to get a party of women and children to Gwened without horses or even an escort?'

The young man shrugged again.

'Oh, take yourself off.' Nicolas spat out the words. 'You'll do so soon enough. I can't keep watching you day and night.'

The boy got to his feet, but made no move to go. 'On the other hand, we could make a bargain. Your women need protecting, so I'll join you on the road to Gwened. But when we reach the city, I go free.' As Nicolas hesitated, he added, 'I can use a sword, and you need help, Sir Nicolas.'

'Very well,' Nicolas said ungraciously. The youth held out a hand, and reluctantly Nicolas took it. 'Wait here, then,' he said, and hurried back across the causeway.

Tiphaine was left face to face with the young man who, she realized, was very handsome. 'It's good of you to help us,' she said at last.

She turned away, in time to see Nicolas reappear, and the little crowd of people he was escorting straggled out after him. Aunt Peronel was there, too, with Mari pushing the cart. Not far behind, Tiphaine spotted Alissende with her baby. The man accompanying her went back to the city in silence.

As the gate closed behind him with a hollow sound, Tiphaine waited for her new acquaintance to catch up, then both turned to face the road to Gwened.

Eighteen

I

King Aymon exhaled in deep satisfaction. Everything – the powerful muscles of his bay warhorse, the smooth upland turf speeding by under its hooves, the bright blue-and-gold banner of Brogall, snapping in the wind of his company's passing, the sun itself smiling on him with favour – conspired to make him certain of success.

The pitiful force Count Fragan had mustered against him had seemed no more than a nuisance. The men of Arvorig fought well, Aymon had to confess, but they had little training in war. They could ply their weapons, but they had no strategy. The troops from Brogall, skills honed from years of skirmishing with the sea raiders on their northern borders, had scattered their opponents like leaves before the wind.

Nothing stood now between Aymon and Roazon.

As his horse breasted a swelling rise in the moorland, a wide tract of country opened up ahead. Aymon raised a hand to signal a halt to the troops behind him, and drew rein. Below him, in the distance, he could see the lake and the city.

The lake lay like a blue jewel among green meadowland patched with squares of stubble, the harvest already gathered, and now parched pale by the sun. Roazon itself glittered in the midst of the water. The king almost felt that he could stretch out a hand and pick it up like a child's toy.

Further still, on the edge of sight, a mass of misty darkness marked the border of the forest of Brecilien. A road led towards it; yet another looped around the lake and struck off in the direction of Gwened. Yet nothing moved in all this landscape.

Of course, the citizens of Roazon would know of his coming, Aymon reflected. Some of Count Fragan's soldiers, fleeing the battlefield, would have brought them the news. The city gates would be shut against him, its walls manned.

Well, thought Aymon, *that only makes it more interesting.*

He drew his sword and raised it high above his head, averting his eyes from a dazzling blaze of white fire as sunlight touched the blade. 'To Roazon!' he cried. 'For God and Brogall, to Roazon!'

He had always known how to hearten his troops.

From behind him, the roar of many voices echoed. 'To Roazon!'

As he set spurs to his horse and sent it thundering down the slope towards the lake, outstripping even his banner bearer, King Aymon was thinking how, if Maugis were still within the city and keeping his wits about him, the siege should not last very long.

2

Alissende blew gently on the first flicker of flame as it crept among the nest of twigs she had arranged for it. Responding, the flame leapt higher; the kindling crackled as it caught. She smiled in satisfaction, squatting back on her heels, and began to feed it with ever larger branches.

Opposite her, across the growing blaze, Tiphaine de Bellière was seated, with Ivona in her lap, clasping her safe as the little girl stretched out her hands towards the brightening flame.

As the sun had gone, the party of refugees had turned off the road to make camp under the trees. The soft murmur of a river was heard through the gathering twilight.

'We must be somewhere near your home,' Alissende said, having by now discovered who Tiphaine was, and all the story of her betrothal to Sir Nicolas de Cotin, who led their party. A week on the road together had consolidated their friendship.

She also remembered where she had seen Tiphaine before: the young girl of her vision in the scrying bowl. Why God had revealed that to her, or why he should want them to know each other, Alissende had not fathomed yet.

Tiphaine nodded. 'A mile or so down the road, there's a bridge that takes the road to Bellière.' She sounded wistful. 'I used to ride through these woods with my grandfather.'

'Don't you want to go back there now?' Alissende asked.

'Oh, if only I could!' Tiphaine cast a longing look in that direction. 'But it's no use wishing. I have to go to Gwened with Nicolas.'

Alissende found that hard to understand. 'Why don't you – ?' She was interrupted as Oliver, their young escort, appeared out of the dusk and dropped a rabbit he had caught at Alissende's side.

'Supper, ladies,' he announced. 'May I share your fire?'

From the first day of their journey, Oliver had befriended them, making no attempt to hide how he admired them both. He seemed very young to Alissende, at the sort of age when he could easily fall in love with any remotely pleasing girl, and Tiphaine at least was very beautiful.

Alissende herself had become adept at turning aside his compliments without being hurtful, and he had never behaved with anything but the utmost courtesy and respect to her. His merry laughter and his singing certainly shortened the tedious road.

Tonight, however, his cheerfulness seemed subdued as he settled down, drew his belt knife and silently began to skin the rabbit.

'Is anything the matter?' Alissende asked at last.

Oliver looked up, his open features betraying uneasiness. He glanced round to ensure no one else was in earshot.

'We're quite close to Bellière,' he said.

'Yes, we are,' said Tiphaine. 'But why should that bother you?'

Oliver hesitated, as if he was wondering whether to continue. Alissende was growing intrigued; so far he had told them nothing of himself.

He paused in his efficient use of the knife, and said, 'I came from there.'

Tiphaine frowned. 'Bellière is my home, Oliver, and I don't—'

'No, lady. I mean I came from there very recently.' Setting the knife aside, he drew closer to them. 'Duke Joscelin is hiding out at Bellière. He's there with some Knights, and my brother Bertrand.'

Alissende felt a tightness in her chest, as if suddenly the forest clearing did not contain enough air for her to breathe. Tiphaine clapped a hand over her mouth to suppress a cry.

'How do you know this?' Alissende kept her voice low.

'I was there with them. We attacked the baggage train

coming from Gwened that Sir Nicolas commanded. That's when I was taken prisoner.'

Almost looking relieved now that the secret was out, he went back to jointing the rabbit.

Alissende prompted, 'Why are you telling us this now?'

'I desperately want to go back to Bellière,' Oliver let out an exasperated sigh. 'But I gave my word to Sir Nicolas, to stay with him until we reach Gwened.' Looking at Tiphaine across the flames, he went on, 'Lady, I thought you might go instead and carry news to my brother Bertrand. Bellière is your home, after all, and you know the way.'

Tiphaine nodded, looking thoughtful; Alissende thought she must be weighing Oliver's request against her solemn betrothal to Nicolas, but when her friend spoke at last it was to say something quite different. 'Is your brother by chance Bertrand d'Acquin?'

'That's right,' Oliver said proudly, with something of his old cheerfulness.

Tiphaine's face had become unreadable, and Alissende thought they would all remember this moment for ever: the hot light that cast moving shadows over their faces, the bitter tang of woodsmoke, the dark encircling trees.

At last Tiphaine let out a long sigh. 'I can't, Oliver. Truly, I want to, but I can't. I'm betrothed to Nicolas.'

Oliver's face showed consternation. 'Lady, you won't tell him what I have revealed?'

'I give you my word,' Tiphaine retorted sharply. 'But I gave it to Sir Nicolas, too. I can't leave now.'

'But I can,' Alissende heard herself saying.

Oliver turned to her swiftly. 'You would do this, lady?'

'If I can. But I have also made a promise,' Alissende said. 'I promised my friends to look after their child. Is that possible at Bellière?'

'Old Nolwen will be there,' Tiphaine assured her. 'She kept house for me and my grandfather for many years. And there's Father Patern, our chaplain, and maybe still some of the servants.'

Alissende felt relieved; she knew the importance of what she could tell Duke Joscelin and his followers, but she would not risk taking Ivona into a soldiers' barracks.

'I'll tell Sir Nicolas you left us to go back to your own village,' Oliver said encouragingly. 'No one will follow you.'

Alissende took a deep breath. 'Very well,' she said, 'I will go.'

Much later that night, when the fires had burned down and the company were sleeping, Alissende wrapped a shawl around Ivona, and slipped off in the dark to Bellière. Tiphaine came with her, stepping silently in her wake until they left the camp safely behind them.

On the edge of the trees, they paused where the rising moon showed Alissende the road stretching straight in front of her.

Tiphaine clasped her new friend's hand in both her own. 'Go safely,' she whispered.

'Thank you. You too, Tiphaine. Goodbye,' Alissende said.

She would have drawn away, but Tiphaine captured her hand for a moment longer. 'When you get to Bellière, commend me to Bertrand d'Acquin.'

She looked so embarrassed, Alissende instantly understood. If Bertrand was as handsome as his brother, Alissende was not surprised. Besides, he would surely make Tiphaine happier than Sir Nicolas could.

Tiphaine released her then, and turned back into the forest. Unseen, Alissende stretched out a hand to her, then settling the child more comfortably in her arms, she set out down the road to Bellière.

3

The wind whipped Lady Marjolaine's hair across her face and she brushed it aside to get a better view of the scene below. She stood on the wall-walk above the causeway gate of Roazon, while below, not much more than a bowshot away, King Aymon's forces were massing.

The gates had been firmly closed now for several days, ever since Aymon and the vanguard of his army had come whirling down from the hills. Not as many as rumour had feared, yet more than enough to deter Marjolaine from joining battle with them. She had few fighting men – the remains of the city guard, who had not left with Count Fragan, and the pitiful few, guards and Knights, who had returned home from the fateful battle in the north. For the rest, the city walls were defended by guildsmen and servants, and Marjolaine would not send those out to be cut down by trained soldiers.

Next she looked north, to see some vast siege engine lumbering down the road. Drawn by draught horses, it was too far away as yet for her to decide what kind of destruction it threatened. More troops escorted it; they were scattered all round the lake by now, the water meadows and the stubble of cornfields defaced by their tents.

The seneschal, leaning against the merlon beside her, raised an arm and pointed. 'Another emissary?'

Following his gaze, Marjolaine noticed movement among

the tents pitched at the far end of the causeway. The herald appeared – a familiar figure by now – and then another man, taller and broader-shouldered, with a lion's mane of hair. Over his mail he wore a blue surcoat blazoned with the golden lilies of Brogall.

The seneschal let out a soft whistle. 'King Aymon himself!'

Marjolaine leant out further, eager to observe her enemy. A strong man moving confidently, lithe and free, he walked out alone to the middle of the causeway and stopped with hands on hips, his head tilted back.

One of the gate guards, a young lad from the armourers' guild equipped with a bow he did not know how to use, slipped an arrow from his quiver.

Marjolaine shook her head. 'Hold off, Rual. He comes in peace.'

The young armourer let out a snort of disgust. Tancred said dryly, 'But don't think we're not tempted.'

'Lady Marjolaine!' the king called out. 'Will you not come down? Let us sit face to face and talk of this. I promise you safe conduct into my camp.'

'And what about a safe conduct out of it again?' the seneschal muttered. 'Does the man think we were born yesterday?'

Marjolaine flashed him a smile. 'I talk with no one who comes against my city in war,' she called out to Aymon.

'We should be allies!' Aymon returned. 'I am here in support of Duke Joscelin.'

'Duke Joscelin does not need your support, sir.'

Aymon launched into a defence of his actions, less eloquent than he might have been because of the need to shout. Marjolaine listened patiently, though he said nothing new or unexpected.

'Open the gates!' the king finished. 'Let us talk as friends.'

Lady Marjolaine laughed. 'I call no one friend, sir, who crosses my borders under arms.'

Suddenly disgusted with this whole profitless exchange, she turned and descended the steps to the inner courtyard, leaving King Aymon to make what he would of her sudden withdrawal. Tancred followed her more slowly.

Down in the courtyard, the guildsmen and guards had gathered close to the gates to listen to the exchange, and Marjolaine heard laughter. One young man called out, 'Well done, my lady!' and then flushed at his own temerity.

Lady Marjolaine smiled at him, but as she moved away with the seneschal by her side, she murmured, 'He will break in sooner or later. Is it wise to anger him?'

Tancred shrugged. 'Wise? Maybe not. But the alternative is just to open our gates to him.'

She halted, head high, pride surging through her, along with the knowledge that the seneschal had intended exactly that. 'Never while I live!' she declared.

Slowly she made her way back up to the citadel, stopping to talk to people on the street. She had never before known the city so quiet that she could hear the soughing of wind in the trees, the calling of birds. The cries of street traders, the shouts and laughter of children at play, had been already silenced. Feeling the grip of cold fingers around her heart, she knew that this was like the desolation of defeat.

'But we are not defeated yet,' she said aloud.

Marjolaine asked herself — as so many times before — whether there was any hope of help from outside. The other provincial lords retained their own guards, and troops of the Legion in their cities. If they banded together they could put an army in the field to confront Aymon. But that must be soon – before he brought down still more of his men from Brogall, or before he managed to break a way into the city of Roazon.

Lose Roazon, she thought, *and all Arvorig is lost.*

But she had no way now of sending a plea for help to the provincial lords, and no way of finding out how they were reacting to events.

All the while, as these thoughts went through her mind, she continued climbing through the streets, smiling at passers-by, and clasping the hands held out to her, responding to the good wishes of her people with a cheerful manner. By the time she reached the citadel square, the sun was beginning to sink, and the cathedral bells were ringing out their summons to the evening Offering.

At the citadel gate, the Grand Master and a couple of men from the bakers' guild were dealing with the last of the queue for the daily food ration. Father Reynaud's air of austerity had deepened, Marjolaine thought, and somehow it did not seem incongruous to see him here with bread in his hands instead of a sword.

Marjolaine turned to observe Tancred, who looked exhausted, his strength diminished to a ravelled thread, yet his bright spirit still glinted out through his eyes.

'Come with me to the Offering,' she said. 'We are all in God's hands now. We can do no more than pray.'

Tancred's mouth twisted. 'I don't know any words that will pray King Aymon away from our gates,' he said.

Yet he took her arm, and walked with her into the cathedral, beneath the defiant, tumbling bells.

4

Val lay on his stomach in the bracken edging the forest. In front of him, the land sloped gently down to the lakeside. Almost straight ahead he could see the green shrubbery of the Pearl of Arvorig, and behind it rose the stone spear that was Roazon. Very faintly in the distance he could hear the cathedral bells.

Marjolaine would be able to hear them more clearly, he thought, and he wondered what she was doing now. His mother, too, but it was Marjolaine's image that would not leave his mind or his heart. Did she ever think of him? It was arrogant to assume she might — and better for her if she did not. Yet her warm beauty seemed to gather before his eyes, until he could almost smell the rose perfume she wore.

Between Val and the city, Aymon's forces lay camped. Thin pillars of smoke began to rise from their cooking fires as the sun went down. At the outer end of the causeway they had set up a mangonel. Val closed his eyes briefly at the thought of the boulders it propelled crashing into the walls and towers of the city that he loved, at the thought of Lady Marjolaine falling into the blunt, predatory hands of King Aymon.

There was a rustling in the undergrowth behind him as Bertrand snaked his way up beside him, until he too could peer out through the concealing clumps of bracken.

'Aymon is well dug in,' he observed.

'I hope you're not planning to attack them?' Val asked.

Since their fight with the baggage train Bertrand had become more circumspect. Instead of direct assault, he had led small groups out, at first to harry Count Fragan's troops, and then turning his force against Aymon's, after the king of Brogall rode down from the north. He would fall on them at night or in the early morning, mounting a quick raid and then away, before their enemies even realized what was happening.

Even so, Val could never be sure his cousin was circumspect enough. He was augmenting his forces, the crowd of his 'lads' swelling daily as word spread about the resistance movement at Bellière. They almost worshipped him, calling him 'the Black Eagle' from the arms of Acquin he wore on his surcoat, and jumped willingly to do his every bidding. Val realized that if Bertrand did order them to mount a full offensive against King Aymon's army they would obey unquestioningly. They would die willingly, but nevertheless they *would* die.

'I'll leave some of the lads here, to act as snipers in the trees,' Bertrand murmured. 'Aymon's men might find that collecting their firewood gets a bit ... lively.

'We'll head back to Bellière,' he added, 'but, before we do ...' He wriggled himself into a more comfortable position. 'Before we do, we'll leave King Aymon a little something to remember us by.'

Val waited apprehensively until the sun had gone, and night lay thick around them. Bertrand's lads had muffled the horses' hooves with rags, and wound thin strips of cloth around the bridles to stop them chinking. Bertrand himself had disappeared off in the direction of a nearby farm, returning after dark with a basket filled with bread and cheese, a flask of oil, and a firepot.

While they all ate, he explained his plan.

'You're mad,' protested Val.

'I know.' Bertrand's black eyes gleamed in the light from the coals in the firepot. 'But it's going to work.'

Mounting Traveller and patting the horse's neck reassuringly as they advanced softly through the darkness, Val was not so sure but, somehow, no one argued with Bertrand.

Aymon's camp had settled down for the night. A few fires still glowed, and lamplight gleamed behind the silken walls of the royal pavilion. As they drew closer, Val could hear the chink of harness from the horselines, and the tramp of a sentry's heavy footsteps over the turf.

'Now!' Bertrand breathed out.

Three of his lads, their bows at the ready, took arrows bound with oil-soaked rags and dipped them in the firepot. As the rags blazed up, they shot the arrows high into the air, to arc upwards and over, and fall in the midst of the enemy camp.

At the same moment Bertrand lit a branch bound with more oil-soused rags, like a makeshift morningstar, and took off, letting out a fearsome screech.

Val leant over, touching his own branch to the coals, and went after him. His allotted target was the mangonel. He urged Traveller into a gallop across the outer perimeter of the camp, aware of men shouting and scrambling around him in the dark. Someone grabbed for his reins, but Traveller trampled him down.

Bearing down on the mangonel, Val tossed his blazing torch into its framework, pausing for a few seconds to make sure the flame would catch. One of Aymon's soldiers threw himself forward to rescue it, but before he could reach the siege engine Val guided Traveller into his path and the man went down.

Val drew his sword, but the man was too stunned to rise, and when Val glanced back at the mangonel he could see flame creeping up its central beam. He stayed where he was, blocking access to it until the engine was well alight. In the terror and confusion there was no serious attempt to put out the blaze.

Meanwhile more arrows were raining down on the camp, most shot at random, but finding enough targets in tents and baggage to set up a dozen fires and drive Aymon's men into further panic.

At first Val had no idea where Bertrand had gone; then he saw the silken walls of the royal pavilion billow out and collapse, flames shooting up into the sky. Bertrand's squat figure became visible briefly against the blaze, standing up in the stirrups and brandishing his sword. His voice rang out over the yelling and crashing. 'For Roazon and Duke Joscelin!'

'Withdraw, damn you, Bertrand!' Val said through his gritted teeth. His own part done, he began to draw off; a moment later he heard a soft explosion behind him, and saw flames spouting from a pile of barrels next to the blazing mangonel. Pitch, he guessed, as he spurred Traveller out of the wave of heat erupting from the pile, meant to be lit and flung over the city walls. Not any more, he thought with savage satisfaction.

As he passed the edge of the camp, a soldier came running out at him, waving a pike. Val's sword sheared through the weapon's wooden shaft, and on the backstroke sliced at the man's arm. Then he was safely through, and galloping for the forest.

Hearing the drumming of hooves on the turf at his side, he realized with relief that Bertrand had caught him up. His cousin's face, smeared with soot, wore a look of wild exultation. Behind them a horn sounded the alarm call, over and over, but no one pursued them.

They slowed down as they reached the three archers, who turned and ran beside them back into the shelter of the trees. At the edge of the forest Val reined in and looked behind him.

Ribbons of fire were spreading right through the king's camp. At the causeway the mangonel and the pitch barrels were now one vast bonfire, shooting a myriad sparks up into the night sky. Smoke drifted out over the city and the lake. Against the red glare, the shapes of men, small at this distance, stumbled and gesticulated and fell to fighting each other.

Val heard Bertrand heave a happy sigh. 'Wonderful!'

'It won't stop the king,' Val warned, through his own feelings of triumph.

'No, but it will make him think,' said Bertrand. 'And it will tell Roazon that they're not alone.'

'Not when the Black Eagle fights for them!' exclaimed one of the archers eagerly.

Laughing, Bertrand bent down to clap the boy approvingly on the shoulder. 'Come on,' he said to his cousin. 'Let's go home to Bellière.'

Nineteen

When she arrived at Bellière, Alissende was disappointed to find that Bertrand d'Acquin was not there, and rather daunted to discover a commander of the Legion in charge in his absence. But five minutes spent with Sir Guy de Karanteg himself had reassured her.

'A remarkable man,' he had commented to her, over breakfast the morning after her arrival. 'He has a whole army of followers gathering out there.' He waved a hand in the direction of the forest. 'Somehow he finds money, and supplies, and has even sent to Acquin for his old armsmaster to come and train them.' He refilled his ale mug. 'They call him the Black Eagle, and they worship the ground he walks on.'

Alissende wanted to share his enthusiasm, but just the mention of an army gathering chilled her. War was spreading out across Arvorig, which had always been so peaceful a land. What did its people know of battles, and how could they fight the mighty King Aymon when so few of them had ever raised a sword in anger?

Sir Guy grew sober again, as if he could read her thoughts by her face. 'Don't worry too much,' he said. 'We'll rout Aymon's army, or die trying.'

'If there must be war,' Alissende said, 'I have healing skills. I'll begin gathering herbs for healing draughts and ointments.'

Sir Guy's weathered features broke into a smile. 'If I were one of these puling priests, mistress, I'd say the Warrior has sent you to us.'

After that conversation, Alissende would take a basket and go daily into the outskirts of the forest, or along the river, to gather herbs. Sometimes she would take Ivona with her; most often she would leave the baby in old Nolwen's good hands.

In the evenings Alissende would go to the Bellière still-room, where she would dry and pound the herbs she had gathered, beginning to build up the stocks that would be needed if ever she had to tend to those wounded in battle.

On these gathering expeditions she saw little of Bertrand's army: sometimes the smell of woodsmoke, or a twig cracking underfoot, told her the forest was inhabited, but the men themselves stayed hidden.

She saw little, either, of Duke Joscelin. He sat down to dine with the company each evening, but remained withdrawn, speaking and eating little. Alissende wondered at how much he had changed since she had first observed him on the hythe, lighting the candle for the late Duke Govrian on the Day of Memories.

By day he seemed to vanish, however, though sometimes he would turn up in unexpected places. Once Alissende found him playing with baby Ivona in front of the fire in the hall; he had folded a kerchief into the shape of a mouse, making the little girl giggle delightedly at its antics.

And once when Alissende entered her still-room, she found him thoughtfully turning over some juniper leaves she had gathered earlier that day.

'My lord,' she said in surprise, dipping a curtsey.

Joscelin turned to her, a sprig of juniper in his hand. 'Mistress Alissende, what is this good for?' he said with his

familiar sweet smile. Until then Alissende was unaware that
he even knew her name.

'Juniper, my lord? Its ashes mixed in water are good for
bathing wounds. And later, when the berries ripen, I can
make an oil that is strong against poisons.'

'Poisons ...' he murmured thoughtfully, twirling the
sprig in his fingers. Then his momentary abstraction lifted,
and with another smile he was gone.

Several days after her arrival, Alissende was taking her
basket into the forest once again, for the day before she had
discovered a tiny, secret stream trickling through the undergrowth. Today she meant to follow it, hopeful of finding
comfrey to help make poultices for wounds.

She had not gone far when she came upon Duke Joscelin
yet again. He sat in the long grass near the edge of the
stream, moulding a handful of clay between his fingers. As
he looked up at the sound of her approach, a ray of sun
striking through the trees burnished his golden hair to a
dazzling aureole, so bright that for a moment Alissende
could not distinguish his features.

Blinking to clear her vision, she bobbed a curtsey, feeling
clumsy and unprepared. Duke Joscelin held out his hand,
the piece of still clay resting in it. 'See.'

From the clay he had shaped a small bird, like a robin
or a sparrow. Though made with little formal skill, yet there
was a liveliness about it, Alissende thought, as if somehow
he had captured the essential spirit of the bird.

His smile reappeared. 'Sometimes,' he began, 'I feel
suffused with strength — something that wells up within
me.' He reached for Alissende's hand, turning it over to
reveal a cut on her forefinger where her knife had slipped
while chopping herbs. His other hand closed firmly over the
wound.

Alissende felt a sharp stab of pain, almost like another blade slicing into her. Then it died away, and Duke Joscelin released her. Alissende drew her hand back, staring at it. Her skin was now unbroken. There was not even a scar.

'My lord . . . this is a wonder,' she said.

She dared to meet his eyes. Blue and guileless, they looked back into hers.

'What am I?' Joscelin whispered. 'Or what must I become?'

Alissende had no answer to the question. *We make plans for him*, she thought. *We discuss, and decide. Even I myself, with my scrying bowl. But what does Joscelin himself want?*

His question repeated itself in her mind. *What am I?*

All his life he had been bounded by the wills of others. Packed off to the monastery as a child because of his father's rebellion. Dragged out again, willing or unwilling, when Duke Govrian died. Finally, driven into exile, by men who were manipulating the Church and the people's faith for their own ends.

Yet here, hiding obscurely in Bellière, he was growing into a power greater than any of them possessed.

Does he want it? Alissende wondered.

Seated before her, his burnished head bowed, he looked young and vulnerable. Alissende wanted to reach out to him, to offer comfort or strength, half aware of how absurd that was, and yet how necessary.

'My lord,' she said, 'whatever you are, we will follow you. We will be whatever you need.' Her voice shook as she spoke.

Joscelin raised his head, and this time his smile was incandescent. 'Sister Alissende.' Joy sang in his voice, like fish flashing silver beneath the surface of a stream. 'You'll find what you need that way.' He was pointing upstream.

It must be a dismissal. Recognizing that her moment was over, Alissende pulled herself to her feet, almost forgetting to pick up the basket.

Sure enough, around the next bend in the stream, she found the comfrey she sought, luxuriant clumps and mounds of it. After what she had witnessed, she barely felt the need to ask how Duke Joscelin had known what she was looking for, or why he had called her 'Sister'.

2

Crowds thronged the streets of Gwened as Tiphaine followed her betrothed towards the fortress. All the rest of their party had left them gradually, some dispersing to villages along the route, others to friends and lodgings in Gwened itself, so that now only she and Nicolas remained, with young Oliver, Aunt Peronel, and the maid Mari.

Her aunt was still complaining, as she had done all the way from Roazon, currently objecting to the crowds, the smells, the weather, the state of her feet. Oliver walked beside her in silence, pushing the handcart with their possessions and gazing around him with a cheerful interest.

Except for Roazon, this was the only large city Tiphaine had visited, and it looked very different. Where Roazon rose to the heavens, bathed in sunlight, Gwened squatted close to the earth. The fortress loured alone, on a bluff above the town, while the town itself straggled down the slopes of a gentle hill as far as the sea. The streets were so narrow that balconies and overhanging rooftops shut out the sky, and even in sunlight most of Gwened lay in shadow. While the gardens of Roazon foamed with green and

constantly exhaled the scent of flowers, Gwened was grey,
and smelt of fish and workaday business.

Other refugees from King Aymon besides themselves
crowded the streets, and mingling with them were soldiers
in the livery of Count Fragan, and other liveries Tiphaine
did not recognize. The followers of other provincial lords
must have made their way to Gwened, and Tiphaine wondered what that signified.

The gate of the fortress was a mighty arch piercing its
thick curtain wall. While Nicolas explained himself to the
guard, Oliver set down the cart and Tiphaine obediently
rooted in their bundles in response to her aunt's demand
for a comb.

She was not at all sure that Count Fragan − if he still
lived − would see them, or care about their appearance if
he did, but it was easier to obey Aunt Peronel than to
argue.

Nicolas' discussion with the guard seemed to take a long
time, and Nicolas was clearly getting annoyed. Tiphaine had
time to comb her hair thoroughly and let Mari fasten it
with a ribbon, before they were finally waved through the
huge gate.

Inside, a narrow thoroughfare wound upwards, flanked
by grey walls pierced with arrow slits. Nicolas began to lead
the way till Oliver, having pushed the cart through the
gateway, stopped and called him back.

Nicolas swung round irritably.

'Journey's end,' Oliver explained amiably. 'I said I would
help you escort your people as far as Gwened, and here we
are, so it's time I went home.'

Nicolas froze for a moment and then moved a few paces
to stand face to face with Oliver. His hand reached for his
sword hilt. 'Home? I don't think so,' he said.

Oliver's cheerfulness was instantly replaced by a mixture of fear and anger. 'What do you mean? We had an agreement.'

'You gave your word!' Tiphaine burst out. 'You shook hands on it.'

Nicolas ignored her. His eyes, narrowed unpleasantly, were still fixed on Oliver. 'I don't make agreements with our enemies.'

Oliver glanced back at the fortress gate, towards the street outside and freedom, only a few yards away. The soldiers on the gate, aware of something unexpected, grew suddenly alert.

'Guards, here!' Nicolas called. 'This man is guilty of attacking troops of Gwened. He is my prisoner.'

As Tiphaine watched, horrified, he slid his sword from its sheath.

The boy had no weapon but his belt knife. 'You bastard, de Cotin.'

'Insults will not help you,' Nicolas sneered. 'You won't leave here without fetching me a ransom.'

Tiphaine saw the colour drain from Oliver's face, but it was anger and contempt that prevailed, not fear. He gathered himself ready to spring at Nicolas and, without thinking, she thrust herself between them.

'Oliver, don't!' she exclaimed.

'Oliver? So you know his name?' Nicolas sounded lazily pleased now. 'Do you know more about him?'

Tiphaine clamped her lips shut as her betrothed seized her wrist and forced her out of his way.

'Don't worry, I'm sure Count Fragan has ways of finding out.'

'You are ... contemptible!' Tiphaine spat out, pulling away from him. 'Do you think I'd wed you after this?'

Nicolas' response was hard. 'You seem to forget, madam, that we are betrothed. Why do you care what happens to this young fool? Or has he been whispering sweet words to you on the journey?'

Oliver pushed forward. 'You're slandering a lady worth a dozen like you. Give me a sword and I'll prove it.'

'Give you a sword?' Nicolas laughed. 'You must think I'm crazy. I don't need to fight you. You're my prisoner.' He raised his sword and laid the point against Oliver's breast. 'Now come with me quietly.'

'Go ... do as he says,' Tiphaine begged, reaching out to touch Oliver's hand. 'Don't let him have an excuse to hurt you.'

The look Nicolas turned on her was murderous. 'Keep your hands off him, you little whore.'

'Nicolas!' Even Aunt Peronel was shocked.

Nicolas grabbed his captive and thrust him up the road, following closely behind with his sword still drawn. Tiphaine cast a glance back at the grinning guards and slowly, hopelessly, turned to follow them.

3

A late flush of roses spilled over the wall, their blossoms barely visible in the sick light of a waning moon, but the heady scent reaching Aurel powerfully, where he paused beneath them to glance up and down the street.

He was still trembling from his latest painful communication with Vissarion, less than an hour before. The ring had burnt so sharply that he wondered his hand was not blackened by it.

Vissarion was growing increasingly impatient. 'You have done *nothing*,' he had snarled venomously.

Aurel could not deny that. He had achieved many things, in Tancred's service, working to strengthen the beleaguered city, but he was still no closer to knowing where Duke Joscelin had gone, or how he might reach him.

Clearly Vissarion did not know either, and his raging frustration was vented on Aurel.

'The gates are shut now against King Aymon, and I can't get out,' he had pleaded.

'Find a way,' Vissarion spat, and even within the tiny compass of the ring, Aurel could discern the anger in his eyes. 'You must leave the city, and find him soon.'

It was that last vicious infliction of pain that had driven Aurel out, in the late watches of the night, to see if he could find some way through the gates, or over the wall. He had begun by approaching the causeway gate, where the guardsmen hailed him in friendly fashion and asked what brought him out so late. Aurel had hastily invented some errand, and withdrawn quickly, defeated.

Next he had climbed up to the wall-walk looking out over the lake. A strong enough swimmer might have dived from there, but Aurel remembered how he had almost drowned, and knew that was one way he could not go.

This time he was approaching the hythe gate. If by some ruse or stroke of luck he could slip out there, he might steal a fishing boat and paddle himself across to the far shore of the lake. But there would be guards here too, he thought hopelessly. He would fail again, and failure would drive him back to the citadel to wait for Vissarion's next assault.

Then, as he stepped softly along the street, clinging to

the deepest shadows under the city wall, he realized that he could not spot any guards. A tendril of fear crept down his spine – not the superstitious dread of Vissarion and his serpent master, but an anxiety more ordinary and practical. What was going on here?

Moments later he found the answer, as he stumbled and fell headlong over something in his path. Biting back a cry of surprise he pushed himself up and found that he had been lying across the corpse of a man. The body lay face down, his cloak making it look no more than a shapeless bundle in the night, and a dark pool was spreading over the cobbles from beneath his head.

Aurel drew in a shaky breath as he realized the dead man was still warm.

A few yards ahead he could make out a second bundle like the first, and beyond that, in front of the hythe gate itself, he detected a movement – no more than a shifting of dark against dark. Then a faint footfall, and a scraping he recognized as the bar of the gate being lifted from its hasps.

Seconds later, the whole gate began to creak open.

Aurel started up, torn between an impulse to flee and the need to know what was happening here. As the opening grew wider, he could see through it the empty expanse of the hythe, and moored beside it some kind of flat-bottomed barge. Rising out of it were dark shapes, that began pouring along the quayside, across the paving-stones of the hythe, and headed towards the gate.

As they approached in silence, Aurel recognized the glimmer of moonlight on chain-mail and drawn swords.

As the first of the invaders pushed their way through the gate, Aurel turned at once and sped back along the darkened street towards the causeway gate.

As he came within sight of the guards there, he yelled out, 'Aymon's men — at the hythe gate!'

The two sentinels on guard snapped to alertness, drawing their weapons and taking off into the night.

Aurel wrenched the gatehouse door open and repeated loudly up the stairs. 'King Aymon's men — at the hythe gate!'

Already others were tumbling down the stairs towards him. As they thrust past him, one paused to speak. 'Take word up to the citadel.'

Then they were gone, all pounding towards the other gate, and Aurel was racing up the main street. As he went, he banged on doors to rouse the townspeople. Shutters were thrown open, angry questions flung into the night, echoing the clamour rising from the hythe gate.

As he stumbled through the entrance to the citadel, he could hear the tocsin clang out behind him. This same bell that had hung above the gate for generations had never been sounded within living memory. Shouts and running footsteps answered it, while Aurel hurried on towards Lord Tancred's chambers.

The seneschal had dismissed all his servants, and now lay sleeping amid tumbled bedding that spoke of the restless tossing and turning of troubled dreams. For all his urgency, Aurel needed to draw breath and paused to gaze down at his master in the light of the last embers from the fireplace.

Even in sleep Lord Tancred looked as if the stresses of the day still clung about him. His dishevelled dark hair strayed across his face, and one hand was flung out wide as if to grasp at something — or perhaps to ward off an evil that only Tancred could see.

Aurel felt an anguish clench within himself. For a few

brief moments it was more painful than anything Vissarion could inflict through that demonic ring – to stand here in Tancred's presence and know that he had nothing to offer which his benefactor could possibly want or need.

Throwing off this self-absorption, Aurel stooped to shake Tancred by the shoulder.

The seneschal came awake all in a moment, starting up with his dark eyes wide and alert. 'What is it, Melin?'

Before Aurel was halfway through his excited account, Tancred was out of bed and wrapping himself in a fur-lined bedgown. He caught up his sword from a chest under the window, snatching his staff in the other hand.

The sound of the tocsin still rose faint but inexorable through the shuttered window. And as Aurel followed his master out into the passage, a terrified servant ran up, and skidded to a halt in front of them.

'My lord ... the gates are breached!'

'I know.' Tancred's response was calm but terse. 'Go at once and rouse the Grand Master. Have him come to the Lady Marjolaine's apartments.'

As the servant sped off, Tancred turned in the opposite direction, and limped rapidly down the lengthy passage towards Lady Marjolaine's chamber, Aurel dutifully following him.

By the time they got there, Marjolaine was already awake. She met them at the door of her anteroom, a dark cloak flung over her nightgown.

'Aymon has broken in,' Tancred announced, his face grim. 'Someone opened the gates for him. So we have a traitor.'

Lady Marjolaine clasped her hands. 'Or Aymon already had spies here. I was afraid of that.'

'And now?' the seneschal asked. 'Lady, command me. Whatever can be done, I'll do for you.'

Lady Marjolaine hesitated, and then slowly shook her head. 'Nothing, Tancred. We always knew it would come to this. Just wait here.'

She retreated into her bedchamber, and Aurel heard her summoning her women before the door closed behind her. Tancred sheathed his sword as he followed into the ante-room, and sat down on a high-backed chair near the empty hearth. Aurel perched himself on a stool nearby.

There was no light in the room except for a guttering torch in the passage outside, slanting through the half open door. Tancred's face was shadowed, his deep eyes beyond Aurel's reading. He wanted to reach up and clasp his master's hand for comfort, but did not dare.

Hurried footsteps outside announced the arrival of a servant — the same one Tancred had despatched to Father Reynaud. Panting, the man gasped out, 'The Grand Master is arming himself. He says he will lead the guard against the invaders ... and the Knights who are left here. He regrets he has no time to come here.'

Aurel could not be sure whether the man's terrified look was from thoughts of King Aymon's soldiery or fear of Lord Tancred's annoyance.

But the seneschal merely nodded. 'Very well. You may go — back to your work, or to your family, or to prepare what defence seems good to you.'

'To the cathedral, sir,' the servant informed him. 'We're going there for sanctuary. Will you not come, too?'

Tancred raised his head, as if listening, and Aurel discerned for the first time, beyond the clamour of the tocsin, the imperative tolling of the cathedral bells.

'No,' the seneschal said firmly, 'my place is here.'
Glancing at Aurel, he added, 'Melin, you must accompany
him, if you wish.'

Aurel shook his head silently, thinking that if he tried
to speak he would only betray his terror.

With a wave of his hand, Tancred dismissed the servant,
then sat in brooding silence until the door of the bedchamber opened. He rose to face Lady Marjolaine, standing
framed in the doorway.

She had dressed in her finest gown of saffron velvet, its
bodice encrusted with flashing jewels, its skirts rich and
heavy with fine embroidery, and sweeping the floor. Her
hair had been drawn up in smooth coils, and netted with
gold and pearls. There were jewels, too, on her fingers and
in her ears.

Smiling, she reached out a hand to Tancred. 'Shall we
go now, dear friend, and receive King Aymon?'

He clasped the hand she offered, raising it to his lips.
'You are a great and most valiant lady,' he declared.

Lady Marjolaine stifled a laugh. 'At least I will not deign
to beg at Aymon's feet.'

Aurel stood a little apart while she and the seneschal
conversed. A wave of black misery was engulfing him as he
struggled with a bitter jealousy of Tancred's love for her.
Even though the Lady of Roazon would never wed her
seneschal, Lord Tancred's heart was truly committed.

Aurel lashed himself. *Did you think he would ever give it to
you?*

He followed a few paces behind as Marjolaine and
Tancred proceeded along the passage and down the stairs.
At one point Marjolaine halted a servant scurrying by. 'Have
some lights set in the Great Hall,' she ordered.

Aurel would not have been surprised if the servant had

simply fled for his own safety, but when they reached the Great Hall there he was, setting light to the torches fixed in their brackets on each pillar, so that a tide of light soon crept up the hall towards the dais at its far end.

Marjolaine went to sit on the high throne that stood beneath a canopy emblazoned in Roazon's silver and black. She carefully arranged her skirts, and rested a hand on each arm of the chair, lightly clasping its carved scrollwork.

Tancred took his customary seat just below her, on the steps to the dais, and laid his staff of office across his knees. His dignity appeared so great that to Aurel the hastily assumed bedgown could have been a prince's robe.

Watching them both, knowing what the end must be, Aurel found he wanted to weep in despair. Instead, he went to stand quietly beside Lord Tancred's chair and received his reward when the seneschal glanced up at him with a wry, almost kindly smile.

The servant, his task finished, vanished without waiting to be dismissed. Already Aurel could hear shouting and the clash of weapons from somewhere not too far off. King Aymon's men must have reached the outer courtyard.

Aurel's palms were prickling with sweat, but he kept his hands loosely linked behind him; it took all his will to stand straight and motionless.

Somewhere a door crashed open, admitting a louder hubbub. A scream and clatter, and the trampling of feet.

Then, from the darkness beyond the doors at the bottom of the hall, a figure clad in mail emerged. His surcoat bore the golden lilies of Brogall, and in one hand he brandished a sword, its blade darkly smeared with blood.

Halting just a moment, he began to stride up the length of the hall until he stood close to the dais. More armed men had followed him, jostling through the doorway and then advancing more cautiously as if they expected some trap.

The leading figure raised his visor, to reveal at last a pair of sharp eyes in a reddened, sweat-streaked face.

'King Aymon,' Lady Marjolaine addressed him evenly. 'Forgive me if I cannot say you are welcome.'

The king hesitated, then let out a short bark of a laugh. 'Welcome or not, lady, what matter? Your gates are wide open, and your pitiful defenders lie dead. Roazon is mine.'

PART FOUR

The Black Eagle

Twenty

'Sister Alissende,' Duke Joscelin began, 'last night you said you would look in the scrying bowl. What did you see there?'

At Bellière the midday meal was over, and Alissende was seated in the tiny courtyard garden. Nolwen had given her linen and thread fetched from the store-rooms, and she was stitching a new gown for the child Ivona, who was growing apace.

The scent of herbs rose around Alissende in the autumnal sunshine; among the leaves of the apricot tree trained along the south wall the last of its ripe fruit glowed like half-hidden lanterns. In a land of scanty harvests, the garden at Bellière seemed an island of abundance.

Since Duke Joscelin clearly knew what she had once been, Alissende had seen no point in concealing it from everyone else. She had told them the story, of how she had left the Matriarchy, repudiating her vows when her family had died, and she had then been persuaded to use her scrying skills for Duke Joscelin's cause.

Now, with her needle poised, she recalled what she had seen on the previous night. 'I saw the banner of Brogall flying from Roazon's citadel,' she said.

'We already know that!' Bertrand d'Acquin got up from his bench and began to pace restlessly back and forth.

'That's no insight of the future. Aymon sits in Roazon, while our master Duke Joscelin is still in exile.'

'Aymon has sent out envoys,' Sir Guy de Karenteg reminded him. None of them had yet come to Bellière but the messages they carried had reached them through Bertrand's network of contacts and gossips in the countryside. 'He claims that he overthrew Count Fragan in our master's name, and bids Duke Joscelin come to take up his own again. But do we consider believing him?'

Bertrand's only reply was a snort of disgust, while Val gave a wry smile. 'Bertrand, let Sister Alissende speak.'

His cousin shrugged. 'Your pardon, Sister.'

Alissende smiled at him. After many days at Bellière, she was still not used to the idea that this man — so dark, rough, clumsy of movement and speech — could be young Oliver's brother, but she had no need of the scrying bowl to know he possessed a good heart.

'I understand your impatience,' she said. 'Sometimes I too am impatient over what the scrying bowl shows me.' She continued, 'I saw a troop of men riding out, though where they were heading I cannot tell. You were among them,' she added, 'riding under the banner of a black eagle.'

Val and his cousin exchanged a glance. 'The banner of Acquin,' Val said.

'But I don't possess one,' said Bertrand, frowning.

Alissende paused, considering. She did not want to tell them that she had seen Morwenna once more, with blood streaming from the places where her eyes should be. That was a vision darker than all the rest, and she did not know what any of them could do to prevent it coming true.

'I saw a dark place under some trees,' she recalled. 'There was a stream nearby, and an old woman crouched beside it, washing linen. She looked up, and smiled, and beckoned.'

Alissende's lips tightened; that smile had not been pleasant. 'Then I noticed that a man stood on the other side of the stream, watching her. It was Lord Tancred, the seneschal.'

'Lord Tancred?' Duke Joscelin looked faintly disturbed. 'Is he not still in Roazon?'

Sir Guy shrugged. 'For all we know.' To Alissende, he added, 'What you saw must be the forest of Brecilien, mistress. As for the old woman—'

'The country people know of her,' interrupted Bertrand. 'They call her the Night Washer, and she washes shrouds.' His hand sketched the sign of the Holy Knot. 'May Lord Tancred have the sense to avoid her.'

'Country tales . . .' Val said, though he sounded uneasy.

'There's more in the forest of Brecilien than you or I have ever seen there, Cousin,' Bertrand retorted. 'We follow the bridle paths and ride safely, but no one knows what lives in the deep, secret heart of it.'

Alissende shivered; she did not want to dwell on that vision any longer. There was nothing any of them could do to help Tancred if what she had scried should come to pass.

'And was there more, Sister?' Val asked courteously.

'One vision more,' she said. 'I saw men being led away from Roazon in bonds. They were guarded by horsemen wearing the blue and gold of Brogall. Of the prisoners many were men, and a few women, and they took the road leading north. Then that image changed, and I saw them camped for the night, ringed by sentries.'

'Prisoners leaving Roazon,' said Val, brows drawn together in a puzzled frown. 'What is Aymon thinking of? And who were they?'

Bertrand gave him an answer. 'Guildsmen – who else? Fragan has already drained the city of fighting men. Now Aymon takes the guildsmen away . . . Less of a threat to him, scattered throughout Brogall, and fewer mouths to feed inside the city. Aymon isn't stupid. Cousin, I'm minded to lead some of our lads up north to free these prisoners.'

Val swivelled round to stare at him.

'I've men in the forest, spoiling for a good fight,' Bertrand went on. 'Sister, how many of Aymon's soldiers did you see?'

Alissende closed her eyes, trying to recall the vision. 'Fifty at least,' she said, trying to decide whether she felt hopeful or appalled to hear what Bertrand was planning. 'All mounted and well armed.'

'And none of them expecting trouble.' Bertrand's chin was thrust out aggressively. 'We'll massacre them.'

'That's all very well.' Val glanced with a glint of amusement at his cousin. 'I'm sure *you* could wipe them out single-handed, but how can you attack if you don't know when these men will leave the city? You can't keep a large force camped near Roazon – not without Aymon finding out.'

Bertrand looked uncertain for a moment. 'Sister?'

Once again Alissende closed her eyes, summoning up the details of what she had seen: the column of men on the road, the prisoners stumbling as the mounted soldiers urged them on, and then their camp at night, the fires leaping high in the darkness, the moon floating low over the hills . . .' She drew in a breath of excitement. 'Yes . . . The night they camp – the moon is full!'

'Ah . . .' Bertrand let out a long sigh of satisfaction, and then began to count on stubby fingers. 'Eight nights – seven days more. Not long to muster our men and ride. Did you see anything more, Sister?'

'No,' Alissende said, 'not in that scrying. But tonight I will try again.'

Sir Guy nodded. 'Thank you, Sister.'

'Meanwhile,' Bertrand said, beginning to pace again, 'we need to decide what to do with these guildsmen once they're freed.' Alissende smiled at his blithe self-confidence. 'They might come and join us here . . .'

'If King Aymon—' Duke Joscelin began, and then broke off, his head raised as if listening carefully. 'More news is coming,' he said.

The outside door from the keep flew open and one of Bertrand's lads dashed, panting and excited, into the garden. 'My lords, there's news—'

Bertrand swung round, eyes gleaming with excitement. 'What?'

The boy gulped for breath. 'The water bailiff brought it in, sir. He heard it from a pedlar, who heard it in a tavern in Gwened.'

'But what is this news?' Sir Guy asked impatiently.

'Count Fragan has sent letters out to all the provincial lords,' the boy said. 'He's calling a Council in Gwened, at the Feast of All Angels, to discuss what they should do about King Aymon.'

'I thought Count Fragan was dead,' said Sir Guy.

'Apparently not,' said Val. 'But does he still think he can steer the affairs of Arvorig?'

'He's a fool if he does,' said Bertrand.

'Of course he's a fool,' said Sir Guy. 'Blinkered to everything but the chance of setting his son Tariec on the throne of Roazon. If he really survived that battle, I'm not surprised he's trying again.'

The three men looked at each other questioningly; Alissende could almost see calculation winging from eye to eye. Eventually Bertrand thought to dismiss the boy. 'I don't suppose Bellière has an invitation to this Council,' he said.

A broad grin spread over Sir Guy's face. 'You wouldn't dare . . .'

Bertrand returned the grin. 'Try me.' He began prowling the garden again, excitement evident now in every move he made, instead of frustration. 'Listen – Count Fragan can only want to persuade the provincial lords to muster an army against Aymon. What other choice has he? And we have men enough here now to become a player in the game. Of course we're going to Gwened. We'll take all the Knights Legionaries with us,' he added, with a nod to Sir Guy, 'and we'll mount a dozen of my lads as escort. Count Fragan will be so pleased to see us.'

Val eyed Sir Guy, who shrugged. 'No point in arguing.'

'In that case,' Alissende said, fastening her needle in the unfinished skirt of Ivona's gown, 'I'd better leave this aside and stitch a banner for you.' She smiled at them. 'Trust me, my lords. The Black Eagle shall ride to Gwened.'

2

Lady Marjolaine de Roazon was standing once again at the peephole in her solar. King Aymon had been keeping her safely confined to her own apartments, except when it pleased him to share her company, but he had no idea that she had this means of spying on him.

The midday banquet was over, when Aymon had summoned her to his table and greeted her with bluff courtesies all the more annoying because Marjolaine knew that they were sincere. Now all her attention was fixed on what was taking place below.

King Aymon himself occupied the ornately carved chair where Marjolaine had waited for him on the night his men had breached the city gates. Sir Baudet de la Roche, the ambassador, released now from his imprisonment, occupied Lord Tancred's seat. The seneschal, Marjolaine's servants told her, was confined as she herself was, and she had seen nothing of him since the city fell. The thought made her anxious — since the uncompromising seneschal was likely to cross King Aymon sooner or later — but she now tried to put him out of her mind and concentrate on the scene below.

Some guards had just escorted Master Eudon, the Head of the Guild Council, into the hall. They prodded him forward with their pikes, until he dropped to his knees at the foot of the dais in front of the King. His face was a doughy white, his mouth slack with fear; sweat beaded on his forehead. Marjolaine pulled back, instinctively avoiding the sight of his humiliation, and then made herself look at him once more.

'You are Master Eudon?' King Aymon's voice was resonant.

The Guildsmaster nodded eagerly, as if relieved that the first question was one he could answer. 'Yes, my lord.'

'Your guildsmen opposed me when I took control of this city.'

This time Eudon's assent was no more than a strangled noise.

'They opposed me, though I came in Duke Joscelin's name, so they are all traitors to their rightful duke.' Aymon smiled as he spoke; though Marjolaine knew it was as false as the king's pretence of support for Duke Joscelin, the assertion carried a spurious ring of truth and honour about it.

Master Eudon could only gibber. 'Traitors ... never, my lord!'

'Traitors,' Aymon repeated. 'And for treason the fitting punishment is death.'

At this, Eudon fell prostrate, babbling pleas for mercy that reached Marjolaine only as an incoherent runnel of sound. Aymon sighed, and nodded to his guards, who grabbed Master Eudon by the shoulders and hauled him to his knees again.

'Yet I will be merciful,' Aymon said. 'Master Eudon, you will take word to all master craftsmen and journeymen in this city — all those who took up arms against me. They are to assemble before dawn tomorrow in the square before the citadel. Let each man carry the tools of his craft, and food for a journey.'

'Yes, my lord ... their tools,' Eudon mumbled obsequiously.

'And have the Guild rolls sent here to me,' Aymon added. 'Inform your guildsmen that each will have his name called out. For each of them who is not present to answer, a fellow guildsman will die.'

There was no threat in his voice, but Marjolaine was in no doubt that he meant what he said.

Master Eudon mopped his face with a kerchief. 'Where ... are they to go, my lord?'

'To my realm of Brogall,' Aymon replied. 'I will not try to hold this city while every street harbours a potential traitor. I shall relieve Duke Joscelin of their presence now, and when he returns I shall find other men, more faithful, to serve him.'

But faithful to whom? Marjolaine asked herself. It was not hard to understand what Aymon was doing. He would both remove a present threat here, and acquire skilled craftsmen for his own realm, where, scattered throughout Brogall, they would be no danger. And if he really meant Duke Joscelin to return here as his puppet, the whole city of Roazon would be filled with men whose first allegiance was to King Aymon.

While she was brooding on this, King Aymon had dismissed Eudon, who backed out of his presence, bobbing and wringing his hands. He was replaced, a moment later, by a shabby and rat-faced stranger. To Marjolaine's surprise, King Aymon grew visibly more good-humoured.

'Maugis, what have you to report?'

'Little as yet, my lord,' the man replied. 'Whenever I send men into the forest, the peasants vanish before them. When we do catch one, he seems to know nothing.' He frowned sharply. 'When I mention this Black Eagle they stare at me with their mouths open, like idiots.'

Aymon snorted. 'Maugis, you've lived all your life in the city, so you don't know about peasants. It's when they pretend to look most stupid that you can be sure they know more than they're telling. Apply torture to one or two — better still, their wives and children.'

'I know what to do, my lord.' Maugis looked stung by Aymon's rebuke.

'Then get on with it, man.' Aymon's narrowed eyes gazed into the distance, as if he could see through the walls of the citadel itself, and out across country to the eaves of the forest. 'He's out there, somewhere. My men can't set foot outside the walls now but he harries them. He raids my baggage trains and my troops arriving from the north. He won't defeat us, but he's a cursed nuisance, and I'll have him, with your help or without it.'

'I've not failed you yet, my lord.'

'No.' Aymon's geniality had vanished now. 'You handed me Roazon when you opened its gates, but you could fail me, just like the next man.' He waved a hand in dismissal.

As Maugis left, his face was like a louring thundercloud.
Marjolaine moved away from her peephole and sat down in
thought. So that was the man who had let the king's troops
into the city. Not a traitor, then, but one of Aymon's own,
planted beforehand. But who was this Black Eagle, who was
causing Aymon so much annoyance?

Caught up in her anxiety, Marjolaine did not hear
anyone approach her door until it began to open. Swiftly
she snatched up her embroidery and was sitting with head
bent demurely over it as the king came into her room.

She rose, but did not curtsey. 'My lord?'

'Lady.' Aymon strode over to the window and poured
himself a cup of wine from the jug on the table there.
Taking a handful of sweetmeats he came back and flung
himself into the chair opposite her. 'Are you well? Is there
anything you need?'

Freedom. My city. My people safe ... Marjolaine reseated
herself. 'No, my lord, nothing.'

The king sat chewing a piece of candied orange, a vaguely
discontented look on his face. Nothing surprised Marjolaine
more than the way he made at least an attempt to treat her
decently, and she could not help wondering what his ultimate
plans for her were. Count Fragan would have married her to
his son Tariec; had Aymon perhaps a younger brother or a
favoured cousin who might be rewarded with her hand? Did
he hope to make her amenable by his attentiveness?

'Lady, nothing would please me better than to see you
wedded to your betrothed,' Aymon said. 'But that cannot be
until we know where Duke Joscelin is. Have you really no
word of him?'

So the wind sits that way. 'Nothing, my lord,' Marjolaine
said aloud. 'And I marvel that you think I might do, kept

confined here as I am. Do you think that birds fly through my windows with messages?'

Aymon chuckled as if he thought she had meant to be amusing. 'No, lady, but you and I know there are other ways. Or you might perhaps have some thoughts as to where Duke Joscelin is likely to have gone. I have already searched the monastery at Brociel, to no avail,' he added.

'Of course, that is the first place you would look,' Marjolaine said tartly. 'Do you think Duke Joscelin is stupid?'

'No, lady, but he may be desperate ... not realizing that I have his welfare at heart.'

'Of course, he is unlikely to realize that,' said Marjolaine. She set a few stitches in her embroidery while Aymon gulped the last of the sweetmeats and sat in ruminating silence. After a while, she said, 'My lord, there is one thing you might do for me.'

'Name it,' said the king. 'Though that's no promise, mind.'

'Some of my women left me before you set siege to the city,' Marjolaine began cautiously, as her idea unfolded. 'I find myself ill-served.'

'If I can do anything ... but there are no women in my retinue. Will you have anyone sent up from the town?'

'There is a woman closer by I might employ, at present kept a prisoner by the Legion,' Marjolaine went on. 'She was detained for questioning over the matter of Duke Joscelin's heresy.' She smiled at Aymon with an attempt at artlessness which both of them knew was false. 'But since, my lord, you support Duke Joscelin's cause, you will think little of the charges against him ... or against this Morwenna. Might she be released to me here?'

Aymon smiled reflectively, turning his cup about; a few beads of wine slopped over the lip. As he drew out a kerchief to wipe his fingers he kept his eyes on Marjolaine. 'And for this, lady, what would you give me?'

'My thanks, my lord. What else have I to give?'

The king grunted, not entirely displeased with her answer. 'Well, you may have her, lady. If only to release her from under the nose of Father Reynaud and those psalm-singing Knights.'

As Marjolaine thanked him, she was aware of a spurt of genuine gratitude. Any truly evil man would have kept Morwenna from her for the exercise of his own power. 'And may I also write a note to her husband, my lord? He is a silversmith, and he could perhaps visit her here,' she added, remembering she was not supposed to know that the guildsmen were being deported from the city.

Her captor shook his head. 'He may not. But write your note – leave it unsealed, so I may read it first, then have it delivered.'

That was no more than Marjolaine had expected. Thanking him again, she reflected that she had manoeuvred him to where she wished him to be. For that he deserved a few days of smiles and compliance – and meanwhile, she would decide what her next move could be.

3

Bertrand raised a hand, pointing ahead to where the winding road vanished around the shoulder of a hill. 'There's Hoel,' he said, a tinge of excitement in his voice.

Val could make out the figure, tiny at this distance, mounted on a hardy moorland pony. All day they had been tracking the men from Roazon, keeping well back except for Hoel, whom Bertrand had sent ahead to act as scout.

Now the sun was going down; before long the full moon would hang in the sky.

'They're making camp,' Hoel gasped as he galloped back up to the head of the column, reining in his mount with a scatter of stones across the road.

'Good.' Bertrand raised a hand signalling his men to halt, and stood up in the stirrups so he could address them. 'Let's rest here for an hour,' he called. 'Eat, and get your weapons sharpened. We'll give Aymon's men time to get drunk and sleepy.'

A gust of laughter swept along the column as the men dismounted, though Val thought he could detect a nervous edge to it. He was not surprised by that; he felt nervous himself. Though most of these men by now had taken part in previous skirmishes, this was to be their first pitched battle.

Val sat down at the edge of the road, pulling bread and cheese from his saddlebag, with a leather flask of water. Beside him, Bertrand was telling a scurrilous story to a group of his lads, something concerning a tavern wench, a priest and a goat. Val was still not quite used to the way his young cousin had grown up in these last weeks. Since they had left Acquin, Bertrand had become more self-confident; he had found poise and authority. Val wondered what Jeanne d'Acquin would think when she next encountered her elder son, and concluded, regretfully, that she would still see no further than Bertrand's ill-made outside appearance.

As they rested, the daylight gradually died, and a full moon lifted above the hills, turning the rough moorland grass to a tapestry of silver. Bertrand rose to his feet.

'Right, lads,' he called out. 'Time to send Aymon's pigs squealing back to the north!'

Laughter and a ragged cheer greeted his words. Someone shouted, 'For the Black Eagle!' and the rest of the men took up the cry. 'The Black Eagle!'

Bertrand grinned and ducked his head.

Val said clapped him on the shoulder. 'They'd follow you to hell.'

For some reason, these words completely sobered Bertrand. 'The Warrior forbid I should ever lead them there, Cousin.' He made the sign of the Holy Knot.

He mounted, and led the column up the road. When they came to the gap between the hills, he halted his men again and rode on with only Val by his side, keeping to the grass beside the road to muffle the sound of their horses.

A little way further, and the road wound round a scatter of enormous boulders, before it dipped into a hollow where Aymon's men had made their camp. As soon as he saw the torch lights, Bertrand dismounted and crept forward on foot, motioning to his cousin to do the same.

From behind a rock, Val peered cautiously down into the hollow. Fires had been lit in a rough circle around the perimeter, inside which King Aymon's men were sitting. Sentries patrolled the outer ring, while in the centre of this circle huddled the guildsmen, roped together, either curled on the ground or sitting with their heads bowed on their knees.

On a strip of grass to one side of the main camp, were tethered the horses, and sentries stood nearby to guard them.

Leaning on the rock next to Val, Bertrand bared his teeth in a grin that held no humour in it. 'Those are fine men,' he murmured, 'and there are many of them. It will be a great pity to see them flee.'

Val saw a deadly purpose in every line of his face, every muscle of his body. Bertrand jerked his head backwards, beckoning Val to retreat, and said no more until they had returned to the main body of his men.

Even there, he had no need to say much, for their plan had been made long before. Sulien de Plouzhel and a handful of the lads abandoned their horses and trod softly up the road, sacks of damp kindling over their shoulders. Val formed up with Lucien and Hervé, the remaining Knights Companions, while Bertrand led the rest of his men.

Quietly they followed Sulien. Among the boulders a couple of men were now tending a pile of smouldering kindling, while clouds of smoke billowed out and over the camp. Val could hear cries of alarm, shouted orders, and the panic-stricken neighing of a horse.

Bertrand drew his sword and lifted it high above his head. With his other hand he raised a hunting horn to his lips and blew a challenge. Then, spurring his horse, he pounded off up the road. No need for concealment now, so Val took off after him, galloping at his shoulder as the road led them down into the hollow, leading his Knights like arrow-flight into the centre of the camp and the captive guildsmen.

Aymon's men-at-arms rose up at them, but the horses trampled them down again. Val reached the nearest guildsmen, who had started up, their fear changing to triumph as they recognized the white surcoats of the Legion.

Val's sword sheared through the ropes that constrained them, then Lucien and Hervé pushed weapons into their hands, which they had carried in sacks hanging from their saddles — swords, knives, maces, whatever they could muster from the neglected armoury at Bellière. Clamour rose up around them as Bertrand joined battle with King Aymon's men, and the first of the armed guildsmen turned on their captors.

Val reined in Traveller, feeling the horse's muscles tense as he responded to the sounds of battle, and bent over to slice through the ropes that bound the rest of the guildsmen's wrists. When at last no more of them were confined, he gave the warhorse his head, and Traveller pounded out towards the camp perimeter again, where the fighting was now thickest.

As one young Guildsman dashed past him, whirling a mace like a flail, his face distorted by a bellow of fury, Val briefly wondered why he looked so familiar, and then realized this was the silversmith Donan, whose messages he had carried at the behest of Lady Marjolaine, in what felt like another existence.

Loose horses were trampling throughout the main camp, after Sulien's men had cut their tethers. Now the smell of smoke and the leaping flames of the camp fires had maddened the beasts, so that Aymon's soldiers could not catch them and were forced to fight on foot, making them easy prey for Bertrand's mounted troops.

Soon the bewildered enemy were fleeing, or throwing down their swords and kneeling to beg mercy. It was quickly over, and soon the clear call of Bertrand's horn rose in triumph.

Val eased Traveller to a trot, until he located his cousin. He found Bertrand dismounted, standing in front of a kneeling man in Aymon's livery. The man had lost his helmet, blood streaking his face and matting his black beard, but his eyes, fixed on Bertrand, were hot with fury.

'This sorry object is King Aymon's captain,' Bertrand said to Val as he approached. 'I wouldn't be in his shoes when he reports this night's work to his master.'

The captain spat a curse at him; Bertrand replied with a genial smile. 'Tell your king,' he went on, 'that the guildsmen of Roazon are not his slaves. Tell him the Black Eagle has ransomed them. And tell him this.' He grabbed a handful of the captain's surcoat and hauled him to his feet, though he overtopped Bertrand by a head. 'Tell your master that Duke Joscelin knows of his treachery. He will not give himself into his hands, or sit in Roazon as his puppet. Soon our master will drive out King Aymon and claim his own again. In the name of the Healer, tell him that.'

He thrust the captain away from him; the man staggered, his gaze black with hatred. Bertrand turned to greet Sulien as the young man came striding up.

'You're in command now,' he said. 'Let them care for their wounded, and allow what provision they wish for their dead.'

Sulien nodded. 'We have dead and wounded too,' he said soberly. He touched Val's arm. 'Come and see.'

Apprehensive, unused to seeing Sulien look so grim, Val followed him across the campsite. In the lee of a clump of gorse bushes, a man lay on his back. His helmet and half his head had been hacked away, and his remaining features were mantled with blood, but enough remained for Val to recognize Sir Lucien de Gwern, youngest and latest of the Knights Companions.

'Dear God, no,' Val whispered, making the sign of the Holy Knot. 'What am I going to tell his mother?'

The words reminded him of his own mother, Regine. Was she still in Roazon? Whatever fate sent her, she would meet it gallantly, he knew. But that did not ease the painful fear of loss.

Beside him, Sulien was murmuring a prayer for the dead. Blinking away his tears, Val looked out over the battle-ground. As the smoke dissipated, he could see a scatter of other bodies, guildsmen and warriors, some moving, others lying still under the cold moon. Not many casualties, fortunately, but a sick regret gathered in his throat for those who would never ride home again. For Lucien especially, for so much promise and eagerness blighted like a winter rose.

Quick footsteps announced Bertrand's arrival. He saw Sir Lucien's body and paused briefly before turning to his cousin. 'We must ride,' he said. 'We can make the forest before the moon goes down. Remember we have an appointment in Gwened.'

Twenty-One

Tancred de Kervel sat huddled in the window embrasure of his main chamber, gazing out hungrily over the steeps of Roazon, the lake, and the fields, brown with stubble now, that lay beyond.

'Damn Aymon,' he muttered. 'They should be ploughing now, before the frosts. The land's blighted enough, without neglect as well.'

Aurel watched him anxiously. On the night the city gates were breached, King Aymon had ordered Tancred escorted straight to his own apartments. Aurel had followed him, unobtrusively, as though he were Tancred's body servant, and no one had tried to keep him away.

Since then, he had taken on the tasks of the servant he pretended to be. Lord Tancred had barely remarked on his presence, pacing the apartments fretfully as if he could not bear to be still, or alternatively sitting for hours, as he sat now, yearning for the freedom he could see so close at hand.

The king's men guarded the door and brought their food. But, for all his efforts, Aurel could glean no more than snippets of news from them: that Lady Marjolaine was a prisoner too; that the Grand Master had been seriously wounded defending the citadel and lay now in the care of the Matriarch. And that no one knew the whereabouts of Duke Joscelin.

There seemed no hope, and Aurel's only consolation was that Vissarion had not sought him out again through the ring.

Suddenly, heavy footsteps sounded outside the door, and a fist banged on it. Tancred did not stir as the door swung open, though Aurel started up nervously. He had not expected anyone until the time of the evening meal.

One of Aymon's guards tramped into the room. 'Sir Tancred.' There was no respect in his use of the title. 'You're to go down to the hall immediately, to attend the king.'

Lord Tancred's head turned sharply at that; Aurel flinched as he saw his master's lips parted as if for a refusal. The scar looked unusually prominent against his chalky face.

Then he relaxed with a weary sigh. 'Very well. Melin, please bring my staff.'

Aurel was already fetching it. Tancred levered himself to his feet and gestured for the guard to lead the way. Still as quiet, as unobtrusive as he could make himself, Aurel followed them. It was the first time either of them had crossed the threshold since the city fell.

In the great hall, they found King Aymon seated on the dais, and Aurel observed him clearly for the first time. A big man, his long blue velvet robe not concealing entirely the muscular body of a warrior. His curling golden hair and beard gleamed as if they had been oiled, but his face was flushed, anger seething in his eyes.

A man whom Aurel did not recognize, with greying fox-red hair and a foxy face, was lounging self-indulgently in the seneschal's usual seat. Aurel was aware of Tancred stiffening when he saw that.

Close by, below the steps to the dais, was a third man,

wearing mail and a blue surcoat with the golden lilies of
Brogall. In place of a helm, a rough, stained bandage circled
his head, and as Aurel drew closer he could see the man's
face was filthy and lined with pain.

'Sir Tancred.' The king's voice was soft and dangerous.
'Our captain here brings me news. Tell Sir Tancred what
you have just told me.'

'They attacked us by night, and freed the guildsmen,'
the captain explained. 'Him they call the Black Eagle, and
his men, they outnumbered us, my lord.' He turned back to
Aymon, pleading in his voice. 'There was nothing we could
do.'

Aymon let out a long breath of fury. 'Repeat the message
this ... Black Eagle gave to you.'

The captain coughed. 'He said ... Duke Joscelin knows
of my master's treachery. He won't give himself over to
him, or hold Roazon as his servant. Soon he will return to
drive out King Aymon and reclaim his own in the name of
the Healer.' Piteously his eyes went back to the king. 'It
was he who said so, my lord, not I.'

Aymon raised a hand to silence him; it was to Lord
Tancred he now spoke. 'He defies me,' he said softly.
'Through the mouth of this renegade Black Eagle, Duke
Joscelin defies me, though I hold Roazon only in his
name.'

A flicker of some emotion crossed Tancred's face at
that, though he kept his silence. The news had pleased him,
Aurel could see.

Aymon snapped, 'Have you nothing to say?'

Tancred gave him a scarcely perceptible nod. 'Forgive
me, my lord, if I fail to commiserate with you.'

King Aymon banged one fist down on the chair arm,
a flash of anger before he controlled himself again. 'Sir

seneschal, you will tell me now where Duke Joscelin is likely
to be found ... and don't bother to mention the monastery
at Brociel, since my men have already searched it.'

'Then I fear I cannot help you,' said Tancred. 'Detained
as I have been, with none but your own guards allowed near
me, how could I have news of Duke Joscelin?'

A feral look settled on Aymon's face. 'Don't play with
me,' he snarled. 'Which of your provincial lords is most
likely to shelter him? Whose alliance did he seek?'

'Duke Joscelin sought no alliances,' Tancred replied
blandly.

King Aymon let out a curse, then took another breath,
and added more calmly, 'I will be merciful. If Duke Joscelin
presents himself to me here in Roazon, at the Offering on
the Feast of All Angels, he shall have his city restored to
him. If not, I shall know he spurns my friendship.'

'And how is Duke Joscelin to know of this clemency?'
Tancred asked.

'You, sir seneschal, shall send letters throughout the
realm. Have the news cried in every town and village. Make
sure it reaches him wherever in Arvorig he may be.'

'Within seven days? Impossible.'

Aymon shrugged. 'That is my firm decision. I grow
weary of this waiting. Go, do as I bid you.'

Tancred straightened up as the knuckles on the hand
that gripped his staff grew white. 'I will not.'

The king glared at him, but the explosion Aurel had
expected did not follow. 'Sir Baudet,' he said, 'did you fetch
the seal?'

The foxy man occupying the seneschal's seat shifted,
and Aurel saw that he held the great seal of Roazon, that
was normally kept in Tancred's workroom. 'Yes, my lord.'

'Then be prepared to use it. I appoint you Seneschal of Roazon.'

Aurel saw Tancred grow tense, as the guard who had escorted him dropped a hand heavily on his shoulder. For a moment Aurel almost expected his master to spring at Aymon, or at Sir Baudet, who was looking on with a smug smile.

To Aurel's relief, Sir Tancred visibly relaxed again. 'Well thought out, my lord,' he said icily, 'since you will never have any service from me.'

King Aymon waved a hand at the guard. 'Take him back to his chambers. And Sir Tancred,' he added, 'make the most of these next few days, for after the Feast of All Angels I shall have more leisure to attend to you.'

2

Tiphaine de Bellière stood before the mirror while her aunt's maid Mari and a Gwened sewing woman crawled around on the floor, pinning up the hem of her wedding gown. So much lace and silk, so many pearls and ribbons and flounces ... And all to join her to a man she hated.

In less than a week, at the Feast of All Angels, she would become Tiphaine de Cotin, Cousin Nicolas's wife. Nothing could stop that now. It was hopeless — had been hopeless ever since their stupid betrothal, when she had been too naive, too deeply sunk in grief for her grandfather, to understand what Aunt Peronel and Nicolas were contriving.

He had never loved her, she could see that now — only the de Bellière wealth. He would own her just as he would own her lands, and she did not even try to pretend to herself that he would treat either new possession with respect.

For a little while she had entertained herself with fantasies that Bertrand d'Acquin would come riding up – on a white horse, no doubt, like a knight in an old tale, she thought dryly – and rescue her from Nicolas. But she had always known that for a fantasy, and Bertrand probably never thought of her any more.

Worse still, at this time when she needed them more than ever, her visions had deserted her completely.

3

In her own room at Bellière, Alissende sat over the scrying bowl. The table was placed in front of the window, so that she could feel the gentle breezes of evening and overlook the rock on which this castle stood sloping away below until it met the river.

Closing her eyes, she murmured the ritual prayers and composed her mind to meditation. When she opened them again, she saw the surface of the scrying water slightly ruffled and reflecting the pale expanse of twilight, broken only by the distorted disc, the tiny image of the waning moon.

She was half prepared to accept that she would receive no visions that night when the blue-grey of evening turned swirling and translucent ... became a swelling sea breaking coldly over the rocks. She was looking down on it from above, as though she stood on a high cliff, with the waves creaming far below. There was nothing to identify this place to her but, as she gazed, she noticed a turbulence begin far out in the water. Black rocks heaved themselves up from it, the sea cascading down from them as slick dark pinnacles

of stone lanced up into the air. At the same time, she felt
herself take wing and swoop directly down upon them. As
the sharp points rose to meet her, she feared she would be
impaled on them.

In rising panic, she let out a cry, and clutched at the
table edge, feeling its rough surface comforting beneath her
hands. As the water in the bowl rippled, the twilight
returned, and the reassuring reflection of the tiny moon.

Alissende leant forward, gasping and trembling. Just
then, behind her, a voice said, 'Sister.'

She whirled, standing up so quickly that she almost
overset the chair. As the table jolted, the scrying bowl was
rocked and water slopped out of it. In the doorway stood
Duke Joscelin.

'Your pardon,' he said. 'I startled you.'

'It's nothing, my lord.'

He gave her his luminous smile. 'I came to call you to
supper.' Quickly he crossed the room and took her hand.
'Sister, you're shaking. I'm sorry, I—'

'No, my lord. It was what I just saw . . .'

'In the scrying bowl?' Alissende felt his grip on her hand
tighten. 'Tell me.'

'I saw rocks suddenly rising from the sea, like a dark
island . . .' She could not convey the sense of dread that had
swept over her . . . that still clung around her.

Joscelin looked puzzled. 'That sounds like what they tell
of Autrys.'

'Autrys?' Alissende stared at him. 'But my lord, that's an
old tale!'

'A tale that lies close to the heart of Roazon, nevertheless,' Joscelin said soberly. 'For Autrys is Roazon's shadow,
and they say that as long as a true lord rules in Roazon,
Autrys cannot return to this world.'

'You do not rule there now.' Alissende could barely keep her voice steady. 'Yet you still live. How can Autrys return?'

She moved closer to him, and suddenly, without her knowing how it had happened, felt his arms round her. His lips brushed hers, a butterfly touch, and then he buried his face in her hair.

Alissende clung to him, joy and terror transfixing her. He was Duke of Roazon – perhaps he was something even greater than that. He was Joscelin, and he needed her.

They stood holding each other for no more than a moment. It was he who first pulled away, his eyes huge in the darkening room.

'You are a sister of the Matriarchy,' he observed, his voice filled with self-reproach.

'I broke my vows.' Alissende's voice rasped in her throat. 'I left the order.'

Joscelin looked down at his hands, then folded them over the icon he still wore. 'And I am betrothed,' he said. 'I was due to wed Lady Marjolaine at the Feast of All Angels.'

Alissende gave a shaky laugh. 'That cannot be, now.'

'One day, it must be,' he said with resignation. 'I am not free.'

'Do you love her?' she asked.

'I thought so.' He smiled a little, his gaze reading her, so closely that Alissende felt as exposed as if she was naked. 'But I felt ... friendship, that was all.' A slight, self-deprecating movement of the hands, releasing the icon. 'And now ... oh, Alissende, I know truly what love is!'

She reached for him, but he recoiled, saying, 'We are not free.'

Alissende wanted to press herself on him, but she restrained herself. It was the hardest thing she had ever done.

She felt her new power pulsing through every vein. She could pursue Joscelin, but the act would break him. His unique integrity would be utterly shattered if she made him abandon his vows. Without the need of the scrying bowl, she realized that if she forced him down that road they would end by hating each other.

She reached out to him again, and this time he let her take his hand. It felt cold, and she clasped both her own around it. 'My lord,' she said, 'I am here. I am what you would have me be.'

'I know. Dear heart, I know.' He raised her hands to his lips and then released himself.

Something within Alissende screamed *Is this all?* She said, 'We should go down.'

Joscelin nodded, and moved back towards the door. 'This vision of Autrys,' he said, 'let us not speak of it. Not to Sir Guy or any of the others.'

Following him, clutching at composure like a ragged cloak, Alissende knew that she could never speak of anything that had just happened.

Twenty-Two

I

Bearing the banner of the Black Eagle, Sir Valery de Vaux led the way up the main street of Gwened towards the fortress. Bertrand rode behind him; their escort was bunched tightly around them, forging a way through the crowded streets.

The sun was going down into a mass of cloud. Torches flared outside taverns, sending a resinous smoke into the air, and in the main square a market was still going on, the stalls lit by oil lamps and tapers. It was the eve of the Festival of All Angels.

Val dipped the banner in salute as he rode up to the main gate of the fortress, addressing one of the guards. 'The Black Eagle of Arvorig rides to the Council.'

He was prepared for the guard to deny ever hearing of the Black Eagle, and refuse to admit them. The man hesitated for a long moment, looking them over; then, whether through deference to the authority of the Knights Legionaries, or Bertrand's simple self-confidence, he made no protest, only gesturing with his ceremonial falchion. 'Enter.'

Bertrand and his escort rode into the courtyard, where it was obvious that the arrival of lords to the Council was expected. Grooms came out to take their horses, and an indoor servant appeared, bowing obsequiously.

Bertrand cut into his elaborate welcome. 'I want to see Fragan.'

The servant flinched. 'My lord count is at supper.'

'Excellent.' Bertrand gave him a friendly slap on the shoulder that nearly knocked him off his feet. 'Take us to him.'

In the end it was only Bertrand and his cousin who followed him into the great hall, thrusting a way through servants scurrying to and fro with dishes or ewers of wine. Bertrand snagged a leg of chicken from a platter as it went by.

At long tables lining each side wall, the nobility of Arvorig sat at supper. As he passed them, Val recognized the arms of Tregor, Malou and Zol, and no doubt all the rest of the provincial lords were there too, with their retinues, ready for the Council to begin on the following day.

The high table was set beneath a silken canopy adorned in the red and gold of Gwened. Count Fragan sat in the highest seat, and, seeing him, Val barely restrained himself from staring. He had never seen a man so changed: the count's iron-grey hair was now streaked with white, his features pale and slack, and he hunched in rich robes that looked too big for him.

Beside him was his countess, but on his other side the seat which his son should occupy was empty. *Is Tariec dead, then?* Val asked himself. He remembered the rumour that both father and son had perished in their battle against Aymon; perhaps it had been partly true.

Bertrand paced boldly up the length of the hall and came to a halt at in front of Fragan.

'My lord count,' he said, 'I think my invitation to this Council must have gone astray.'

Val suppressed a grin as the countess drew an outraged breath and courtiers further along the table put their heads together, whispering avidly.

Fragan's mouth twisted. 'I know you, Bertrand d'Acquin. So it is you who call yourself the Black Eagle now?'

'My men call me that, at least.' Bertrand tossed the remains of the chicken to one of the hunting dogs sprawled under the table.

'And your companion.' Count Fragan's gaze flicked to Val. 'The captain of the Knights Companions, I believe?'

Val bowed in assent, but did not speak.

'The last time I saw either of you,' Fragan continued, 'was fleeing the hythe at Roazon, by boat.'

'With Duke Joscelin,' Bertrand agreed cheerfully.

Is he mad? Val wondered. He half expected the count to call his guards, and have them both strung up by the thumbs until they confessed where Duke Joscelin was hiding.

Fragan, however, gave no such orders. His sunken features adopted a secretive look. 'We have much to talk about.'

Bertrand was still genial. 'That's why we're here, my lord – to take part in your Council.'

Fragan's brows rose. 'The lords of Arvorig will sit in Council tomorrow, it is true. Do you place yourself on a level with them?'

'I think so, my lord.' Bertrand grinned. 'I have men now, and ... other assets. Enough to bargain for a place in your Council chamber.'

Fragan gestured for a servant to refill his wine cup, and did not speak until he had drunk deeply. 'Very well,' he said, ignoring the look of shocked disdain his countess gave him. 'We will assemble at noon, in the Church of the Holy Lance, to dedicate ourselves to our enterprise. You are welcome, Black Eagle.'

He nodded as if to dismiss them, but Bertrand stood his ground.

'My lord, there is another matter. You have in your service a knight called Nicolas de Cotin. Is he present here?'

The count merely nodded, and gestured towards one of the lesser tables.

Bertrand swung round, the cheerfulness now wiped from his face; he looked dangerous. 'Sir Nicolas de Cotin!' he called out, 'I must have words with you.'

The chatter in the hall died totally. All heads turned, waiting to see what the intruder would do next.

Nicolas de Cotin was seated halfway down the table. He looked annoyed as he got to his feet.

'What is this?' he began. 'D'Acquin, have you no more courtesy than to thrust yourself among your betters? I think you—'

He never finished, as Bertrand shot down the hall like a bolt from a crossbow, thrusting two of the seated courtiers aside so that he could grab his target by the front of the tunic and drag him across the table into a dish of roast venison. A wine ewer crashed over and flooded the linen cloth with crimson.

'You treacherous bastard, what have you done with my brother?' Bertrand hissed.

Nicolas gasped, barely able to breathe in his assailant's grip. One hand seized a belt knife and slashed wildly at Bertrand's arm. But the knight seated beside him grabbed his wrist and pinned it to the table. At Bertrand's grateful nod, he murmured, 'My pleasure.'

At last Bertrand loosened his grip, enough for his purpling adversary to take in a crowing breath. '*Where is my brother?*' he repeated dangerously.

'Your brother?' Nicolas coughed. 'What do I know of your brother?'

'My younger brother whom you took prisoner.'

'My prisoner is your brother?' Nicolas choked again. 'Then you may take him and welcome. His ransom . . .'

'Ransom?' Bertrand roared at him. He thrust him away, so that the knight almost overbalanced backwards off the bench. 'I'm told you swore to release him – and you dare ask ransom?'

Dripping sauce, Nicolas sat up, grasping vainly after his lost dignity. Before he could answer, Bertrand had ripped off one mailed gauntlet and threw it in his face.

'That's all the ransom you'll get from me, de Cotin.'

Nicolas did not touch the glove. Massaging his throat, he said, 'You are no knight. You cannot challenge me.'

'Coward!' Bertrand snarled in fury.

'Coward indeed.' The knight beside Nicolas spoke, smiling pleasantly, but with cold disdain in his eyes. 'Now I *am* a knight, de Cotin, but I'll wager you'll not challenge me.' He released Nicolas's wrist, but Nicolas made no more attempt to use the knife. He drew back instead, not meeting his neighbour's eyes.

'Accept the challenge!' urged someone from further down the table. Immediately a chorus of voices broke out in agreement.

An older man, seated at one end of the high table, rose to his feet. He called out, 'I'm Lord Henri de Zol, young Eagle, and I'll knight you myself!'

Bertrand bowed courteously to him. 'I thank you, sir, but I will take knighthood from my own liege lord, or not at all.' As he turned back to Nicolas, his courtesy vanished again. 'Meet me tomorrow, de Cotin, with spear and sword, or I'll beat you with my bare hands all the way from here to Roazon.'

Sir Nicolas glanced from side to side, meeting nothing but contempt and laughter. With a last attempt at bluster, he announced, 'I'm due to be wed tomorrow.'

'And I must sit in Council.' Bertrand spat on his hands and rubbed them together eagerly. 'We'll fight at daybreak in the main square, and then on to our other business.'

Nicolas realized he was trapped; Val could see it in his eyes. He snarled something incoherent, snatched up the glove, and left the table, pushing his way past the derisively cheering courtiers.

The knight who had sat beside him got up, holding out a hand to Bertrand. 'I'll follow him and make sure he appears tomorrow – and that your brother doesn't meet with any accident in the meantime.'

'I thank you, sir,' said Bertrand, gripping the proffered hand. 'May I know your name?'

'I am Francis de Montroulez. I wish you well, my friend.'

The knight moved rapidly after Nicolas, catching him up at the main doors.

'Come, sir,' one of the other men invited, 'sit here and join us.' He moved further up the bench, making space for them, and called for a servant to clear the mess. 'By the Warrior, I wouldn't have missed that for the world. It's time someone took that young snot down a peg or two.'

Bertrand took his seat and began helping himself to the various dishes that were passed to him. The talk and laughter rose louder than ever. Music struck up from the gallery above.

Then Val noticed something that made iron bands

clutch around his heart. At the far end of the high table sat a man he had not noticed before, dressed in the linen robe of the Knights Legionaries. His cold eyes were trained on Val, as, Val guessed, they had been since the first moment he had set foot in the hall.

It was Sir Girec d'Evron.

2

Alissende was working in her still-room, boiling up alder bark for a decoction to bathe battle wounds. Storm clouds had covered the sun as it set, and now rain and wind rattled the shutters. Earlier she had lit rushlights, and the gentle bubbling of water, the warmth of the brazier, soothed her into peacefulness. On the floor at her feet Ivona staggered happily about in pursuit of a ball.

Crumbling more bark into the water, Alissende thought she could hear sudden voices at a distance. Presently quick footsteps moved along the passage, and old Nolwen opened the door.

'Sister, the men are back from Roazon.'

Alissende felt an unpleasant tightening in her stomach. Bertrand and his cousin, of course, had returned and gone off again several days ago; they should be in Gwened by now, bearing the banner of the Black Eagle which she herself had stitched. The main body of their troops, accompanying the guildsmen, were to follow more slowly, along with their wounded. Now they had arrived, there would be work for her to do.

'Have the injured brought up here,' she instructed. 'See that the rest have fire and food.'

'Yes, Sister.' Nolwen bobbed a curtsey. 'I'll spread mattresses in the great hall.'

As she hurried off, Alissende drew the pot off the brazier, then ran an expert eye over the shelves of salves and distillations she had been preparing ever since she first came to Bellière. At least she was ready.

When she reached the hall, leading Ivona by the hand, some servants were already dragging in mattresses, placing them in lines between the pillars. Another servant was lighting the fire; it burnt smokily as yet. The doors at the far end of the hall were wide open, and men came tramping through.

The first Alissende recognized was Sulien de Plouzhel, looking mud-spattered and weary. He came up to her smiling, his teeth white in his filthy face.

'It's good to see you, Sulien. Are there many wounded?'

Sulien's smile vanished; he looked suddenly older. 'Too many — and some dead. But it could have been worse, the Warrior knows.'

Alissende made the sign of the Holy Knot. As more men appeared — some merely limping, others with arms in slings or heads bandaged — she suddenly realized the size of her task. She had treated wounds before, in her days as a holy sister: a leg broken from a fall, perhaps, or an arm accidentally slashed by a reaping hook; but never in war until now.

She was kneeling beside one of the guildsmen, bandaging his arm with a poultice of yarrow and toadflax, when she realized that Duke Joscelin was standing over her.

'What can I do?' he asked her.

Alissende glanced up at him, but before she could reply she saw four men-at-arms manoeuvring a litter through the hall doors. Someone lay very still upon it, and Alissende got quickly to her feet. 'Finish fastening this bandage,' she said. 'I must see to him.'

Vaguely aware of an embarrassed rumble behind her as the guildsman realized that the Duke of Roazon himself was binding his wound, Alissende hurried over to the advancing litter. It was a makeshift affair of branches lashed together. The man lying on it, covered by a couple of cloaks, soaked with rain, was limp and unmoving, his hair plastered over a chalk white face.

Alissende drew a long breath of fear and pity as she recognized Donan. He looked smaller than she remembered, and somehow younger.

Reaching out, her fingers close to his lips, she detected just a faint flutter of breath. Quickly she ordered the men to set down the litter and lift Donan on to a mattress. As gently as she could she stripped off his torn, mud-soaked tunic. His right hand and arm were swathed in bandages, deeply stained with blood and sodden with rain.

One of the soldiers brought a lamp and set it at the head of the mattress so she could see better. Then Joscelin was beside her again, holding a bowl of water and some linen cloths. Alissende took her knife and slit the bandages, sponging Donan's swollen arm to ease away the fabric where it stuck to the wound.

She exposed a long slash, running from his shoulder almost to his wrist, crusted with dried blood and pus, and more was oozing out of it. Long red streaks ran from the wound itself over his neck and shoulder, and across his hand.

Alissende felt a sudden piercing pain behind her eyes. She knew that a wound so badly infected, left untreated for six or seven days, would not heal easily. Donan would likely lose the arm, or he would die.

She remembered him in his workshop, spinning beauty out of silver. Without his craft, he would be crippled, not only in body, but in mind. She thought of Morwenna, forbidden to paint, and their child removed from them. 'God, this cannot be your will,' she whispered.

'Alissende?' A murmur at her shoulder from Duke Joscelin.

'I shall have to take off his arm.' She could feel tears beginning to slip from her eyes, and was furious with her own weakness. 'He's a silversmith, Joscelin. He's Ivona's father.'

Blue eyes intent, Joscelin knelt beside Alissende and took Donan's hand in his. The patient roused, tossing his head from side to side, and then relaxed suddenly.

Alissende felt that the whole world had shrunk to the yellow circle of the lamplight.

Joscelin began massaging Donan's hand, then let his fingers move up the arm on either side of the wound. Alissende caught her breath painfully. She knew what she was going to see, and yet something within herself would not let her believe it.

The red streaks of infection began fading, as if shrinking away from Joscelin's touch, as if gradually the wound itself was closing. Donan's breathing became steadier, and he looked as if he slept.

Joscelin swayed back, and Alissende slid an arm round his shoulders, bracing him. His face was whiter, now, and for a moment Alissende thought he would faint.

Then he drew a shaky breath. 'Alissende, is he . . .?'

'He is recovering.' Alissende could find nothing in herself that was surprised, only a growing wonder and delight in the healing power in Joscelin.

She looked past him into the hall, growing lighter now

as two of the servants applied tapers to the torches fixed on
the pillars. There were perhaps twenty men still waiting for
her assistance. She could hear moaning from one of the
mattresses nearby, and further away someone muttering a
prayer.

'Can you?' she asked. 'Have you the strength?'

Joscelin swallowed. 'I must. You'll help me, Alissende?'

'You know I will.' She kissed his forehead, not demanding now, wanting nothing but to offer him what he needed
to receive. 'That's why I'm here.'

3

In the great hall at Roazon, as the evening feasting was
drawing to a close, King Aymon shifted restlessly in his
raised seat, staring down at the assembled company, but all
the while aware of the woman who sat at his right hand.

He had lately allowed the Lady Marjolaine a certain
measure of freedom: to walk in the garden under the eye of
an escort – though in the chill autumn weather that was less
of a privilege – and now to sit at table with him. Damnably,
she seemed quite insensible of the honour he was doing her
and, although unfailingly courteous, she always gave him the
impression that she was the one conferring the favour.

She would learn better soon, the king resolved.

It was the eve of the Feast of All Angels, and as Aymon
had ordered, appeals had gone out through all of Arvorig,
bidding Duke Joscelin to return. There had been no
response yet; Aymon had not expected one. But it was
necessary to maintain the fiction that his offer of support
to Joscelin had been thrown back in his face.

In less than twenty-four hours, at the festival Offering

itself, he would be rid of Joscelin for good and all. The king let out a chuckle of satisfaction.

'You are merry, my lord,' Lady Marjolaine said.

She had scarcely touched her wine, and half the food on her plate remained uneaten. You would almost think, Aymon reflected, that she was one of those bloodless sisters of the Matriarchy, except that blood all too clearly flowed through her veins. Aymon found himself growing heated at the very thought of what passions she might conceal.

His wife, that tediously pious woman, being great with child, had remained in Brogall. So, when he looked at the Lady Marjolaine he felt a lust arising after enforced abstinence.

'How could a man be anything but merry, in your company?' he responded.

Marjolaine raised her brows. 'You find me a cause of mirth, sir?'

Aymon stammered, 'Through joy, lady, not mirth.'

'I fear you are easily pleased, sir,' murmured Marjolaine.

An easy compliment sprang to his lips, but he kept it back. He would say nothing that she might find offensive, not because he feared to do so, but because he would not have her alerted to the plans that had begun to take up residence in his mind.

Now that Tariec de Gwened was dead, two people alone bore the Roazon bloodline that these superstitious fools here in Arvorig valued so highly. Lady Marjolaine was the last in the direct line of descent from Duke Govrian, so would he himself not sit more securely on the throne of Roazon if he might marry her? A son of theirs would then carry the bloodline, and inherit the city with the blessing of all Arvorig, even its over-scrupulous priests.

Yet he was already married. *But women die in childbirth,*

Aymon thought to himself, and, policy aside, it would be a sweet relief to be free of his queen's continual praying and preaching.

Yet she was in Brogall, and he here in Arvorig. A word to Maugis would see the job done, of course, and yet Aymon knew how foolish he would be to share such notions even with Maugis, thus putting himself in the man's power for ever.

No, he decided, a letter must go to the queen, bidding her to journey and join him in Arvorig at once. He could explain that her babe would rule after him in Roazon, so it pleased him that it should be born there. He had no doubt that the queen would obey him.

She might even miscarry on the journey, Aymon thought optimistically. And he would be free to wed the Lady Marjolaine, to take all that ripe, rose-scented beauty for himself. God, he would make her a better husband than that monkish Joscelin — or that boy Tariec.

Smiling in satisfaction, Aymon snapped his fingers for the harper to take his customary place in the centre of the hall. Everything would fall into his hand, he knew; after tomorrow's Offering he would rule Roazon in his own right, and before she knew it he would rule the Lady Marjolaine too.

Twenty-Three

On the morning of the Feast of All Angels, Val rose while it was still dark, blundering about the tiny attic room of the tavern where he and Bertrand were lodging, until he managed to find a taper and light it.

The wavering flames showed him Bertrand still snoring on his back, with a grin on his face that suggested his dreams were happy ones. Val prodded him hard. 'Get up. You've got an appointment.'

Bertrand grunted a protest and sat up, blinking at Val with bleary eyes.

'Daybreak?' Val prompted him. 'Nicolas de Cotin? Your brother Oliver?'

Bertrand sprang up, suddenly alert. For a moment his cousin had been afraid that Bertrand had drunk too much of Count Fragan's wine the night before.

'Ah, yes.' Bertrand slapped his chest. 'Better order us a decent breakfast, Val. Settling that bastard will give me an appetite.'

Instead, Val called for water for them to wash with. As they let themselves out of the tavern and into the street, it was still dark. Cloud covered the early morning sky and an icy drizzle was falling.

Until now, Val had never doubted that Bertrand would win his forthcoming duel, but as they walked through the cold, unwelcoming city, he could not help feeling less certain.

Their adversary was already waiting in the main square as they arrived. Amongst the small group of men who stood around him was Oliver d'Acquin. Bertrand let out a glad cry and went bounding over to grip his brother's hand.

People were beginning to gather around the edges of the square, and Val could see lights burning in the windows of houses, whose shutters were thrown back so spectators could lean over the sill.

Francis de Montroulez came over to greet them. 'This is the best entertainment Gwened has seen in years,' he said wryly. 'Bertrand, I've a message for you from a lady. She says she's confident you will win.'

Bertrand was squinting along the blade of his sword. 'What woman would know about that?'

Francis's grin grew broader. 'But this is a special lady, my friend. She is Tiphaine de Bellière, who will wed Sir Nicolas later.'

Bertrand froze and, in the cold grey light that was oozing over the square, Val saw that he was flushing deeply. 'Lady Tiphaine?' he stammered. 'She sent a message to me?'

Francis clapped him on the shoulder. 'Relieve that idiot of his head, and the lady could be yours.'

Thoroughly disconcerted, Bertrand shook his head. 'This is a fight for my brother only. I don't want to kill.'

He stood still while Val laced on his helmet. Then both Val and Francis stepped away, and the two combatants were face to face. 'Fight until one or the other yields,' explained Sir Francis. 'Bertrand, if you prevail, then your brother Oliver goes free. If Sir Nicolas wins, then you pay the ransom he demands.'

Both contestants nodded their agreement.

'Then may the Warrior see right prevail.'

Val pulled his cloak closer against the cold drizzle, watching Bertrand and Nicolas still cautiously testing each other, scarcely within reach of each other's sword. Like a dancer, Nicolas moved lightly: the careful pupil of a good swordsmaster, doing everything correctly. Bertrand, in contrast, planted his feet firmly on the ground as if expecting to take root. He gripped his sword two-handed; when he moved in to slash at Sir Nicolas, his adversary parried easily and slipped aside.

Bertrand would spin round, follow him up, but Nicolas was never quite where his blade fell. At one point, instead, he slipped his sword below Bertrand's guard, and pinked him under the arm.

'First blood,' Val muttered.

Oliver said nothing, looking agonized, as if realizing for the first time that his brother could lose.

The touch of Nicolas's sword seemed less to hurt Bertrand than madden him. He pressed forward, aiming a flurry of blows as his opponent retreated, dodged aside again. But this time his foot slipped on the rain-soaked paving, and he went down on one knee.

'Now!' Oliver urged.

Instead, Bertrand retreated, gesturing to his opponent to rise.

'Damnable chivalry!' Oliver groaned.

Once Sir Nicolas had recovered his feet, they joined battle again — closer now, the blows falling faster, their footwork more intricate. The crowd, who had been yelling encouragement, fell silent — no sound at all in the square except the clash of swords and the thudding of boots on the ground.

Then – so quickly that Val failed to follow the movement – Nicolas de Cotin twisted his blade, and Bertrand's weapon went clattering out of his hand. Val hoped for Sir Nicolas to step back, allowing Bertrand the grace he had been granted himself. Instead, he swept his sword round for a killing blow.

Oliver gave a cry of anguish. Val gripped the boy's shoulder. He expected Bertrand to retreat, but instead he sprang forward. Ducking under the scything blade, he rammed his head into de Cotin's chest, propelling him backwards with Bertrand on top of him.

Nicolas's sword had gone flying too. Pinning him down with a knee on his chest and one hand on his shoulder, Bertrand drew his dagger and slashed through the helmet lacing. He tossed the helmet aside, and crashed a mailed fist into Nicolas's face.

The knight let out a yell, more of outrage than fear or pain, but Bertrand was kneeling on top of him, both hands tightening around his throat. 'Do you yield?' he growled. 'Do you give me back my brother?'

Sir Francis de Montroulez strolled over and looked down at them. 'Let him breathe,' he suggested. 'How can he answer you if you strangle him?'

Val could guess what was going through his cousin's mind. If Nicolas died, Tiphaine also would be free. The mailed fists seemed intent on choking out Nicolas's life.

'Bertrand!' Val cried urgently. 'Remember your oath to my mother. Never to fight but with a noble weapon!'

To his vast relief, Bertrand relaxed his grip.

Nicolas coughed for air as he tried to form the words. 'I yield,' he said at last. 'Take your brother, damn you.'

With a grunt of satisfaction, Bertrand scrambled to his feet.

'Well, honour is satisfied,' Sir Francis confirmed. He slid a hand under Nicolas's arm, to raise him. 'Sir Nicolas, come. You must dress for your wedding. It wouldn't do to keep your bride waiting.'

Bertrand watched them retreat, then swung round on Val and Oliver as they hurried over to him. 'Why are we all standing here?' he demanded irritably. 'I have a Council to attend.'

2

Tiphaine de Bellière stood in the narthex of the Church of the Holy Knot and tried to stop her hands from trembling. Nicolas, her betrothed, had just stalked past her into the church with barely a greeting. He looked to have the beginnings of a black eye, and his temper was even blacker.

Mari, coaxing one of her ribbons to twine through her hair, whispered, 'Lady, you look very lovely.'

'Thank you,' said Tiphaine, pulling away from her to reach a hand towards Sir Francis de Montroulez, who was following her future husband into the church.

The knight bowed, laying a hand on his breast. 'At your service, lady.'

'The combat ... you were present?'

Sir Francis nodded. 'I regret to tell you that Sir Nicolas lost, lady. But he is not much hurt.'

'And his opponent?' Tiphaine did not care how much she was giving away.

'A little damaged too, lady, but glad to have his brother restored to him.'

And what about me? Tiphaine thought dismally, realizing

now that she had loved Bertrand since the day of that tournament, when he rode up to receive her favour.

But now it was too late: the church doors stood wide. As she paced slowly up the aisle, with only Mari in attendance, she could see the priest already waiting in front of the altar, and Nicolas standing with his back to her. Except for them, and Aunt Peronel, the church was almost empty. In Roazon, of course, it would have been a much more splendid gathering, so Tiphaine was grateful for that, at least.

Within a few moments she would be married to a man who had no love for her, who wanted nothing but her wealth. And no one would help her, because that was how things were done.

Men had different standards from women, she reflected bitterly.

Suddenly, between one step and the next, as she approached her betrothed's side, she finally knew what she must do.

Her mind whirling, the first words of the ceremony passed over her in a blur. She did not come to herself again until the priest turned to ask her, 'Will you take this man for your wedded husband?'

Tiphaine took a deep breath. 'No,' she replied.

From somewhere behind her, Aunt Peronel let out a tiny shriek. Nicolas looked thunderstruck, his damaged face reddening still more.

'What do you mean?' he demanded shrilly.

The priest held up a hand to silence him. 'A moment, sir.' Turning a look of mild inquiry on Tiphaine, he continued, 'Daughter, you know that you are lawfully betrothed? That means you are already joined to this man.'

'I know, Father,' said Tiphaine, 'but I *will* not marry him. I repudiate him.'

'You can't!' Nicolas exclaimed, but the priest ignored him.

'What grounds have you, Daughter?'

'Because I have found he has no honour in him,' Tiphaine said. Anger lifting her like a wave, she recounted briefly how Nicolas had broken faith with his prisoner. How he was not the honourable knight she had been persuaded to marry.

'Is this true?' The priest turned to de Cotin sternly.

Nicolas opened his mouth but said nothing.

Of course, thought Tiphaine, *he dares not admit the truth. Perhaps he could bring himself to lie, even before the altar, if he did not know that his dishonour could so easily be proved.*

The priest's face grew sterner as once again he asked his question. 'My son, is this true?'

Nicolas could not look at him, just gave an infinitesimal nod. 'Yes.'

'Then, Daughter, your cause is just, and your repudiation stands.' The priest flicked through his prayer book, and began to speak the holy words that would release her.

Tiphaine felt as if the dimly-lit church were suddenly flooded with sunlight as she listened, while Nicolas stood silently in a furious sulk, and Aunt Peronel gave way to her usual hysterics.

3

Sir Nicolas de Cotin, still wearing his wedding finery, lurked in an alcove near the Council chamber as the assembled lords began to drift along the corridor to take their places.

They had dedicated themselves in the Church of the Holy Lance, and after that Nicolas had been forced to hang about while they regaled themselves with an interminable banquet.

He himself could not have eaten a thing, though he craved wine. His stomach felt stuffed with leaden weights, and he had a raging headache. He still could hardly bring himself to believe that since the day before his life had crashed down around him.

He owed money here in Gwened; even the clothes he was wearing were not yet paid for. Tradesmen had been delighted to give him credit as the betrothed husband of the heiress Tiphaine de Bellière. Even the ransom he hoped for in exchange for Oliver d'Acquin would have settled his debts. Now he had lost both wealthy wife and the expectation of ransom, and his creditors would be hammering at his door before the day was out.

There were creditors left behind in Roazon, too, who would be demanding their money if ever he got home. Nicolas could only see one way out of the troubles that beset him.

Count Fragan — he had pledged himself to his cause before the count had even moved to depose Duke Joscelin. That must be worth something, even though Fragan's attempted *coup* had come to nothing. He was openly Fragan's man, and the Count must surely help him now.

He looked out of the window at the dripping afternoon, and wondered where he would find the money to pay for his lodgings, or even to eat. Unfastening his purse, he tipped its contents out on to the window sill: a few coins, and a heavy gold ring he had discovered lying forgotten in a compartment of the travelling chest he had brought from Roazon. He could sell that, he supposed, and stave off disaster for another few days.

Nicolas was reaching out for it when voices from the far

end of the passage heralded the arrival of Count Fragan himself. He was flanked on either side by the lords of Zol and Tregor, with other councillors following just behind. One foot dragged as the Count walked, legacy of that disastrous battle; his face was grey with ill-health. Chilled, Nicolas wondered what would become of himself if Fragan were to die.

Straightening, he stepped out into Fragan's path, and bowed. 'My lord count—'

'Not now, de Cotin.' Fragan steered a path around him, not even breaking step. 'I'm busy.'

'But my lord—'

No response as Fragan disappeared into the Council chamber, leaving Nicolas to stare frustratedly after him.

As a hand fell on his shoulder, he started and turned, half-prepared to see a guard ready to eject him. Instead, he found himself looking up into the chilly eyes of Sir Girec d'Evron, the Knight who had taken command of the Legion in Gwened after Sir Guy de Karanteg turned traitor and went off to seek his heretic lord.

So d'Evron has fallen on his feet, Nicolas thought resentfully, remembering the night when the pair of them had crossed the lake to visit Count Fragan in his pavilion.

'De Cotin, a word.' D'Evron drew him back into the window embrasure while the last of the councillors filed past them. Out of the corner of his eye, Nicolas spotted Bertrand d'Acquin, and turned away, not wanting to face him.

'What do you want?'

D'Evron eyed him in silence for a moment, then asked, 'What is your business with Count Fragan?'

Nicolas considered ignoring this, then replied brusquely, 'He owes me favour.'

D'Evron made no comment about that. Frowning a little, he touched his pectoral Knot. 'Your prisoner ... this Oliver d'Acquin,' he began at last.

'What of him?'

'His brother, and his cousin Valery de Vaux, were two of those who escaped from Roazon with the heretic Joscelin.' D'Evron leant over until their eyes were just inches apart. 'De Cotin, where did you encounter the boy?'

Nicolas had opened his mouth to reply before he realized what d'Evron was asking him. 'Oh, no,' he said, 'I know what you're thinking.' He grinned as he realized what an asset he held. 'Do you really think I'll tell you, just like that?'

D'Evron sighed. 'What do you want then, de Cotin?'

'Money. Preferment.'

D'Evron looked austere. 'As a Knight of the Legion, I have embraced holy poverty.'

'Maybe you have — but Count Fragan hasn't.' Nicolas gestured dismissively towards the few coins and the ring, scattered on the sill where he had left them. 'Damn it, man, I haven't two pennies to rub together!'

As d'Evron glanced where he pointed, his gaze grew fixed. He reached past Nicolas, and took up the ring, examining the intaglio with minute attention.

'What ...?' Nicolas began uneasily.

Girec d'Evron held out the ring so that de Cotin could see its carved design. 'The arms of de Montfaucon? Just where did you come by that?'

Nicolas felt like a man who has missed his step in the dark, and goes plummeting down into nothingness. He remembered how, years ago, the ring had been Aurel's love gift to him.

'I don't know what you mean,' he said.

'Oh, come. A ring bearing the arms of a noble house is

not given lightly, or just bought in the marketplace.'
D'Evron's face held a curious expression, a mixture of
horror and satisfaction. 'And we all know the vile reputation
of Aurel de Montfaucon. Is that how you got this, de
Cotin? Did he give it to you? A payment for sin?' The
words were spat out. 'Do you share his filthy lusts?'

Nicolas knew, as his mind spun crazily, that there must
be a safe answer to d'Evron's interrogation. There must be
some respectable excuse for obtaining the ring, but he could
not think what it might be, and his very hesitation condemned him. He said nothing.

Girec d'Evron gave the ring even closer scrutiny. 'I fear
it may be my duty to bring this to the notice of the
Church,' he said.

'No!'

D'Evron's eyes met his, with that same chilly stare, his
hand moving in the sign of the Holy Knot. 'I ask myself
whether it would be sin on my part to conceal it. If I am to
help you, I should need some persuasion.'

'All right, you damned bastard,' Nicolas croaked. 'I know
what you want.'

Girec d'Evron smiled, glancing towards the door of the
Council chamber. 'I must take my place now. Ask a servant
to show you to my rooms, and wait there for me.'

Nicolas suddenly found that his legs would not support
him. He slumped into the window-seat, defeated, muttering,
'I'll be there.'

Girec d'Evron turned away, then glanced back. 'You are
mine now, de Cotin, and don't you forget it.'

He closed his hand over the ring and went into the
Council chamber.

4

The Council chamber in the fortress of Gwened was an austere room, the single fire at one end failing to drive out the raw cold of the day, the shadows in the vaulted roof not banished by the torches burning in their sconces.

Bertrand d'Acquin took his seat at the long table, between the lords of Tregor and Malou. Gralon de Tregor gave him the sort of dismissive look he would have given to a peasant who dared usurp a place at his dinner table, while Rivalin de Malou, Bertrand's own liege lord, merely nodded curtly and ignored him thereafter.

Bertrand treated each of them to a friendly grin. 'A foul wet day, my lords,' he said. 'I'd rather be sitting in front of a tavern fire than freezing my backside off here.'

Chilly stares met this statement, but neither lord replied.

At the head of the table, Count Fragan was already seated, as Girec d'Evron slid into the vacant chair at his side. The Count tapped for attention.

'My lords,' he began. 'We sit here on this unhappy day to decide what we must do for the defence of our beleaguered country. Roazon lost its authority when its lord turned heretic. My son Tariec should have sat upon the throne of Roazon, by right of inheritance through his mother.'

To have ruled as instructed by you, Bertrand translated silently.

'But my son is dead,' Fragan went on, 'cut down untimely in battle. And no one now remains of the true bloodline of Roazon. With that in mind—'

'Just a minute.' His chair scraped back noisily as Henri of Zol got to his feet. 'The last I heard, the Church had still not declared Duke Joscelin a heretic. Are you speaking treason here, Fragan?'

Fragan gave him a look of distaste. 'Be seated, my lord, and ask yourself, how many men of Arvorig, nobles and commons alike, will follow a lord who flouts the teaching of Holy Church.'

'Not the men of Tregor!' Gralon growled.

'Nor Brieg.' Lord Geoffrey spoke peevishly. 'Roazon rules through the Church. It always has, always will. Why should we go to war in order to put Joscelin back in his position when he shows no respect for what that position means? When he became duke, he swore to uphold the Church, not challenge it.'

'But if not Joscelin, then who?' Henri of Zol asked. 'Count Fragan, if you're trying to claim Roazon for yourself—'

They were all suddenly on their feet and shouting at once. Bertrand could not recognize individual voices in the clamour, but he caught the gist of what was said. Most of them asserted Duke Joscelin's heresy — not out of piety, he thought cynically, since all realized that with the sovereignty of Roazon broken they might gain more power for themselves.

Most of them, however, were wary of Count Fragan. None of them wanted to be free of Roazon only to bow to the ruler of Gwened.

The only man seemingly loyal to Duke Joscelin was Henri of Zol — the smallest and poorest province of them all. Perhaps Henri realized that if power in Arvorig were sliced up afresh, he could not hope for more than the last leavings.

As the clamour persisted, Girec d'Evron leant towards

Count Fragan and spoke softly into his ear. Fragan seemed hardly to listen at first; then his features grew suddenly alert. As his cold gaze fell on Bertrand, he felt a stab of uneasiness. What could d'Evron have told the Count about him?

Then he recalled seeing Girec d'Evron and Nicolas de Cotin together in a window alcove outside the chamber. What could those two have to say to each other? And what was their link with him?

The answer came to him like a douche of icy water. After the attack on the baggage train there, even Nicolas de Cotin might guess that Bertrand was based at Bellière. And since D'Evron would have recognized him among the rescuers of Duke Joscelin, on the hythe at Roazon, combining such information would suggest that Duke Joscelin too must be hiding out at Bellière. Had d'Evron just passed that information on to Fragan?

Bertrand's seat in that Council chamber suddenly became much less desirable. In fact, it was downright foolish for him to stay there any longer. There was clearly no hope, in any case, of his influencing this crowd of self-seekers. Desirous of power for themselves, they would never join together in support of either Joscelin or Fragan.

But how to get out? Bertrand needed to be on the road, riding for Bellière to warn Duke Joscelin. But if Count Fragan now knew what Bertrand suspected, he would surely never let him go. Bertrand did not fancy his chances of fighting his way out. Dressed for the Council, he was not even wearing his sword.

Well, he thought, *no one can count the score until he throws the dice.*

By this time, Count Fragan had managed to get the unruly lords under some kind of control, and the clamour around the table was dying down. Back in their seats again, they all glared furiously at Fragan. No one was paying the slightest attention to Bertrand.

As the count opened his mouth to speak, Bertrand rose to his feet. 'My lord, I thought this was to be a solemn Council.' He tucked his thumbs into his belt and stared round him. 'Yet all you do is brawl.'

'Don't try to lesson us, boy,' snarled Rivalin de Malou.

Bertrand ignored him. 'No one has yet mentioned what we should be considering,' he said. 'King Aymon holds Roazon. What do you propose doing about that?'

Count Fragan let out a snort of irritation. 'There's much to do before—'

'No, my lord count. While we sit here, Aymon brings down more troops from the north. He grows stronger by the day, and before we know where we are, he'll be marching on Gwened – or Malou. Together we could defeat him.'

'Don't be a fool, boy,' said Gralon de Tregor. 'Aymon holds Roazon, and it's known to be impregnable.'

Bertrand examined his grubby fingernails. 'King Aymon got in,' he pointed out.

'And I suppose you're the one who's going to get him out?' said Geoffrey de Brieg.

The sneer gave Bertrand the opening he wanted. He turned to de Brieg with his widest smile. 'Yes, my lord,' he said. 'I will retake Roazon. I, the Black Eagle, pledge you my word.'

There was a frozen silence, broken only by derisive laughter from one of the lords sitting across the table. Taking advantage of this, Bertrand spun round, pushed his chair aside, and strode out of the chamber.

He was poised to sprint off down the passage, expecting Count Fragan to summon his guards. But the order did not come: only a babble of voices and more laughter rising behind him.

So. Girec d'Evron had not passed on his suspicions yet. Bertrand continued walking at a normal pace, aware of the eyes of the guards upon him. But the door into the courtyard was not far away now, and after that his escape route would be clear.

Bertrand began to relax as he reached the open air. Then he halted, for approaching him along the path leading down to the street, were his cousin and Oliver and, just behind them, the Lady Tiphaine. She was muffled by a dark cloak worn over an elaborate silken gown that was surely her wedding dress, and clutched tightly the arm of Sir Francis de Montroulez.

'Cousin?' said Bertrand, as Val reached him.

'This lady has been seeking you,' de Montroulez announced.

'Seeking me?' Bertrand did not understand, and for a moment the danger right behind him slipped out of his head.

'Since she has not wed Sir Nicolas, she needs your protection.'

'Not wed?' Bertrand stood gazing in puzzlement at Tiphaine – more beautiful than ever in her agitation – and then recollected himself. 'We have to get out of here, and ride at once for Bellière. Tell me more as we go.'

His hand poised over his belt knife, he led the way down to the gate. There was one perilous moment as they passed the guards, but soon they were out in the street, and putting the fortress well behind them as quickly as they could.

'Now, tell me everything,' Bertrand said, as Tiphaine

hurried along beside him, her skirts caught up so as not to impede his progress.

'I repudiated him at the altar,' she panted. 'He had dishonoured himself, so the priest released me. I'm not betrothed any more.'

'She is a valiant lady,' said Francis.

'Sir Francis has been so helpful!' Tiphaine turned a glowing look on him. 'He escorted me back to my lodgings to pack up all I needed.' She indicated the leather bag de Montroulez was carrying. 'Together we found your inn, and your cousin and Oliver were there . . .'

She came looking for you, a small voice told him, wonderingly.

'They said you were in Council with Count Fragan,' Tiphaine finished triumphantly, 'and so here we are!'

'I'm ready to serve you, lady, in any way I can,' Bertrand said.

It was Francis de Montroulez who replied. 'Escort to her home in Bellière. I wish I could come with you,' he added, 'but I'm vowed to attend my lord of Leon. Yet I'm Joscelin's man, and have no stomach for what goes forward here.'

While he was speaking, they reached the archway to the inn yard. Bertrand gripped his hand. 'My thanks, sir.'

'No need.' Sir Francis smiled. 'May the Warrior go with you, my friend. And may we meet again in a happier time.' With infinite courtliness he kissed Tiphaine's hand and hurried away.

As the others entered the inn yard, Bertrand sent Oliver off to order their horses saddled.

'What happened at the Council?' Val asked.

'Nothing but wrangling,' Bertrand said disgustedly.

'There's no help there. Aymon will die of old age before any of them can agree long enough to move against him.'

'So you walked out.'

Quickly, Bertrand explained how he had realized the need to warn Duke Joscelin, so he had created a diversion to let him leave.

'You swore you would retake Roazon?' Val was staring at him with the anxious look he had worn all too often lately. 'You're mad!'

Bertrand shrugged.

'Cousin, you'll be forsworn,' said Val. 'Dishonoured.'

Bertrand had always known it. But he had thought his own disgrace was not too high a price to pay for Duke Joscelin's safety. Now, as he met the look of admiration Tiphaine gave him, he felt a surge of new courage and resolve – and, yes, madness.

He grinned. 'Don't look so worried, Cousin,' he said. 'If the sun can get in, I can.'

Twenty-Four

On the Feast of All Angels, Father Patern conducted the Offering ceremony in the tiny chapel at Bellière. Assisting him at the altar, Alissende fed the incense pot before the sanctuary.

Duke Joscelin himself was present, escorted by the few remaining Knights Companions. Donan was there too, restored to health now, and reunited with his child, Ivona. Alissende prayed fervently that Morwenna would soon join them.

Nolwen and the servants filled the rest of the benches, and when the ceremony was over Father Patern led them down to the edge of the forest to bring the blessings of this festival day to the men camped under the trees.

As she followed behind them all, Alissende drew her cloak closer around her against the chill wind. Brown leaves whirled in the air, the last rags of autumn, and the sky was heavy with cloud.

Descending the steep path from the castle, she could see men begin to emerge from the shelter of the trees, while Father Patern, in a voice surprisingly firm for his age and frailty, began a holy chant.

As the little procession approached the men waiting, the clouds parted and a thin ray of sunlight lanced down. As if it was seeking something, it finally came to rest on Duke

Joscelin, who stood transfixed, his hair burnished like golden fire, a strange look of wonder on his face.

Alissende thought she could discern a shimmer in the light, the movement of wings, as if angels were making it a stairway between earth and heaven. Could Joscelin see that splendour unveiled, she wondered. He seemed almost poised to be gathered into it, leaving the stains and trouble of the world behind.

The clouds shifted again; the ray of sunlight was cut off. Whatever Duke Joscelin had seen was gone. He stood surrounded by his followers, a little of that celestial glow still on his face.

As Father Patern still intoned his chant, Alissende realized that her face was wet with tears.

2

Since his arrival in Roazon in the guise of Melin, Aurel had never once entered the cathedral. As Aurel, he was excommunicate, and in his bitterness against the Church he had not greatly cared.

Now, in thrall to Vissarion and his serpent master, sealed to them by the power of the ring he wore, he was afraid to enter a place of such holiness. But there was no way to avoid attending the ceremony of the Offering on the Feast of All Angels.

He would have preferred to go with Lord Tancred, but even though deprived of his office, the seneschal would be seated in one of the ceremonial stalls in the chancel. With his fellow clerks, Aurel was bundled into a pew close to the front of the nave.

It was the first time he had left the citadel since King

Aymon's invasion, and the very sky outside seemed strange. The cathedral was stranger still, though Aurel vaguely remembered coming here with his father once.

He gazed around him, his eyes beginning to sting from a billowing cloud of incense as the thurifer paced past him at the head of the procession, followed by the Knot-bearer, the acolytes and the choir. The carved angels gazed down at him, half veiled in smoke.

Did *they* see past his disguise, Aurel wondered. Did *they* know him for what he truly was? The Judge would see, Aurel had no doubt of that, and yet no fire rained down on him, no voice from Heaven condemned him, nothing was heard but the sweetly interweaving chant of the choristers. Aurel felt lost, anonymous in that vast holy building, no more than a dust mote in the light lancing down from the narrow windows.

His anxiety ebbed. This could be borne, and perhaps for a little while he could imagine that even for him there might be a way back to grace.

He looked for Lord Tancred, but could not see him. Instead, he had a good view of King Aymon, enthusiastic in his seeming piety, intoning the responses louder than all the rest, though his attention seemed to wander as the Archbishop preached.

Beside the king sat Lady Marjolaine, calm and attentive, and beside her Master Eudon, head of the Guild Council. Beyond him again was Father Reynaud, wearing a plain black cassock adorned with a pectoral Knot.

Though surprised to see him there, Aurel was even more surprised that the Grand Master took no part in the Offering. Apparently he had been wounded when the city fell; at one time rumour had it that he was on the point of dying.

The festival Offering drew on with all the lavish ceremonial and music the cathedral could muster, yet the
Archbishop's sermon seemed short: perhaps to please
Aymon, perhaps to avoid political issues the Archbishop
would rather not confront. The prelate confined himself to
thanking God that they were all delivered from their recent
dangers, and praying for continued faith and strength in the
difficult days lying ahead. From beginning to end there was
no mention of Duke Joscelin.

Aurel's head began to swim from the aromatic incense;
its smoke filling the cathedral looked like solid bars of silver
where the light cut across it. The repetitive chanting grew
soporific, the crowded building becoming heated and stuffy.
Aurel increasingly longed for a breath of clean air.

At length the Archbishop pronounced the final blessing,
reaching out to the congregation with the sign of the Holy
Knot. The acolytes and choir began to move into position,
and the Knot-bearer raised his staff.

But before the procession could move off, King Aymon
himself got to his feet and moved to the head of the chancel
steps, where he beckoned the Archbishop to his side.

A rustle passed through the congregation: shock, or
apprehension. Even Aurel knew that no diversion might
interfere with the traditional ceremony of the cathedral,
especially on a day of high festival.

The Archbishop's face mirrored the general shock. 'My
lord king—' he began.

'Silence,' Aymon ordered brusquely. He moved to the
bell, hanging from one of the chancel pillars, which the Knot-
bearer would ring at the most holy moments of the Offering,
and tugged on it several times. At his signal, the west doors
of the cathedral were flung open, and two files of King

Aymon's soldiers entered. Each man carried a sword in one hand, a flaming torch in the other.

Some of the armed men marched down the central aisle and stationed themselves at the foot of the chancel steps, separating Aymon and the rest of the nobility from the general congregation in the nave. Others moved to line the outer walls. The doors were closed again, two men standing to guard them. At last, King Aymon spoke.

'My lord Archbishop, the city of Roazon has been too long in strife. You know how I rode to Duke Joscelin's aid, believing his error to be no more than the fruit of youth and inexperience.' He heaved a deep sigh. 'Alas, I was mistaken.'

He paused, and in all that vast building there was no sound, except for the cooing of pigeons outside the east window.

'I have held Duke Joscelin in friendship, and have sent word throughout Arvorig, begging him to return. But he has ignored me, and in his name some peasant they call "the Black Eagle" has attacked my men. I cannot hide from the truth any longer. At his induction he swore to uphold the Church.' King Aymon's voice rose to a shout. 'I name him oath-breaker! He has given up the right to rule!'

'My lord—' The Archbishop tried to interrupt again, and again the king would not let him speak.

'Archbishop, this has gone on long enough. Here and now you must declare Duke Joscelin a heretic and a renegade.'

The protest, when it came, was from Father Reynaud, who rose from his stall and moved to stand beside the king. Aurel thought he looked shaky, and yet even in his plain black garb he seemed to hold more authority than the Archbishop.

'My lord king, you cannot do this,' he began.

'You dare tell me, *cannot*?'

The clear menace in the regal tone did not intimidate Father Reynaud. 'You cannot, I say,' he repeated. 'This is, and always has been, a matter for the Church.'

'But the Church has made no pronouncement,' said Aymon. 'Come, Father, by all reports, you yourself spoke loudly against this Healer.'

'My opinions are my own,' Father Reynaud retorted. 'The Church will announce its decision in its own time.'

'That time had best be now,' said Aymon. He turned back to the Archbishop. 'Strip Duke Joscelin of his office forthwith, or I fire this cathedral.'

A babble of voices rose up all around Aurel. From behind him, someone screamed. An old man across the aisle from Aurel started to scramble out of his seat, only to subside as the nearest swordsman took a step towards him, with weapon raised. Gradually the babbling faded to a frightened silence.

Aurel glanced around him. The city was stripped already of the young and the strong; most of the guildsmen were gone too; many of the women and children had escaped before Aymon set the siege; men had died with Count Fragan or at the king's taking of the city. Those who remained were men and women too old to make the journey to safety, and the few younger people who had refused to leave.

The men at arms held the torches ready, their smoke and flame thickening the air; Aurel swallowed the panic that surged into his throat. The wooden pews would burn; the rafters above, with their carved angels, would burn; the silken banners of the Guilds would flash into flame. Within minutes the body of the cathedral could become a raging furnace.

King Aymon himself, and the rest of the nobles in the chancel, could make their escape through the vestry door, leaving the congregation to struggle out of the inferno as best they could. Aurel could imagine the hell of panic and screaming that would erupt as they fought each other to reach the doors.

He clasped his hands together tightly, willing himself to stay calm. The clerk sitting beside him had his head down, muttering a monotonous stream of curses. Behind him were voices raised in prayer, and someone sobbing.

The Archbishop remained silent for what seemed like a century. When at last he spoke, it was only to mouth a feeble protest. 'My lord, you cannot mean this!'

'When I sound the bell again,' said the King, 'my men will start the fire.'

As he raised a hand to grip the bell-rope, two other people rose from the ceremonial stalls and moved towards him. One was the Lady Marjolaine; the other was Tancred the seneschal.

Aurel could see the strain in his master's face, and longed to be at Tancred's side. Crippled as he was, and weakened by his long confinement, the seneschal would be swept away in a panicked rush for the doors.

Worried by these dark thoughts, Aurel could scarcely attend to what the seneschal was saying, his voice sounding sharp with disgust. 'My lord, if you do so, the men of Roazon will curse your name for generations.'

'Let them curse the Archbishop, then,' Aymon replied indifferently. 'The decision is his.'

Even from his seat in the nave, Aurel could sense

Tancred's helpless frustration. At that moment, Lady Marjolaine stepped forward, sinking to the ground in a curtsey at Aymon's feet.

Her voice rang out clearly. 'My lord, have mercy on our people here. Destroy this sacred building if you must, but let them free first.'

'Madam, if any voice could sway me, it would be yours,' the king said. 'But this matter must now be concluded with no more delay. Archbishop, speak your verdict.'

Lord Tancred gave his hand to Marjolaine and raised her up. They stood side by side, waiting for the Archbishop's response, for what seemed to Aurel like another hundred years. The Grand Master, face tight with outrage, moved quietly to join them.

The aged Archbishop stood with head bowed in prayer, then looked up. 'My lord Aymon,' he began. As soon as Aurel heard the quavering voice, he knew what the churchman's response would be, and while his fear began to ebb, a pang of fierce regret thrilled through him.

'The Church has laboured long to decide this,' the Archbishop went on. 'Duke Joscelin has indeed begun to worship the Healer, though the divine being has never manifested himself so – nor do we know whether this aspect is pleasing to him.'

He paused, till the king snapped, 'Get on with it!'

'Moreover,' the Archbishop continued, even more shakily, 'our scholars have considered whether a divine vision might be granted to a common woman, and a painter, instead of to scholars and churchmen.

'And thirdly, we have taken thought for the people of our city, whose fear of this new doctrine was made clear in riots recently. We might say—' he cleared his throat '—we might say that our long peace is broken because of the divine anger that we have not made our decision before now.'

'A comfortable thought, you old fool,' Aymon muttered.

The Archbishop's gaze flickered fearfully towards him and away. 'In short,' he went on, 'it seems plain to me that this idea of the Healer is indeed a heresy, and that Duke Joscelin in holding it has renounced the authority our faith gives him.

'I therefore pronounce him heretic and excommunicate. He is no longer Duke of Roazon.'

As he finished, he covered his face with his hands. Lady Marjolaine turned to the seneschal beside her, who clasped her hands and comforted her. Father Reynaud looked ill with silent anger.

King Aymon released his hold on the bell-rope and moved away to stand at the top of the chancel steps again. At this gesture, the guards by the west door flung it open and the soldiers with their swords and torches began to file out. A frightened babble rose up again from the congregation as the recessional procession formed up once more.

Meanwhile the light from the windows slowly faded, as clouds began to mass above the cathedral.

3

Storm clouds were building, too, in the sky off Kemper. All day the air had been clammy with heat, but now a fugitive breeze sprang up, fluttering the surface of the sea beyond the harbour mouth, or stirring tiny dust devils in the streets, and plucking blossom from the frangipani trees.

Townspeople returning from the Offering ritual scurried for their homes, bolted their doors behind them and slammed the shutters closed.

Down in the harbour the fishermen preparing to set sail unstepped their masts instead, and lashed protective canvas covers over their boats. Tavernkeepers left the lanterns over their doors unlit.

Silence gathered as the day drew to its ending, as if the ears of the town itself were stopped. A few fat drops of rain spattered in the dust, but the storm did not break. The sun began to set in a smudge of sullen crimson, while the world waited.

Suddenly lightning split the sky, a jagged finger of incandescent silver pointing down to the surface of the sea. The crack of thunder followed almost at once, rolling over the rooftops, but instead of dying away it built and built, sounding as if it echoed through caverns of rock, and the whole world was being ripped apart.

Another bolt of lightning crackled and, in the last of the daylight, the spot where it seemed to touch the sea began to boil. Pinnacles of rock, serrated like knives, slashed upwards, black against steel. The thunder continued to reverberate as the rocks grew mountainous, water cascading from towers and steeply pitched rooftops as they heaved themselves higher into the air.

Finally, gradually, the thunder died away.

Off the coast of Kemper now lay an island city, newly emerged from the sea. Obsidian walls ringed it round, pierced opposite the harbour mouth by an iron gateway barred by a spiked portcullis. Buildings crowded behind the encircling wall, in a slender pyramid that at last met the sky in the spires of a black cathedral.

The turbulence continued spreading, until waves lashed

the harbour walls of Kemper, smashing the boats at their moorings, and rising until seawater spilled over the quayside and battered the doors of the waterfront taverns.

The sky was a mosaic of lightning as, against its crackling silver, huge winged creatures vaned lazily downwards, circled the topmost spires of this new island, and plummeted down to perch on gables and finials, until iron doors and shutters were flung open to let them enter.

As rain lashed down, Vissarion stood on the roof of the house on the headland, laughing ecstatically and extending his hands into the storm.

Autrys had returned at last.

PART FIVE

Pilgrims of the Night

Twenty-Five

Alissende sat on a stool before the fire, lining a hood with rabbit fur for Ivona. Her needle flashed steadily in and out; firelight fell warm on the crimson wool.

Duke Joscelin was seated on the opposite side of the hearth, his elbow on the arm of his chair and his chin on his hand, staring into the flames. Alissende wondered what he saw there.

They might have been an old married couple, she thought, he resting after his day's work, she stitching for their own child. *Never.* The word was like a bell tolling inside her head. *Never* that ordinary human comfort. Limitless glory, she suspected, more than she could imagine, but not that. She thought her heart would break.

Since the Feast of All Angels, Alissende thought that Joscelin was waiting. In a land where war was rife, where men grappled for power and she herself had seen the return of evil in the scrying bowl, he was the still centre. Alissende could not help believing that his silence carried more weight than all the rattling fury around him.

She did not know what he waited for, though sometimes she caught a look of dread in his eyes, as if he himself knew all too well the part he would have to play. Yet he did not speak of it, and she herself dared not ask.

A glittering drop fell onto Ivona's hood, and soaked into

the wool. Furiously Alissende blinked her tears away. *He needs nothing from me, except to wait with him,* she told herself. *Well, if that is so, then I will wait.*

2

Sudden pain in his hand woke Aurel while it was still dark. He lay – as he had lain every night since he came to be lodged with Sir Tancred – on the couch in the seneschal's sitting-room, curled among the cushions with a blanket wrapped round him.

He stirred restlessly, too fogged by sleep to realize at first where the twinge of pain originated, and then snapped suddenly awake as he recognised the faint, blood-red glow cast by the devilish ring.

Half sitting up, he looked down at its stone. Vissarion's face, tiny and perfect, stared back at him, smiling. The pain, this time, was almost gentle, almost like a caress.

Vissarion's voice was heard. 'Aurel, you have failed me. Duke Joscelin still lives.'

Aurel braced himself, expecting spasms of pain that did not come. 'I'm a prisoner here,' he protested. 'I can't—'

Vissarion was still smiling. 'You will, my dear. But your task is less urgent now. Can you guess why?'

Bewildered and relieved, Aurel shook his head. Even within the tiny scope of the ring, he could see the blaze of triumph in Vissarion's eyes.

'Can you really not guess? Autrys has returned.'

For a few moments Aurel could do nothing but stare back at the tiny image in the stone. He understood that until now, in spite of all he had seen of Vissarion's evil, and the serpent lord who inhabited the dark chamber beneath the hill, he had never truly believed in the existence of Autrys. He had never managed to separate it from the folk tales his old nurse had whispered while he ate his supper by the fire in his father's house.

Vissarion was still waiting for his response, and at last Aurel murmured, 'So Duke Joscelin need not die?'

For an instant he caught a glimpse of venom behind the smile. 'Stupid, of course he must die. All those of the Roazon bloodline must be destroyed, for until they are gone, Autrys will not be truly safe.'

'But with Autrys returned, you have power – you have other servants?' Scarcely daring to plead, Aurel added, 'Vissarion, I beg you, let me go.'

Again the venom lancing out of Vissarion's eyes. 'Truly stupid, my dear. You are mine – and my master's. There is no going back.'

Aurel had not really expected any other answer. 'What must I do?' he asked resignedly.

'Find Duke Joscelin.' Swiftly anticipating Aurel's protest, he went on, 'The chance will come. Take it, when it comes. And once he is dead, my servants will speed your journey back to me.' Vissarion's tongue crept out, travelling over his smiling lips, in a gesture of anticipation that made Aurel shrink in terror. 'When you return, you shall experience all the delights Autrys has to offer.'

Then the light faded, the pain in his hand died away, and Aurel was left shivering in the dark.

Later that same morning, Aurel and Lord Tancred were finishing breakfast when heavy footsteps sounded outside the door. The day had dawned cold, with the sting of sleet in the wind, so Aurel had closed the shutters again and lit the lamps.

As Aurel sat in silence, he thought again about what Vissarion had told him earlier of his cold intent to destroy every one of the Roazon bloodline. With a shudder he realized that meant Duke Joscelin himself, and the Lady Marjolaine.

Was there any way of warning her, Aurel wondered. Could he maybe bribe one of the servants to take a message to her? And how would he convince her?

'Visitors?' the seneschal murmured, pushing his plate away and standing up as the door swung open.

A couple of Aymon's usual guards were standing there. 'You're to come with us to my lord,' one of them announced.

Tancred's brows twitched a little at the peremptory tone, but he said nothing. Taking his time, he rose and took up his staff, which was propped against his chair.

Meanwhile, the second guard strode into the room, glanced around quickly, and snatched down the little icon of the Healer, which Tancred had set in a niche above the hearth.

'What need have you of that?' the seneschal asked abruptly.

'My lord asked for it,' was the only response.

As they escorted Tancred out of the room, Aurel followed, unobtrusive as always, and once more no one tried to prevent him.

As before, Tancred was taken to the great hall, where Sir Baudet de la Roche was again in attendance on the king, lounging in Tancred's former seat, with the seneschal's chain of office draped across his shoulders.

The guards led Tancred in front of the dais, and one of them stepped forward to offer the icon to King Aymon, who examined it curiously.

'So small an object, to create such a stir,' he said. 'Tancred, how many other people possess these?'

'I don't know, my lord,' Tancred replied frostily. 'The painter created the one Duke Joscelin has — and then this one. She was arrested soon after.'

The king nodded and looked up. 'By possessing this icon,' he said, 'and your deference to the heretic, Joscelin, you give me cause to doubt your loyalty.'

'You mistake me,' Tancred said dryly. 'There has never been cause to doubt my loyalty. It lies where it always did.'

A brief ugliness peeped out of Aymon's eyes, and his tone hardened as he snapped, 'Don't match wits with me.'

'I wouldn't presume.'

Aurel waited apprehensively. King Aymon, he judged, was not stupid, and would catch the subtle insult in Tancred's words. He wanted to warn his master to be careful, but dared not speak in case he was thrown out.

Aymon turned the icon in his fingers for a moment. 'You were in the cathedral, Sir Tancred, when the Archbishop declared Joscelin heretic.'

Tancred was abrupt. 'You know that I was.'

'Yet you persist in keeping this icon in your possession.'

Aurel saw Tancred's mouth become a thin line, and his grip on the staff tighten.

'What the Archbishop did on the Feast of All Angels was out of compassion for the citizens whom you were threatening with a hideous death.'

Aymon snorted. 'Compassion! Fear, most like.'

Tancred shrugged. 'Call it what you like. One thing is certain: it was not his true opinion. So the matter of heresy is still undecided.'

'Are you suggesting the Archbishop himself cannot speak for the Church?'

'I say that he cannot speak honestly under such coercion.'

This retort kept the king silent for a moment, and Aurel dared to hope that this might end the confrontation. His hope grew as Aymon levered himself to his feet, as if preparing to leave.

Then he realized how wrong he had been. Aymon let the icon fall to the floor, and ground it into the paving with one booted foot.

'So dies heresy,' he declared and, in a grotesque parody of piety, made the sign of the Holy Knot. 'And as for you, Sir Tancred, you are banished. You will leave Roazon today.' King Aymon waved a hand dismissively. 'You have an hour to make what preparations you will — and you may take your servant here with you.'

At the last words Aurel felt a strange surge of joy. For all the danger that must lie ahead, he could think of nothing now, with the precious hour already beginning to slip away, but what needed to be done.

Tancred said nothing to him as they were escorted back to his chambers. After the guards had withdrawn, he prompted his silent master, 'My lord, we must pack. Will the king provide us with horses, do you think?'

'Aymon will provide us with nothing.' Tancred limped across the room and flung open a small chest that stood near the hearth. Kneeling, he began pulling out papers and feeding them to the flames.

Aurel left him to it and went into his master's bedroom, where he chose Tancred's warmest clothes, rolled them up in a blanket, and trussed the bundle with one of the cords from the bed hangings. He then took up the sword Tancred had given him and thrust it into his belt.

Returning to the outer room, he asked, 'Where shall we go, sir? Have you estates of your own?'

Tancred was still burning papers, and replied without looking up from the task. 'No, the Kervel estates were swallowed up long ago. As for where we go . . .' He shrugged.

Aurel thought rapidly. Going on foot would be hard for Tancred, so he briefly considered stealing a boat, and travelling down river, but that would take them right through Gwened. Tancred would prove no more popular with Count Fragan than he was with King Aymon.

That meant a journey on foot, to Naoned or Zol – with Zol being perhaps the nearest. It also had the advantage amongst all the provinces of Arvorig, of being furthest from Kemper and the newly risen island of Autrys.

Aurel began to pack up the rolls and fruit that remained from their interrupted breakfast. He did not want to think now of Vissarion's instruction to search out Duke Joscelin and kill him. Anyway, he could not abandon Tancred in his hour of need. If Vissarion punished him, he would just have to endure the pain.

Then he recalled Vissarion's strange promise. 'My servants will speed your journey back to me.' He did not know what that meant, or what to expect, but his heart grew cold to think what Vissarion might achieve now that Autrys had re-emerged.

Rising from the fire, choked now with the ashes of his documents, Tancred rested a hand on his shoulder. 'I'm glad to have you with me, boy,' he said abruptly.

Aurel was too overwhelmed by emotion to reply, and just then footsteps sounded again in the passage outside, the guards come for them before the promised hour was up. Now it was time to follow Tancred outside, to hear the door of the citadel slam shut behind them, to descend the stairways leading down through the city mountain that was Roazon, right down to the causeway and the road beyond.

Into exile, or freedom, or an imprisonment more oppressive still, Aurel could not know.

3

Valery de Vaux flung open a wooden chest and looked down at the half dozen rusty swords it contained. Bertrand had already raided the armoury at Bellière to supply his lads, and the weapons that remained had obviously been neglected for years. No wonder, when peace had lasted so long in Arvorig.

Bertrand himself was seated on a bench with his back to the wall. On a whetstone attached to a leather strap across one knee, he was patiently honing a spearhead. Close by him, Tiphaine de Bellière was shaking out a quilted jerkin she had pulled from another chest, blinking in the cloud of dust that billowed out of it. She and Bertrand seemed to be very carefully avoiding looking at each other.

Val suppressed a smile, and then a sigh. He knew how Bertrand felt about her, and anyone — except Bertrand himself, perhaps — could see her interest in him. But Bertrand's mind was fixed on redeeming his oath — and for too long he had assumed that no woman would accept his ugliness.

But that, Val thought, was the least of their current worries. 'How long do you think, before Fragan turns up?' he asked.

Bertrand squinted along the spearhead, and, satisfied, laid it to one side, and took up another. 'A few days more.

He'll need to gather troops, and before then we'll have an army in the field, on our way to Roazon.'

Val grunted, examining a sword that was more rust than blade, and tossed it back in the chest. 'What about the garrison here?'

'Bellière has never been captured,' Tiphaine intervened. 'Leave us just a few men, with Sir Guy to command them.'

Bertrand nodded, still intent on his work. Tiphaine glanced at him, then went on beating dust out of the jerkin, her swift, forceful movements telling of her frustration more clearly than any words.

'And Duke Joscelin?' Val asked. 'Will he come with us, or stay here?'

'Duke Joscelin will do what he wants,' Bertrand replied.

Suddenly the door swung open and Hoel stood there, holding out a sealed paper. 'There's word from Acquin,' he explained.

Bertrand rose and accepted the message, turning it over in his hands. 'My father's seal,' he muttered.

He frowned at the folded document for a moment, before breaking the seal and reading what was written there, his frown deepening. Finally, he held it out to his cousin, and Val noticed that he had grown pale, his eyes distant.

The letter was brief: Sir Robert d'Acquin reported that his wife was sick, perhaps to death. He begged Bertrand and Oliver to come to their mother's bedside.

'Bertrand, I'm sorry . . .' Val began.

'No matter.' Bertrand's voice was gruff. 'How can I go? I'm needed here. But we can spare Oliver.'

'But if your own mother's dying,' Val protested.

'Do you think she sent for me herself?' Bertrand snatched the letter from his hand and thrust it at Hoel.

'Find my brother and give him that. Tell him to saddle up and go at once.'

Hoel hesitated, then disappeared rapidly. As his footsteps died away, Tiphaine said softly, 'Bertrand, there's enough time for you to go to Acquin.'

Bertrand rounded on her. 'My mother hates me. She tried to have me disinherited. When I last saw her, I took Oliver away from her, and borrowed her jewels to pay for this campaign. Do you think she would want to see me now?'

Tiphaine stared at him. 'Jewels? Does she care only for jewels? Take mine to her, then! I brought jewels from Gwened, and there are more here at Bellière. Take them all if they'll please her! Do you think I wouldn't give you everything you asked for—'

She broke off, slapping a hand over her mouth. Bertrand's black eyes were shining. As if unaware of Val, he moved to stand over her.

Val could not prevent a smile as his cousin drew her into his arms and kissed her. When at last they broke apart, they still could not stop gazing at each other.

'Oh, lady . . .' Bertrand breathed out. 'I will ask for more, I swear it, when my honour is redeemed.'

Tiphaine, recovering herself, reached out and grabbed his wrist. 'Come with me, and we'll find the jewels your mother thinks so precious. And you *will* ride to Acquin with your head held high.'

As she dragged him out of the room, Bertrand went without a protest.

Grinning quietly, Val sat down on the bench and picked up the whetstone.

Twenty-Six

King Aymon shifted uneasily in his seat in the Great Hall, where the tables were spread with snowy linen, the silverware gleamed, the company was assembled, and yet there was no sign of the feast.

He hardly liked to admit to himself that these matters had been better ordered under Sir Tancred's supervision. Sir Baudet de la Roche had served him well as ambassador, with a fox's skill at diplomacy, but he had little idea of the requirements of the seneschal's office.

At least, the king reflected, he had Lady Marjolaine sitting by him, and although she showed him no reaction warmer than mere courtesy, his plans in that direction were slowly coming to fruition. He had summoned his wife; with her customary obedience the irksome woman might already be on the road. And once she reached Roazon, Aymon could engineer his freedom. He needed a good deal of self-restraint not to speak words of love to the Lady Marjolaine, words that she would certainly find displeasing until that freedom was his.

Ah, at last. The doors at the far end of the hall swung open, and Aymon caught a glimpse of serving men beyond, bearing platters of food. The first of them entered, ceremonially bearing a charger containing a roast sucking pig. Aymon could imagine its savoury sauces already wafting to his nostrils when there came a yell of terror from the passage outside. The serving man swivelled round suddenly, and the dish and its contents went crashing to the floor. The man following cannoned into him, and from further back along the column of servants sounded another crash.

The king let out a curse and sprang to his feet, trying to see what had alarmed the men. He caught a glimpse of something moving fast, too far down the passage to make out ... something the size of a boarhound but moving with the scuttle of a spider.

Without turning his head, he snapped at the page who stood behind his chair. 'Go and find Sir Baudet de la Roche, and ask him what in God's name is happening.'

When there was no response, Aymon finally turned his head to find that his page had vanished. The door at the rear of the dais, leading to his private staircase, was swinging open on its hinges. Cursing the boy, Aymon turned back to the hall and saw the passage beyond the doors was empty of servants now, though strewn with discarded dishes and salvers. An icy wind blew in, fluttering the flames of the lamps and extinguishing some, so that the hall was soon plunged into semi-darkness.

Sudden cries of alarm rose from the tables all around, and Aymon now noticed that about halfway down the room a set of window shutters was bulging inwards. As the king stared it gave way in a shower of splintering wood.

Something glistening slithered over the sill – like a giant serpent or slug, Aymon could not tell. Its head quested blindly from side to side as it coiled in the rest of its length, while a mouth opened up in its underside, lined with spiny teeth.

The guests at the nearest table scrambled away in haste, the table rocking and crashing over in a chaos of wine and silverware. The creature moved on in labyrinthine coils, nosing over this wreckage with a hideous sucking sound, leaving a sticky trail behind it as it edged further into the middle of the hall. One of Aymon's fleeing knights slipped in the slime it deposited and fell full-length, and before he could get up the thing was upon him. The man shrieked and struggled, vainly clawing at the scented rushes that covered the floor, as the creature sucked him gradually into its maw.

By now the feasting guests were panicking. King Aymon got to his feet and bellowed, 'A sword! Someone fetch me a sword!'

But screaming and shouting drowned his words, and no one responded. Already other shutters were giving way, as a variety of monstrous creatures slithered and plummeted into the enclosed space of the hall. Aymon blinked, his mind refusing to make sense of what he saw, reducing everything to a whirl of scales and feathers, claws and predatory mouths. A lamp stand crashed over, spilling burning oil; its flames caught in the rushes and licked at the bottom edge of the tapestries, and soon clouds of smoke billowed through the hall.

The king drew his belt knife and began to back away towards the open door leading to his private rooms. Curses spilled from his mouth. His eyes darted back and forth and he sidestepped to avoid a creature, as thick as his forearm, that drew its coils tightly round a broken body still twitching in its death throes. The snake-like beast turned its head towards him and Aymon started back as he saw it wore a beautiful woman's face. The mouth smiled at him — then darted out a lascivious forked tongue.

He was still groping behind him for the door when a beast borne on leathery bat wings erupted from the roiling smoke above his head and plunged at him, claws striking at his face. As it knocked him backwards to the ground, Aymon hit his head on a bench, and lost his grip on the knife.

Claws raked his face; he screamed in pain that pierced deep into his head, and the sight of one eye was extinguished. His hands still battered at leathery membrane as he tried to reach the creature's neck to throttle it, while blood gushed from his arm as its razor bill slashed across it, plunging deep into his belly. The king's last sensation, as darkness rose up around him, was the sound of the creature beginning to feed.

2

Sir Baudet de la Roche had been one of the first to escape the great hall. Skirting the knots of terrified servants in the passageways, he left the building by the door into the kitchen courtyard.

The guards had already fled from the postern gate in the outer wall, so Sir Baudet let himself out through the wicket, and paused briefly in the street outside. To his left rose the buttresses and spire of the cathedral. Something huge and serpentine was flapping around up there, emitting long, harsh cries. As Sir Baudet stared at it, a bell began to ring, a single urgent note, at whose sound the creature sheered away, plunging down below the roof line and out of his sight.

To his right the street was dark and silent. Treading cat-silent, he followed the outer wall until he heard cries and the clash of weapons warning of danger ahead of him.

Then he slid into a narrow stairway, leading steeply downwards, till the comforting silence encompassed him again. His throat was dry and his heart was hammering as he descended further, choosing always the steepest and narrowest stairs, crossing wider thoroughfares at a crouching run, ignoring the cries, the sounds of shutters being flung open, as the city woke to its peril.

He had one fearful moment, turning a street corner, as he stumbled to a halt only paces away from a coiled and scaly creature that blocked the way in front of him. He thanked God that its head was turned away from him, nosing at something that still writhed and moaned on the cobbles as a lolling tongue rasped over it.

Sir Baudet swallowed vomit and retreated with cringing care until he reached the same corner again and left the hideous thing behind him.

The city gates were closed when he reached them, but the guards still held to their posts. Adopting a haughty demeanour, Sir Baudet snapped out an order to them for the portcullis to be raised.

'What is it, sir?' one of the guards asked, as the iron grille creaked slowly upwards. 'What's come to us?'

Sir Baudet considered not replying, then changed his mind. 'Attack,' he answered briefly. 'I ride for help from the north.'

The guard saluted him uncertainly as he strode through the gates and across the causeway.

Flames were beginning to arise from the upper levels of the city, as he hurried along the lakeside road towards the stables where his own horses were kept. Pounding on the door, he roused a groom and ordered a horse saddled at once.

Waiting, sheltered in the doorway from the treacherous sky above, Sir Baudet looked out towards the forest. Uneasily he considered that somehow it looked darker tonight, and closer – and his own shaken nerves persuaded him that the line of darkness was moving.

I'm no coward, he reassured himself. *They cannot say I fled. For someone must take word to Brogall.*

When his horse was brought to him, he tossed a coin to the groom and mounted, taking the road to the north. A black shape flapped in the sky over his head, as if pointing out the road to him. Sir Baudet recognized it as a raven, and shuddered to remember the old folk tale that a traveller guided by a raven would never return.

Urging his horse to a canter, he glanced back at the burning city and settled himself firmly into the saddle. He would ride through the night, and not stop until he was well away from this accursed place. The raven was surely a good omen; returning here was the last thing he wanted.

Yet that glance behind had revealed something else. He had not been imagining things. There was indeed a shifting darkness, something that spread across the open space between the forest and the city walls, like ooze rising from the bottom of a swamp.

An icy chill pricked his skin and he shivered, longing for something warmer than the silken robe he had worn to attend the feast. Yet the solidity of the horse under him was comforting, its muscles bunching and relaxing in a strong rhythm as it bore him to safety.

He was drawing level with the head of the lake, where the Rinvier river poured into it with an endless murmur, when he caught a glimpse of movement over to one side. Glancing in that direction, he saw something keeping pace with him, too far away to discern its shape. A bear perhaps? There were plenty such up in the mountains, though only the fiercest winters drove them down this far.

He lost sight of it, and was telling himself it had been no more than imagination when he saw it again. But now it was not alone. More shapes flowed along with it; the tide of darkness from the forest was pursuing him.

His breath rasping, he spurred his horse and it leapt forward, galloping headlong up the road in front. Trees spun out of the night and vanished behind, but the dark presences remained alongside him.

Now he saw, with a first whimper of terror, that they were encroaching between him and the river. They were drawing ahead, surrounding him, so that he galloped in the centre of a circle of darkness.

No sooner had he realized this than his mount slammed into the first rank of it. With a neigh of terror, the horse reared, striking out with its hooves. Sir Baudet caught a whirling glimpse of myriad dark shapes, half human and half beast, of shaggy forms and sharp claws reaching out for him. Most horrible of all, they were quite silent.

He had no weapon but the belt knife he had worn for King Aymon's feast. Drawing it, he slashed out wildly, but the blade met nothing except yielding darkness. Desperate for speed, he dug his heels into his horse's side, but they could not break through the thronging shapes surrounding them.

His mount reared again, throwing Sir Baudet backwards, his reins snapping as they took his full weight. He grabbed vainly for the saddle bow, and slid helplessly to the ground in the midst of his steed's trampling hooves. One struck his shoulder, and he heard the bone crunch.

Sobbing with pain and terror, he stared upwards into the pairs of red, flaring eyes moving in on him. Clawed hands reached for his throat, as the hellish creatures gathered tighter round him on little goat feet.

Though he drew another breath, he did not have time to scream.

3

In the priest's house attached to the chapel of the Pearl of Arvorig, Father Cornely was dozing over the fire. Roused by terrible shrieks from the city, he stepped out into the clearing in front of the chapel. Flame spurted up on the heights, and clouds of smoke billowed across the towers of the citadel. While he stared upwards a foul stench wafted over him as some huge winged creature vaned lazily overhead.

Muttering a quick prayer, Father Cornely ducked inside the chapel and came back out bearing the emblem of the Holy Knot, carved from cedar wood, that hung behind the altar. Stumbling along the path in near darkness, he reached the bridge leading to the hythe.

Men and women were swarming over the hythe itself, scrambling for places in the fishing boats still moored there. More boats were already out on the lake, and, as Father Cornely stared in horror, a thing like a winged serpent, jetting flame, dived out of the sky. One boat was instantly wreathed in fire, its sail flaring up like paper and then the wooden hull. The unfortunates on board became a screaming, struggling tangle of flame as their hair and garments burned. Father Cornely thought he could hear a hissing as the lake swallowed them.

A second boat, tacking to evade the creature, had capsized, and heads bobbed in the water all around it. Something like a spider scuttled over the surface of the water and picked them off, shrieking, one by one.

'Come!' Father Cornely called out. 'Come here! Take refuge in the chapel!'

None of the panicking crowds still on the hythe could

hear him, but the serpent – or another like it – did. Father Cornely became aware of the flap of leathery wings, and raised his head to see the jet of flame directed at him an instant before it struck. He threw up the Holy Knot against it before his eyes were scorched out; the last thing he saw was the threefold emblem outlined in fire, as his body fell, jerking in agony.

4

Master Eudon, head of the Guild Council, was likewise dozing in front of his fire, comfortably seated in his solar with a good dinner inside him and a cup of spiced wine close at hand. His wife had long gone off to her sister in Plöermel, so there was no one to complain if he took an extra cup and went to bed pleasantly warm and mellow.

When commotion in the street roused him, at first he thought it was a crowd of revellers being turned out of the tavern at the corner – ruffians who couldn't drink quietly in their own homes – until he caught an unmistakeable note of terror. Muttering a curse, he heaved himself to his feet and stumbled across to the window overlooking the street.

Master Eudon pushed open the shutters. Outside the sliver of moon cast little light, but he could just make out a crowd in the street below, shoving and grappling with each other as they fled down from the citadel. He could not see any sign of what had frightened them.

As he peered down, even the faint moonlight was blotted out. The street became a dark abyss, terrible shrieks rising from it. Involuntarily, Eudon glanced upwards, half expecting to see thick cloud covering the moon, though the sky had been clear at sunset.

What he saw instead made him start back with a gurgling cry of shock. Something huge and winged had just flown across the moon, and its thin rind of light was revealed again as the shape swooped lower, and settled on the gable of a house opposite. Its claws gripping the ridge tiles, it uttered several raucous cries and flapped its wings, sending a warm wind loaded with the stench of decay into Eudon's face.

Suddenly unpleasantly sobered, he clapped the shutters to, but, before his view of the street was cut off, he caught a glimpse of something moving on the wall of his own house just below. From outside came the sound of something sucking across the gilded wood. As Master Eudon stared in alarm, one shutter splintered inwards, and a slimy head slid into the room, trailing ropes of mucus. It had three eyes, and a mouth full of teeth like needles as it smiled at him.

Instantly Master Eudon was out on the landing with his back against the door, shaking and swallowing vomit that kept rising in his throat. From inside the solar came an unpleasant squelching sound.

He hurried into his bedchamber and strapped on the money-belt he had kept in readiness ever since these troubles had begun. Next he thrust inside the breast of his tunic a leather pouch of unset gems, and crammed half a dozen of the most valuable rings from his jeweller's stock onto his plump fingers.

Quickly belting a furred velvet gown around him, he went back onto the landing, and yelled down the stairwell for his servants. No reply came — only the unspeakable noises from his solar. Of course, that pack of cowards had abandoned him long since.

A sticky ooze began to trickle under the solar door.

Shuddering away from it, Eudon half fell down the stairs and pushed the street door open just a crack. He could see nothing outside, and, after a few moments of agonized indecision, ventured out into the street itself. The panicking crowd had passed on, but more shouting and screaming sounded from further up the hill, nearer to the citadel. Turning away, ducking when possible under the shelter of projecting balconies and roofs, Eudon fled.

He was sweating from fear and exertion by the time he reached the city's lowest levels and paused, chest heaving, at a street corner. The open space before the main gates was packed with a swaying mob. Those at the rear were trying to press forward towards escape, while those in the gateway itself were trying to retreat from a tide of ... something black that flowed across the causeway and into the city.

Eudon took one look, with eyes and a mind that refused to differentiate shapes within the writhing mass, and turned to lumber towards the hythe gate. But within a few paces he was caught up in the crowd, tossed and buffeted around, barely able to keep on his feet as the terrified mob poured along the street.

Once through the gate and onto the hythe itself he could pause again, retrieving his breath, and snatching vainly at the rags of his shredded dignity. Boats were putting out on all sides, sails rising jerkily, while the citizens of Roazon fought for places on them.

Eudon strode over to the nearest, thrusting through the crowd, pulling off one of his rings as he drew near to the fisherman in the stern, who was unfastening the mooring rope. 'Here, my payment for passage over the lake.'

The fisherman spat back, 'Too late, we're full.'

'I'll give you gold ...' Eudon made a desperate grab at the gunwale, but the fisherman had already pushed off, and he stumbled down three or four steps into the lake water. It slopped over his soft leather boots and soaked the hem of his velvet gown. After a moment's frustration as the boat slid out into the lake, he climbed the steps again, cursing freely.

Another boat nearby was getting ready to leave. This time Eudon did not make the mistake of trying to bargain. Instead he barrelled his way on board, thrusting one man aside, and wrenching himself free from a hand fastening in his hair to impede him. Three or four others followed in his wake, before the fisherman managed to cast off, and the overloaded boat wallowed away from the quayside.

Master Eudon looked back at the crowds still thronging the hythe, and at the city above it. Flames leapt up from somewhere close to the summit, casting a red light on the water around him. Then he noticed, with a lurch of pure terror, that all of the fire did not come from the city. Over to the left of them another boat was burning. As he watched, it disintegrated into gouts of flame, pitching its screaming passengers into the water.

Just then another winged creature swooped overhead, the flame spouted from its jaws searing another vessel that became an instant bonfire in the darkness, then hissed out.

'Turn back!' Eudon shouted at the fisherman who now sat at the tiller. 'We'll all burn out here!'

Some of the others near him took up the cry, while others started to protest that there was no safety back in the city. Suddenly the boat canted over, and an icy wave washed over the gunwale. Eudon had scarcely time to cry out before the overburdened craft sank under him, and he found himself floundering in the lake.

The clamour of the drowning was all about him, but air trapped in his voluminous velvet gown helped to buoy him up as he thrashed about clumsily, making for the steps. But eventually the garment's heavy folds encumbered him, and the money-belt seemed to have multiplied in weight, dragging him down.

The Guild Master's inexpert splashing made little headway. His arms began to ache and, as he sank lower, he lost sight of the steps. He gasped for breath, swallowing a mouthful of water. 'Help me!' he choked. 'I'm drowning!'

Something gripped the back of his collar. Coughing up water, he started to sob in pure relief, but as he twisted to grab hold of his rescuer, his hands encountered something chitinous and spiked with bristles. He flung his head back and gagged in terror at the insectile head that lowered over him.

As its mandibles gaped open, his last coherent thought was that drowning would have been an easier fate.

5

Lady Marjolaine began by holding open the private door behind the dais, and urging all those around her through it. She saw the king fall and knew there was nothing she could do for him. No one else was nearby, so she slipped through the door herself, closed it behind her, and sped up the stairs to her own chambers.

So far the rest of the Roazon citadel was quiet, but she could not believe it would remain so for long. Those evil creatures – whatever they were, wherever they came from – had easily breached the defences and soon would be everywhere. She had to find another refuge quickly.

At the foot of the stairs up to her own apartment, she met one of the chambermaids coming down with an armful of soiled linen. She grabbed the girl's arm. 'The citadel is taken,' she said. 'Go straight to the cathedral. Go now!' she urged, as the girl just gaped at her.

Not waiting to see if this order was obeyed, she hurried on. In her bedchamber, Morwenna was laying out a nightgown for her new mistress. Rapidly Marjolaine explained what had happened, and Morwenna, blessedly asking no questions, immediately gathered together a bundle of clothes, and fetched both their cloaks.

'Where shall we go, lady?' she asked. 'You're welcome to my house . . .'

Marjolaine shook her head. 'Too far. These things will be all over the streets. We must go to the cathedral.'

Morwenna followed her as Marjolaine led the way along passages and down staircases, making all the while for the rear of the citadel and the postern gate that led onto the cathedral square. All the while she was alert for the sound of the evil creatures breaking in, but all was deathly quiet, as if they had so far confined their attack to the great hall.

Passing an armorial display upon the wall, she snatched down one of its crossed swords for herself, and gave the other to Morwenna. She had never been trained to use one, but at least she would not die totally helpless against tearing teeth and gouging claws, and the rough hilt in her grip was comforting.

When they came to the rear door she paused to listen a moment, before edging it open. Outside all lay dark and silent. Briefly Marjolaine fancied that something huge and unseen was hovering in the night sky above her head, but she pushed the thought away, lest it lead to panic and a useless death.

Motioning to Morwenna to follow her, she crept out into a courtyard lined with workshops – deserted now –

along one side, and the barracks of the Legion on the other, ending in the squat turret housing the captain's quarters. For a moment she wished that Sir Valery was still with her, and then pushed that thought away, too.

In the barracks one or two lights were burning, but no one was in sight. Marjolaine could see a torch flaring beside the postern gate, though the guards themselves had gone and the gate stood half open. From somewhere outside, by the cathedral square, came faint cries and the clash of weapons, almost drowned out by the rhythmic tolling of the cathedral bell.

Fear pulsing through her, she hurried across the courtyard, and they slipped through the postern then up the flight of steps that led to the square itself. As they reached halfway up, the clash of weapons grew louder, amid raucous cries and the beating of wings in the sky.

'Wait,' Marjolaine murmured.

She crept a few steps higher, until she could see clearly what went on in the square. Light spilled out of the cathedral windows, and by this she could see the Grand Master and a group of the Knights Legionaries, defending themselves against more leathery-winged predators like the one that had slaughtered King Aymon.

The Knights held their shields aloft and slashed away at their adversaries. The beasts wheeled easily away, but kept their distance, and the Knights were gradually winning their way towards the cathedral. Marjolaine realized that they were clustered round some townspeople, protecting their way to safety.

But Marjolaine could not linger there to watch. She and Morwenna were defenceless, and they could never reach the cathedral under that ravening sky.

She crept back down the steps to where she had left her

companion, gesturing back to the postern gate. 'Let's hide for now,' she murmured, 'and try again later.'

In the courtyard she hesitated, reluctant to return inside the citadel. But while she hesitated the door of the barracks opened a crack, and a dark figure beckoned them. 'Over here!'

They sped across to the partly open door and slipped inside. Drawing a breath of relief, Marjolaine turned to thank their rescuer, and was struck silent with astonishment to see it was the Matriarch.

Still dressed in her white robes edged with blue, the old woman had her sleeves rolled up, and wore a sacking apron. 'Welcome, my lady,' she said.

Marjolaine knew she was staring at her stupidly, then recalled how at her own Council the Matriarchy had vowed to care for the wounded in the citadel barracks. It had not occurred to Marjolaine until now that they would still be there.

'Thank you, Mother,' she said at last. 'There's great evil abroad in Roazon tonight.'

The Matriarch nodded. 'We have seen a little of it, and that's more than enough. Come, lady, there's supper laid, if you have not eaten.'

She held out a hand, graciously directing the two women to a nearby room, which was laid out as a refectory with long tables and benches. A small group of people were seated at the end of one, some blue-robed sisters, and a few women from the town, among whom Marjolaine recognized Regine de Vaux.

The women all rose to their feet as the Matriarch escorted the newcomers over. One of the sisters cried out, 'Lady, what news? What is out there?'

'I don't know,' Marjolaine said, feeling suddenly

exhausted. Her legs trembling, she was glad to sink down on the bench. 'I only know that it's truly evil.'

'Mother, what shall we do?' one of the younger women asked.

'What we have always done,' the Matriarch answered tranquilly. 'We do the tasks laid in front of us, and we trust in God.'

Twenty-Seven

I

Aurel scrambled up the last slope to the crest of the moorland and turned to give a helping hand to Sir Tancred. Together they stood, hair blown about by the stiff wind, and looked down a further slope towards the sea.

The springy moorland grass was interrupted by line after line of standing stones, grey and roughly shaped, casting their shadows towards the two men as the sun went down behind them. Aurel shivered involuntarily. He knew nothing of the ancient peoples who had placed these stones, or what was their purpose, but he felt them ominous.

By now they must have crossed the border. The town of Zol was hidden still by some fold of the land, but another day or two should bring them there. And that might mean safety, at least for a time.

Sucking in the cold air, Aurel remembered uneasily the red glow in the sky towards Roazon, that he had seen the night before. Lord Tancred, already sleeping, had known nothing of it, and Aurel had not enlightened him. But something had happened there – perhaps a great burning?

High above, in a sky growing greenish as evening approached, a hawk hovered on widespread wings. Aurel imagined its piercing eyes alert for the movement of some prey, and felt suddenly exposed there on the crest, as if he and Tancred could be the quarry the predator sought.

'Shall we go on, sir?' he asked.

Lord Tancred let out a weary sigh. 'I'm sorry, Melin, but I'm finished for today. Let's go down a little way and find a more sheltered spot to lie in.'

Aurel murmured assent, though he would have preferred to travel on, at least beyond the standing stones. But he could see his master's face was strained from weariness and the pain in his crippled leg.

Tancred bracing himself with his staff, they moved slowly down the slope until they reached a sandy hollow scooped out of the hillside, hedged around by thorn trees and watched over by one of those grey monoliths. Its surface was patterned by sulphurous lichen and stonecrop, and it stood canted at an angle, as if about to fall over and crush them. The place made Aurel feel profoundly uneasy, but he did not protest when Tancred sank down with a sigh and muttered, 'Out of that damn' wind, at last.'

The sun was going down in flame over the distant line of the sea. Aurel unwrapped his bundle of their possessions, laying out their remaining food. The scanty provisions they had brought from Roazon were long gone, but they had managed to buy more from farms in the hill country – bread, cheese and apples, and a leather bottle of cider.

They ate in silence while scarlet faded from the sky and the stars appeared. By this time tomorrow, Aurel thought half-regretfully, they could be in Zol. While they journeyed, he had been almost content. He wanted nothing more than to be with Sir Tancred, and the demands of the journey had proved easy compared with the imprisonment they had left behind. But tomorrow his master would take up his rightful place again – in exile, yes, but still Lord Seneschal of Roazon, with a part to play in events that moved the world. Aurel – or Melin the clerk – would scarcely be needed then.

Without realizing it, Aurel let out a sigh. Barely visible in the twilight, Tancred turned to him, one eyebrow cocked. 'Something on your mind, boy?'

Aurel shrugged. 'I was wondering . . .' His voice trailed off. He was suddenly more aware still of the standing stone above their hollow, a black shape looming above their heads, blocking out the stars. For a second he entertained the absurd notion that it had edged closer, like an eavesdropper.

A soft susurration passed through the grass, and Aurel's uneasiness deepened into shivering fear. He felt Tancred's hand fasten round his wrist. 'Something just moved – down there,' the seneschal said.

Aurel peered down the slope, but he could see nothing except the dark ranks of the stones. 'Maybe a sheep,' he said, his voice trembling.

As they waited, there was no more sound or movement, but the prickle of horror did not leave him. Softly he murmured, 'Sir – can we go on now?'

Tancred nodded, reaching for his staff. In silence Aurel bundled their possessions together again. He froze in the action of holding out a hand to help Tancred get up.

Something *had* moved. He had caught it from the corner of his eye, but when he whipped his head round he felt he had just missed seeing some of the nearer stones shuffling and realigning before they settled. Aurel wondered if his master had noticed too, and dared not ask.

Sir Tancred struggled to his feet, and they set off again. The way to Zol lay down and to the right, but before they had gone many paces they found a stone blocking their path. Rounding it, they came upon another. Aurel never spotted the stones moving, but always what had seemed to be a clear space was closed once they reached it. In a nightmarish fancy he imagined the monoliths wavering across the hillside like a line of dancers in complex figures that were always about to begin, or just completed, when he turned to look. He half expected to see great scars in the earth where the stones had torn their way through it, but the tough moorland grass was unmarked, as if the stones could swim through it and have it close behind them like a ship's wake.

Whatever the truth – whether the stones moved, or whether the travellers' own fear betrayed them, or whether something evil from outside was acting on their minds – Tancred and Aurel were driven aside from the route they wished to take. The stones gradually herded them south and east, away from the safety of Zol, and back into the hills.

Tancred's breath was rasping and he stumbled more than once. As Aurel took his arm to steady him, he said, 'No good, boy. If we made a stand . . .'

Almost as soon as the words were out, another stone loomed up in front of them. Lord Tancred thumped his staff on the ground and faced it squarely. At his side, Aurel glanced back and saw that they were now surrounded by a tight circle of monoliths. As he stared, he felt the cold touch of stone pressing up against his back.

'No!' he gasped. 'They'll crush us!'

He thrust Lord Tancred through the last remaining gap. Thrown off balance, the startled seneschal missed his footing and fell, rolling a few feet down the slope until he fetched up at the foot of yet another stone.

Aurel cried out in anguish, ready to see the thing grind over him and crush him into the ground. He flung himself at his master and dragged him to his feet again. While the stone loured above them, Aurel caught the sense of an implacable waiting.

'Let us go!' he yelled. 'We mean you no harm.'

The stretch of moorland to their left was still clear. Tugging Tancred along with him, half supporting him, Aurel stumbled up towards another ridge. As he reached it, he looked back, to see the lines of monoliths where they had always stood, dark and secret, guarding the approach to Zol. Aurel realized that he and his lord could not go that way.

He turned and looked ahead. The moorland fell away steeply in front of him, into a valley where a stream glinted under the rising moon. Beyond the stream rose a gentler slope cloaked with dark trees, and moonlight revealed the edge of the forest of Brecilien.

2

Bertrand d'Acquin had always loved the forest. Unhappy as he had been as a child, out of place in his own home, it had provided a refuge. He had explored it and fought mock campaigns through it with the peasant lads who were his only friends. He had learnt to hunt in it — not with hawk and hound and all the panoply of a nobleman, but quietly, with snare and arrow and the poacher's knowledge of his prey. Sometimes he had slept there.

Now, on his way from Bellière to Acquin, he did not understand why the same forest suddenly felt alien. Its dark places had grown darker still. He began to hear unexplained rustlings and cries that sounded like no bird or beast that he had ever encountered. When he and Oliver lit their evening cooking fire, the night crowded round them as though it watched and listened.

For the first time he could remember, Bertrand felt relieved to ride out of the trees and see the fields of Acquin in front of him. Even without knowing what he would find there, he was still glad to leave the once hospitable forest behind him.

His mind was in turmoil. Early in the morning, before he left Bellière, he had become betrothed to Tiphaine in the chapel. He was still not sure how this had come about. He had dreamed of her often, but in his dreams he had ridden off to war in Roazon and returned to her loaded with honour, a knight at last, so that his dazzling splendour might blind her to his ugliness. But Tiphaine had not seemed to care about any of that – only himself. Bertrand was still stunned by the wonder of it.

But set against his bewildered happiness there was the sense that the forest had rejected him, and darker still the thought of meeting his mother at the end of his journey – and hers. He prayed for her recovery; he prayed too that if she was really to die she might turn to him at the last. He did not expect either prayer to be answered.

He had refused, in the end, Tiphaine's offer of all the Bellière jewels, except for an emerald collar, a glittering extravagant thing far finer than anything Jeanne had ever owned. It would be a gift to her from Tiphaine, his betrothed. Surely, Bertrand thought, his mother must find some worth in him if he had won the heart of Tiphaine de Bellière.

The weather was cold, with cat-ice at the edge of the river and the slap of sleet in the wind. Lamplight shone warm in the windows of the manor house as Bertrand and Oliver dismounted in the courtyard and gave their horses to the elderly groom who came out to meet them.

'Go in, masters, go in,' he said, his voice a mere croak. 'Your father's expecting you.'

Sir Robert d'Acquin himself flung open the door as

Bertrand approached, and stepped outside to embrace his two sons. Not until they reached the brighter light of the hall did Bertrand see how much his father had changed.

He was much thinner, and what flesh remained hung on his bones. The last of the bright chestnut had vanished from his hair. His face was gaunt, marked by illness as well as trouble, Bertrand suspected.

'Father, what's happening here?' he asked.

Robert motioned to the steward, Graelent, to fetch wine, and urged his sons to take seats by the fire. Sitting opposite, his hands on his knees, he explained, 'Marsh cough. We think one of the stable hands picked it up at the horse fair in Malou. It's gone right through the estate.' He cleared his throat, thumped his chest, and went on, 'I had it too, but it's clearing now. Your mother . . .'

His voice trailed off.

'What about Mother?' Oliver asked. 'Is she . . .?'

Robert shook his head. 'I rode to Malou and brought Lord Rivalin's own physician to her. He gave her syrup of elecampane, but . . .' His hands moved together convulsively, scarred fighter's hands. 'She wastes away. She cannot breathe.'

Oliver stood up, waving away Graelent who was bringing the wine. 'Take us to her, Father.'

Robert led the way to Jeanne's solar, Bertrand bringing up the rear, with his head bowed. He knew his first instincts were right: he would not be wanted here.

Fine beeswax candles burned in the solar, and a fire leapt on the hearth. A maidservant sat by the window, embroidering a design on a fall of white silk.

They found Jeanne d'Acquin seated in her usual chair by the fire. For a first breathless second Bertrand's heart leapt.

It had all been a joke! There was nothing wrong with her — how could there ever be anything wrong with Jeanne d'Acquin, always so indomitable, so much in command?

Then he looked more closely.

She was dressed in one of her finest gowns, crimson silk finely worked with gold thread and tiny gems at the throat and on the edging of the sleeves. Rings glittered on her hands, and her hair was coiled high, covered by a gauzy headdress. But cushions propped her up in the chair and, always so consciously graceful, she sat stiffly like a wooden doll.

Her face was turned towards the fire, so the reflection of the flames cast a glow of health on it. As Robert led the way inside the room, she raised her head, her eyes, hard sapphires still, looking out from behind a mask of paint. Her beauty had always been a mask, Bertrand thought confusedly, so that you looked at that, and not the woman herself. Now he thought he might almost lift that mask away — would there be emptiness behind it?

'Oliver!' Jeanne stretched out a hand to her younger son. 'So you're home at last! Come and sit by me and tell me everything.'

No sign of the shrieking fury she had unleashed when Oliver left. She was gracious now, smiling at him, and the sight of a smile on that dead countenance made Bertrand shiver. Her breathing sounded like the tearing of silk.

Oliver took her hand and sat down beside her on her footstool. Robert drew his elder son further into the room and said, 'Here's Bertrand too.'

'That clown!' Any hopes he might have felt died under the scorn in his mother's voice. 'I wonder he dares show his face here.'

Hesitatingly Bertrand stepped forward, the familiar embarrassment, anger and helpless frustration washing over him.

'Mother, I wanted to see you,' he began awkwardly.

'I can't imagine why.'

'I – I've news, Mother. I'm betrothed, to the lady Tiphaine de Bellière.'

'Betrothed!' Jeanne's high laughter spilt briefly into the room, followed by a fit of coughing. As Bertrand watched, horrified, she bent over, gasping for breath. The maidservant snatched a cup from the table, and Robert tipped his wife's head back, helping her to drink. When some of the liquid trickled down her chin, Bertrand noticed old dribbles of it, crusted and sticky, on the front of her gown.

When she had recovered, dabbing her mouth with a napkin that smeared her face paint, she stared at her son with cold hostility.

'The wench must be crazed to want to wed you, Bertrand,' she hissed. 'To feel those crude peasant hands on her.'

Bertrand felt a dull throb of anger, and beneath it an uncertainty that he had never yet put into words. He feared exactly that – perhaps when they came to the marriage bed, Tiphaine would find him repulsive.

But he remembered the glow in her eyes when Father Patern had joined their hands.

Gently he laid in his mother's lap the soft leather pouch that held the emerald collar. 'She sent you a gift, Mother.'

Jerkily, his mother loosened the drawstring and tipped out the emeralds to flash in the firelight. Bertrand heard a gasp, from Robert or from Oliver, but his eyes were fixed on his mother.

'She knows her duty then.' White fingertips flicked the stones. 'A little gaudy, maybe.'

'Would you like to wear it, Mother?' Bertrand asked, knowing her well.

Jeanne nodded. 'Robert, you do it,' she commanded her husband, pointedly holding out the emeralds.

Carefully, exchanging a glance with Bertrand over his wife's head, Robert fastened the collar in place. The gems cascaded, glittering, over the stained gown. The maidservant brought a mirror, and Jeanne stared into it, contemplating herself with a small smile creasing the paint around her mouth.

Did she still see beauty there, Bertrand wondered.

She was completely withdrawn from them now, so Robert touched Oliver's shoulder and motioned towards the door. As they went out, Robert softly closing the door behind them, Bertrand was not sure if she had even noticed them leave.

Urgent knocking at his bedroom door roused Bertrand in the middle of the night. Blinking sleep away, he saw the door open and Oliver standing there, a taper in his hand. He beckoned to Bertrand.

'Father says we should come.'

No need to ask why. Bertrand wrapped himself in his cloak and padded after Oliver along the passage to his mother's room. The flagstones chilled his bare feet but he scarcely noticed; the real chill was in his heart.

Another taper burned beside the bed, its twin flames casting a pool of light over Jeanne d'Acquin where she lay propped up on pillows, her unbound hair spilling over them.

Her face was pallid now, without the paint, her breathing a shallow rattle.

The chaplain, Father Corentin, sat near the bed's head, his beads slipping softly through his hands. At the other side of the bed Sir Robert was kneeling, his wife's hand clasped in his own.

He looked up as his sons came in. 'She . . . she leaves us now,' he said.

Oliver went forward to kneel on Jeanne's other side, but Bertrand hovered beside the door. He was not sure how long he stood there, his breathing falling into the rhythm of his mother's, whose each extended exhalation he thought would be her last.

Longer still he stood, the tapers burning right down, a pale light beginning to leak through the window shutters. The door opened again to admit a nursemaid with the two little girls, their faces white and scared.

Then Jeanne convulsed and Robert's grip on her tightened as she let out a wordless cry. Then she fell back on her pillows, and the rattling breath was stilled for ever.

After long moments of silence Sir Robert suddenly spoke. 'When I first saw her, she was dancing with her sisters, on the Feast of Birds. She was the most beautiful thing on God's earth, and when she smiled, the sun shone. I never expected that she would even look at me.'

He let his head fall on to the embroidered bedcover, and sobbed in despair.

3

Each day in the citadel barracks would begin with the Offering ritual, led by the Matriarch. Lady Marjolaine always made a point of attending, for among the daily worries of scarce food supplies, dwindling salves and dressings and the herbs of healing, it was too easy to forget God. Most of all, in the face of the horrors which she knew hovered just beyond the barracks walls, it was hard to remember that God held all — even the demons who had devastated Roazon — between his cupped hands.

The Offering completed, she went with the others to the refectory, for the piece of bread and cup of water which made up her breakfast. Crumbling the dry bread, she wondered for the thousandth time why the demons did not simply break in and destroy them all. They could do it; she had seen enough of their power on the night they attacked to be sure of that.

Perhaps somehow they could see through the walls, she imagined, and derived more amusement in watching their patient efforts to survive than in inflicting a quick kill. Yet she did not feel that the leather-winged creature who had disembowelled King Aymon was capable of such subtlety.

No, she decided, they were waiting for something. She and the others with her were being reserved for another fate. And she herself must necessarily be the focus of it: as Lady of Roazon, last but one of the Roazon bloodline, she would have to be stupid not to realize that. Her courage almost failed as she wondered what her end would be.

Breakfast finished, Marjolaine made her way to the Knights' Dortour, where the Matriarch and her sisters were already tending the wounded. Outside the laundry, she caught up with Morwenna, struggling along with an enormous basket of clean linen.

'Let me help you with that,' she said.

Thankfully, Morwenna let her take one of the handles.

In these days, it was scarcely worthy of comment that the Lady of Roazon would help to carry a laundry basket.

'Today is Ivona's birthday,' Morwenna said, with a tight smile close to tears. 'She's one year old, but I wonder if anyone else will remember.'

'I'm sure she's safe with your friend Alissende,' Marjolaine replied, answering the doubt behind her friend's words.

'Oh, I know . . .' Morwenna sniffed, and wiped the sleeve of her other arm over her eyes. When she next spoke, her voice sounded determinedly cheerful. 'Well, wherever my child is, she's better off there than here.'

'Perhaps you'll see her again soon.' Marjolaine tried to match her false optimism. 'Soon the whole of Arvorig will know what has happened here, and they'll send an army to drive those foul creatures away.'

At this thought, a wave of longing swept over her, for in her mind's eye one of their rescuers must be Sir Valery.

'They'll come soon,' she repeated. 'This evil won't triumph for ever.'

'What touching faith.' A silken voice spoke. 'And how misguided.'

Marjolaine jerked to a halt. They had almost reached the end of a passage leading to the Dortour. Just ahead was a small hallway with a door into the yard outside.

Now that door lay open and a man stood on the threshold, behind him a close-packed darkness of eyes and claws. A dry, sweetish odour of decay drifted in around him, like something embalmed in myrrh and myrobalon from an ancient tomb.

Morwenna gasped and dropped her handle of the basket. Marjolaine set down her own more carefully, matching her gaze with the intruder's. At first she thought she was looking at a young man, and very beautiful — tall, with long dark hair and alabaster skin. Then she noticed fine wrinkles at the corners of his eyes and mouth, and the deadness revealed by the eyes themselves. He could have come, himself, from that old tomb.

When he smiled, Marjolaine thought that terror might unseat her reason. 'Who are you?' she asked, making every effort to keep her voice steady.

'My name is Vissarion.' His voice was serpent-soft, soft as the black velvet he wore. 'And I seek the Lady Marjolaine of Roazon.'

For a moment Marjolaine stood frozen in shock, and in that moment Morwenna acted. She took a step forward, her hands clasped at her waist, and declared, 'I am Marjolaine. What do you want of me?'

Vissarion's smile stayed fixed, but venom flashed into his black eyes. 'Oh, no, do you think I'm foolish? *This* is the Lady Marjolaine I seek.'

He stepped forward, his hand stretched out as if he was about to lead Marjolaine into the dance. 'Lady, you shall come to my realm now,' he said. 'You shall exchange Roazon for Autrys.'

'I'll go nowhere with you!' Marjolaine said, her paralysis falling away. She whirled to flee, and heard Morwenna cry out. Somewhere further inside the barracks a door crashed open.

But it was too late for help. The darkness gathered behind Vissarion was now flowing inwards. One coil was already wrapping itself around her, looking insubstantial, stronger than cords of steel. Out of its end a serpent head coalesced, its neck arching over her, its tongue the flicker of dark lightning. Marjolaine sucked in breath to scream, but found her throat had closed up as if she fought with nightmare.

The creature drew her, still struggling vainly, out into the open courtyard, and spread its bat wings gleaming with iridescent darkness. As her feet left the ground she heard Vissarion say to his servants, 'Bring the other one too. She may provide some amusement.'

Then a dark fog rolled over Marjolaine's senses, and she knew nothing more.

Twenty-Eight

Sir Tancred eventually halted, leaning on his staff, and spat out a curse. Glancing over his master's shoulder, Aurel saw that the path they had been following petered out in a tangle of briars and bracken.

'You would almost think this damned forest knows we're here,' Tancred said. 'I'd swear it's trying to trap us.'

Aurel felt a deep uneasiness that the seneschal might be right. He had never walked beneath the trees of Brecilien until now, but the forest had figured largely in the tales his childhood nurse had told him. Sensible folk, she said, did not go that way, but now he and Sir Tancred had been given no choice.

On its outskirts, he had felt little of the fear those old tales had once roused in him. There the trees were widely spaced, letting plenty of light through, and in hazel brakes and bramble thickets there was food to be found. There were even paths, trodden by foresters or villagers who pastured their pigs on fallen acorns and beechmast. In a few days, Aurel had reckoned, by clinging to the forest's western edge, they should come to Sant Brieg or Pempoulle.

He should have known better, for all the paths they followed seemed to lead deeper into the heart of Brecilien, and if they tried to retrace their steps soon they found themselves in swamp or thicket, or on the edge of a bluff which Tancred could not hope to climb down.

If standing stones could move, and obstruct them from their goal, then Aurel believed that the forest could also play with them.

Wearily they retraced their steps to a point they had passed perhaps an hour before, where two paths crossed. They had barely turned into the new direction when Sir Tancred halted again, reaching out to grip Aurel's arm. 'Listen.'

From somewhere ahead of them sounded the creaking of cart wheels. Aurel's first reaction was relief: this must be a farmer returning home from his labours. He would be able to give them directions, perhaps even food or shelter. Then uneasiness crept over him, and, even though he did not understand why, he could see his master shared it, so he made no protest when the seneschal drew him into the shelter of some bushes beside the path.

Peering through the tangle of branches, Aurel saw the cart approach. It was drawn by a black mule, and the driver was tall and thin, in tattered black robes, with wispy white hair escaping from under a flat, broad-brimmed hat. He was gazing from side to side as he came, his head swivelling stiffly on his shoulders. As his glance swept across the bushes concealing Aurel and Sir Tancred, Aurel caught a glimpse of a green flame flaring in empty eye-sockets.

His throat closed in terror; he felt Tancred's grip on his arm tighten. Frozen, he waited for what seemed like an eternity, while the cart drew abreast of their hiding place and passed on down the path. From his nurse's old tales Aurel knew what he was seeing: the Ankou, servant of Death.

At last the creaking of the cart wheels died away, and

they dared to emerge. Aurel shivered, all his body bathed in an icy sweat. Sir Tancred was chalk white, his mouth set. He took a few steps further along the path, and then paused, looking back at Aurel. 'Call me a fool,' he said grimly, 'but I don't like the look of this.'

Ahead of them, the path wound onwards, bordered by briars and clumps of fern, until it was lost among the trees. Its surface seemed smooth, almost inviting. Aurel swallowed. 'Nor do I.'

With a sense of inevitability, he was unable to rid himself of the feeling they were being watched. Autrys had risen, and all the evil in Brecilien — perhaps in all Arvorig — had risen to meet it. Now he and Sir Tancred were trapped in the midst of it. Aurel could scarcely think coherently for his fear.

Sir Tancred was looking upwards, to where a shaft of cold light broke through the tree canopy above. After a moment's thought, he gestured with his staff. 'That way.'

He stepped out into the bracken, and Aurel followed, trying not to remember his nurse's stories of foolish travellers who left the forest path and were never heard of again.

At first they made good time in their new direction. The rhythmic swishing of the bracken as they strode through it soothed Aurel, until he realized that it was the only sound he could hear. No birdsong, no small scurryings of creatures in the undergrowth. The whole of Brecilien seemed to have fallen into a listening silence. Aurel became acutely conscious of his own accelerated breathing and the pounding of his heart, and tried to tread more softly.

'Sir,' he began nervously, 'do you think—'

He broke off as his master stumbled, failed to right himself with the staff, and crashed to the ground. Darting towards him, Aurel himself was thrown off balance as the ground fell away into hollows, concealed by the luxuriant growth of fern. A natural hazard, he thought ... or was it another trick of the forest?

Reaching Sir Tancred, Aurel helped him to sit up. The seneschal was cursing, softly and viciously.

'Are you hurt, sir?' Aurel asked.

The man's face was pale as he answered. 'No. Just this damn' useless leg ... Melin, you were a fool to come with me.'

Aurel wanted to hug his master and reassure him that even now there was nowhere in the world he would rather be, but he had the good sense to restrain himself. That was not what Sir Tancred wanted to hear – not from him.

'Rest here for a few minutes, sir,' he said instead. 'I'll see if I can find some food for tonight.'

Tancred, sitting with his head in his hands, did not reply. Aurel stood looking around, but there was nothing in sight that would yield them nourishment. The food they had bought from the hill farms was finished, and even the nut bushes and brambles were rarer now.

But without food, Aurel knew, they would weaken, until at last they could only lie down and die. Was that what Vissarion intended for him?

As despair threatened to overwhelm him, he pushed it aside. If Vissarion had decided to discard him, that was all to the good. He would not give up without a struggle, for that would be to endanger Tancred's life too.

Standing very still, he began to realize that another sound had crept into the silence of the forest – a faint trickle of running water. Once Aurel had pinpointed its direction, he turned to his master.

'Sir, there's a stream over there.'

Tancred looked up, alert again. 'That's good – we need the water. Here, boy, hand me my staff.'

Aurel searched among the bracken until he found it; then they struck out in the direction of the hidden stream. There might be cresses there, Aurel thought, or even fish that they could cook over a fire. But the thought of kindling a flame to burn the wood of Brecilien chilled him. He swallowed uncomfortably; well, raw fish would be better than nothing.

Soon they came to a dark and secret trickle straying among the roots of trees. Sir Tancred took his bearings from the sun again and decided, 'We should follow this stream. Sooner or later it should flow into the Rinvier.'

Hope quickened in Aurel again. He stooped to drink and filled the water flask, while Tancred quenched his own thirst. The water was clear and ice cold.

When they were ready to continue Aurel took the lead, following the twisting line of the watercourse and offering a hand to his master when trees threw out knotty roots across their path.

They had been journeying like this for about an hour, and the daylight was dying fast, when the level ground they walked on fell abruptly away and the stream cascaded down into a dark pool. Flecks of foam eddied on its surface and the rocks on either side were slick with spray.

Aurel crouched on the edge of the ridge and examined the slope below. 'This doesn't look too difficult, sir,' he said. 'I think you could get down there if I help you.'

As if the sound of his voice had animated it, something he had assumed to be a boulder by the side of the pool unfolded itself, revealing an upturned face, pale in the twilight, the shape of its skull clearly visible beneath tightly stretched skin. Aurel realized that he was looking down at an old woman in a black robe. As he stared, she drew up a length of white linen from the water with one skinny hand, while with the other hand she beckoned to them.

'The Night Washer.' Tancred murmured, and Aurel glanced up to see the seneschal standing over him. 'Which of us do you want, old woman? Whose shroud is that?'

The crone made no reply, only beckoned again, her toothless smile growing wider.

Aurel scrambled to his feet and grabbed his master's arm. 'Don't look at her, sir. Don't go down there.'

For a minute of heart-stopping terror he thought that Tancred might plunge into the pool to embrace his death. He placed himself between his master and the waterfall, blocking his view of the beckoning woman.

'Sir, we must go this way — across the stream.'

Tancred shook his head sharply, as if shrugging off a bad dream. 'Yes, lead the way.' Then he added quickly, 'And don't look back.'

So they splashed across the stream and into the cover of the trees on the other side. As the gurgling of the water diminished behind them, Aurel thought that it held the sound of a little, chuckling song. He did not dare to release Sir Tancred's arm until the song had faded to nothing.

2

Like a border of grotesque, late blooming flowers, brightly coloured tents had blossomed along the river bank beneath Bellière. Beside them, banners snapped in the wind. Count Fragan had raised the plain ermine of Arvorig along with his own arms, the red lion of Gwened. The Holy Knot

banner of the Legion stood a little way apart, and still
further along the bank Alissende could make out the colours
of Zol, Brieg and Malou. Others still were lost to her sight
as the ranks of their besiegers curved round the walls of the
castle.

She had climbed up to the wall-walk more than once
since the armies of the provincial lords were first spotted
approaching along the road from Gwened. Surprising herself, she did not feel afraid: it was all as she had expected it
to be. Once Nicolas de Cotin had revealed what he knew,
Duke Joscelin's whereabouts had drawn the lords to him as
a lodestone attracts iron.

Sir Valery had already departed at the head of their own
troops, to rendezvous with his cousin Bertrand in the forest
near Roazon. Alissende did not know what their plan might
be to retake the city, or even if they had one yet. Only a
few men remained under Sir Guy's command to defend
Bellière. Everyone was moving, Alissende thought, into the
positions they must take to bring about an end, like pieces
on a chessboard – or like masses of cloud shouldering each
other across the sky before the storm breaks.

Only Duke Joscelin had not moved, or not yet, and
Alissende knew that the stillness of his meditation would
hold the key to Arvorig's survival, more than all the
posturing of the men in arms.

As she watched from the shelter of a merlon, she noticed
a movement in the camp. One of the Knights Legionaries,
fully armoured but for his helmet, was mounting his horse,
as a small escort of other Knights formed up behind him.
The whole group set out at a trot towards the bridge.

Footsteps sounded on the boards beside her, and Sir
Guy de Karanteg rested a mailed hand on her arm. 'Best go
down, Sister,' he said. 'There might be trouble.'

'Who is that?' Alissende asked, not moving.

Sir Guy snorted. 'Girec d'Evron. A natural-born, fully-fledged bastard, and now calling himself Commander of the Legion in Gwened. Don't trust him, Sister.'

He strode off along the wall-walk towards the gatehouse, and Alissende followed him, heading for the steps which would take her into the comparative safety of the courtyard below.

The group of Knights crossed the bridge, and began ascending the road which led to the castle gate. One of them carried the black and silver banner, and another a totally plain white flag. A parley, then, Alissende assumed, loitering at the top of the steps to hear what Girec d'Evron would say. His look was arrogant as he faced up to Sir Guy.

'Open the gates, de Karanteg, and yield up the heretic,' he demanded.

Smiling pleasantly, Sir Guy invited him to perform an act of astounding obscenity.

Girec d'Evron retorted with the sign of the Holy Knot. 'No more than I would expect of a renegade to our order. Will you yield up Joscelin? If not, you will be excommunicate!'

Sir Guy let out a gust of laughter. 'You terrify me.'

'In defying me, you defy Holy Church herself,' d'Evron replied. His voice rose. 'The Judge will strike you down for your blasphemy, both you and the heretic you protect!'

He wheeled his horse and rode down the hill and back to his camp.

Once d'Evron had gone, Alissende withdrew to her still-room, and began checking the shelves: earthenware crocks of ointments, wooden boxes of dried herbs. Now that the siege was set, there would be no chance to gather more.

The astringent scent of the herbs managed to soothe her, and she could almost imagine herself in the role of a housewife, putting up simples against the months of winter. Intent on her task, she did not realize she was not alone until a voice spoke behind her.

She turned to see Tiphaine, who looked pale and nervous. 'Sister ... having been trained in the Matriarchy, you can foresee what is to come?'

So many credulous people had asked her that question, ignoring the disciplines of fasting and prayer that the art of scrying demanded; so many feather-headed girls thought she could tell them who they would wed. 'We merely look in the scrying bowl, and see the visions sent to us.'

'Sister, I have seen such things, too.'

Alissende froze with her hands on a box of dried thyme. 'Tell me.'

As Tiphaine stumbled into an explanation, Alissende did not understand most of what she said, but she did not need to. She set the box of thyme in its place and turned to face the younger woman.

'Sit down.' She pointed to one of the stools beside the table. She brought over two of her earthenware bowls and a pitcher of water, and took the stool opposite. 'I'll show you what we do in the Matriarchy.'

She tipped water into each of the bowls, then spoke the prayers. All the while Tiphaine watched her with wide eyes.

'Now,' Alissende said eventually, 'look into the bowl. Whatever you may see, you may not describe until the visions are ended.'

Tiphaine nodded, bending over the water. As soon as

Alissende looked into her own bowl, the reflection of her face vanished, to be replaced by a picture of dark forest branches and dead bracken, under falling snow. That blinked out almost immediately, and she saw a bewildering sequence of scenes: Bertrand riding under his banner of the Black Eagle; Sir Valery de Vaux and others of the Knights at prayer; a narrow, derelict street with a huddled body face-down on the cobbles; the provincial lords of Arvorig taking up their banners as they formed a column to ride away.

The siege will be raised, she thought, wondering when that might be. As the water in her bowl cleared again, she realized that she was looking at a grey expanse of sand and pebbles, beyond which lay the hard, grey line of the sea.

Her scrying vision swung round and she saw a causeway, built of roughly dressed blocks of grey stone curving out across the beach. At its further end loomed that same dark island, with saw-toothed pinnacles cutting into the sky.

Tiny winged things wheeled about the topmost turrets, and on the causeway, a man was walking away from her, towards the island. Though the sky was heavily covered with clouds, he seemed to move in sunlight that gleamed on his golden hair.

As Joscelin moved on, the gates at the far end of the causeway gaped open. Another man stood there, robed in night as Joscelin wore the sun. His smile was the desecration of all that was good and true.

'Oh, no!'

At once the water in the bowl shivered and grew clear again. Alissende looked up to see her friend was white, tears in her eyes.

'I saw Duke Joscelin . . .' she whispered.

Pure dread seized Alissende. 'Tell me what you saw.'

'He was walking out towards a fortress. Its gates opened, and there was someone waiting for him.'

Alissende's fear hardened till she felt cased in ice. Scrying with her sisters, she had learnt how rare it was for two of them to see the same vision. Experience showed that such moments held the most truth.

She reached out and took Tiphaine's hand in hers. 'I will think of this,' she said. 'Meanwhile, say nothing to anyone.'

3

Snow was drifting from the sky, beginning to load the bare branches of the trees and lying like white dust on the forest floor, as Bertrand and his brother Oliver rode to their rendezvous near Roazon.

Huddled in his cloak, Bertrand was oblivious of the snow except to curse it as one more obstacle. King Aymon's men would be snug inside the city walls, while Bertrand's own troops froze.

Since leaving Acquin, he had done his best to put thoughts of his mother's death out of his mind, and had almost succeeded. But deep inside his head a bell was tolling: *she will never know me now.* He was a man now, with a man's concerns, but he could not quite relinquish that consuming hope from his childhood, even though he knew that it was futile.

For all his brooding, he was still aware of the forest, still uneasy here where he had always felt so much at home. From time to time he could have sworn he saw narrow, malicious faces peering at him from branches or thickets, though when he turned to confront them there was nothing there. The strange cries he had heard on the way to Acquin returned, seeming louder now and closer, as if unseen beings were tossing words back and forth in a language he did not understand. Were they being pursued? Bertrand rode with one hand on his sword.

The short winter day was drawing to an end when he began to hear the sounds of a large company in the trees ahead. Before he reached them, a man stepped smartly out of the undergrowth in front of him, his crossbow cocked, and demanded, 'Who rides in Brecilien?'

Bertrand recognized Donan the silversmith. 'It's me, Donan,' he said wearily, pushing back the hood of his cloak. 'Where's Sir Valery?'

The sentry straightened up, and pointed. 'That way.'

Bertrand grunted in acknowledgement, and turned his horse down the path Donan had indicated.

'I hope there's a pot on the fire,' Oliver said. 'I'm so hungry I could eat King Aymon himself!'

'He'd give you bellyache,' Bertrand retorted sourly.

The red glow of fire began to appear among the dark treetrunks. Men and horses had passed this way earlier, trampling the snow into grey slush. Then the path came to an end at the edge of a clearing, where men sat hunched around a camp fire, dark silhouettes against the flame.

One of them sprang to his feet, and Bertrand heard his cousin's voice calling his name. He dismounted, and almost at once Val was embracing him.

'Bertrand, thank God! I thought you might not get here.'

'Why not?' Bertrand thrust his cousin away at arm's length, noticing that he looked drawn and worried. 'What's happening?'

Val tried a smile, but with that darkness still in his eyes. 'There's news, Bertrand. Things have changed since you went off to Acquin. Come to the fire, and I'll tell you all.'

The men around the fire shifted to make room for them, and platters of roast meat and bread were thrust into their hands. Someone hooked a pot off the flames and began pouring hot ale into horn beakers.

Val squatted down beside Bertrand. 'Your mother?' he asked quietly.

'Dead,' Bertrand replied, his eyes burning into Val's. There was so much he would have liked to tell his cousin, if they had been alone. As it was, he said no more, except, 'Tell me the news.'

Val accepted the beaker of ale held out to him, and Bertrand ate ravenously while he listened. The snow grew thicker and hissed into the fire.

'Roazon first,' said Val. 'I don't know if King Aymon himself is still there, but there's something else in there with him. One of our watchmen swears he saw a giant snake, slithering along the top of the wall. Twenty feet long, he claimed, with a woman's face.'

Bertrand snorted. 'He should go easy on the ale.' He drained his own beaker and held it out for more.

'That's what his friends told him at the time,' Val replied with a half smile. 'But since then others have seen it, too — and there's more. Huge spiders have been seen crawling around the hythe and over the lake. Sulien says he spotted a creature like a bat, but much bigger, flying over the citadel. Then yesterday it passed over here — dear God, the stink! There are evil things in Roazon, Bertrand, and I don't know if we can contend with them.'

Bertrand shook his head. If anyone else but Val had told him all this, he wouldn't have believed it, and yet his

account seemed to fit with the strange presences he had
sensed in the woods.

'Where did they come from?' he asked finally.

'That's the other thing,' said Val. 'Master Segondal,
come and tell my cousin what you told me earlier.'

One of the others around the fire looked up. Bertrand,
looking more closely now, saw that he was a stranger. He
was a small man, with straggling fair hair, and the cloak he
held tight about him, though filthy and tattered, was of
velvet lined with silk. Rings flashed on his hands as he
moved closer to the two cousins.

'They've taken Kemper,' he croaked and started to
shudder.

Val laid a hand on his shoulder. 'You're safe here. Just
tell it from the beginning.'

Master Segondal pushed hair out of his eyes with a hand
that shook as if he had fever. 'I'm a merchant in Kemper,'
he began. 'Or at least I was, before all this. Silks and vel-
vets . . .' As Bertrand stifled an exclamation of impatience,
he went on quickly. 'There was a huge storm, so we put
up the shutters and lit the blessed candles, before we sat
down to have supper. Then there was a colossal noise as
if the whole earth was being torn apart. People were running about and shouting in the street. I was worried about
my warehouse, so I headed down to the harbour, and I
saw . . .'

He started shaking again, so Val put a beaker of ale into
his hands and he gulped it convulsively.

'What did you see?' Bertrand urged, trying to curb his
impatience.

'An island had arisen offshore.' Master Segondal's voice
was hushed. 'An island city, like Roazon, but black, all

black. It's Autrys, that the Lords of Roazon banished from this world. It's come back.'

'Autrys!' Oliver exclaimed. 'Our old grandmother used to tell us stories about Autrys. Do you remember them, Bertrand?'

His brother nodded. His grandmother had been a shrewd and wise old woman; Bertrand remembered her sitting by the hearth in the great hall at Acquin, while he begged her for a story, and she began, 'Long, long ago, when chickens had teeth . . .' It was one of the few warm memories of his childhood; he would crouch by the fire and listen attentively, until his mother would chivvy him away with complaints of how he wasted his time. His grandmother and mother were both gone now, but the stories remained clear in his mind.

'What happened then?' he pressed.

The little merchant's eyes stayed dark with fear. 'Demons came flying over, and something inside Autrys let them in. Inside, mark you! Something had been waiting there, under the sea, for all those years . . .'

'And then?'

'Lord Rebius was away in Gwened, so his seneschal sent a courier to Roazon. And the local commander of the Legion set his Knights to watch at the harbour wall.' Segondal emitted a peal of hysterical laughter, then pressed a hand against his mouth. 'As if that would do any good! When the demons came, they butchered everyone they found out in the streets, they tore down house walls as if they were pie-crust . . . We fled, all those of us who could. Some of us made for Roazon, thinking we would be safe there. But they've taken Roazon, too. They'll take the whole world soon, and nowhere will be safe!'

He covered his face with his hands, and began to weep.

Val turned to Bertrand. 'What do we do now?'

Bertrand shrugged and wiped his mouth on his sleeve. 'We do what we always planned to do. We retake Roazon.'

Val looked uncertain, and Oliver protested, 'But if it's full of demons . . .?'

'I swore I would do it,' Bertrand retorted. 'Demons or no demons, I'll keep my word, or die trying.'

His brother grimaced. 'Mad,' he muttered to Val.

'It was hard enough to begin with,' Val said. 'It's even harder now.'

Bertrand held him with a look. 'Your mother is still in there,' he said.

For the first time Val's calm wavered. 'I know.' His voice was scarcely above a whisper. 'And Lady Marjolaine too. What will they do to them?' He scrubbed a hand over his eyes. 'Oliver's right, it's madness. We haven't enough men.'

'Not here, no,' Bertrand agreed, his spirits starting to rise again as he realized what his next step must be. 'But I know where we can find them — well armed and mounted, too.'

'Where?' Val challenged him.

Bertrand grinned. 'I reckon they should be at Bellière by now.'

Twenty-Nine

The Lady Marjolaine de Roazon looked out of her narrow window and down the black steeps of Autrys to the sea far below. At low tide a causeway joined the island to the coast, but now waves were washing over it, and even as she gazed its dark line vanished. She had watched the sea engulf it several times now over recent days, and each time she felt even more isolated.

Beyond the causeway rose cliffs, the coast of Arvorig. Marjolaine did not recognize the area, though if the old tales were true then Kemper should be a mile or so up the coast. She shivered when she thought what might have happened to the inhabitants of that wealthy, beautiful, complacent city.

On the long flight from Roazon she had lost count of time. The winged serpent had brought her into Autrys by night, letting her drop on to the obsidian flagstones of a circular courtyard beneath walls so high she felt as if she was lying at the bottom of a well. She had immediately tried to get to her feet, but her legs, still stiff from lying immobile in the serpent's grip, would not support her.

Then rough hands had seized her on either side and pulled her upright. On seeing the creatures who held her, she barely stifled a scream. From the waist up they were men, though rough hair covered their naked skin; they had the shaggy haunches and prim cloven feet of goats. Their faces looked human but slack-featured, their eyes dull as if no reason lit the minds behind them. Marjolaine could sense their animal desire for her like a stink in her nose, and shuddered as she wondered what other power restrained them.

'My lady, welcome to Autrys.' That silken voice again, and Vissarion moved into her field of vision. He was poised, elegant, as if he had somehow bypassed the long journey from Roazon and had groomed himself in preparation for her arrival.

'What is this place?' Marjolaine demanded. 'What have you done to Morwenna?'

Vissarion gestured with a slender hand, as a great lord might invite his guests to look over his luxurious estate. 'This is the island of Autrys, my lady.'

'Autrys?' Marjolaine looked wildly round at the soaring pinnacles of stone. 'But that's just...'

'An old tale?' Vissarion finished for her. 'But as you see, some old tales are true.'

'After Joscelin was declared heretic...' Marjolaine said, struggling to understand. 'And when no true lord sat in Roazon...'

'Excellent.' Vissarion nodded approval, as a master would compliment a bright pupil. 'Then Autrys returned. And now it's *my* task to make sure it stays here.'

'You'll never do that!' Marjolaine drew herself up, despite the demibeasts who still gripped her by the arms. 'You'll never find Duke Joscelin, or destroy him.'

Vissarion raised his brows. 'No? Even when I can pluck the Lady of Roazon out of her own citadel? There are many things I can do, lady, and destroying the Roazon bloodline is perhaps not the most difficult.'

For all her efforts, Marjolaine's expression must have changed. Vissarion smiled. 'Oh, yes, lady, you must die too. But not quite yet. Now I have you safe, I can afford to wait. There are several quite amusing things that we can do together before that moment comes.'

Impotent fury at his sneering tone was growing stronger even than Marjolaine's fear. She flung herself at him in rage, only to be hauled back by his creatures, who shook her roughly until she thought her neck would snap.

'Gently,' Vissarion cautioned. 'I don't want her damaged yet. Take her to the chamber prepared for her.'

As they dragged her away, Marjolaine twisted her head to see her captor standing easily with the dark towers behind him. 'What have you done with Morwenna?' she cried.

'Your friend is here too, and quite unharmed,' Vissarion said. 'How many times do I need to tell you — killing quickly is so wasteful.'

Marjolaine turned to study to the room she was confined in. Its walls were bare stone, ribbed and stippled as if from the long lapping of the sea, and gleamed strangely with a faint, nacreous light. There was a bed, a chair, a table, and a closet concealing a privy. The door was locked and bolted, and the window too small to escape through, even if she had dared climb out over such a dizzying drop beneath.

Yet another of the demibeasts had brought her a basin of water to wash, a comb, and a fresh gown. She was adequately looked after, yet she did not fall into the trap of believing she would be safe. She thought she understood Vissarion all too well.

Turning back to the window, she was disturbed a

moment later by the sound of the bolts being drawn back. By the time the door had fully opened she was on her feet. Vissarion entered with an escort of his creatures.

'Good day, lady,' he said. 'Should you find your quarters tedious, I've come to distract you a little.'

'How kind of you,' Marjolaine replied icily.

An ugly flash of anger crossed his face. 'Kind indeed,' he said. 'You shall now see a little of Autrys, and join our revels.'

'Your pardon,' Marjolaine said, seating herself at the window again, 'but I have no mind for revelry.'

'Not even if I give you the chance to see your friend?'

Morwenna? Marjolaine turned back to face him. She tried not to seem too eager. 'Yes, I'd be glad to see her.'

'Then gown yourself, as befits a lady of your rank.'

For the first time Marjolaine saw that a woman had followed Vissarion into the room. She was tall, holding herself like a great lady, with dark hair piled up on her head, and a gown of scarlet silk. But, as she moved forward from the shadows around the door, Marjolaine noticed the faint markings decorating the skin of her exposed arms and bosom, like the diamond patterning of snakeskin. When the woman smiled, a forked tongue flickered between her teeth.

In her arms, the snake woman carried a gown made of silk, so fine that Marjolaine could not help wondering at it – layer upon layer in black and grey and silver. It was so beautiful, but as she touched it she could not repress a shiver of revulsion, as though it were spun out of cobweb, and the spider still lurked within it.

'Gown yourself,' Vissarion repeated.

Marjolaine stared at him icily until he withdrew, the demibeasts with him, leaving her with the woman, who helped her put on the new gown, and combed her hair into a headdress of glittering jet.

As she made ready, the last of the day died in the sky outside, and lights began to spring up in the city below — red flares dancing on the jagged lines of walls and rooftops, as though the whole place burned.

Music drifted faintly upwards, its notes wavering into subtle discord, the rhythms uneven, as if the phrases could never come to resolution. Marjolaine tried to imagine the dance that might accompany it.

When she was ready, Vissarion returned, and held out his hand with a grotesque parody of courtesy, leading her through his fortress like a great lady escorted by her knight. All the time, the demibeasts escorted them.

A twisting stairway led down and down, so far down that Marjolaine fought with the fancy that they were plunging deep into the earth. She did not bother to ask her escort.

At last they came to the foot of the stairs and he opened a door. Cold air flooded in, and that same leaping red light. Marjolaine stepped out into a narrow thoroughfare bounded on one side by the fortress and on the other by a blank wall. In the strip of dark sky visible above her head, no stars pierced through the canopy of cloud.

She turned to face Vissarion. 'You said you would take me to Morwenna.'

'And I will.' The glint in his eyes showed how her protest had pleased him. 'We shall meet her at the revels, and then you shall see a little of my city.'

'*Your* city? You command here?' Marjolaine asked sharply. Though she had seen no one of higher rank than Vissarion, she somehow did not believe that he was ultimate lord of this place.

Vissarion gave a slight, elegant shrug that rippled the black velvet of his robe. 'I have a Master greater than myself,' he said. 'He has given me Autrys for my own, and I command his servants here to do his will.'

Marjolaine was not sure she understood, but she asked no more questions.

Vissarion led her on down the street, with his creatures shambling behind them. The road led steeply downwards, twisted to one side, and became a stair. At the bottom lay a square with a fountain in the centre, where three stone serpents entwined, their gaping jaws vomiting a dark stream into the basin. With a start of horror, Marjolaine caught the reek of blood.

Down, and yet down. Clearly the tower where they kept her captive was one of the topmost pinnacles of this city, and all Autrys lay below it. The place was, she realized, a twisted parody of her beloved Roazon, but the familiar white walls exchanged for steel and obsidian, the tree-lined walks become cramped and arid alleyways, the spilling roses replaced by contorted vines that clung to wall and column, bearing poisonous clusters of scarlet berries.

Sometimes an archway to one side would lead into a courtyard beyond. In one Marjolaine caught a glimpse of a barbed wheel turning unceasingly; in another was a cage in which something dark and shaggy snarled and slavered at the bars. Once, high above her head, she heard a terrible scream.

At length they reached another square, the largest expanse Marjolaine had seen so far. The jangling music grew louder here, crowds thronging the open space. At first they seemed like a noble company, richly dressed and masked for carnival; then Marjolaine realized that they were not fully human: men with the heads of birds; women with webbed hands and hair writhing snake-like around their heads; figures like small children with ancient, dead eyes. Sometimes she could not be sure whether what she saw were masks or living distortions of flesh.

At first she could do nothing but stare at them in fascinated horror, but at last she tore her gaze back to Vissarion, who had paused beside her with a satisfied smile.

'Where is my friend Morwenna?' she asked him coldly.

Vissarion gestured towards a colonnade on his right, where tables had been set up, furnished with goblets of wine and dishes piled with sweetmeats. At one of these tables sat Morwenna.

Marjolaine could scarcely recognize her at first, so richly gowned in copper-coloured silk, and with her hair netted into a tower of copper wire. Yet beneath the extravagant headdress her face was white and watchful, and her eyes lit up with relief as she spotted her mistress.

'Lady – what have they done with you? I've been so afraid.'

'I'm sorry,' said Marjolaine. 'It's my fault you're here.'

'Lady, enough,' Vissarion interrupted her. 'Tonight is for revelry – see.'

Marjolaine turned to see that he now wore a triangular black mask with a gleaming surface. In his hands he carried two other masks, one silver and one copper, which he held out to them. 'Put these on, I pray, and then you will be ready for all the delights Autrys can offer you.'

Morwenna tentatively accepted the copper mask from him, turned it over in her hands, then raised it to her face.

As soon as its surface touched her, tiny claws sprang out from the edges and buried themselves in her face. She let out a strangled cry, and tried to tear it off, but the claws held it tight as threads of blood trickled down her neck.

Marjolaine rushed to help her, but she could not prise it loose. She had one horrifying glimpse of Morwenna's eyes staring out in terror before more tiny claws sprang out around the edges of each eye-hole, and curved back inwards.

Morwenna's frightened cry spiralled up into a thin shriek of agony. Blood gushed from the slits of the mask as she crumpled into Marjolaine's arms.

Vissarion merely smiled as the music jangled on.

2

'Melin.' Sir Tancred's voice was a rough gasp; his chest heaved. 'This is no use. I have to rest.'

He was leaning on Aurel, as he had for many hours now while they struggled through the forest. Since the snow had fallen, the ground was more treacherous than ever, the white mantle covering it deceptively soft and smooth, though it concealed hummocks and hollows and twisting roots. Aurel had lost count of the times they had stumbled. Their clothes were soaked in snowmelt, ice matted in the fibres, and he could not remember ever feeling so cold.

He used the edge of his cloak to brush snow off a broad tree root, and lowered his master to sit down on it. The seneschal leant back against the trunk, his eyes closed.

'If you had any sense, lad, you would leave me here.' His voice sounded low and defeated.

Every muscle in Aurel's body was aching too, but he realized that if he sat down to rest too, neither of them would ever get up again. Gripping a lower branch for support, he looked round with the faint hope of finding food or shelter. He had forgotten when they had last eaten, and he was light-headed with hunger.

A pale light suffused throughout Brecilien, its trees stark black against the snow. Aurel gazed up at the full moon through a tangle of branches and reflected that with the snowfall their last hope had vanished. They might as well lie down here and find a little warmth together before all was over.

With death facing him so starkly, Aurel longed to tell Tancred that he loved him. Was he to sink down into the eternal dark with his heart unspoken? And yet he held back, unable to bear seeing that scarred and beautiful face turned towards him with a look of disgust.

So instead he reached down, rested a comforting hand on Tancred's shoulder, and said nothing.

For an unknown time he stood there, his breath silently clouding the air, till gradually he became aware of a weight of oppression, as if he was being jostled in the middle of a huge invisible crowd. From the corners of his eyes he caught glimpses of flickering movement, as if unseen creatures kept creeping through the undergrowth, but once he turned to face them, they were gone. And all the time he felt aware of malign eyes watching them both from the dark places underneath the trees.

In his fear, he almost roused Sir Tancred and urged him to press on, but soon recognized how futile that was. Neither of them had the strength to escape. If something evil was closing in on them, as well face it here as anywhere.

Then he noticed a golden flush on the snow, and that a branch, broken and half buried, was casting a blue shadow as though the sun rose.

Aurel looked up. A few yards away, beside a thicket of

juniper, stood Duke Joscelin. He was clad in the same plain linen robe that he had worn in Roazon, and his hair was burnished with sunlight. He smiled at Aurel, and beckoned, then disappeared behind the thicket.

For a second Aurel stood motionless with astonishment. With the figure now gone, he assumed that he must have been dreaming, his mind giving way to fancies as his strength failed. But he dared not disbelieve, so he stumbled forward, plunging towards the trees where Duke Joscelin had disappeared. Somehow, that sense of oppression was gone.

Breaking through a tangle of undergrowth he found himself reaching the edge of a clearing. Snow glittered silver in the moonlight, flushing again to gold just where Joscelin stood at the foot of a broken wall of rock. Smiling still, he raised a curtain of bramble, revealing a dark hollow beneath, and beckoned to Aurel again.

Shelter? Hope flooded through him again, but at the same moment something was gnawing at Aurel's mind — a sense that something was not quite right here. Was this some evil vision sent by Vissarion, offering hope that was only the road to a deeper despair?

'My lord, wait for us!' he called to Joscelin, and hurried back to fetch his master.

The seneschal, barely conscious, protested irritably as Aurel tried to rouse him. Taking almost all the man's weight, Aurel guided him stubbornly through the under- growth and across the clearing to where Joscelin had shown him the cave.

His uneasiness returned as he saw that the figure had vanished, but again he pushed that aside until he should have Sir Tancred safely in shelter.

'Look, sir,' he said, drawing aside the brambles. 'We can rest here.'

The seneschal emitted a harsh crack of laughter. 'Just like a tomb — how suitable.'

'I'll go in first,' Aurel said, ignoring that irony.

He reached inside his tunic and drew out the serpent knife. *One scratch brings death*, Vissarion had warned him. Well, if anything evil was lurking deeper in that dark cavity, Aurel would soon find out if he spoke true.

At first, the roof of the cave was so low that Aurel had to stoop. His own presence cut off the light from outside, but within a few paces he could sense that he stood in a much larger space. Cautiously, he straightened up and listened.

Everything was silent, except for his own breathing and the shuffling sound of Tancred dragging himself along the tunnel on his hands and knees. Aurel stood gripping the knife still, poised to strike, but as more seconds slid by he began to relax.

With a grunt and a long sigh, Tancred slumped to the floor. Now a faint light was able to filter in, showing Aurel that the seneschal had collapsed half inside and half outside the tunnel.

Sheathing the knife, Aurel knelt beside him, fumbling desperately for his heartbeat. He found it at last, weak and unsteady, but all his efforts to rouse his master failed.

'What can I do?' he asked aloud, then sat back on his heels and looked around.

Becoming more accustomed to the dim light, he began to realize that the cavern was not as empty as he had first thought. Dark shapes like boxes or bales were ranged along one wall. Against the other was a mound of something unidentifiable, and other shapes crowded in the darkness at the farther end.

With a sudden quickening of excitement, Aurel crawled back down the tunnel, past his master, and looped back the bramble curtain to let in more light. Returning, he stood and stared for several minutes, hardly able to believe what he saw.

Someone had been living in this cave. At the far end a semi-circular bay contained the ashes of a fire and an iron trivet for a pot. Logs were stacked beside it, with a basket of kindling. A niche in the wall held an oil lamp and a tinderbox.

Up against the wall was a pile of sheepskins, while on the opposite side one wooden chest held blankets, and another one earthenware bowls and an iron cooking pot. Earthenware jars held flour, and meal, and dried beans. Several joints of smoked meat hung from the roof of the cave.

Aurel was trembling with relief, half inclined to weep, as he realized that they would not die after all. Slowly he dragged Sir Tancred over towards the mound of sheepskins. Fumbling with hands that were stiff with cold, he managed to strip off the seneschal's wet outer clothes and wrap him in a blanket. Tancred did not rouse; his breathing was very shallow.

'Don't leave me now,' Aurel whispered. 'You can't, not now we're safe.'

For a little while anyway, he added to himself. He wondered briefly what would happen if the normal occupant of the cave returned, but then he resolved to dismiss such worries. The ashes of the fire were cold, and a spider had spun its web across the niche above it. Everything here suggested that the cave's owner was long gone.

Once he had settled his master, Aurel lit the lamp and then made a fire. Its bright flames flickered wildly in the cold air flowing into the cave mouth.

He went to let the bramble curtain fall again, and took with him the cooking pot to collect snow; he would melt it over the fire and get some hot porridge ready.

Outside, the snow still glittered under the moon, and as Aurel scooped some into the pot he glanced back across the clearing and saw the dark, wavering line of their footprints.

Then his heart grew cold as the snow he collected, and he realized what had been troubling him before. The mysterious figure of Duke Joscelin had left no footprints.

3

As they rode through the snow towards Bellière, Val felt quite convinced that his cousin was mad, and that he himself was mad to follow him. It could be nothing else that was sending them back into the hands of their enemies.

Yet Bertrand's reasoning made a crazy kind of sense. If evil had arisen, then it was the duty of every good man to drive it out.

'Be damned to all this nonsense about heresy,' Bertrand had said. 'What does that matter now? Not even Fragan would hand Arvorig over to a pack of demons.'

Frost sparkled under a pale wintry sun as they emerged from the forest and saw the tents of the lords of Arvorig encamped around Bellière. The smoke of cooking fires rose into the cold, still air.

As the horsemen approached – Bertrand and Val, with no greater escort than a couple of Bertrand's lads – a shout rose from the camp ahead. Moments later their way was barred by four spearmen – two in the livery of Gwened, and two Knights in surcoats so white they could almost have been carved out of the surrounding ice and snow.

'Who rides to Bellière?' demanded one of the men-at-arms.

The other gripped his arm. 'That's Bertrand d'Acquin,' he muttered. 'him they call the Black Eagle. The count will want to see him.'

'I'll wager he does,' Bertrand said cheerfully. He flipped out a square of fabric that might once have been white too, and waved it under the man's nose. 'Recognize this? It's a flag of truce. Now take us to your master.'

Count Fragan's tent was a haven of warmth in that frosty landscape, draped with fur and deerskin, rugs spread on the floor, and a brazier burning near the entrance. The Count himself, looking older and more infirm, was seated on a chair well padded with cushions, a fur-trimmed mantle wrapped around him.

He half started up as the cousins entered. 'D'Acquin!'

'Yes,' Bertrand agreed He untwisted the purse strings at his belt and tossed the purse to the floor at Fragan's feet. 'Payment for your baggage train,' he said. 'And you might let me have the name of your wine merchant.' Glancing round, he added, 'We wouldn't say no to a cup now.'

Ignoring the purse, Fragan snapped his fingers at one of the servants as Bertrand seated himself on a nearby bench and Val went over to sit beside him.

'Now,' Bertrand loosened his cloak and pushed its wet folds off his shoulders, 'we've news, my lord count, that you might not have heard yet, stuck out here in the back of beyond.'

Fragan raised his brows. 'I doubt that,' he growled.

Bertrand gulped some wine with a sound of satisfaction. 'So you know that Autrys has returned? You know how the demons have destroyed Kemper and taken Roazon?'

'What?' Fragan started to rise, and then sank back into his chair with a spasm of wheezy laughter. 'You've impudence and to spare, d'Acquin.'

'It's true, my lord,' Val said seriously. 'I saw the demons myself on the walls of Roazon.'

The count opened his mouth to reply, then snapped it shut again. His eyes focused sharply on Val, who thought he could read uncertainty there.

'We're here to ask your help, my lord,' Val went on. 'Now that these evil things are loose in Arvorig, we must put our differences aside.'

The count said sourly, 'For all I know, this is some trick intended to stop me from smoking out your heretic lord from Bellière.'

Bertrand bristled at the implication, and Fragan glanced away, plucking at his furs, avoiding the challenge that must come if he said any more. Val was surprised into a sudden pang of pity for his increasing frailty.

'My lord,' he said, 'we only speak what we know to be true. We can save Arvorig from this evil, but only if we band together.'

Fragan snorted, and instead of replying to him, clapped his hands for one of the guards. 'Fetch me Sir Girec d'Evron.'

Val finished his cup of wine, while Bertrand shifted impatiently. The count just stared down at his own clasped hands, as if he could read the answer to his dilemma there.

A few moments later Girec d'Evron himself arrived, wearing the off-duty woollen robe of a Knight Legionary,

with a black cloak over it. He bowed to the Count. 'You
sent for me?' He broke off suddenly as he noticed Val and
Bertrand, and stiffened.

'They're here under truce,' said Fragan, 'with dire news
for us all.'

As Val launched again into his story, d'Evron listened to
him with a fixed sneer. 'And you believe this, my lord?' he
asked the count, once Val had finished.

'Somehow I do,' said Fragan tiredly.

D'Evron let out a faint sound of contempt. 'Do you
think he would scruple to swear to a lie? A renegade Knight,
and a follower of the heretic?'

Fragan sat back, steepling his fingers. Suddenly he
looked more like the man he had once been, the hard-
headed warrior and politician. 'I said I believe him. What
would you do in my place, d'Evron?'

D'Evron looked shocked. 'If this story is true, then
clearly it is a punishment for heresy. The best way for us to
drive out these demons is to capture the heretic and make
an end of him.' He made the sign of the Holy Knot, his
face the image of sanctimonious piety.

'You're wrong, d'Evron,' Val argued, new certainty welling up inside him. 'That's not the way. Through many
centuries Autrys was kept out of our world by preserving
intact the Roazon bloodline. What we must do now is
restore Duke Joscelin to his rightful place.'

'Restore a heretic!' D'Evron's shocked outburst went
unnoticed.

'And how do you propose that?' Fragan asked.

'We must recapture Roazon,' Bertrand said eagerly, 'and
force the Archbishop to reinstate him.'

A gleam of amusement came and went in Fragan's eyes.
'Very well. Tonight at supper we shall sit in Council with

the other lords who have accompanied us here. If they all agree, we shall march on Roazon tomorrow.'

D'Evron backed away towards the tent flap, his face convulsed with venom and a kind of sick disgust. The man's faith might be twisted, Val thought, but clearly it was genuine, and somehow d'Evron managed to be unaware of his own hypocrisy.

'You will excuse me, my lord,' the departing Knight said coldly. 'I will not attend your Council, nor will the Legion ride to Roazon.'

'The Legion will do as it's damn' well told,' said Fragan.

D'Evron almost smirked. 'You do not rule the Legion, my lord, but I do. The Knights will stay here until Bellière falls and the heretic Duke Joscelin is delivered into our hands.'

Thirty

Blinking in the cold light, Aurel emerged from the cave and rubbed a handful of snow over to his face to wake himself. No fresh snow had fallen in the night, and the clearing was criss-crossed with the spiky tracks of birds, the pads of foxes, and other prints that Aurel preferred not to examine too closely. A pale winter sun slanted through the trees.

Following his routine of the last few days, he skirted the clearing as far as a hazel brake where he relieved himself, and then continued to the snow-covered dome of a charcoal-burner's clamp, and the rough shelter beside it where more logs were stacked. Discovering these had explained the provisioning of the nearby cave, though Aurel could not help wondering if the charcoal-burner had returned to his village at the onset of bad weather or if his absence had some other, more sinister explanation.

Collecting an armful of logs, he hurried back to the cave, where the embers of last night's fire still smouldered under turf. Now Aurel carefully built it up and coaxed a flame. Once he had set the pot to boil, he turned to Sir Tancred.

The seneschal lay curled on his side, his hands feebly clutching the sheepskins. Since entering the cave, he had done little but sleep, as if their struggle through the forest had consumed all his resources. His weakness — for one who had always been so competent — sent a pang of pity through Aurel, and yet it was mixed with a kind of joy, that the seneschal should need the care Aurel could offer.

Gazing down at him now, Aurel dared to draw one finger down the back of his master's hand, then to touch the hair, silvering a little, at his temple. The physical contact roused Sir Tancred; his dark eyes opened, and he smiled at Aurel drowsily.

Aurel's starvation for love overcame him. Stooping, he let his lips touch Tancred's, and he realized too late how he had betrayed himself. He drew back, appalled.

'I'm sorry, sir,' he stammered.

But there was no disgust in Tancred's face. The look he gave Aurel was questioning, uncertain. 'Melin, I—'

'I'm sorry,' Aurel repeated. He drew further away, wanting to flee the cave, to hide himself, knowing that he had thrown away so much that was precious in one unguarded moment.

Sir Tancred reached out and fumbled fingers around his wrist, keeping him by his side. 'There's nothing to be sorry for. Dear God, don't leave me now, not when . . .'

As his voice failed he looked away, shaking his head helplessly. With a shock, Aurel realized that Tancred shared his fear, and with that knowledge a warm confidence began to grow inside him. He stooped over again, and turned Tancred's face towards him. 'My dear lord,' he said.

There was a glitter of unshed tears in Tancred's eyes. He had been alone for so long — how long, Aurel wondered — showing nothing but that harsh exterior to the outside world. Was there anyone, even the Lady Marjolaine, who truly knew the man behind this façade?

Gradually, as Aurel still bent over him, he saw his

master's smile return. In the seneschal's dark eyes gradually grew an incredulous delight.

'I won't leave you.' Aurel's voice cracked. 'As long as you're not angry with me.'

Tancred tightened his lips on an outburst of shaken laughter. 'Not angry, Melin. It's what I hoped for.'

Aurel felt his chest tighten, as if he was going to suffocate; there was suddenly not enough air in the cave. He sat gazing down at Tancred, paralysed by happiness, until with a hiss the pot boiled over, sending clouds of steam and smoke up into the cave. Aurel scrambled to rescue it, and tipped in some oatmeal with shaking hands. The first breakfast of their shared love was destined to be a disgusting mess.

As he set the pot back over the fire the flames glinted on the silver ring he wore. Aurel shrank from this reminder of Vissarion – and yet, the ring had been quiescent for days now. Perhaps he had been forgotten, or with Autrys returned to the world Vissarion had other, more important matters to deal with. Whatever the reason, Aurel hoped fervently that this silence would continue. Aurel de Mont-faucon was an outcast who had wasted his own life. Melin was loved.

When the oatmeal was bubbling steadily, Aurel went back to sit at Tancred's side. 'I thought you loved the Lady Marjolaine,' he said.

'I do,' said Tancred, 'but as a brother.' He sat up, and Aurel shifted the sheepskins so he could lean back against the cave wall. 'I loved her father, Lord Primel. I was his squire,' Tancred went on, his tone making the words a confession. 'I thought the world could not hold a man so noble or so beautiful.' He shrugged. 'But he was a man for women. And then he died, stupidly, unnecessarily. And I never wanted anyone else ... until now.'

Shakily Aurel said, 'I'm not noble or beautiful.'

Tancred's eyes glinted. 'At the risk of sounding like some drivelling poet, you are both, to me.'

He leant over and returned Aurel's first, tentative kiss.

2

The sun was rising as Alissende stepped out into the courtyard of Bellière, drawing her cloak around her against the cold. The snow had been trampled to mud, and straw laid down to provide a more secure footing between the door of the keep and the gatehouse. A few hens pecked among its battered stalks.

Since the siege was set, she had fallen into the habit of beginning her day with a climb up to the wall-walk. There was little to see from there, but she longed for the day recalled from her vision, when the besieging troops would pluck up their banners and go.

She could hear raised voices from the camp beyond the walls. Something of note was happening there. As she crossed the courtyard, she saw Sir Guy standing on the battlements, his armoured figure silhouetted against the paling sky. He seemed unafraid of making himself a target, but something in his poise told Alissende that he was watching what occurred below with intense interest.

She picked up her skirts and hurried over to climb the steps to join him. Sir Guy greeted her with a jerk of his head towards the camp below. 'Look there.'

Alissende reached his side to see a string of pack mules

standing ready along the road, while men at arms loaded their panniers. Some of the bright pavilions had already vanished; as Alissende watched, another of them collapsed in a billow of silk.

'They're leaving us!' she said.

Sir Guy grunted. '*Some* are leaving.'

It took a moment for Alissende to understand. Then, as she watched the busy scene below, she realized that the banners of the Legion still remained in place, their black and silver pavilions being drawn in an even tighter cordon around Bellière.

'It seems the provincial lords are leaving the siege in the hands of the Legion,' Sir Guy said. 'I'd give a month's pay to know where they're going.'

As Alissende watched, she realized the split was not a clean one; while some of the lords' followers still remained, a few of the Knights Legionaries were leaving too. Then she recognized a couple of familiar figures, riding across the bridge towards the castle gates.

She gasped, touching Sir Guy on the arm. 'Look there – it's Bertrand and Sir Valery.'

A grin spread over her companion's face. 'Now we'll hear some real news.'

He waited until the pair were close to the gate, then leant over the battlements. 'Hey, what's going on?'

'A horde of demons has taken possession of Roazon,' Bertrand replied.

'*What?*' Sir Guy leant further out. 'Has the world gone crazy?' He paused, then, glancing at Alissende, added, 'Sister, Duke Joscelin should hear this news. Will you find him for me?'

Alissende turned and hurried off down the steps. At this hour Joscelin would likely be at prayer in the chapel, as so often these days. She felt that he was drawing away from the whole world, into some remote place where no one could reach him. Where she herself could not reach him. There was an immense distance in his eyes.

When she edged open the chapel door she saw him kneeling on the sanctuary steps in a cold winter light, his hair a gleam of gold among the muted tones of wood and stone.

Reluctant to disturb him, she crept forward silently, but he must have become aware of her presence, for he signed himself with the Holy Knot, then rose and turned. He listened intently to her message. 'Then Autrys has returned,' he said, 'and they would naturally turn to Roazon next.'

'Your betrothed, Lady Marjolaine, is there,' said Alissende.

He nodded. 'I will give Bertrand a special weapon,' he said.

He took up the processional Knot, a silver emblem on a staff of ash, from its resting place, and Alissende followed him outside.

On the way back to the courtyard, they passed the door of the library. On impulse, Alissende pushed it open, knowing that Tiphaine spent much of her time there, cleaning and restoring her grandfather's books after the neglect they had fallen into since his death.

'Tiphaine!' she called out.

The girl appeared from behind a massive reading stand carved of oak, her hair escaping from its knot, and her woollen gown filthy. She carried a bound volume in one hand and a cloth in the other.

'Bertrand is here,' Alissende announced.

Joy flooded into Tiphaine's face. 'Has he lifted the siege?'

Nothing, Alissende realized, was impossible for Bertrand in her friend's eyes. 'Not exactly,' she said. 'But come and see.'

Tiphaine set down the book and hurried out after Alissende into the courtyard.

On the battlements, Sir Guy was exchanging news with Val and Bertrand below, while Duke Joscelin stood listening to them.

'My lord,' Bertrand was explaining as they reached the wall-walk, 'vile creatures now hold your city! In the Warrior's name, will you not lead us?'

Joscelin looked briefly surprised, as if that thought had never occurred to him. 'No — not yet.'

Then what? But Alissende could not ask the question out loud.

'This is *your* task, my eagle,' Joscelin went on, looking suddenly joyous, as if he was offering Bertrand some great privilege. 'You're vowed to it, and you will perform it honourably.' Leaning forward, he went on, 'Do you know how to breach the gates of Roazon?'

Bertrand rubbed a hand over his brow. 'I had a plan when I thought I'd be dealing just with King Aymon. Whether it will work now . . .' He shrugged.

'It will work,' Joscelin promised him, sounding so sure. 'And I will give you a weapon to drive out the demons.'

He unfastened the cord from his woollen robe, tied it to the centre of the Holy Knot, then let the sacred emblem down from the battlements. Val manoeuvred his horse into position to catch it by the staff.

'Raise it when you come within the walls of Roazon,' said Joscelin.

Bertrand was looking bewildered. He trusted in his sword, not in pious gestures.

Sir Guy moved back, to let Tiphaine take his place; she leant over perilously, as if hoping she might reach Bertrand and touch his hand before he rode away.

'Lady!' Bertrand called exultantly as her face appeared. 'Is all well with you?'

'It would be better if you would come home to us,' Tiphaine replied.

'Soon, I promise, lady. Not all the demons hell ever spawned could keep me away from you for long.'

A shout from the far end of the bridge interrupted him. By now the provincial lords had assembled all their troops, and the columns were ready to move off. Alissende watched in silence as Bertrand and Tiphaine gestured their farewells and he began to ride away.

Duke Joscelin turned to Alissende, and with relief and joy she realized that he truly saw her again. He reached out a hand to her, and they stood together on the battlements until the whole bright cavalcade had wound its way along the road and out of sight.

3

'We can't hide an entire army,' Bertrand said. 'It's now or never.'

With Val at his side, he stood on the outskirts of the forest looking across the snow-covered ground to Roazon. Nothing stirred inside its walls; nothing hovered in the sky above. The sun was setting under a sulky covering of cloud.

Val turned to contemplate the bundles of wood piled at the edge of the trees, and the handcarts to carry it. He had left his horse some way back, and had covered his armour with the filthy sacking tunic Bertrand had thrust at him.

Planted in the snow beside him was the staff of the Holy
Knot that Duke Joscelin had given them.

'This might have worked when King Aymon was in
occupation,' he said. 'I'm not sure it will now. What would
demons want with firewood?'

'Who cares,' Sulien de Plouzhel murmured, 'provided
they open the gates to us.'

'Oh, they'll do that.' Bertrand gave him a tight grin. 'If
only to have fun with us.' He swung round as more nervous
muttering broke out behind him. 'Except it's we who'll be
having the fun, don't worry.'

Val was not sure, but he was not going to argue in front
of Bertrand's lads. Any one of them would have followed
their eagle unhesitatingly into battle, but no one could be
expected to face what was inside Roazon without some
misgivings.

'Let's get going, then,' Bertrand said. As Val plucked up
the Knot staff, he warned him, 'Keep that out of sight.'

Val thrust the staff deep into the pile of wood on one
of the handcarts. His sword, and a spear or two, were
already concealed there. Standing between the shafts, he
found the right balance and began to haul the cart forward,
Sulien pushing it from behind.

With a bundle of wood on one shoulder, Bertrand led
the way as they trudged over the snow. His lads were strung
out behind him, like a long file of peasants bowed under
their burdens, seeming no threat to anyone in the city
ahead.

Commanded by Henri de Zol, the troops from Bellière
were waiting in the forest. They would sweep down on
Roazon once Bertrand and his party had got through the
gates.

If the gates were ever opened. As Val drew closer he could still see no movement on the city walls, but he felt a prickling sensation, as though he was being watched intently.

The same silence continued until Bertrand, heading the column, had reached the causeway. As soon as he set foot on it, the gates ahead of him swung slowly open, though no one could be seen.

Bertrand continued under the archway and into the square beyond. There he set down his bundle, while his cousin lugged the handcart up beside him and let it stand.

The instant that the last of Bertrand's lads had stepped through the gates, a harsh cry sounded from one of the towers of the gatehouse. From the corner of his eye Val saw something black come plummeting down at him, and whirled round to see a huge crow-like creature fasten its claws into the back of one of Bertrand's lads who lay face down in the snow.

A second later a crossbow bolt spat past, to bury itself in the creature's feathers. The thing gave another harsh cry and fluttered upwards, while the bleeding man it had attacked rolled away to safety.

'Scatter!' Bertrand yelled, and his men were already running for the walls that bounded the square. They had pulled their weapons out of the bundles of firewood, and now they headed for cover, while their archers kept their bows trained on the gates, to keep them open.

In the distance Val could hear the sound of a horn, and the approaching thunder of horses' hooves. He pulled out his sword, then stuck it in his belt, and raised the Knot staff. By now he was all alone in the middle of the square.

Bertrand had ducked under a nearby balcony on the street leading up to the citadel, gesturing frantically for Val to join him under cover.

Val looked beyond him, to see what was coming down the street. Dragging itself on sharply clawed forefeet was a giant lizard that filled the thoroughfare from side to side, its armoured hide scraping destructively against shop signs and gables. Its tail swatted back and forth, casually splintering shutters, its gaping jaws letting out a constant high-pitched shrieking. Val suddenly caught the foul stench that rolled ahead of it and almost vomited.

Bertrand slid another quarrel into his crossbow and aimed at the monstrosity. The bolt struck it full in the chest; its shrieking redoubled – but it kept on coming. Val had a premonition of carnage as the approaching horsemen swept through the gates and slammed into it unaware. They might eventually destroy the beast, but at what cost?

He raised the Knot staff of Roazon above his head, with both hands. 'For Roazon and Duke Joscelin!' he cried.

Instantly the Knot emblem flashed with silver fire. Its three separate branches lashed out like whips, the curves squirming outwards until Val held a staff crowned with a thicket of silver tendrils, reaching out for the monstrous aggressor.

Between awe and terror Val almost dropped the staff, then stepped forward, thrusting the Knot at the monster until the writhing branches touched. At once they wrapped themselves about it, enfolding it in a net of cords that burnt silver so incandescent that Val was dazzled. The lizard monster screamed, but it was cut off abruptly as the net of fire around it tightened. A black rain of dust floated down into the street – the lizard was gone.

With a thundering of hooves, a flashing of banners,

Henri of Zol and the troops of Bellière poured through the gates.

Bertrand grabbed his cousin's arm. 'Don't let's stand here gawping! On to the citadel.'

Val swung round, still holding the Knot staff and expecting to see some other horror that he must battle against. Instead, Sulien was dodging through the crowd towards him. He carried three billets of firewood bound together in a rough approximation of the Holy Knot. As he reached Val's side he touched it to the silver branches.

Light flashed from Val's Knot staff to Sulien's, and the whole square was illuminated in the flaring radiance. Sulien gave a hoarse cry of triumph; calling some of Bertrand's lads around him, he ran back across the square towards the street to the hythe gate.

No sooner had he gone than others were pressing around Val, with more Knots made from firewood, claiming their own gift of dazzling light. Passing them from hand to hand, they scattered to assail the heights of the city. Standing half-blinded in the square, Val imagined he could see a silver radiance crawling up the streets, rising like the tide to engulf Roazon, and cleanse it.

At length the crowd thinned out. Gazing up the main street, Val saw Bertrand halted at the foot of a stairway. A couple of Knotbearers fought off a crowd of bat-like creatures that came pouring down on them, flapping into the air on stunted wings.

Val ran to join them, and the last of the hellish creatures, recoiling from the flaring branches of the Knots, vanished into the night. Bertrand led his party on. There were obstacles: a serpent, coiling down from a balcony, its jaws dripping fire; an eagle, with the head of a snarling lynx, stooping from the sky; a shapeless, vast slug, sucking its way out of a deserted house; nearby a fleeing crowd of shaggy, goat-footed creatures. At each encounter, the Holy Knot emblems came to life, wrapping the demonic creatures within their tendrils, and reduced them to nothingness.

At last they reached the square fronting the cathedral. The skies above them were clean. Looking back, Val caught glimpses of yet more flares of silver, as Henri de Zol and his followers slew their demonic enemies in the lower reaches of the city.

Val swung round at a noise behind him, but it was only Sulien and his followers, arriving up the steep stairway from the hythe.

Bertrand loped across the square and beat a thunderous summons on the cathedral doors. At first there was no response; then sound pealed out from above, bells clamouring their joyous message over the city.

A wicket in the great doors of the cathedral opened, and the Grand Master stepped out. He looked gaunt and exhausted, but his head was high and he held a sword in his hand.

'Sir, the city is cleansed,' said Val.

'Or will be,' Bertrand added practically. 'I'll wager it'll take some time to root out all the damned things from where they're hiding.'

Father Reynaud stared blankly as if at first he could not take in what they were saying to him. 'We have held out,' he said finally, 'but so many are dead. So many of the Legion. And the Archbishop ... the Archbishop's heart burst as he made the Offering.'

'Go back, Father,' Bertrand said. 'Keep your people inside until the streets are safe.'

Father Reynaud drew himself up, with a ghost of his old intransigence in his eyes, but before he could argue he was interrupted by a shout from the square. A couple of Bertrand's men were running across from the postern gate into the citadel.

The group behind them included several sisters in the distinctive blue robes of the Matriarchy. Val's heart leapt at seeing that his mother was among them.

One of the lads rushed up, halted beside Bertrand and gave him a rough salute. 'Survivors in the barracks,' he reported. 'They say—'

A second man interrupted him: Donan the silversmith. He grabbed Bertrand's arm, insane with fear and grief.

'They've taken Lady Marjolaine away to Autrys!' he shouted, shaking Bertrand fiercely. 'And my Morwenna with her!'

Thirty-One

I

Aurel was cooking flat cakes of bread on a griddle over the fire. Briefly he glanced at Tancred, as he neatly cut slices from one of the quarters of ham which had hung from the ceiling.

'Are you really fit to go on?' Aurel asked anxiously.

'As fit as I'll ever be,' said Sir Tancred. 'We can't stay here for ever. And the weather will get worse, the longer we wait.'

His servant knew he was right. In the last few days, the weather had turned warmer again, and the early fall of snow had vanished, except for a few hollows under trees where the sun scarcely ever penetrated. It was time to move on, and yet Aurel would have welcomed an excuse to delay.

He did not want to leave their cave. He had never been so happy, and this time he knew his happiness was built on a firm basis. Sir Tancred was worthy of the trust Aurel placed in him.

Tancred glanced up and Aurel met the warmth in his eyes. The unknown charcoal-burner, he thought, had given them so much — not only food and warmth and shelter, but the chance to find each other. It was a debt that could never be repaid.

They set out the following morning, carrying what provisions they could manage. For several days they walked, in a late autumn landscape of bare boughs and leafmould clotted underfoot. The forest seemed to have opened up; there was more light and air, and they saw nothing evil stirring.

On the fifth day, they came to the Rinvier river. Its wide waters, usually busy with shipping, were deserted now, except for a small rowing boat bobbing at its mooring line. With scarcely a word exchanged they cast off, to be carried several miles downstream until the current drove them up on a pebbled spit of land on the opposite shore. Aurel could not stifle a growing conviction that their journey was guided – but he could not tell whether that guiding hand was for good or evil.

They ate sparingly, but their supplies were dwindling and Aurel began to be anxious again. At last they came to a well-defined footpath. Aurel was nervous of turning into it, but he followed Sir Tancred, alert for any sign of being watched, and started as Tancred exclaimed, 'Look at this!'

The path skirted a clearing, at whose edges rough shelters had been built of branches interwoven with bracken. Burnt patches on the forest floor showed where fires had been laid, and the grass around them was worn away by the trampling of many feet. Here and there objects – like a broken arrow – lay discarded.

Tancred was thoughtful. 'Perhaps we're getting some-where at last.'

He was right. As they followed the path, and the trees thinned out, Aurel began to hear the sound of running water. Shortly they stood on the forest perimeter: a stretch of rough ground that led to the edge of a gorge where a river swirled along through rocks. Further downstream was a bridge, and beyond it stood a castle, grey and stark on a bluff above the water. At the foot of its slope, on both sides of the gorge, were pavilions, and banners standing straight in the stiff breeze. Aurel's eyes widened as he recognized the black and silver colours of the Legion.

Tancred's voice cut into his thoughts. 'At least I know where we are now. That's Bellière. The last I heard, it was empty.'

'It looks like a siege,' said Aurel, 'but why would they besiege an empty castle?'

'Not empty now,' Tancred said, and pointed. The plain ermine banner of Arvorig flew from Bellière, beside the arms of Roazon. Aurel turned to Tancred with a question in his eyes.

'I think we know where Duke Joscelin might be,' said Sir Tancred.

Aurel's mind was spinning. After so many days out of the world, away from the problems that beset him, he was suddenly plunged back into them. Was he still meant to reach Joscelin – to kill him?

Tancred had seated himself on a rock near the edge of the gorge, his staff across his knees, his fingers drumming on its smooth wood. 'Of course...' he said. 'The damn' Legion trying to get their hands on a heretic.'

While he spoke, movement caught Aurel's eye. Three horsemen in the armour of the Legion had left the camp and were spurring towards them. Aurel moved closer to his master, who rose and planted his staff on the ground, as if gathering authority around him.

The Knights circled loosely round them, their horses snorting out clouds of breath into the frosty air. The Knights themselves were faceless behind their helmets; only glittering eyes showed through the slits. Aurel, though longing for his master's reassurance, clasped his hands behind his back and kept his head high.

'Who are you?' demanded one of the Knights. 'And what do you want here?'

The seneschal gave him a look of frozen disdain. 'I am Sir Tancred de Kervel, Seneschal of Roazon,' he replied.

For a moment the Knight did not reply, as if taken aback. 'You'd best come and speak to our commander,' he said at last. He gestured to where a pavilion larger than the rest had been erected near the bridge. Two more Knights guarded the entrance, and as Tancred and Aurel approached one of them said brusquely, 'You're to go in.'

We're prisoners, then, Aurel thought.

Tancred led the way inside, where the furnishings were austere, but comfortable. The man sitting at his desk was waiting with almost a hungry look. He was tall and thin, with brown hair falling lank on either side of a narrow face and pale eyes. Aurel felt that he should have been familiar, but could not recall where he had seen him before.

'Sir Girec d'Evron!' Tancred exclaimed.

Then Aurel remembered. Years ago, this Knight had come to Kemper, with letters from the Grand Master to the Commander of the city's garrison. Then Aurel's father, a noble merchant assiduous as always to please the Church, had hosted a welcome banquet for them on behalf of the merchants of Kemper.

Aurel had spent the time afterwards pursuing acquaintance with one of the young Knights of Sir Girec d'Evron's escort, and was making good progress with him until the man had recollected his sworn piety and fled.

But Sir Girec d'Evron had no personal quarrel with Melin — had never set eyes on him before.

'You're Commander here?' Tancred did not bother to hide his incredulity. 'The last I saw of you, you were packed off to Gwened in disgrace.'

Girec d'Evron smiled thinly. 'Where I now command the Legion, under the Warrior.'

Tancred's brows went up, but he made no comment. 'What do you want with us?' he demanded.

Sir Girec paused, toying with a pen. Aurel's nervousness increased as he sensed the man's satisfaction. 'You will now take your orders from me,' the Knight began eventually. 'You are—'

A shout from outside cut him off, and a rising clamour swept up to the pavilion they stood in. A Knight stumbled inside. 'Sir, out there in the sky—'

'What do you mean?' D'Evron rose to his feet and pushed his way outside.

Aurel and Tancred followed, to see that all the Knights were staring upwards. Over Bellière, a whole segment of the sky had darkened. At first he thought it was a storm cloud; then he saw the wings and claws: a packed army of demonic creatures hovering above the castle: winged serpents, and crows and other shapeless horrors that Aurel could not discern. Crimson lightning flickered around them, as their wings beat a hot stench down on the men below.

As Aurel stood frozen in terror, he heard Tancred's voice say quietly, 'Well, d'Evron, you've banished the Roazon bloodline, and this is the result. I hope you're satisfied.'

2

The shouting from the courtyard outside alerted Alissende. She went out of her bedchamber, to be met in the passage by Nolwen, with little Ivona in her arms.

'Don't go out there,' the older woman warned. 'There

are evil things in the sky. We should all shelter in the chapel.'

Alissende followed her. Somehow, she was not surprised by Nolwen's news. Having seen the return of Autrys in her scrying bowl, she had never been in any doubt that sooner or later the evil would come here to attack Bellière, to reach Duke Joscelin and destroy him.

Inside the chapel the servants were already assembling, Father Patern ascending the steps to the sanctuary, but there was no sign of Duke Joscelin. She halted. It was now her job to find him.

Passing Tiphaine on the way, Alissende continued as far as a window which overlooked the courtyard, and looked up to see the sky filled with a writhing darkness. Her heart beat hard and fast; what use could swords be, against the monstrous shapes that flew over Bellière? And where was Duke Joscelin?

As if he answered that question in her mind, a shaft of golden light cut into the shadow outside and he appeared. He carried no lamp, yet he seemed to walk in sunlight as he crossed the courtyard, calmly, unhurriedly, with Sir Guy de Karanteg beside him.

Alissende left her viewpoint and ran down the stairs. She was just in time to reach the gatehouse door before it was closed. Slipping through, she saw from the light that spilt down the winding stair that Duke Joscelin had gone that way, a couple of soldiers gaping upwards as if they could not believe what they had seen.

Following the same light, Alissende came to the stretch of battlements between the two gate towers. Sir Guy was with Duke Joscelin, and men at arms clustered around them. One of them said, 'What are we to do, my lord?'

Joscelin paused to look over the battlements. Below, in the camp of the Legion, men were running here and there, as if they did not know how to defend themselves. Others stood rigid, staring upwards. As Alissende gazed across, she saw a winged serpent swoop down and snatch up an armed Knight, to bear him struggling into the sky. His shrieks reached her for a moment, then were abruptly cut off.

Duke Joscelin said, 'Open the gates.'

'M'lord?' The man sounded astonished. 'And let the Legion in?'

'Yes,' said Joscelin. 'And let the Legion in.'

The man stared for an instant longer, and then made for the stairs.

Shadows surged thick around the castle, but on Bellière itself lay the tranquil sunlight of a summer day. Shading her eyes against this brightness, Alissende could just make out winged demons battering themselves against it in a vain effort to breach it. Avid to fall on the castle and destroy it, their howls of fury seemed to sound from a great distance.

But outside the protection of the golden light lay only darkness, where fire raining from the sky had turned silken pavilions into crackling towers of flame. The cries from the Legionaries grew louder, more panic-stricken, as these hell-ish creatures hovered over them. Their horses, driven mad with terror, reared or bolted, throwing their riders. Through the shimmer of light Alissende realized that the Knights were trying bravely to make a stand, but against the flying enemy they were hopelessly outmatched.

A glimmer of light fell on the path leading down to the bridge as the gates were pulled open. Duke Joscelin raised his arms. 'Knights of the Legion!' His voice rang out with renewed authority. 'Knights of the Legion, come in!'

Through the chaos below, Alissende could not be sure if

they heard him, but clearly some of them had noticed the opening gates.

Two or three men broke away almost at once and stumbled up the path to safety. They vanished from her sight as they entered the courtyard below.

Duke Joscelin beckoned again, but a shout came from below. 'No!' One of the Knights near the bridge raised his sword, as he tried to control his plunging horse. 'Stand firm! The Warrior alone will protect you!'

'That damn' lunatic d'Evron,' muttered Sir Guy de Karenteg.

The bulk of the Legion's forces were trying to hold their formation around d'Evron, but the attack became fiercest there, and moment by moment their numbers dwindled as serpents swooped down to blast them with jets of fire, or clawed them out of their saddles and up into darkness.

A few men broke away and tried to flee across the bridge to the castle, but by now their hellish adversaries were cutting off their escape. Alissende watched, transfixed with pity and terror as she saw one Knight below bravely hacking at a giant serpent with a woman's face. But it eventually coiled itself almost lovingly round him and crushed the life out of him.

Others flung themselves into the river in panic, where the weight of their armour sank them, or tentacles emerged from below to drag them down. On the further side some tried to escape into the forest, where a seething darkness swallowed them up under the trees.

Though some of the Knights accepted the sanctuary of Bellière, most of them tried to obey d'Evron's injunction to stand firm.

'Dear God,' Sir Guy whispered. 'Our Legion's destroyed.'

Only a few men now were left around their commander, who had lost his helmet, his white surcoat stained with blood. He still slashed wildly at the adversaries who hovered just above him, out of range of his sword.

'More courage than I'd ever have given him credit for,' Sir Guy murmured.

But at that moment d'Evron broke. Wrenching his horse round, and thrusting his way through the last of his men, he rode for the river, galloping down the rocky slope into the gorge. Alissende clasped her hands over her mouth as he tried to swim his horse across. As he reached the middle of the river, his mount suddenly disappeared, plucked down into a rolling surge, leaving the Knight floundering.

His cries for help could be heard briefly above the dying clamour, then the current bore him down to a projecting rock, which he clung to desperately; Alissende could see his white face upturned towards the battlements.

Duke Joscelin reached out a hand, as if even at that distance he could bear him up to safety. But as d'Evron clung to his rock, Alissende watched in horror when a huge mouth opened up in the water's slick, black surface. D'Evron shrieked as its jaws closed on his wrist and began thrashing in a frenzy to free himself from it. Then a claw emerged from the river to peel off his breastplate like a fruit rind and sank itself deep into his flesh. Alissende had covered her eyes before the spasmodic jerking of his body died away.

Shuddering with sick revulsion, Alissende went down into the courtyard. There she saw one or two of the Knights were kneeling in prayer, but most stood dizzy with fear, or lay flat, as if dead.

Then Alissende noticed two unarmed men, one seated by the gatehouse wall, the other stooping anxiously over him. Suspecting a need here for her healing skills, she began making her way towards them. But when a hand reached up and grabbed her skirts as she went by, she halted to look down into the face of Sir Nicolas de Cotin.

'You must help me ... you must speak for me to Duke Joscelin. I was never a traitor!'

Alissende did not trouble to hide her distaste for him. Given a choice between Duke Joscelin and Count Fragan, Nicolas had chosen wrong, and now all he could think of was his own wretched skin.

She tried to pull away, but he clung to her, babbling, and she had still not managed to extricate herself when Duke Joscelin himself came down the steps behind her.

Nicolas finally released her, turning to the lord he had betrayed. Joscelin merely stretched out his hand and said, 'Welcome.' Alissende caught the glint of tears on his face as he called out to the gate guards, 'Close the gates. It's over. It's all over.'

3

On the morning after the demonic assault on Bellière, Aurel left his master sleeping and ventured down the stairs from the tiny tower room where they were lodged. The seneschal had taken a wound in the shoulder from some clawed beast that had flapped down on them as they struggled up the path to the castle gate. The scratches were not deep, and had been efficiently bandaged, so Aurel thought he could go in quest of breakfast.

He had not ventured far before he realized he was lost. Opening a door that he thought might lead to the kitchens, he saw that, instead, it led into a tiny courtyard garden.

Seated on a stone bench, facing away from Aurel, was Duke Joscelin himself. Birds fluttered around his feet, and Aurel realized that he was tossing them scraps of bread.

He felt the serpent knife squirm against his side, and drew it out. In his mind, Vissarion's voice urged, 'Strike now!'

Aurel stood rigid with tension, uncertain whether to plunge the blade into Duke Joscelin or into himself. Duke Joscelin turned to him.

Smiling, he said simply, 'Aurel?'

Aurel started at the mention of his real name. 'You mistake, lord,' he said. 'My name is Melin.'

Still smiling, Duke Joscelin shook his head. 'Let's have truth between us, Aurel.' He held out a hand. 'Don't be afraid. Come, sit by me.'

Closing the door behind him, Aurel trod hesitantly across the grass to where Duke Joscelin was scattering the last of the crumbs. The birds fluttered away as Aurel approached him.

When he reached the bench he did not sit as Joscelin had invited him, but knelt before him and laid the serpent knife on the ground at Joscelin's feet. He did not dare look up into Joscelin's face.

'Tell me, Aurel.'

Aurel took one quick glance at him. 'You came to save us in the forest,' he said, 'showed us where to shelter.'

'I?' Joscelin smiled. 'No, that was a sending.'

The blue eyes that regarded Aurel were filled with kindness and understanding, which Aurel found harder to face than Vissarion's predatory amusement. He looked down again, at his hands twisting together, and the knife on the ground between them.

'Aurel, tell me all,' Joscelin repeated.

There was no avoiding his persuasion any more. Stumbling over his words, Aurel told Joscelin everything: how he had consented to Vissarion's evil, how he had come to Roazon, what his task had been.

When this recital was over, and he had fallen silent, he continued staring down at the knife. He did not dare look up to see Joscelin's kindness replaced by condemnation.

At last, Joscelin reached down to him and caught hold of the hand that bore the ring. 'That is what holds you in this shape?' he said gently. 'And Vissarion controls you through it?'

Aurel nodded, for the first time wondering why Vissarion had done nothing to prevent him from revealing the truth to Duke Joscelin. Had he truly discarded Aurel? Or was there some other, darker reason?

Before he could resolve those questions, Joscelin said, 'Then that is soon mended.'

Simply and easily, he drew off the ring.

A shiver went through Aurel, and he lifted his hands to his head. His fingers encountered clustering curls, not Melin's neat crop, and he realized that he was Aurel de Montfaucon again — that Melin the assassin was gone.

'No,' he whispered. He could feel tears springing up. 'I wanted to be Melin.'

Duke Joscelin's hand rested on his brow, forcing him to look up. 'Why?'

'Lord Tancred is my lover — Melin's lover.' Now at last would come the disgust he had expected all along. 'Aurel is lost in evil.'

'Not lost.' Incredibly, Duke Joscelin's eyes were still warm. 'Aurel, you are free of evil now. Learn to know forgiveness, and tell the truth to Sir Tancred.' He added, 'Believe me, in the end all will be well.'

Dismissed, Aurel could think of nothing to do but renew his search for breakfast. Now the distorting veil Vissarion had cast around him was removed, and he was returned to his own appearance, he felt as if he was walking around stark naked, but none of the other servants in Bellière gave him a second glance. The old woman in charge of the kitchens thrust a tray of warm rolls and fruit at him without even asking who it was destined for.

His heart began to pound uncomfortably as he opened the door of the tower room. Sir Tancred was sitting up, propped against pillows, his face white as the linen. As Aurel manoeuvred the tray inside he said, 'Breakfast – thank you. Have you seen my clerk anywhere?'

His crisp tones, his blank lack of recognition, were worse than anything Aurel could have imagined. His hands beginning to shake, he quickly set the tray down in the window embrasure.

'Tancred . . .' He choked into silence.

The seneschal's brows snapped up at the familiarity. 'Do I know you?'

Aurel wanted to sit on the bed beside his lord, to take his hands, to draw strength from him as he told the truth at last, but he knew how Tancred would recoil from such an assumption of intimacy.

'My lord . . .' His voice rasped in his throat. 'My lord, I am Melin.'

Now Tancred's blank look was replaced by irritation. 'What nonsense is this?'

'The ring I wore—' He gestured with the hand that was

free of sorcery now. 'It held me in that shape. This is what
I truly look like – but I'm Melin, just the same as I always
was.'

Gazing down at his master, he saw such chaos of feeling
in Tancred's dark eyes that he knew how truly Melin had
been loved. 'Do you expect me to believe that?' The tone
was defensive, as if Tancred was hopelessly trying to reject
what he already believed. 'All right – convince me. Tell me
why.'

Once more Aurel stumbled into the explanation of
Vissarion's murderous intentions. 'I never wanted to harm
Duke Joscelin!' he swore. 'I only wanted to stay with you.'

Tancred made no comment on that. 'Well, boy,' he
murmured, 'you're either raving mad, or the story's true.
Who are you, then, if not Melin?'

Aurel closed his eyes in despair. 'My name is Aurel de
Montfaucon.'

Silence. When Aurel dared to look again, the seneschal
had turned his face away. His voice cold, he said at last,
'That explains a great deal.'

Terror flooded through Aurel, and he fell to his knees
beside the bed. 'Tancred, I know you'll be ashamed of
me.' In his desperation the words were spilling out of him.
'But I've finished with all that, I swear it. I love you – only
you. I would never drag your name into the mud. Please
don't—'

'Aurel de Montfaucon.' Tancred tested the sound of the
name. Turning back, he scanned Aurel's face intently, as if
he was trying to find something he could recognize, some
hint of the features that were gone for ever. Then his gaze
slid aside again, and he raised a hand to his head. 'Just let
me think.'

'Please . . .' Aurel repeated. Between love and anguish, he

was losing self-control. 'I'm still the same as I was, out in the forest, and the cave. Does anything have to change?'

In his urgent need for reassurance, he reached for Tancred's hand, but his master drew back. 'I loved Melin.' The seneschal's voice was raw with pain. 'I don't know you.'

A sob torn out of him, Aurel scrambled blindly to his feet, and stumbled across the room towards the stairs. He could not help listening for Tancred's voice to call him back, but no sound came.

In despair, Aurel went on down into the courtyard. It was deserted now, except for a couple of guards at the gate. Aurel walked across, and, without speaking to them, unlatched the wicket. He had no plan, no intention except for his instinct to get away from there. And if it meant leaving the sanctuary of Bellière, it was no more than Aurel de Montfaucon deserved. Clearly none of Duke Joscelin's earlier words of hope and forgiveness could be meant for *him*. He pulled the wicket open and stepped through.

The day outside was cold and grey as Aurel headed down the path to the bridge, the gate banging ominously behind him. Crossing the bridge, he took the road that would lead him into the forest. But just before he reached its fringe of outlying trees, a winged serpent emerged – as he had known it would – out of the forest canopy. It circled him once, then hovered a little in front of him.

Sitting easily on its neck, Vissarion said, smiling, 'At last you have come back to me.'

4

Death, thought Sir Tancred de Kervel, must be something like this. A sense of frozen detachment from everything around him, and the certainty that while in some remote world the sun still shone, he himself was prisoned in darkness.

All the rest of that morning, Aurel did not return. By midday, Tancred realized that he would have to go and look for him. Somehow they would need to make their peace with each other; Tancred doubted there could be any more.

He was dressing, ready to begin his search, when a servant came to his tower room to tell him that Duke Joscelin wanted to see him. Warily, Tancred followed him, wondering what the duke would have to say about the story Aurel had told him.

The servant escorted him into a small room hung with faded tapestries, lit by oil lamps and the warm glow of a fire. Duke Joscelin himself was there, with Sir Guy de Karanteg and the woman they called Sister Alissende.

'Come, sit down,' Duke Joscelin said as Tancred entered.

The others were seated round a table where food and drink was set. Tancred took a vacant place, and let Sir Guy pour him a cup of wine, relaxing a little as he realized this meeting had nothing to do with Aurel.

'I still say we should ride for Roazon,' Sir Guy said, evidently picking up an argument that had been in progress. 'Bertrand needs you there.'

Joscelin shook his head. 'Bertrand will manage very well without me.'

'There's been no word,' Alissende reminded him.

'It's early days yet,' said Sir Guy. 'Seneschal, what can you tell us about Roazon? Did you see these evil creatures there?'

Tancred stared. 'Evil...? No.' He listened, almost incredulous, as Sir Guy told the story of what had been seen in Roazon. A hard knot of fear gathered in his stomach. 'Lady Marjolaine?' he asked urgently. 'What news of her?'

'Nothing,' said Sir Guy.

Tancred wanted to leap up and call for a horse, to ride straight away to Roazon. But he knew how futile that would be: himself a cripple, still exhausted from the journey here, his fighting skills half a lifetime away. Sick with self-disgust, he knew he could do nothing to help his lady now.

A knock sounded at the door, which opened to reveal a man at arms. 'Beg pardon, my lord,' he said, 'but there's a man at the gate. He wants to speak to you.' Seeming embarrassed, he added, 'None of us likes the look of him, sir.'

Sir Guy let out a snort of contempt, but Joscelin kept his eyes fixed intently on the guard, as if he had been expecting this.

'Bring him here to me,' he commanded.

Everyone sat in silence until the man returned, and another with him. The newcomer was tall, with flowing dark hair and pale features – a beautiful face, if you disregarded its cold, dead eyes. He wore a black velvet tunic, more suitable for a lord's feast than a winter journey, with a cloak of sables draped over it.

As he entered, Tancred heard Alissende let out a gasp. Joscelin glanced at her, for silence, then dismissed the man-at-arms and turned to his visitor. 'May we know your name?'

The newcomer laid one slim white hand on his breast and bowed. 'My name is Vissarion, Lord of Autrys.'

'Lord of an old wives' tale? What nonsense is this?' Sir Guy exclaimed.

Vissarion smiled. 'Are you really so isolated, here that you do not know that Autrys has risen again?' He nodded to Joscelin. 'I'm sure that's no news to *you*, my lord.'

Joscelin said nothing, just kept staring at Vissarion.

Sir Guy looked uneasy. 'My lord, is it really true?'

'After all you saw yesterday,' Vissarion snapped disdain-fully, 'do you really need to ask that?'

'What do you want with us?' Joscelin asked finally.

'A bargain,' Vissarion said.

'And what have you to bargain with?' demanded Sir Guy.

Vissarion's unholy smile returned. 'The Lady Marjolaine de Roazon.'

Involuntarily, Tancred made the sign of the Knot. 'No!' he whispered.

'Oh, yes, sir Seneschal,' Vissarion said. 'And more. I can offer you the Lady Marjolaine, the woman Morwenna, and Aurel de Montfaucon.'

At the sound of Aurel's name, Tancred thought that he would fall into darkness. Through a mist and a roaring in his ears he saw Joscelin touch the icon he wore, and heard him say, 'What do you want in return?'

'Yourself, my lord,' said Vissarion.

Sir Guy shot to his feet in anger. 'Hold him here,' he snarled. 'Exchange him for the Lady Marjolaine.'

'Hold me? Do you really think you could?' Vissarion's brows rose in delicate contempt. 'Silence your fool, lord,' he added to Joscelin. 'He grows tedious. It's *your* answer I want.'

'My answer?' Joscelin was thoughtful. Leaning over the table, he poured wine and offered the cup to Vissarion. 'Renounce Autrys. Drink with me in peace,' he invited.

Vissarion's countenance was darkness itself. Moving fast as a serpent strikes, he dashed the cup from Joscelin's hand. 'Your answer – now,' he repeated.

Duke Joscelin's robe was spattered with crimson, and wine pooled on the table in front of him. 'You have it,' he sighed. 'I will come to Autrys.'

A gleam of triumph lit in Vissarion's eyes. Ignoring Sir Guy's protest, he continued, 'I can offer you quick and easy transport. This affair may be over within hours.'

'I think not,' Joscelin said evenly. 'I shall make my own way there. That's what you want, isn't it? For the Duke of Roazon to walk submissively into your city?' Vissarion's avid look showed that was exactly what he wanted, as Joscelin added, 'If you harm your hostages, the bargain is void.'

'Understood.' Vissarion's voice was a satisfied purr. 'I shall go now and await you in Autrys, my lord.' He bowed and went out.

Alissende was weeping. 'I want to come with you.'

Joscelin shook his head. 'No, dear heart, how can I ask that?'

'How can you refuse it?' Her voice was bitter.

Joscelin's blue eyes were fixed intently on her. 'Very well,' he agreed at last. 'As far as the coast – but not into Autrys itself. I shall need a boat,' he added to Sir Guy, before Alissende could argue. 'Something fit to sail down-river and along the coast. To leave tomorrow morning.'

'I'll organize it right away, my lord.' Sir Guy went out.

'I'll come with you, too,' Tancred said, surprising even himself.

Joscelin gave him a sharp look. 'Tancred, that isn't . . .'

'I need to be there, lord,' Tancred said painfully, 'For the Lady Marjolaine . . . and Aurel. Besides,' he added harshly, 'I know how to handle a boat, which I'll wager neither of you can do. You need me there.'

Duke Joscelin nodded assent, and Alissende murmured, 'I'll go to make ready.'

Joscelin escorted her to the door. Tancred stayed in his seat, dropping his head into his hands. The tears came, slow and difficult, as shame sluiced through him like a rising tide.

At a touch on his shoulder he looked up to see Duke Joscelin standing beside him. Clumsily Tancred stood up.

Joscelin gripped him by the shoulders and looked deep into his eyes. 'Tancred, dear friend,' he said, 'don't weep. All will be well.'

'I sent him away.' Tancred could not prevent the words breaking out. 'I turned from him when he most needed me.'

'No,' Joscelin interrupted. 'I tell you, all will be well.'

He drew Tancred into a fierce embrace, and Tancred felt something like a bolt of lightning pass through him, pain and fire and light all at once. Without Joscelin's support he would have sunk to the floor.

Joscelin drew back, though he still kept a grip on Tancred's shoulders. Bewildered, Tancred realized that he felt no pain any longer. The nagging ache in his crippled leg, that he had borne for so many years, was gone. He lifted one shaking hand to the scarred side of his face, and touched smooth skin.

Duke Joscelin was smiling, and his eyes danced. 'Well, Tancred?' he asked.

Thirty-Two

I

Their boat slipped quietly along the coast as the night drew to an end and the stars grew pale. Kemper rose as a dark mass to the right; no lights showed there, nor the smoke of morning hearth fires. Alissende sat facing forward, a rope in one hand to trim the sail as Sir Tancred had taught her. At her feet in the bottom of the boat Joscelin lay in tranquil sleep.

She herself had slept little during the night just past. Sir Tancred still sat at the tiller, intent on the movements of wind and tide, but with a distant look in his eyes that told her his thoughts were somewhere else entirely.

The wind bore them on past the harbour mouth, and round the curve of the coastline. Suddenly Sir Tancred raised an arm and pointed. 'There.'

Autrys was perhaps smaller than Alissende had imagined it, but nothing she had imagined could come near to the menace pouring out of it. Briefly she toyed with the fancy that it might be the spiked fin of some immeasurably huge sea monster, which, in a moment more, would open its jaws and suck down their boat in a cataract of seawater.

Seconds later the keel grated on shingle, and soon they were running up on to the beach, within sight of the causeway leading out to Autrys. Tancred leapt from the stern and held out a hand to help Alissende. Just then Duke Joscelin roused himself.

His gaze fell first on Alissende and Tancred, then he looked outwards to the dark island. Alissende saw a shadow fall over his expression.

As the three of them dragged the boat high above the water line, the sea hissed and sucked behind them, hungrily dragging pebbles back and forth until Alissende thought she could hear dark voices in its rhythm.

From the beach, they had to climb to reach the causeway, over black rocks heavily encrusted with shells. On the landward side, the rock rose almost perpendicular, a narrow stair cut into it to reach the cliff top.

Seabirds swooped overhead, crying out like the voices of the damned. Alissende wanted to cry out with them.

As they stood gazing at the city gates ahead, she could not help asking him, 'Joscelin, why this way? You could have gone back to Roazon, and taken up rule again ... Wouldn't that banish Autrys from this world?'

Joscelin gave her a sad smile. 'No, not when half of Arvorig thinks I am a heretic.'

She held out her hands to him, and he caught hold of them. 'I found that a temptation,' he admitted. 'To go to Roazon, and wield power as its lord again.' There was a catch in his voice. 'But it must end now.' He released her hands. 'This is the only way.'

'My lord,' said Sir Tancred.

Alissende looked round, and a pang of fear lanced through her. Smoothly, silently, the gates of Autrys were opening for them.

When they stood wide open, a figure paced out onto the causeway. Alissende recognized him as Vissarion, who had come to Bellière, with desecration in his eyes.

'Joscelin,' she whispered, 'You could enter Autrys and destroy it. You could come home to Roazon.'

He touched her lips for silence, and then bowed his head to slip off the icon, and placed it around her neck. 'Goodbye, dear heart,' he said. 'Don't come any further, either of you.'

He turned and walked out along the causeway, to meet his enemy.

2

Sir Valery de Vaux was ready to leap out onto the quay as soon as the barge glided towards it. The journey downriver had seemed agonizingly slow, with the thought of Lady Marjolaine's peril never far from his mind.

'Take care, Cousin,' Bertrand warned. 'We don't know what might be lurking out there.'

He had redoubled his watch on sky and river as their barges approached Kemper, but no more of the demonic beasts had yet appeared. The waterfront taverns and warehouses were dark and silent as they slid by. There were no lights, no signs of movement. Kemper seemed a city of the dead.

As if to confirm this, a faint stench of decay wafted across the deck. Val shifted uneasily. 'Is there no one left alive?' he asked.

Bertrand grunted. 'Anyone still alive would have got out by now.'

In the east, the sky was paling towards dawn. A rack of cloud floated over the sea, and the hills, rising gently on either side of the Rinvier, hid Autrys from their sight.

One of the crew jumped ashore to make a rope fast to the bollard. Behind them, the other barges carrying troops from Roazon tied up each in their turn.

Bertrand raised his voice to a bellow. 'Stay on board and keep watch. Wait till I give you the word!' He turned to Val. 'Now, Cousin . . .'

As he leapt on to the quay, Val handed him the Knot staff, then followed, gazing intently at the dark line of buildings opposite, alert for enemies.

But everything was still and silent.

Treading softly, Bertrand led the way along the quayside to where the river mouth broadened into the harbour itself. Bobbing there were several fishing boats, their oars shipped and their sails neatly folded. Val smelt the stench first, heard the buzzing, saw a cloud of flies rise up, before he noticed the corpse curled in the bottom of one of the boats, one arm and part of its shoulder torn away.

Pulling his cloak over his nose and mouth, he followed his cousin up the steps of the harbour wall. From there, at last, they had their first sight of Autrys.

The city rose from an island of dark rock, and its slick, grey walls might have been forged from steel. Within them rose towers like the sharp spikes on some ancient instrument of torture, as if poised to impale the sky. If Roazon was a spear raised to salute heaven, Autrys defied it.

Between the island and the mainland ran the causeway of grey rock, a pebbly strand stretching on either side of it, already threatened by the first ripples of the incoming tide.

Figures were moving along the causeway. They looked human in shape, though Val could not be sure.

They watched this movement on the causeway for a moment longer. Then Bertrand said, 'We must get out there before they realize who we are.' Abruptly he turned and bounded down the steps again. 'We need one of the lads who can handle a fishing boat.'

3

Lady Marjolaine could not remember exactly how long she had been a prisoner here in Autrys. Remembering her life in Roazon was like looking down a long, dark tunnel to the picture of a sunlit garden she was unable to enter any more.

Since the night of the hideous revel, they had let Morwenna stay in her care. Though she pleaded, they did not send a healer to tend the painter's damaged eyes, but the wounds were beginning to heal.

Morwenna spoke very little, but spent each day seated by the window, her hands folded in her lap, her face turned outwards, as if she could still see the pinnacles of Autrys and the sea beyond. Once she startled Marjolaine with words of crystal clarity. 'I see him, always. I shall see him until I die.'

One dark morning came when Marjolaine was roused from sleep by the silent opening of her door. Into the room was carried a lamp, and she was urged, with the usual inarticulate grunts, to rise and dress both herself and Morwenna.

Once they were ready, the demibeasts herded them out of the fortress and down the steep streets of the island city until they reached a square opposite the main gates. All the while, Marjolaine held Morwenna's hand and guided her.

By now a grey light was seeping from the sky. The air was heavy with moisture beading every surface with irides-

cent patterns like moth wings. Even the city gates reflected
a quivering gleam.

Vissarion was standing before the gates, a group of his
creatures gathered around him, armed with barbed spears
and triple hooks. Beside him, with Vissarion's fingers laced
round his wrist, stood a golden-haired young man Marjolaine did not recognize. Only the fear in his eyes was
familiar.

Vissarion released him as Marjolaine approached. 'Lady,
this is Aurel de Montfaucon. And in a moment you shall
meet some other friends.'

When Vissarion gestured, unseen hands within the gatehouse began to open the gates. 'You should thank me, lady,
for I bring you what you most desire.'

As the gates gaped wider, Marjolaine could see the
causeway stretching out ahead. At its far end stood three
figures stood, and as Marjolaine watched, one of them
detached himself and began to head towards the island
city.

Though no sunlight penetrated to Autrys itself, a golden
light rested on him, and Marjolaine recognized Joscelin.

She wanted to cry out, to warn him to go back, but all
that came out was a whispered: 'No.'

'Follow me,' instructed Vissarion.

Graceful as if he approached the dance floor, he stepped
out on to the causeway. Marjolaine followed, Morwenna's
hand still held tightly in hers. The young man named as
Aurel walked on her other side, the demibeasts crowding up
behind them.

As they met Duke Joscelin at the midpoint of the
causeway, Vissarion stood aside, to let him confront Marjolaine face to face.

'Why have you come?' Marjolaine whispered. 'There's nothing but evil here.'

Joscelin smiled. 'It is the only way.' He took her face between his hands and kissed her on the lips for the first time as a man might do – and yet she felt it was a sign of renunciation and farewell.

His face filled with a bright resolve, he slowly drew off the ring he wore given to him at his induction, and placed it on her finger.

Marjolaine stared at it. 'Joscelin, I can't.'

'You must. You are the last of the Roazon bloodline,' he said. Smiling, he added, 'Wed, and be happy, and bear children, to keep our world safe.'

Marjolaine thought that her heart would break.

Joscelin reached out to clasp Aurel's hand briefly in reassurance, then turned to face Morwenna.

'Is it you, lord?' she asked.

'Yes.' He took her hand from Marjolaine's and drew her close to him, then laid his palms against the scarf covering her ruined eyes.

Her lips parted in a low, shivering moan. Gently, he loosened the knot of the scarf and let it fall. Morwenna gazed up at him, her eyes clear and restored.

Marjolaine felt her tears spill over.

'Don't weep,' urged Duke Joscelin. 'Soon everything shall be healed.'

Suddenly incensed, Vissarion let out a snarl and leapt forward. He grabbed Joscelin by the arm and flung him among the demibeasts. Crowding around, they fastened onto him.

To Marjolaine, Joscelin said, 'Go now, quickly. This is the only way.'

But Marjolaine felt frozen in place as Vissarion gestured to his obscene creatures. They dragged Joscelin to the causeway's edge and hurled him down to the beach below. Then they swarmed down after him and pinned him on his back, the first shallow lapping of the tide foaming around him.

More demibeasts swarmed out of the gates of Autrys, and Marjolaine fought vainly against their grabbing hands. A shout came from the shore, and she recognized Tancred and Alissende, running along the causeway in a hopeless attempt at rescue, only to be seized in their turn.

Winged demons took off from the towers of Autrys and hovered over them, while Vissarion leapt down onto the beach at his victim's side. 'Fool!' he said. 'Did you really think I would keep that bargain? With you dead, and your lady in my dungeon, I shall rule in Arvorig for ever!'

He snatched up a spear and skewered one of Duke Joscelin's hands into the sand.

A cry was finally torn out of him, as Vissarion rammed home another spear – then a third one through both Joscelin's feet together, so that he lay splayed out in a grotesque parody of the Holy Knot. His life blood was sluiced away by the rising tide.

Vissarion gestured his creatures away, and stood over his enemy as the water rose, gazing down in an ecstasy of hatred. Marjolaine saw his lips move, but what he said was drowned out by Joscelin's raw screaming.

Marjolaine wanted to turn her eyes away, but she could not. She had to bear witness. Duke Joscelin fought desperately against the constraining spears, but could not free himself. And though the water was rising swiftly now, his torment seemed to stretch out for an eternity.

At last his struggling grew weaker. His screams were stifled as the sea finally covered him. There was a moment of turbulence where he lay – then nothing.

Vissarion stood a moment longer with the tide swirling round him. Then he climbed back to the causeway and gestured to his followers. 'Bring them all.'

Too stunned to move by herself, Marjolaine was propelled back along the causeway, towards the city gates. The world had turned dark, and all hope was gone.

The tide was racing in now, swift as a herd of wild horses. Before they reached the gates, sea water was spilling over the causeway, tossing spray into the air. Black clouds shouldered each other across the sky, dousing the pale morning light that was growing in the east. A chill wind cut through the clammy air, and the roar of thunder, when it came, sounded as if the whole world was being torn apart at the roots.

As lightning gashed the sky, Marjolaine flinched from its searing brightness. When she looked again, it was to see the thin black line of a crack zigzagging from the topmost pinnacles of Autrys, down through its walls and towers, over rooftops and across pavements, until it reached the archway of the gate, and the whole island was split in two.

The clouds crashed open overhead, releasing a torrent of rain and stinging hail. Sea water was welling around Marjolaine's knees, and showed no sign of abating.

Vissarion checked, and then began to wade more rapidly towards the gates, yelling at the demibeasts to follow. Some abandoned their prisoners and broke into a shambling run, while the rest milled about on the causeway, as if they realized that there was no safety ahead. In the midst of the confusion, Tancred grabbed one of the creature's spears, using it to stab through its owner's throat, then slashed out at another.

With a wild cry, Alissende snatched up the other one's spear, but terror at the storm had already overwhelmed the survivors. They broke for safety, running towards the island city, or even back to the shore.

'Back.' Tancred gestured with the spear. 'That way . . . there's a boat . . .'

Lady Marjolaine tried to push Morwenna and Aurel in front of her, while reaching a hand out to Alissende, but already the water had risen to their waists, and it was impossible to make swift progress against it. The surface of the causeway had vanished under the waves, and they could easily to step off the edge of it. Spray constantly buffeted her face, and she feared each successive wave would sweep her away.

At last they could do no more than cling together, trying to stay upright, step by step towards the shore, but Marjolaine knew it could be no more than moments before they were swept into the churning sea. Beside her, Morwenna gazed wonderingly at the miracle of sea and sky, at the light she had thought never to see again.

Marjolaine glanced back to see that the fissure splitting Autrys from top to bottom had gaped wider now, its two sections rapidly peeling apart. She could hear hideous cries, and see dark creatures scrambling out of doors and windows, jostling each other as they sought to escape from the ruin of their island city. Others tried clinging to walls and columns, only to be shaken off as Autrys shuddered again and began to disintegrate.

Near the gap where the gates had been, a panic-stricken crowd was trying to launch a large boat. By the time they cast off, the craft was overloaded and settling lower in the water. Wind ripped at the sail as they tried to hoist it, and the vessel tossed helplessly until swamped by surging sea water. Slowly it foundered, leaving its shrieking occupants to grapple together in the icy sea.

From the inmost depths beneath the island the demons themselves came, clawing their way out of the widening fissure. They lumbered into the air on bat-like wings, but the lashing storm soon shredded the leathery membrane to tatters and propelled them down into the surging waves where they floundered awkwardly until the sea swallowed them.

As the tormented island began to subside into the waves, flames jetted into the sky and played across the water until Marjolaine feared that she was foundering in a sea of flame. In the midst of it a dark form took shape: a giant serpent with a wedge-shaped head and burning eyes. As its glistening neck arched above the ruined towers, with horror Marjolaine saw that it held a struggling human figure in its jaws. She could feel no doubt she was witnessing the hideous end of Vissarion.

Outlined by flame, he writhed helplessly in the serpent's fangs as the fire consumed him. The serpent parted its jaws to let out a shriek of rage and defeat, then it seemed to collapse inwards on itself, and the water covered it. The towers of Autrys tumbled into the sea with a terrible roar, until nothing was left above the waves but a mound of steaming rock.

Sea water was washing around Marjolaine's shoulders, and she could barely keep on her feet. Just then she heard Morwenna cry out, 'Look, there!'

Sailing from the harbour mouth was a single fishing

boat. As the wind lifted it and brought it skimming over
the waves towards them, a silver gleam radiated from it.
When it drew closer Marjolaine saw that the emblem of the
Holy Knot was bound to the mast.

Then she spotted Sir Valery and his cousin leaning over
the side, reaching out to pull her and her companions on
board. One by one they were hauled to safety and crouched
shivering in the bottom of the boat. Marjolaine could hardly
believe that they were safe at last, that no trial remained for
them but to get home and begin the long work of
restoration.

But before the boat turned for the harbour, a golden
gleam appeared on the water. One of the crew uttered a
hoarse cry. Looking up, Marjolaine saw the jagged heap of
dark rock, the last remains of Autrys, beginning to spilt
open, and golden light pouring out of it.

From the fissure, a shape burst upwards into the air. Its
wings spanned the sky, each separate feather etched in
burning gold. Fiery sparks trailed from the tail feathers. Its
crest was flame. It sang a single note, pure and high-pitched.

'A phoenix!' Val whispered.

Marjolaine drew in a breath of wonder as the bird
mounted into the sky and headed towards them with slow,
steady wingbeats. Behind it the last remnants of Autrys
finally crumbled into the sea. The surface of the waves was
a sheet of molten gold.

As the phoenix reached their boat, with its bedraggled
crowd of survivors, it circled once above them and golden
light spilled over them. The creature's song became a
complex harmony, like a whole choir announcing the joy of
victory.

Marjolaine's silently watched the miraculous bird soaring on towards the land, shedding its healing light over Arvorig. As its fiery radiance dwindled, the song faded and was gone.

The storm now over, the clouds were clearing, and the sun was rising in the east. Light shimmered on the expanse of water that covered the ruins of Autrys and all the evil it had tried to spread.

And somewhere, under the glittering surface, lay the tormented body of Duke Joscelin.

EPILOGUE

Sprigs of Juniper

'Joscelin, go with God. May this light shine in your memory.'

As Lady Marjolaine spoke the words, she set down the wreath of roses on the surface of the lake. The candle burnt bravely, a flicker of light against the darkening waters, as the eddies spun it away from the edge of the hythe.

Above her, the spear that was Roazon still soared towards the heavens. The lake shore beyond, hidden now in the gathering twilight, was rich with the growing crops of the most bountiful harvest Arvorig had seen in years. The land was learning to laugh again.

And on the following day, Marjolaine herself would attend the induction ceremony and take her place as Duchess of Roazon. She knew herself equal to the task.

Meanwhile the fragile candle burned, and Duke Joscelin's body, recovered from the sea, lay encased in stone beneath the stone paving of the cathedral.

'Tariec, go with God. Let this light shine in your memory.'

Count Fragan stepped back, and his son's wreath, bobbing on the water, blurred as unaccustomed tears welled into his eyes. He could not hide the truth from himself; his ambition had killed Tariec as surely as the northern spear.

He had redeemed himself a little, perhaps, when he won over the provincial lords and sent troops to the relief of Roazon. Lady Marjolaine had pardoned him and received him as Lord of Gwened.

But it was not enough. It would never be enough.

'Jeanne, go with God. Let this light shine in your memory.'

Bertrand watched his father as Sir Robert knelt on the cobbles of the hythe and entrusted his lady's circlet of white roses to the lake. Oliver stood close by with his little sisters, and Bertrand held Tiphaine's hand tight in his.

The tension in him began to relax as the wreath's pale blossoms drifted out into the dark. It was over now: no more need to struggle for an approval he could never win. He had accepted knighthood from Lady Marjolaine; he was Sir Bertrand d'Acquin now, and his new family were his lady Tiphaine and the child she was carrying. So why should the tears persist?

Tiphaine turned and kissed him on the cheek. 'Don't weep, my love,' she said. 'Soon we'll go home to Bellière.'

'Mathurin, go with God. May this light shine in your memory.'

As Father Reynaud set down a wreath for the dead Archbishop, he could not help remembering the fluctuations of the year gone by. He was Grand Master no longer, the Legion was dispersed, and power had slipped from his hands like melting snow. Now appointed chaplain of the Pearl of Arvorig, he would live in that tiny priest's house beside the chapel, and there would beg forgiveness for his former pride and stubbornness.

And so he took another wreath from the acolytes, lit the candle, and spoke the parting words.

'Cornely, go with God. May this light shine in your memory.'

'Cado, go with God. May this light shine in your memory.'

Almost surprising himself, Aurel felt true regret as he laid his dead brother's wreath on the waters – regret mostly for the hatred between them. If Cado had survived the assault on Kemper, Aurel would have tried to heal the breach between them, but it was too late for that.

A light touch on his arm. 'House Montfaucon is yours now,' said Sir Tancred. 'What will you do?'

Aurel faced him. He could read uncertainty, still, in the man's dark eyes, as if Tancred feared he might want to return to Kemper and adopt the life of a rich merchant.

Aurel gazed at the unscarred face, the straight body, Sir Tancred looking ten years younger than the weary, pain-racked man Aurel had come to respect and love. But for all his newfound vitality, the uncertainty still remained.

Aurel could have answered his question with a kiss, but there was no cause to set tongues wagging.

'I have made up my mind. I belong in Roazon now – with you.'

'Girec, go with God. May this light shine in your memory.'

As Valery de Vaux launched his wreath into the lake, he was aware of all those others pressing up to the edge of the hythe: mothers and fathers, brothers and sisters, waiting to say a last farewell to the fallen Knights of his order. Yet Girec d'Evron had no family, and so Val, who had been briefly his commanding officer, had taken the duty on himself.

The previous day, Lady Marjolaine had summoned him to her. He knelt before her, but she had raised him up, and sat with him by a window looking down over Roazon.

'We are resolved to initiate a new order of knighthood, dear friend,' she explained. 'The Knights of the Juniper — and you shall be their commander.'

As he gasped at the honour she did him, she smiled mischievously. 'This time,' she said, 'there will be no vows of celibacy.'

'Joscelin, go with God. Let this light shine in your memory.'

Alissende had attended the Offering in the chapel on the Pearl of Arvorig, but she had not followed the rest of the congregation to the hythe. There Lady Marjolaine would light the official candle for Duke Joscelin, and that was fitting, for she had been his betrothed. But Alissende needed to make her own farewell. So she had plucked a few of the roses that twined around the chapel door, twisting them into a wreath. She had taken a votive candle from the box beside the altar, and lit it from the sanctuary lamp.

Holding the wreath in one hand, and gathering up her robes of Matriarchal blue in the other, she made her way through the bushes to the lake shore, and laid the fragrant blossoms on the softly lapping water.

She whispered the words of farewell, and let her tears fall freely. The candle flame fractured into orbs of golden light as the current carried it away from her, out into the dark. As she watched it, unable to turn away, the flickering light seemed to coalesce and grow in size and take form.

Brushing away her tears, she saw Duke Joscelin's likeness walking towards her across the water.

He came to where she stood at the edge of the lake, and seemed to put his arms around her.

'Alissende,' he said at last. 'Don't weep for me. All's over now.'

She drew back and looked up and saw he was smiling. There was sorrow and love in that smile, but very little triumph.

Part of her wanted to say, *It will never be over. For I've lost you, and nothing can change that.* But this impulse was swallowed up in a greater joy that he had won at last, had kept faith with what he was meant to be, and come back to manifest himself to her through the waters of death.

'And Roazon lives again.' Joscelin's gaze shifted beyond her, through the trees, to where the cathedral spire was just visible against the darkening sky. 'You have work to do now, to heal, and pray. But one day ... one day we will be together always.'

His words seemed as inexorable as the tolling of a bell, and Alissende thought her heart would fail her from both joy and sorrow.

'Goodbye, my love,' Joscelin murmured and moved away from her. Alissende would not let herself reach out as if to cling to him, or do anything that would diminish the wonder of the renewed faith he had given to her.

'Goodbye,' she whispered as he turned away and walked back out over the lake. As he withdrew, the light surrounding him seemed to divide, and it was as though two other figures stood there with him: a warrior with a stern yet joyful face, and a judge clothed in age and wisdom. They reached out their hands to him, then all three were gone.

Alissende stood a while, staring out across the ruffled water. Then she wiped her face on her sleeve, and walked slowly back along the path, past the chapel and towards the bridge and the hythe, where she knew her friends would be waiting for her.

Afterword

The character of Bertrand d'Acquin in the novel is based on Bertrand du Guesclin (1320–1380), a minor Breton nobleman who became Constable of France.

Because of his ugliness, Bertrand du Guesclin was rejected by his parents and denied the upbringing proper for someone of his birth. Instead he grew up among the peasant lads of his estate, some of whom remained with him for the rest of his life.

As a young man he fled from his family home and took refuge with an aunt in Rennes. The events of the tournament which followed are a well-known story, though it may be apocryphal. Other episodes of his life which I've adapted include the affair of the baggage train and the combat to release his brother from imprsonment. I've also used a few of du Guesclin's recorded sayings, including that speech of sublime arrogance when Bertrand d'Acquin contemplates the retaking of Roazon: 'If the sun can get in, I can.'

Bertrand du Guesclin is now regarded as one of the great French heroes, and lies in St Denis along with so many French kings. As well as being Constable of France he acquired a long string of titles and honours, but he never forgot his upbringing among the peasantry, and to his lads – *ses gars* – he was 'Bertrand' to the end of his life.

www.ingramcontent.com/pod-product-compliance
Ingram Content Group UK Ltd.
Pitfield, Milton Keynes, MK11 3LW, UK
UKHW040641280225
455688UK00002B/58